PRAISE FOR CHRISTI CALDWELL

"Christi Caldwell's *The Vixen* shows readers a darker, grittier version of Regency London than most romance novels . . . Caldwell's more realistic version of London is a particularly gripping backdrop for this enemies-to-lovers romance, and it's heartening to read a story where love triumphs even in the darkest places."

—NPR on *The Vixen*

"In addition to a strong plot, this story boasts actualized characters whose personal demons are clear and credible. The chemistry between the protagonists is seductive and palpable, with their family history of hatred played against their personal similarities and growing attraction to create an atmospheric and captivating romance."

—*Publishers Weekly* on *The Hellion*

"Christi Caldwell is a master of words and *The Hellion* is so descriptive and vibrant that she redefines high definition. Readers will be left panting, craving, and rooting for their favorite characters as unexpected lovers find their happy ending."

—*RT Book Reviews* on *The Hellion*

"Christi Caldwell is a Must Read."

—*New York Times* bestselling author Mary Balogh

"A story that not only touches, but plays at every string of your heart . . ."

—Chandrani Shome

"Two people so very broken in different ways, and their journey to becoming whole again. This is Christi Caldwell at her absolute best!"

—Kathryn Bullivant

"Christi Caldwell has a way to redeem dark, broken characters and make you forget their past sins and fall in love with them."

—Sharon Coffey

The GOVERNESS

TITLES BY CHRISTI CALDWELL

Wicked Wallflowers

The Hellion
The Vixen
The Governess

Sinful Brides

The Rogue's Wager
The Scoundrel's Honor
The Lady's Guard
The Heiress's Deception

The Brethren

The Spy Who Seduced Her
The Lady Who Loved Him

The Heart of a Scandal

In Need of a Knight
Schooling the Duke

The Theodosia Sword

Only for His Lady
Only for Her Honor
Only for Their Love

Heart of a Duke

In Need of a Duke
For Love of the Duke
More Than a Duke

The Love of a Rogue
Loved by a Duke
To Love a Lord
The Heart of a Scoundrel
To Wed His Christmas Lady
To Trust a Rogue
The Lure of a Rake
To Woo a Widow
To Redeem a Rake
One Winter with a Baron
To Enchant a Wicked Duke
Beguiled by a Baron
To Tempt a Scoundrel

Lords of Honor

Seduced by a Lady's Heart
Captivated by a Lady's Charm
Rescued by a Lady's Love
Tempted by a Lady's Smile

Scandalous Seasons

Forever Betrothed, Never the Bride
Never Courted, Suddenly Wed
Always Proper, Suddenly Scandalous
Always a Rogue, Forever Her Love
A Marquess for Christmas
Once a Wallflower, at Last His Love

Danby

A Season of Hope
Winning a Lady's Heart

Brethren of the Lords

My Lady of Deception

Nonfiction Memoir

Uninterrupted Joy

The GOVERNESS

CHRISTI CALDWELL

This is a work of fiction. Names, characters, organizations, places, events, and incidents are either products of the author's imagination or are used fictitiously.

Published by Montlake Romance, Seattle

www.apub.com

ISBN-13: 9781503903425
ISBN-10: 1503903427

Cover design by Erin Dameron-Hill

Cover illustration by Chris Cocozza

Printed in the United States of America

To Joy

You were the first person ever to read one of my books...
and entirely by accident.
I'm so glad for the day I handed over my laptop with the manuscript open. You helped me see a talent in myself when years of rejection began to wear on my confidence.
Thank you for remaining supportive all these years later.
I love you, Grandma.

Prologue

London, England
Spring 1826

Killoran, I am coming for you . . .

Broderick Killoran, proprietor of the Devil's Den, had survived falls from grace and violent battles in the streets. But *this* could be the one that destroyed him.

It was why he now stood in the heart of the Seven Dials, those cobblestones no sane man would wander at night—unless one had been born to them or one's life depended upon it.

For Broderick, the latter held true.

Where in hell are they? I need to find them . . .

Broderick reread the note he'd received, the words there already etched in his mind.

"Ye sure ye dinna want me to handle this one, Mr. Killoran?" the burly guard, MacLeod, called out, cutting across Broderick's dread.

Settling a flinty stare off into the shadowed mist of the early-morn London fog, Broderick refolded the letter. Tucking it back inside his jacket pocket, he pulled out the pair of leather gloves that rested alongside it. "Quite sure," he said, his hushed tones infused with cheer as he drew the leather articles on with meticulous precision. "I will handle this meeting, MacLeod."

The guard cast him a sideways look. "Ye certain, sir? Ah'll gladly find him an' gut him myself for ye." MacLeod spoke the way one might offer to pay for a bottle of whiskey to share between them. "Wouldna be no trouble." The friendly cheer to that thick brogue was contradicted by the slashing gesture he made at his throat. "Real quick it would be. We could be off and at the clubs faster than ye could say 'the blighter deserved it.'"

That willingness to kill for the Killorans was a loyalty that went back to when Broderick had saved the man from his own miserable circumstances and appointed him to a position of power within Mac Diggory's gang.

"I'll see to this one, Mac." In one fluid motion, Broderick withdrew the dagger tucked in his riding boot. The hiss of metal, an ominous echo of danger and death, filtered through the London quiet. "Stand watch."

Worry darkened the other man's eyes. The first hint of it. He doffed his hat and slapped the article against a thigh thicker than most tree trunks. "There's Miss Gertrude and Master Stephen to think about."

Gertrude and Stephen, two of his siblings of the streets, were the reason Broderick was here even now, in the early-morn hours, and not at his gaming hell. The Devil's Den would be brimming with patrons—most of them drunk and loose with their purses, and it was therefore a time he never left the walls of the kingdom he'd built.

His family's survival, however, mattered more than even his own existence.

Broderick's fingers curled around the hilt of his dagger. "I don't need you to remind me of my responsibilities." That whispered warning sent the color fleeing from MacLeod's cheeks.

"Nah insult meant, Mr. Killoran. Ah merely—"

Broderick held up a silencing hand. Laying swift mastery to the demons of old, he fixed on the task at hand. "I will not be long." He touched the tip of his right index finger against the knife, testing the sharpness of his blade. The metal pricked through the leather fabric of his glove and pierced his skin.

With MacLeod standing guard alongside their mounts, Broderick stalked the streets of the Dials, the rancid alleys he'd had, for a brief time, the misfortune of calling home.

Back then he'd been a sniveling, terrified boy. Now he moved with purpose, a hunter on the prowl, fighting for survival, determined to succeed, and intent on getting the scum of the streets before they got to him . . . and everyone he cared about. Most men would have taken smaller steps, lost themselves in the shadows, and chosen concealment as the safest option. But not Broderick. His every stride sent his cloak swirling in the dank, thick fog hanging on the London streets.

Broderick narrowed his eyes, taking in his surroundings. He'd discovered early on that timidity was oftentimes more perilous than boldness. As such, he'd never been one to mince steps or words, or to present himself as anything other than the leader of London's underworld.

He abruptly stopped.

His senses immediately went on alert.

Doing a quick sweep, he raised his knife close.

A whore with heavily rouged cheeks and unkempt, oily black hair stepped out of the shadows. "'ey, guvnor, want a good toime?" she purred, her barely discernible King's English roughed by Cockney and misery.

He nudged his chin in a silent order that she step aside. "I've other pleasures awaiting me this night, love."

Desperation glittered in her bloodshot eyes. "Ya looking for a man to dicker? Oi can find ya one of those, too. If ya let me?" she whispered. Desperation or stupidity? Or mayhap a combination of both made her careless. She stretched her callused fingers out past his knife and ran cracked, dirt-filled nails along the lapels of his cloak. "Or mayhap a lass or lad?" she asked, her voice brightening.

Repulsion snaked through him, along with something else: long-buried disgust for the person he'd been a lifetime ago. Nay, how much he *had* been just like her. The street rat's presence stirred reminders he didn't want. Not at this time. Not when he was at his most vulnerable. But the door had been cracked open earlier, and the memories would not stay buried, forcing Broderick momentarily back to himself as a lad. Once pampered and then orphaned, new to East London. His father's sins and mistakes had left Broderick alone, with his honor for sale and the hunger to survive strong. Begging for a scrap, selling the whereabouts of others if it meant he didn't have to be buggered against a wall by men who at the time had been bigger and more ruthless than Broderick.

Self-loathing for the weak boy he'd been soured his mouth and renewed his purpose.

Broderick fished out a small purse and tossed it over. Her reflexes were slowed from drink, and the sack slipped through the woman's fingers.

Like the rats the men and women of the Dials were forced to be, she tossed herself prostrate upon the meager offering and then scurried off, her figure disappearing within the swirl of grey fog.

Broderick resumed his hunt.

He stopped at the corner of Monmouth Street. Holding his dagger close, he worked his gaze over his surroundings. In no more than three hours, this place would be brimming with barefoot children hawking fraying boots and old shoes they'd filched from dead bodies or slumbering drunks. Pickpockets would be weaving amongst a crush of bodies out to buy or sell their wares.

But at this hour, battered souls surrendered to the grip of exhaustion and a too-brief respite from the hell that was the Dials.

The Wood Yard Brewery stood, an impressive redbrick structure, as a deceptive facade of respectability lent to a godless, soulless place.

At the entrance of Mercer Street is where you'll find them . . . They rise at three and start thieving at three thirty . . .

The Runner's report echoed in his mind as he slipped along the Seven Dials' cobblestones.

Life, after all, had taught him there were greater dangers to face than the physical hurts to be dealt in London's East End.

Rats chirped the Dials' symphony as Broderick moved deeper into an alley the Devil himself knew not to enter . . . and then stopped.

The half-moon's glow slashed down between the narrow slats of the buildings, casting an eerie light off the heavily scarred bastard stretched out on the hard stone.

He's here.

Broderick resumed his march over to that prone figure.

With every step, hope—a rare emotion to these streets—spiraled through him.

He'd found him. The bastard who'd kidnapped Broderick's youngest brother, Stephen. The man who'd passed off that same boy, a nobleman's child, as a street orphan. And now Broderick's very existence hung on a thread because of it.

But I've found him . . .

Broderick stopped over him. He kicked the prone man in the side with the tip of his boot. A hiss of pain whistled past the drunkard's lips as he jerked awake. Broderick took a perverse pleasure in the fear that replaced the confused glint in the man's eyes.

"You," the man rasped.

Broderick smirked. "Me."

"Oi didn't think ya'd find me." The faint slur hinted at a man with a weakness for cheap spirits and a carelessness that should have seen him with a blade in the belly long ago.

"You should think less and run more, Walsh." Broderick gleefully doled out the first advice Mac Diggory had given him, a blubbering mess of a boy scared of his own breath.

The greying man struggled up onto his elbows. "Why would Oi run?"

"Because you kidnapped a marquess's son." *A boy who became a brother to me.* Broderick forced an icy smile. "Because I now intend to drag you to that very marquess himself." Only this visit would not be one of empty words about what had happened that no nobleman would ever trust, but one with the thug truly responsible for those crimes in tow.

Except . . .

There was a marked calm to Walsh.

He was . . . *too* calm.

Broderick swiped his blade back and forth over his gloved palm. "You are not the only one I'm searching for." He did a sweep of the narrow alley, all the while knowing the other wretch he sought had gone. But he had one, and for now, that was enough.

A cocksure smirk marred Walsh's gaunt face. "She ain't 'ere."

Bloody fucking hell. Broderick flashed a hard grin. "I'll find her later, then. For now, I'll deal with just you." He ground the bastard's hand under the slight heel of his boot.

"Ahhh!" Those cries carried forlornly and familiarly around Monmouth, cries that would be heard and invariably ignored in these merciless streets.

"You deserve this." Broderick buried his foot in the bastard's stomach. He'd brought a stolen child into Broderick's life, and that same boy who'd become a brother to him would now go on to another—to his rightful family.

Agony spearing him, Broderick kicked Walsh again.

The street rat rolled onto his side. Clutching dirt-blackened hands around his middle, he glowered up at Broderick. "Ya think torturing me will make a bloody difference," he panted. "Ya're strong, but ya're nothing compared to a bloody nob."

Aye, that much was true. Having been born to a powerful nobleman's man-of-affairs, Broderick had known precisely how the world was ordered and his place in it. "Ah, but you see . . ." Leaning down, he stuck his blade against the man's enormous Adam's apple. Walsh's throat bobbed wildly, and Broderick reveled in the scent of fear that clung to Walsh, more pungent than even the cheap whiskey on his breath.

"I don't need to be more powerful than a nob," he whispered, trailing his knife tauntingly back and forth. A crimson bead pebbled on Walsh's skin and trickled a winding path down his threadbare, stained white shirt.

"P-please," Walsh sputtered. A damp circle formed on the front placket of the coward's pants.

Broderick chuckled, and with one hand he dragged the man to his feet. Gripping his throat, he shoved him against the building. Fragments of a shattered brick sprinkled around them. "I'm not pleased with you, Walsh." The thief's face grew a mottled red as he struggled in vain against Broderick's grip. "You gave me *bad goods*." Even uttering that latter part left a jagged mark upon Broderick's soul. For these weren't watered-down spirits or rotted shank they spoke of. His grip tightened reflexively, and he reveled in Walsh's near noiseless rasping.

The man's thin lips moved, but speech was impossible because of Broderick's hold. He kept the pressure there and then released his hold.

Hands rubbing at his throat, Walsh fell hard to his knees. He sucked in great, gasping breaths. "Diggory a-asked for a ch-child."

Broderick backhanded him. "I asked you for an orphan, you pisser," he hissed. Diggory had been running the clubs, and acting as his second at that point, Broderick had been calling the proverbial shots on his master's behalf. "*I* asked you for a fatherless babe, and you brought me a fucking marquess's son."

"D-Diggory l-loved the n-nobs," Walsh said in weak, graveled tones.

"I asked you for the child." Broderick seethed. "I gave you the orders." What had been his attempt to save some boy from the fate he himself had known as a young lad had been twisted and turned and warped into an evil act perpetrated by the one before him.

But I can get to the marquess. I can give him the ones he really seeks. The ones truly deserving of his wrath and ire.

"*Pfft*, the babe came to ya in foine garments. Ya knew precisely what he—*aheee*," he howled as Broderick buried his fist in his nose, reveling in the crack of shattered bone and the spray of blood.

And yet, with Walsh twisting and squirming at his feet, the dread that had wound about him since he'd learned Stephen was in fact a marquess's stolen child blossomed. Guilt stuck in his gut, sharp in its intensity. "I didn't order you to do that," he said hollowly. "You stole that child. You and that whore who served as nursemaid."

Broderick's family's only hope for surviving this was in turning Walsh and Lucy Stoke over to the marquess . . . before they paid him that favor first.

While the man writhed and groaned on the hard ground, Broderick's mind raced.

There would be no mercy for the soul who found himself in the vengeful sights of the nob whose son had been stolen. Broderick's sources had turned up a file on the Mad Marquess, as the widowed gent was known. His wife burnt to death in a fire set by this man before Broderick, and his only child and heir stolen, the Marquess of Maddock wouldn't forgive a single soul linked to Diggory.

But if Broderick could hand-deliver to the marquess the ones who'd wronged him, and present himself and his family as the saviors who'd given Stephen a home, then he could escape ruin—escape ruin, at the expense of losing Stephen.

Agony swept through him. With a curse, he dragged Walsh back to his feet. He forced the smaller man on his tiptoes and stuck his face in his. "You will pay the price. I'll have my meeting with Maddock, and he'll know precisely what you and your whore wife have done."

He welcomed the flash of terror and the frantic pleading . . . that did not come.

A slow, hideous chuckle rumbled from Walsh's concave chest until his entire frame shook with the ugly expression of mirth. "Ya're a day late to that meeting."

For the first time since Broderick had set out to find the pair who'd stolen Stephen and drag them to the marquess for their belated day of reckoning, unease pitted in his gut.

"What do you mean?" When Walsh only continued laughing, Broderick propelled him against the wall once more. "I said . . . what do you mean?"

But he knew. Knew it with an intuition that had saved his life countless times in the streets.

"I got to His Lordship. He knows ya ordered a nob's babe for Diggory. And . . ." Walsh's lips curved in a triumphant smile. "He believes me."

All the air left Broderick on a swift rush.

His hands went slack. "Impossible."

Walsh struggled out from his hold, and with the tables now turned, the vanquished became the victor. "Not so impossible? Ya thought yarself better, but to that nob, we're the same."

They were. God help him.

Walsh crowed. "Not so tough now, are ya?" He spat at Broderick's feet. "Only a matter of time before His Lordship comes a-calling with the constables in tow to take down the one who filched his boy."

Broderick stumbled back a step. *No.*

Walsh smirked. "Yes," he said, confirming Broderick had spoken aloud.

Dread slithering through him, Broderick backed away from the street rat, and with Walsh's triumphant laugh trailing after him, he took off running.

Chapter 1

At that same time
Grosvenor Square

For all the crimes upon your black soul, you'd attempt to foist a street rat born in the gutters off as my son? That is the least of the vile deeds you'll pay for . . .

As a young woman who'd once watched over her younger siblings and then stepped into the role of governess, charged with the care of a nobleman's three daughters, Miss Regina Spark had extensive experience looking after children.

Not a single one of those previous charges, however, had been a jot like the one she'd shadowed from the Dials all the way to the West End of London.

The fancy end, where she and those she now called family were unwelcome, and the last place Reggie cared to be.

And yet, this night, she had no choice.

Her eleven-year-old quarry, Stephen Killoran, more than a foot shorter than Reggie, darted quickly around a corner, disappearing down Park Lane. What he lacked in stride he made up for in stealth.

Running through a litany of curses that would have scandalized the family she'd once had, Reggie increased her pace and followed suit until she lost him from sight.

Her chest rising and falling, Reggie stopped and did a sweep of the quiet streets. She surveyed Somerset House in the distance. The moon bathed those grounds, a blend of buildings and gardens that didn't know if they wished to be in the crisp English countryside or a part of the metropolis they, in fact, were.

Where are you . . . ? Where are you . . . ?

Panic pounded in her breast. *I am too old to be running after a boy who doesn't want to be found.* She should be seeing to her own business, setting up the future she dreamed of for herself. And yet . . . this child was like family.

And Reggie's obligations—for now—belonged to Broderick Killoran, the proprietor of the Devil's Den. Gathering her coarse wool skirts in hand, she rushed in swift pursuit.

At last, he stopped. So quickly, so unexpectedly that Reggie stumbled to a halt, catching herself against a stucco townhouse.

Stephen doffed his cap, a threadbare article better suited to the pickpocket of years ago and not the beloved boy whose family had more money than Croesus.

Reggie's breath settled into an even cadence as she willed him to lose himself in the shadows once more. With Ophelia, the middle Killoran sister, only recently sprung from Newgate, they could not lose Stephen to that merciless gaol.

As it was, after Stephen had set the rival club, the Hell and Sin, afire, destroying the establishment in one reckless move, it was a miracle he'd not already found himself hanged for his crimes. Society didn't discriminate amongst the age of sinners. Desperate children, men, and women swung equally, as a reminder to all that to the world, the only lives that mattered were those born to the *ton*.

Given that, Reggie should jar him from his endlessly motionless state in the middle of the street. And yet she forced herself to remain frozen to her spot.

Waiting.

Watching.

Trying to sort out what it was about this enormous brick residence with its limestone accents that made him careless enough to stand in plain sight.

In the far distance, the rumble of carriage wheels upon the stone thoroughfare jerked him from his reverie.

Giving his head a shake, Stephen took off running once more. Not breaking stride, he caught the ineffectual black fence erected around the white limestone double residence and hefted himself over. His cap flew backward, landing forlornly on the pavement, forgotten by the child who was already rushing off. But who was also always in possession of it.

Regina once again raced forward. When she reached the same gleaming black fence, she scooped up Stephen's forgotten hat and stuffed it between her teeth.

Her heart pounded, and she waited for the hue and cry to go up. She scaled the fence and swung one leg over, straddling the structure. Her skirts tangled about her legs, and the cool night air slapped at her exposed limbs. In her haste to find Stephen, she stretched her boot to the ground, miscalculating the distance.

Reggie went down hard, landing on her back in the midst of a small designed garden under an arched window.

She winced as pain jolted from her buttocks all the way up her back and down to her feet, radiating agony down to the soles of her serviceable black boots. A handful of stars peeked out from behind a thick cloud cover, twinkling overhead as if in celestial amusement.

Wincing, Reggie shoved herself to her feet. She hurriedly pushed her skirts down and bolted along the side of that grand residence.

Oh, bloody hell.

I am not meant for this . . . She'd been rot at sneaking and subterfuge when she'd first joined the Killoran family, and she was just as rot at it all these years later.

Still for that truth, this family had become the family she'd lost, and she'd scale the bloody Tower of London in order to save a single one of them, if she must.

Reggie had reached the back of the endless building when something hurtled at her, knocking her hard into the side of the townhouse.

She opened her mouth to scream when a pair of accusatory, anger-filled eyes met her own. "Ya're following me, Spark." The absolute frost in his gaze chilled her.

He's just a boy.

Just a boy, but one who had an age-old wariness in his jaded eyes that most grown men wouldn't have in seventy years of suffering through this existence.

Reggie made her lips move up in a smile. "You forgot this," she whispered, holding out his cap.

He stared at her as if she'd sprung a second head. "This is what ya came after me for?"

By that suspicion-laden query, he'd not remembered losing the article. Questions perked at the back of her mind. Unimportant ones for now, but their meaning surely mattered and would be explained later.

"Does Broderick have *you* watching me now?"

That unenviable task fell to the boy's eldest sister, Gertrude. Partially blind, however, Gertrude wasn't one to rush off through the streets of London. "No. I saw you sneak out." Reggie settled her features into her sternest governess expression. "What are you doing here?"

Stephen spat at her feet. "Ain't yar business. Ya ain't a Killoran."

He was a mere boy whose life had been endlessly harder than any adult's, let alone a child's, and even knowing that and telling herself that, it didn't make Stephen's well-placed barb hurt any less. Reggie leaned down, sticking her face close to his. "No. I'm not." *Not by blood.* "But regardless, I'm not leaving you to snoop around some nobleman's household." Not when he'd a history of setting fires all over London that had very nearly seen people killed.

Stephen's eyes said "go to hell" more loudly than had he shouted the words into the early-morn quiet.

The sharp bark of a lone dog echoed around the night sky. Reggie's heart jumped.

"Scared of a fucking dog," he taunted. "Wot Oi'm doing here 'as nothing to do with ya." The boy pressed his hands against her stomach and shoved hard.

A smaller person would have gone down under that impressive shove. Reggie stumbled but caught herself against the townhouse.

Stephen was already running around back.

She briefly closed her eyes. And all those years ago, she'd believed her charges a challenge. Not a single spider in her tea nor a poorly hiding girl could have compared to this.

Nor was this boy merely an assignment to her, either.

Setting out after him, Reggie crept along the same path Stephen had followed until she reached the mews 'round back. The eight-door, brick stables covered in meticulously groomed ivy could comfortably sleep the entire staff of the Devil's Den.

She skimmed her eyes over each wood panel and then snagged her gaze on the sixth door, cracked slightly.

Drawing in a silent breath through her tensed lips, Reggie hugged the building one more moment before sprinting across the courtyard. The heel of her boots striking the graveled grounds thundered loud. Or was it merely fear that magnified her damning footfalls?

At last reaching that cracked doorway, she let herself in.

To an empty stall.

Reggie blinked frantically in a bid to adjust her eyes to the dimly lit space. There were few places any person could hide here.

"Stephen," she hissed, venturing forward. The straw cracked and crunched under her feet. "Stephen," she repeated, peering at the stacks of hay that lined the left-hand side of the stall. She reached them in two quick strides, leaning over.

Furious eyes met hers. "Oi said get the hell outta 'ere."

"No," she clarified. "You said what you were doing here had nothing to do with me, which it doesn't. It does, however, have to do with *you*, and because I care about you, I choose to be here," she said practically, using her most matter-of-fact tone. Having known this boy well enough since he'd been an orphan, she knew he'd reject any kindness or gentleness shown.

"Care about me?" he scoffed. "You're just looking to court my family's favor."

"You're wrong. I do care. And you know that. Even if you are too stubborn and angry to admit it," she said calmly, refusing to give rise to his baiting. "We have to leave."

Fate interjected in the form of a horse's hoofbeats.

Oh, blast.

Reggie rushed around the stacks of hay and dropped onto the ground beside Stephen.

Her heartbeat throbbed harsh and unsteady against her rib cage. Reflexively, she sought Stephen's fingers and curled her coarse, callused palm around his. And the same boy who'd always rebuffed any show of affection or human contact clung to her.

The thump of boots striking the stones outside the stable reached Reggie, ratcheting up her panic. Her cheek layered to the floor; the hay scratched at her face, tickling her nose, torturing her bid at absolute stillness.

Go away. Go away.

Time and life's miseries should have shown her the inherent foolishness in prayer.

Those sure, powerful footfalls came closer, ever closer.

Reggie tightened her grip. Stephen winced, and she forced herself to lighten her hold.

Do not breathe . . . do not move . . . do not breathe . . . do not move . . .

That alternating mantra pulsed in time to the stranger's approaching steps and the click of a horse's hooves.

Too often, people believed fear was simply an emotion. But it was more.

With all of an inch between her face and the child alongside her, Reggie felt it pouring from Stephen's still frame. Smelled it in the faint rasps of his breath.

"Shh," she silently mouthed, pleading with her eyes.

And this boy who'd seemed to make it his life's mission to disobey everyone—including the Killoran clan he called family—complied.

Reggie strained her ears. No servant had come forward? Where was the stable hand to take that mount?

The door opened, with the heavier footfalls marking the stranger as a man coming first, then the clip-clop of the horse following him.

She bit down hard on her lower lip, the metallic tinge of blood flooding her nostrils. What gentleman tended his own horse? Especially at this hour. Gentlemen traveling about London now either returned by carriage . . . or rode horses back from the very wicked club that employed Reggie. Those lords left drunk and sloppy, and this man's smooth, near-silent, methodical movements as he removed the saddle and returned it to the opposite wall spoke of one in complete control.

No, this was no mere drunken wastrel of a patron from the Devil's Den Stephen had sought out.

This was another sort of nobleman. And a far deeper-seated terror held her in its grip. A drunkard was careless. They were the ones easiest to sneak away from. Composed, clearheaded nobles were the ones who'd never stomach two Seven Dials street toughs sneaking about their properties.

Surely you're not so dim-witted that you'd believe I'd ever welcome a match between you and my son . . .

Reggie closed her eyes, willing her past back to the grave where it deserved to stay buried. When she opened them, she found Stephen staring back.

"Shh," she repeated that noiseless reminder.

After an eternal stretch of time, the gentleman took his leave, closing the door in his wake.

They were so close . . . so very close . . .

Elation built in her breast, a thrilling sense of victory that could come only in escaping certain doom. And it harkened back to another triumphant escape.

Her joy was short-lived.

Stephen jumped up and, scrambling over her, rushed to the front of the stable.

"Stephen," she hissed as she struggled to stand.

The horse, an enormous black mount more beast than stallion, stamped its hoof and whinnied.

Or mayhap he sought to alert the master who'd gone off, unsuspecting that his stables had been invaded by strangers who had no place here.

"Get back," she pleaded in a frantic whisper.

Either failing to hear or not caring about her admonishment, Stephen layered himself to the front of the stable doors and, stretching up on his tiptoes, peered out.

Squinting, she searched for the object of the boy's focus. Her gaze landed on a tall, powerfully broad gentleman striding away from them. He cut such a quick path through the mews, his midnight-black cloak whipped furiously about his ankles. Not even the distance between them could hide the high quality of that garment.

A flash of silver glinted in the stables.

The black stallion snorted nervously, stamping his hooves.

Reggie's gaze locked on the familiar sapphire hilt of Stephen's dagger.

The boy reached for the handle.

What in blazes . . . ?

She grabbed his collar and yanked him back, hard. The blade sailed to the floor, flashing a shadow about in its descent, until it landed with a muffled thump upon the hay.

The stallion squealed, rearing up in the small space.

Reflexively, Reggie pushed the boy down and covered his body with her own. Her pulse thundered loud in her ears, muting the furious whinnies of the horse. She hunched forward, curling her body tight around Stephen.

The creature's front hooves landed close to her head, trampling errant strands of her hair and tearing them from her scalp. Tears popped up behind her eyes.

And when the world at last righted itself, Reggie straightened.

Stephen scrambled out from under her; his eyes glinted with outrage. "Ya shouldn't've done that."

Reggie held his gaze. "Yes. Yes, I should have." For so many reasons. If he wandered deeper down the path of violence and destruction, he'd ultimately be destroyed by it.

The boy glowered, his fury palpable.

Offering a truce, she rescued his dagger and handed it over.

The stallion intercepted her efforts.

A searing agony burnt Reggie's ear, and she fought back a silent scream. She shot her hand up to apply pressure to ease the throbbing. Something warm and wet coated her fingers. She drew them back.

Blood soaked her palm, the darkness of the stables lending shades of black to the crimson stain.

Horror filled Stephen's eyes. "Ya're 'urt."

"We have to go," she whispered, yanking the hood of her cloak back into place. Pressing her hand hard against the sore flesh, she sought to staunch the flow once more with the coarse wool fabric. Blood immediately seeped through, coating her fingers. With her spare hand, she took Stephen's fingers, and he hesitated.

She stared questioningly back.

There was a faint pleading in the proud boy's gaze. "Don't tell Broderick."

"I won't," she said, squeezing his hand.

He searched her face. "You promise?"

"You have my word." The longer they remained, the more they risked discovery at the nobleman's residence. "Now we have to leave."

This time, Stephen went unresistingly.

Making a slight crack in the slat, Reggie peeked out.

Empty.

Soon, however, these well-tended stables would be overrun with that nobleman's staff.

And she had no intention of either her or Stephen being around when that happened.

Chapter 2

You will pay. Not today. Not tomorrow. But when you least expect it . . .

Broderick tossed the reins of his mount to a waiting servant outside the Devil's Den.

What a bloody disaster.

With the hem of his cloak whipping an angry rhythm in time to his movements, he climbed the steps and sailed through the front doors thrown open for him.

"Mr. Killoran," the butler greeted with a deferential bow of his head.

Not breaking stride, Broderick continued forward.

At nearly five in the morning, the crowd had already begun to thin, but the tables still remained crowded enough to cause a raucous din. Any other night the rapid clink of coins striking coins and drunken revelries of the nobles present would have the same calming, victorious effect it always did.

This day, however, was different.

I got to His Lordship. He knows you ordered a nob's babe for Diggory.

That smug deliverance from Walsh played over and over in his mind.

All that remained was his word against Walsh's.

He'd been bested, and by the scum of the streets who dealt in the sale of children.

He growled, fisting his hands.

"Mr. Killoran." Nerrie, the second guard behind MacLeod, rushed over, falling into step beside him.

Broderick's mind raced. That meeting had been his only hope, and it had been a slim one at that. "Not now."

Undeterred, Nerrie matched his stride.

What course did he have? What options were available to him?

None that were—

"If I may, sir?" Nerrie tried again.

"You may not."

They reached the base of the stairwell to the private apartments, and the guards on duty there parted, allowing them to pass. "I understand you have other matters to attend to, Mr. Killoran."

God, had the blighter always been this damned thick?

"It sounds like there is a 'but' there. Do not let there be one," Broderick warned tightly, taking the steps quickly. The young guard, near to his twentieth year, had been one of the more recent hires and had proven himself very nearly obsequious in his efforts to please.

Trailing behind him, Nerrie hurried to keep up. "But . . ." They reached the main landing, and another set of guards on duty allowed them entry.

"I said, not now." Broderick stepped around a maid carrying a pitcher of water, that small slip of a girl waylaying the deuced persistent guard dogging his footsteps.

The usually quiet-for-this-hour corridor saw a flurry of servants rushing about, while other uniformed maids knelt on the Axminster carpet, scrubbing the wool. "What in blazes?" he muttered, stepping around the sea of his staff.

"Yes, sir. It is just . . . that . . ."

Whatever the young guard had to say could wait. Broderick was clinging to the world he'd built with his bare hands.

The other man swallowed loudly. "There was a problem while you were out," Nerrie blurted just as Broderick turned down the hall to his apartments.

He abruptly stopped. "Why didn't you say that?"

Nerrie cringed.

Maddock. A frantic energy thrumming through him, Broderick gripped the other man by his arm and dragged him over. "What. Problem?"

The guard's massive Adam's apple jumped. "M-m . . ." *Maddock.* "Miss Spark," the young man squeezed out on a ragged exhalation.

Through the panic sawing at his mind, he registered that most unexpected of names. "Miss Spark?" Broderick echoed dumbly, his grip going slack.

"Your *assistant*," Nerrie ventured.

"I know who my damned assistant is," he snapped, releasing the other man. Broderick thinned his eyebrows warningly on Nerrie's whitewashed face. "Careful about what you have to say concerning Miss Spark."

In his employ for more than ten years, she'd been both friend and confidante and had also dedicated her life to caring for the Killoran siblings. None had proven themselves more loyal to the Killoran family and the Devil's Den.

"No, of course she's not a problem, sir," the man stammered, looking one more misstep away from sobbing. "That is . . . she's *encountered* a . . . problem . . . sir."

Nerrie's statement penetrated the earlier fog left by his street meeting.

Now he took in those details that had previously escaped him: the sea of servants busy at work in the hall, the carpet marked with fresh stains of blood. "Where is she?" he barked.

"H-her rooms, s-sir," Nerrie called after him.

Readjusting his path, Broderick forced his feet into a measured calm he didn't feel. To reveal a hint of weakness or emotion only offered others a weapon to use against oneself. He reached the stairwell leading to the next floor and took the steps quickly.

Not bothering with a knock, Broderick tossed the door open. He shot a hand out to keep it from slamming back in his face.

Four sets of eyes met his: three human and one feline. From where he sat beside Reggie's feet, Gertrude's latest rescue, Gus, hissed. Broderick looked past the eclectic gathering and found Reggie. She held a cloth stained red with blood pressed to the right side of her face. Blood had matted the already crimson tresses to her cheek.

"Broderick." Gertrude was the first to greet him. She finished winding a bandage about Reggie's ear. "There."

He growled.

With another hiss, Gus bolted out from under Reggie's chair and darted under the corner bed.

"Get out," he ordered.

"I am fine," Reggie protested in those placating tones she used on disgruntled serving girls arguing over a patron.

Gertrude was already abandoning the linens in her hand. She stalked over to Stephen and said something quietly to the boy seated with his legs dangling over the edge of Reggie's bed.

When he refused to budge from his spot, Gertrude grabbed him by the hand and tugged him from his perch.

"Don't see why we can't stay," Stephen groused.

"Because it isn't our business," Gertrude explained.

"Ya can't say that for sure unless we 'ear 'im out."

Broderick fixed a hard look on his brother.

"Foine, foine. We're going," he muttered.

A nearly imperceptible glance passed between Reggie and Stephen, that look so infinitesimal it might have been imagined.

Stepping deeper into the room, Broderick allowed his siblings by. He looked to Gertrude, the eldest of his siblings, who, in the whirlwind of Cleo's and Ophelia's marriages, had slipped into the unfamiliar role of leader in the club. A role she'd shown marked ease in taking on.

"Call for the—"

"I've already called for Dr. Craven," Gertrude interrupted.

He yanked off his gloves. "Do not—"

"I'll not allow him abovestairs until you've summoned him." She raised a brow. "Is there anything else?"

"That's all." He faced Reggie.

Behind him, he registered the soft click as Gertrude shut the door.

Before he could put a question to her, Reggie spoke. "I really am fine, you know," she muttered, quitting her chair. Her modest skirts settled into place and put on full display the amount of blood she'd lost. She took up a place at the makeshift station of medical supplies Gertrude had abandoned.

Cursing, Broderick set aside for now his meeting with Walsh and hurried to Reggie's side. "Who did this?"

The stubborn woman who'd served as his assistant since he'd taken over ownership of the club dipped her cloth in the water and wrung it out. "It's merely a flesh wound," she said placatingly. Any other woman on his staff would have already been reduced to tears by the hint of blood.

It did not escape his notice that she'd failed to answer his question. But then, since he'd found her at London Bridge all those years ago, that is precisely the way she'd gone about answering any questions about herself . . . or her past: she didn't.

Shedding his cloak and then jacket, Broderick layered both over the back of the chair. "Sit," he ordered, dragging over another seat.

Reggie's lips formed a perfect, plump circle.

"I said, sit, Reggie." He unhooked the cuffs of his shirt and shoved his sleeves up. "No man, woman, or child who works for me comes back looking as you do now. Not without someone paying a price." And particularly not this woman, who'd become his closest confidante outside of his sisters.

Grudgingly she released the cloth. It landed with a *plunk*, pinging drops of water over the edge of the porcelain bowl and marking the oak side table.

"You're making something out of nothing," she muttered after she'd sat.

Time should have given him plenty of lessons on how to handle—or rather, deal with—this woman. Reggie, however, wasn't one to be handled, by him or by anyone. She possessed a calm pragmatism and control over her speech that could have run circles around the best barristers in London. And if she wished to hold on to a secret, she'd clamp her lips shut and deny herself breath before conceding to the one putting demands to her.

"Here," he urged. "Let me see." Taking her chin, he tipped her head sideways so he could assess the extent of her injuries. His heart twisted, and in that instant the sword hanging over him and his family was forgotten. "Reggie, you look dreadful." Dried blood splotched her cheeks and caked her hair. At some point, it had also formed a paste that matted loose strands to her face.

"My, aren't you the charmer," she said drolly.

Grabbing the forgotten cloth, Broderick washed the grime from her cheeks. His hands shook with a staggering weakness that should have appalled, but instead fury, frustration, and something worse weighted him: *fear*.

When staff changed, Reggie had been the steadfast one inside this hell. The scared girl he'd escorted from London Bridge had been so transformed over the years, into someone indomitable . . . or rather, that's how he'd allowed himself to see her. *What would I have done if she'd been hurt?*

But she was safe. Here with him, still.

With me?

She winced.

"I'm sorry," he murmured, steadying his palms.

He knew so much about this woman, and yet . . . how had he not known until now the satiny softness of her skin? And suddenly what had been a perfunctory task became something more. The air crackled around him. It sizzled like the earth right after a lightning strike. And damn if he hadn't always been drawn to that danger.

He released the soggy cloth.

Hooding his lashes, Broderick tucked the clean strands behind her uninjured ear and availed himself of an unobstructed view of her heart-shaped face.

The first time his guards had discussed Reggie Spark had been three years ago when Broderick had first inherited the Devil's Den from the scourge of the Dials. Seated around the breakfast table, awaiting Broderick's first meeting to commence, the kitchens had buzzed with bawdy talk about the different girls on staff.

Four guards had made the mistake of speaking ill of Reggie, deeming her too ugly to bed and too clever to marry. They'd been tossed out on their arses—they had worked their last day at the Devil's Den.

That had also been the last time anyone had spoken ill of her.

As an employer who'd vowed never to take advantage of those females on his staff, he'd been outraged at the bastards who'd besmirched Reggie's reputation. Now he saw past that fury to something else: the truth about how wrong they'd been.

The mass of loose curls drew his gaze to Reggie's face. Her wide eyes were a beguiling blend of greens and blues. Those aquamarine pools beckoned in their depths the crisp Cheshire countryside, blue skies and rolling emerald hills all at once.

Her crimped red curls, always drawn tightly back, now lay in a tangle about her shoulders, framing her face. What was once severe was now softened by that crimson waterfall. A pert nose, high cheeks, and a wash of freckles splashed upon luminous skin. Her rounded lips with a peaked Cupid's bow, made for kissing and more.

Reggie stared back with a question in her wide aquamarine eyes. "What is it?" she whispered.

Look away. Look away from whatever this momentary madness is.

And yet—Broderick swallowed hard—he'd proven weak in ways he'd never believed himself. "Reggie," he croaked, barely recognizing that gruff voice as his own, incapable of offering anything other than her name. The name of this woman who was a friend and confidante and employee. She was that, too. Nonetheless, he slid his fingers through her hair, those silken curls caressing his palm. Reggie's thick crimson lashes fluttered.

Hunger sang in his veins like a discordant symphony that made no sense and never would, but it was one he wanted to continue playing forever.

Her lips parted, and the softest of sighs slipped past her lips, a breathy invitation. Or did he merely hear what he wanted? Then, she tipped her head back, and there could be no mistaking that unspoken invitation.

Like the sailor drawn to the siren at sea, Broderick lowered his head, closer, closer. Craving something he'd never known he wanted . . . or needed . . .

And in this instant, it didn't matter that in lusting after Reggie Spark, he was devoid of honor. Only this need to feel something other than the fear that had gripped him these past days took hold and would not relinquish him.

I am my father . . .

Choking on his swallow, Broderick yanked away, drawing his hands back.

And mayhap he'd merely conjured her response out of his own yearnings.

Those crimson lips which he'd just been lusting after tipped at the corners into a troubled little frown. "That bad?" She felt around her head. Slightly crooked front teeth worried at that flesh, making a mockery of his notice.

Bloody hell. "It's not," he said in hoarsened tones. *I am. Lusting after a friend and woman on my staff.* Broderick gathered up the cloth and tossed it back into the wash basin.

Avoiding his gaze, Reggie came swiftly to her feet. "Then I'm finished." The spindly legs of her chair scraped along the floor.

"Stop." He encircled his hand gently about her wrist. "You're not. I'm not, that is."

She puzzled her brow. "What?"

"Through inspecting your wound," he clarified. By God, he was rambling. And all because he'd realized that Reggie Spark was . . . a woman. Of course it was natural to note those details. In fact, one might argue that it was unnatural that he'd not noted them before now. Guiding her back into her seat, he made to release her but stopped. "What in blazes happened here?" Broderick raised her palms closer, inspecting one and then the other. A faint dusting of scratches and bits of gravel remained embedded in the creases of her palms, those bilateral wounds indicating she'd come down on her hands. And by the hint of black and blue forming there, she'd come down hard.

At her silence, he looked up.

She shuttered her expression. "I fell."

"What rot." Regina Spark moved with an elegant grace at odds with every other woman who called this hell home—his sisters included. "You've never so much as stumbled or missed a step as long as I've known you."

"You're misremembering," she muttered.

"I don't *misremember* anything." Broderick gathered her heavy hair slicked with blood; those luxuriant tresses slid between his fingers like the fine satin sheets he'd commissioned for his bed upon taking ownership of this hell. Threading his hands through her curls, he drew them away from her face. Desire bolted through him. Shocking in its intensity and shaming for who it was he sat here lusting after, a woman who'd been like another sister . . . and when she was injured, no less.

Only, there was nothing fraternal in this desire to continue running his hands through the crimson tangle that was her hair.

Fighting that dangerous pull, he focused on his task. After all, not even Broderick himself operated under any illusions that he was a gentleman—in any way. Using the loose pins scattered on the table, he proceeded to tuck the strands into a messy topknot.

With Reggie still stubbornly silent, Broderick continued to probe, inspecting her scalp and cheeks for further hint of injury. Each mark a clue that he filed away. He trailed the tip of his index finger along her right lobe.

She winced.

"My apologies," he murmured, lightening his touch even further. "It does not escape my notice that you are being deliberately evasive." Broderick lowered his voice. "In the event you've forgotten, Reggie, I ultimately find out . . . *everything*."

Chapter 3

I hold your secrets. And soon everyone else will, too . . .

For one glorious moment, Reggie had believed Broderick was going to kiss her. His eyes had burnt with hot emotion that had stroked her like a physical caress.

Until the heady cloud she'd hovered upon had come crashing back to earth.

You bloody fool. Of course he wasn't going to kiss you . . .

Everything with Broderick, even his care of her ear, was all business. That was all that had ever existed in their relationship.

I ultimately find out . . . everything . . .

From under her lashes, Reggie searched Broderick for some indication that he'd gathered her plans. That even now, he simply toyed with her, knowing very well the lies she was guilty of.

As he separated the bloodstained rags and dragged over the handful of remaining clean ones, she studied him.

Or mayhap it was simply that his lashing out at her for those sins against him would be easier than . . . this. His kindness.

For his tender ministrations and concern about her well-being only intensified the guilt that sat low in her stomach.

"I told you, I'm fine," she calmly repeated when he made to pick up another makeshift bandage. He stopped, midtask, and shot her a probing look. "You really should be on the floors, you know," she said, her voice creeping up a notch.

I'm not made for this . . . Lying. Deception. Trickery.

"Eager to be rid of me, I see, love."

Her heart did a funny little jump. *Love.* "I trust that is a rarity," she said with forced brevity. Every serving girl, prostitute, and servant sighed as he passed.

"What? Ladies wanting to be rid of me?" He paused. "Quite," he added with a waggle of his brows that pulled a laugh from her.

And just like that the world righted. This was Broderick. And she Reggie, and this easy, comfortable relationship was all there would ever be.

It is why you're *leaving . . .*

An increasingly familiar melancholy took hold.

He quirked a golden brow. "May I continue?" He gestured to her injured ear.

Blast, he was tenacious. There wasn't a battle he'd concede. Nor did she believe he'd been content earlier with her evasiveness.

She offered a curt nod. "Fine."

Unwinding the bandage Gertrude had applied, he tossed it aside. The small gash at the top of her ear seeped blood, oozing a warm trail down her cheek.

A hiss exploded between his pearl-white, even teeth. "Bloody hell, Reggie."

Fury rolled off his frame, and the evidence of that concern for her sent warmth spiraling through her.

"Who did this?" he demanded again.

"I told you, no one." Which wasn't an untruth. That furious mount was not of the human species.

Some of the rage eased from his shoulders, and he dusted an open palm over her cheek.

Her breath quickened, and she leaned into that slight touch.

"Poor Reggie," he murmured, and for the first time, that hated moniker as it rolled off this man's lips was transformed into a seductive caress. That dizzying web he'd cast over her senses lifted at his next words. "You've always been rot at subterfuge." He let his hand fall.

A blast of cold swept over her, stealing the fleeting warmth of his touch.

He knows.

She clawed at the fabric of her skirts until the stiff wool crunched damningly. Reggie abruptly stopped.

Most people who survived in the Dials did so by ruthlessly taking what they wanted, when they wanted, without a single damn for those they trampled over on the path to their success.

But that had never been Reggie. She'd not developed that edge of ruthlessness after Lord Oliver's betrayal.

It was why, with Broderick caring for her as he now was, that guilt weighed on her chest, constricting her airflow and making it impossible to muster a flippant lie.

For in the first time in ten years, she kept not only one truth from this man who'd saved her but two.

And just then, she couldn't sort out which was the greater of them.

Broderick silently continued his work, cleaning her wound and applying pressure.

Collecting an untouched linen, he dunked it and set to work wiping the blood from her cheeks. "Your ear will not require stitches."

"It looks worse than it is." Reggie folded her arms at her chest. "*You* recall better than anyone just how badly the ear bleeds."

A half grin curved the right corner of his mouth, that honest expression of his amusement so very real and so very different from the affected, cynical smile he wore for the benefit of the patrons and gaming hell staff. "Yes." During one street fight between Broderick and a river rat with a propensity for too much jewelry, his opponent's damned ring had snagged his ear, and afterward, Broderick had left a trail of blood through the streets of London. He held Reggie's gaze, a faint accusation there. "I also recall you insisted on looking after my injury, as well."

"It wasn't at all the same," she said, her voice rich with exasperation. "Your wound required stitches." Ones that she'd herself expertly threaded when he hadn't trusted the task to another in the gang. Not even to his sisters.

Broderick lowered the rag, inspected her wound, and then applied a faint pressure. "Turn."

Reggie presented to him her throbbing ear. "You were out earlier," she observed, shifting the question to safer ground.

He paused; it was an infinitesimal stretch of time, so brief she might have merely imagined it.

She watched him from the corner of her eye. Broderick didn't leave his club in the early morn. Those were the hours it was busiest, and he ceded control of his post to no one. Never in all the years he'd led this club had anything called him away from it during those times. "Nothing to say?" she pressed.

He brushed his fingertips along her chin, tipping her gaze back to his. That butterfly-soft touch set her skin burning from the point of his touch. "Trade a secret for a secret?"

Her heart flipped. Those had been the first words he'd ever uttered to her. During her time serving Broderick and his family, he'd turned them on her, more teasing than anything. She returned her usual reply, delivered this time as a faintly breathless exhalation. "I've no secrets I wish to share."

"You're more stubborn than God," he muttered.

"Oh, is he?" She puzzled her brow. "Stubborn, that is."

Broderick flashed a half grin so empty it struck like an arrow in her chest. "I ceased believing in God long ago."

A chill scraped along her spine. There was an emptiness to his tone which she'd never heard from this man in all the years she'd known him, and she wanted to chase back the stark desolation there. Those raw, tormented sentiments had no place in his gaze . . . this man who shared nothing with anyone. And yet this was the closest he'd come to ever offering her a piece of his past. "Yes, well, if we cease to believe in Him, it makes the prospect of what comes after this rather grim, does it not?"

He chuckled. "Only if one is not content with what one possesses or does in their time here."

Reggie went still, again searching for a sign that he'd discovered her intentions. That he even now dangled her along in a game that would end with her secrets all laid out before them.

Releasing the cloth, Broderick continued his examination of her wound. "You see, Reggie, I shared the name of my assailant all those years ago because there was no one I cared to protect." Tommy Lassiter had robbed corpses and slaughtered cornerside whores, all to sell to body snatchers.

"I'm not protecting anyone," she said calmly.

"Where were you when it happened?"

"The stables." Which wasn't altogether untrue. They just hadn't been his stables. "It was a horse, Broderick," she said with a sigh. That much was true. It was just the foreign stables she'd been in and the boy she'd been chasing after that truly mattered.

"A horse?" He shook his head. "Horses do not bite."

"Oh, I assure you, they do. I've been bit on the thigh. That hurt like the Devil but didn't bleed nearly as much. Another nipped at my shoulder." She motioned to the spot of a long-ago wound. "My—"

He arched an eyebrow.

She abruptly stopped, hating that age-old penchant for rambling when nervous. It had been the curse of her childhood and just one of her many struggles in trying to fit in with the people of the Dials.

"My horses do not," he clarified.

No, they didn't. They were as obedient as any other member of his staff. Bloody hell, he was unrelenting. He wouldn't give in until he had an answer. She waged an inner battle with herself. Stephen would never forgive her for sharing his secret with Broderick. But Broderick was deserving of the truth. *Bloody hell.* "It happened when I was following Stephen."

All his muscles tensed. "What—"

She interrupted him and proceeded to provide a vague telling of Stephen's actions and how she'd come about an injured ear. She took care to avoid mention of the fancy end of London he'd been wandering around.

When she finished, Broderick cursed. "I told him he wasn't to be out on his own."

"But he's accustomed to it. One cannot simply just change their ways and habits."

"He can," he said bluntly. "He no longer has a choice."

Reggie searched his face. "What do you mean?" She knew this man enough to know there was more at play. He'd never limited the boy's actions before this. Not even after the fire he'd set that had destroyed their rival's gaming establishment.

Broderick immediately veiled his features and presented that mask he donned with everyone else in the clubs. "I meant nothing by it." He pushed his sleeves down. "I want you resting." Next, he collected his cloak and jacket. "I still intend for the doctor to see you. Regardless of the seeming innocuity of the wound," he spoke over her protestations. He started for the door. "I'd have you remember Jack Spier," he said, reaching for the handle.

Reggie snorted. "Jack Spier was stuck with a rusted blade, covered in dirt. I hardly think the two wounds are the same."

He inclined his head. "Ah, yes. And the mouth of a horse who eats shite and hay is a good deal cleaner," he drawled.

"Do you know your sister's equine books indicated that if a horse eats dung it's an indication there is a problem with his diet. In fact, it is known as coprophagy and—"

"Reggie."

She sighed. "Very well. Send him."

He flung his garments over his opposite arm. "Take the remainder of the day to rest," he instructed, starting for the front of the room.

"Broderick?" she called after him. He spared her a glance over his shoulder. "He needs to be more carefully guarded . . . but go easy on him."

Reggie stared at the oak panel long after he left. Broderick had been upset with the information she'd sought to keep from him this day.

What would he say when he learned just what she'd kept from him all these months . . . and the plans she had for her future?

Chapter 4

Which would you prefer? To spend out your days in Newgate? Or a hanging? Either way, your fate is the same.

She'd been looking after his brother.

Not a single sane man, woman, or child would go dashing through the streets of the Dials, and certainly not for a miserable, surly boy like Stephen.

And yet . . . that is precisely what Reggie had done.

Mayhap it was that the end was rushing up quick to meet him. Or mayhap it was the early-morn hour and the days without sleep, but an appreciation stirred for the courageous spitfire who'd throw reason and caution aside to look out for another.

Nay, not just appreciation. This went far deeper. People didn't put other people's well-being before their own. Why, his own coward of a father was testament to that. And then there was Reggie: fearless.

Courageous. Undaunted. And *beautiful.* She was that, too. He just hadn't noticed that inconvenient fact—*until now*.

Walking briskly through his private suites, Broderick choked. *You bloody fool.* The noose was tightening. His future had all but been decided a short while ago in the alleys of the Dials, and here Broderick was, lusting after Regina Spark. Swamped with self-disgust, he loosened his cravat.

Nay, it had been a momentary lapse in sanity that had very nearly seen his mouth on hers. The reality of his own mortality . . . of the impending doom about to rain down upon him . . . had chased off all reason.

Knowing that, however, didn't make him feel any less caddish.

Focus on your bloody situation.

After all, he had far greater matters to set to rights.

Broderick strode past servants still hard at work cleaning the bloodstains from the carpets. Whether he'd almost kissed Reggie, wanted to, or dreamed the entire interlude was irrelevant in the scheme of the peril that faced him: Walsh and Lucy.

Nay, more specifically . . . the Marquess of Maddock.

I cannot make this go away.

He dragged a shaky hand through his hair. He was at a loss. Just as he'd been when he and his father had been turned out by his father's employer and Broderick's godfather, the Earl of Andover.

Broderick's father had proven himself useless in helping them survive.

And if I do not see all my family cared for and looked after . . . I'm very much his son.

He hardened his jaw. No, he'd not leave his family in the same sorry state his miserable excuse of a sire had left him. Each sibling would be looked after and their futures settled. Broderick neared the stairway where his head guard stood on duty.

At his approach, MacLeod straightened.

"Where is my sister?"

"She was called to the stables." The burly man's lips twitched. "Problem with one of the barn cats."

Yes, that had forever been Gertrude. She was the most tenderhearted of his sisters. Absent of the same pitilessness that drove Broderick, Stephen, Cleo, and Ophelia, she was the only soft one of the Killorans. The one who'd always required protecting . . . *and I failed her.*

Just as I'm failing her again, now.

A sick sense of shame gripping him, Broderick found his way through the mews.

All the hands and grooms stood in a circle outside the stone stables, smoking cheroots and quietly talking.

Harry, the most recent street urchin rescued by Ophelia and set to work at the Devil's Den, immediately snapped to attention. Following the boy's focus over to Broderick, the well-clad servants immediately tossed down their cheroots and cigars and pocketed their flasks.

Broderick motioned for them to continue as they'd been as he let himself in through the wide, curved white doorway. The scent of hay and horses immediately filled his nostrils.

He blinked, attempting to bring the darkened space into clarity, searching for Gertrude . . . and finding her at the far end of the stables.

Back presented to him, she lifted a finger warningly.

With a careful tread, he picked his way over the errant pieces of hay that littered the floor.

He stopped beside his sister.

"How is Reggie?"

"She will be fine." Intractable as always, but her wound would heal. "I see you've given my entire stable staff the morn off."

Gertrude again touched a silencing finger to her lips. "He's being mulish," she whispered softly, ignoring that droll jest on Broderick's part.

Broderick followed her stare overhead.

A pair of gold eyes twinkled in the otherwise dark space. *"Meowwww-meowwww-meowwww,"* the black cat wailed, remaining firmly planted on a narrow beam.

The extent of his experience with those feline creatures of course was aged information that came from his time with Lord Andover, but Gertrude had taken the fickle animals in enough over the years for him to know just how self-reliant they were. "A cat has nine lives. For three he plays, for three he strays, and for the last three he stays."

Gertrude quietly snorted. "What rubbish. You've escaped death and danger. No one dares believe you are in possession of nine lives. Why should Master Brave?"

For all the hell of that morn, he found himself grinning. "A cat who's gone and gotten himself caught on a beam and can't get down without assistance is richly misnamed."

"Oh, hush," she chided, jabbing a sharp elbow into his side. He winced. "Don't listen to him. You are far braver than all the horses and dogs in the whole of the stables," she crooned to the still mournfully moaning creature overhead.

As if there were some magic to her tone, Master Brave stopped.

Gertrude held her hands up.

The black cat darted back and forth on the beam.

Sighing, Gertrude let her arms fall.

They remained there, brother and sister silently following Master Brave, and Broderick searching for the words to put his request to Gertrude.

The very request he'd put to her was the same he'd put to each one of his sisters before . . . only this time, the reasons were different. This time, it was about something more: seeing everyone—his siblings, his staff, his business—secure.

Bitterness stung his insides. For it was just further proof of how his life had spiraled out of control, and he couldn't get a handle on it. He inhaled slowly. "Gertrude—"

"If I'm to have a Season, I'll have certain terms met," she cut him off, bringing him up short.

"How did you . . . ?"

"Know?" She arched an eyebrow. "First Cleo. Then Ophelia. It didn't take much to gather that I'd be the next in line you'd try and find a noble husband for." She moved her determined stare from that damned cat over to Broderick. "If I'm to do this for the club, I want concessions from you."

Of course she'd assume it was about his business. Why should she believe anything different? None of his siblings or staff would. He'd lost the right to that faith. And he was not so very selfish that he wanted her or any of their siblings to know the truth. Either way, it was easier for all that they carried that low opinion. "Very well." Unable to meet his sister's eyes, he studied Master Brave's frantic pacing. "What are your terms?"

"My animals come with me."

She expected he'd send her off with one of their sisters. He'd made the mistake of sending Ophelia off to Cleo, and though Ophelia was happy, she'd nearly found herself hanged because of her love for Connor O'Roarke. "I'm accompanying you." And he'd be there to look after her, as long as he was able. *As long as that bastard allows you . . .*

Gertrude's eyes formed circles. *"You?"*

"And I'll . . ." He loosened his cravat further. "Allow the cats."

"All of them, Broderick. Or I'm not coming."

Oh, bloody hell. He tugged free that strip of white silk and slapped it against his leg. They'd have an entire menagerie in the Grosvenor Square townhouse he'd rented for the remainder of the Season. "Fine. All of them. Rodents and cats." An unlikely, incompatible lot of creatures she'd assembled, as only Gertrude could.

She launched her next demand. "Stephen accompanies us."

His heart squeezed. "Of course." He'd also keep his brother close as long as he was able. Then, God willing, if all went to plan, Gertrude would be the one with access to that world where a Killoran could properly watch after Stephen.

"And I continue overseeing his lessons."

"It is not possible." Broderick stuffed his cravat into the front of his jacket. "Nor is it because I don't believe you've done an admirable job with his schooling to this point," he interjected when she made to speak. Gertrude had been assigned the unenviable task of instructing a boy who'd rather be picking pockets than sitting in a schoolroom, and despite that had taught him to read anyway. "You'll be occupied, attending formal events and gatherings." All her energies needed to go toward making her match . . . securing her future . . . being settled.

Gertrude snorted. "You have an optimistic view of my Season."

"Don't disparage yourself." Broderick pressed his fist to his chest. "You're a Killoran."

"I'm blind," she said bluntly, without self-pity. "No one wants a blind wife."

"You'll find an honor . . ." Before Broderick's sins against the Marquess of Maddock had come to light and he'd discovered his role in the theft of that nobleman's child, he'd have been able to offer the eldest of his siblings assurances. That no longer held true. He and Gertrude were those beloved mice being toyed with by Lord Maddock, whose claws would be out when they least expected. "You'll marry a respectable gentleman who'll overlook your *partial* blindness," he settled for.

"Blind is blind," she muttered.

"Your worth is far greater than your eyes," he said quietly.

A sound of frustration escaped her. "I'm not relenting on this, Broderick." She refocused on the black cat, motioning again for the creature to come down.

The cat batted at the air with his paw but remained rooted to his spot.

"Very well," Broderick said, quickly adding, "but you'll only do so if you do not have previous engagements."

Gertrude shook her head. "That is not good enough." She moved so that she stood directly in front of him. "Stephen requires routine, Broderick. As all children do," she spoke in strident tones. "He needs some sense of order in his disordered life, and at the very least we can provide him that before he . . ." She bit down on her lower lip.

Oh, Christ. Broderick closed his eyes. *He is going to be lost to us . . .* "Two hours each morning," he managed to get out.

"Three."

Had she always been this tenacious? "Three," he capitulated. But he needed her to know . . . "This arrangement, Gertrude . . . there will be benefits to you. Your security. Your safety. Marriage is just"—Gertrude stared expectantly back—"a business arrangement." Just as all life was. A contract entered into between two people that proved mutually beneficial.

Gertrude snorted. "*That's* a lot of rot."

"It's the truth," he said simply. All relationships were based on what one could both do for another and receive for themselves in return.

"They're not. But I'll not debate the point with you. I have another term."

"What is it?"

His sister drew her shoulders back. "I want Reggie to serve as my companion."

"Absolutely not." Impossible. Not after what had nearly transpired between him and her. She'd been oblivious to his lustful thoughts, but to have her close . . . ?

His flat rejection was met with a scowl. "And whyever not?"

Because he didn't trust himself. Because he needed some distance with which to return their relationship to the platonic, businesslike one that had defined it for . . . all the years they'd known one another. "Because I might not have been born to the peerage, but I know enough the requirements for a lady's governess or companion." God, even as that admission left his mouth, he inwardly cringed at the pomposity of it.

Gertrude scoffed. "What a supercilious thing to say."

Yes, it was. He deserved to be called out on it. And yet he'd still rather his siblings took him for a self-important prig than know the truth: that he was a bounder lusting after a loyal employee and woman who'd been like family to them. Broderick fiddled with his collar. "Although I call Reggie friend and trust her with my very life, Polite Society will never prove as accepting," he brought himself to say. Which wasn't *untrue*. There was no one he trusted more. No one as loyal as Reggie. Those bastards, however, wouldn't see her worth or her strength. They'd merely see her bloodlines—or rather, lack of—and both she and Gertrude would pay the price in the *ton*'s disdain.

"Since when did you become so bloody puffed up?" Gertrude shot back. Master Brave hissed; that sound sent nervous whinnies up around the stables. "Oh, my apologies, love," Gertrude crooned, Broderick summarily forgotten. The cat darted farther down the wood beam. "I shan't do it again."

"Gertrude," Broderick began, needing her to let the matter of Reggie go. "You require someone who can perform proper introductions and who knows the social norms of the peerage." *Liar. You're just afraid to have Regina Spark there, now that you've noticed the hue of her bow-shaped lips and can't stop thinking of what it would be like to claim them.*

"Reggie can do all those things, and the continuity will be good for Stephen," Gertrude said, matching Master Brave's back-and-forth pacing.

Yes, there was nothing Reggie couldn't do. But he could not have her there. She'd be a distraction . . . that he couldn't afford. Not now.

"Furthermore," Gertrude said, "I'm not sure if you've ever listened to or observed Reggie, but she wasn't born to the streets."

That brought him up short. Yes, Reggie spoke in flawless King's English and exuded propriety and decorum in a place wholly stripped of either, but that did not mean she was also familiar enough with that world to ease Gertrude's way. As his sister continued to cajole that black cat overhead, Broderick caught his chin in his hand.

Nay, Reggie hadn't been born to Polite Society, but she, as Gertrude aptly pointed out, was more skilled than any of the governesses who'd tutored his sisters on proper decorum. More than that, she could wield her tongue with the same skill she could a blade but without Cleo's and Ophelia's loose tempers. With a fierce protector such as Reggie Spark at her side, there could be no doubting Gertrude would be defended if—when—need be, while having a companion who also knew how to conduct herself amongst the peerage. And that mattered more than his own sudden fascination with the young woman.

"Very well."

Gertrude spun around. "What?"

She hadn't thought he'd concede that term, then. "Reggie will serve as your chaperone," he said clearly for his sister's benefit. His mind was already going to what needed to be done before Reggie took on that respective role. She'd require a new wardrobe, one that would mark her position of influence and wealth.

An image flashed behind his mind's eye of Reggie as she'd been a short while ago, with her hair in a tangle of crimson curls around her nipped waist, and he stripped her of those drab brown skirts, replacing them with purple ones.

His mouth went dry.

Nay. A rich emerald green of diaphanous satin that clung to Reggie's long, supple frame—

"At last!"

Broderick jumped.

Master Brave scrambled down the sloping beam and rushed into the corner stall. A moment later he bolted out from under the opening in the door and raced over to Gertrude. She scooped him up and murmured soothing, nonsensical words to the troublesome creature.

His ears burning, Broderick started for the front of the stables.

"Broderick?"

He turned slowly back. And for a horrifying instant he believed she'd seen those wicked thoughts that had gripped him.

Gertrude arched a brow. "I suggest before you're so confident in your promise that you speak with Reggie." Even dimly lit as the stables were, he caught the sparkle in Gertrude's eye. "And I suggest before you do *that*, you wash the stench of sweat and horse from your person."

He snorted. For everything that had proven beyond his control and influence, his sister had at last charged him with a task he could succeed at. Broderick would pay a visit to the one person who'd never denied a request he'd put to her in the ten years he'd known her.

Chapter 5

Soon you'll know what it is to lose everything you care about . . .

> "Over the mountains
> And over the waves,
> Under the fountains
> And under the graves,"

Reggie softly sang.

> "Under floods that are deepest,
> Which Neptune obey,
> Over rocks which are the steepest,
> Love will find out the way."

Seated at her desk, she tapped her pen back and forth in time to the beat of the familiar ballad. The long-forgotten joy she'd always known as a girl singing those beloved melodies filled her. How much she missed music. And soon, if she was successful, she and Clara, the former madam who had been placed in charge of the female Devil's Den staff, would have a whole life devoted to that love. She glanced down as her current work companion—Gus, the grey tabby found 'round back of the Devil's Den—yawned widely.

"How shameful," she chided. With her spare hand, she ruffled the smooth fur between his brows. "I just sang my heart out, and not so much as a meow?"

My girl . . . you've a voice that would make a whole choir of angels weep with envy . . .

The unexpected echo of her father's voice, coupled with her once innocent laughter, filtered around the chambers of her memory. It had been so long since she'd thought of them. It had been so long since she'd *allowed* herself to think of him. Or her brothers.

Gus lapped her palm with a coarse tongue, snapping her back to the moment. *"Meow."* He purred, nudging his head into her hand. Just one of many animals rescued by Gertrude Killoran. Reggie had developed a kindred connection to Gus. A snarling, snapping, terror-filled creature scrounging for scraps in the alley, he'd been so very much like Reggie. Despite his world wariness, he'd become a reliable, comfortable companion.

"*Pfft*, now you'd offer your feline praise." Reggie tossed down her pen. "Just like every man, you are. Making a lady beg for your attentions and oblivious to how she's feeling." Reggie softened that chastisement by lifting the nearly weightless creature into her arms. She held him close, his wet black nose pressed to hers, his accusatory green eyes staring back. "Oh, very well. You are correct. I am . . . being deliberately avoidant, but you are so very sweet that it makes it easier to do."

Avoidant, just as she'd been since Cleo Killoran had wed Adair Thorne of the rival gaming hell and the fabric of Reggie's existence—a *family* member—to the Killorans had begun to unravel. Her ordered life within the Devil's Den as assistant to Broderick Killoran was coming to an end.

And then where would she be?

The smile she had for Gus dipped, and she glanced over at the clock ticking away incessantly in the corner.

And with it, reality crept back in.

Reggie dropped her gaze to the pages spread out before her. A jumble of numbers and calculations that all added up . . . to a possible new future.

Away from the Devil's Den.

Away from when Gertrude, the last unwedded Killoran woman, married.

And away from Broderick Killoran . . .

Why had he been so blasted nice that morning? He'd tended her ear and sent a doctor to inspect her injury.

And each of those kindnesses vastly complicated everything Reggie had dreamed of, plotted, and intended to carry out.

Reggie dropped her head and banged it against the surface of her desk.

Gus dug his claws into her thigh, kneading her brown wool work dress.

"I know, I know," she groaned. "I'm a bloody fool."

"Meowwww."

"Oh, now you'll share some feline attention. Traitor," she grumbled into her papers. She petted Gus down the middle of his soft back.

He arched, as if to break free, but then turned his lithe body close to her belly.

She cradled the oft-skittish cat on her lap and forced her efforts back to the documents sprawled before her.

Absently stroking the tiger stripes that stretched from his neck to his tail, Reggie redirected her attention to the closest page.

No matter how many times she'd gone through the mathematics of it, the number remained the same: ten thousand pounds was what it cost for that new beginning.

And that didn't include the weekly and bimonthly and annual costs for drinks and food and a modiste, nor salaries for the staff and workers and . . .

Groaning, she lowered her forehead to the table and banged it in a silent, rhythmic knock.

For one of Broderick's obscene wealth, such a sum would not even be worthy of a second glance. But this, her venture—something that had never been done before—would require every last, precious fund she'd accumulated in her tenure within the Devil's Den.

And betrayal. Rolling her head sideways, she stared at the names assembled upon another page of eleven of the serving girls at the club and one head guard—her venture also would require a betrayal.

"It's not a betrayal," she muttered, grabbing another page that contained possible properties. All of which had been crossed out. "Not really." *If* Reggie went forward with the purchase of her own establishment, it wasn't a rival gaming hell.

But she would be in direct competition for clients who'd hopefully seek out an alternate form of entertainment where women were at the front and center.

Women who, in the name of her security as much as theirs, she'd steal out from under Broderick. Though honorable her intentions might be, that sentiment meant far less in the Dials than loyalty. These were different streets than the one she'd called home a lifetime ago.

A rhythmic knock sounded at the door.

The grey tabby hissed and unsheathed his claws. Reggie winced as he scrambled down her body, leaving a trail of scratches in his wake before bolting under his usual spot, her corner bed.

"Come in," she called out.

Leather folio in hand, Clara Winters, who was responsible for overseeing the female staff, entered. "Are you all right?" she asked without preamble as she dragged a chair over to the desk and set herself down alongside Reggie.

Previously employed by their rival club, Clara had been treated as an outcast by the staff of the Devil's Den since she'd arrived. It was a sentiment Reggie could sympathize with all too well, as she'd once been shunned by Diggory's gang. That had created a kindred bond between the two women. From the moment Clara had caught Reggie defending her to the guards, they'd struck up a special friendship.

"I'm quite fine," she assured Clara, rolling shoulders that were tight from hours of being hunched over her papers.

Clara gave her a long look. "Following the boy around?"

"Shh." Reggie whipped her head around. One never knew who was about and when, and given the recent trouble Stephen had found, if the wrong person overheard a single thing about the child, he'd swing. "How . . . ?"

"How do I know?" Clara tossed the folder in her hands down atop Reggie's papers. "I saw you sneaking out. He's not your job."

Her stomach sank. "Did anyone else see?" she asked, ignoring that latter reminder from Clara. Family looked after family.

"The club was busy."

Some of the tension left her.

"You deserve better than this," Clara said matter-of-factly. "Spending your days chasing around after a child who doesn't want to be chased and filling the role of all-purpose servant for a man who'll never see you."

Reggie flinched. So Clara had gathered Reggie's greatest secret, the humbling one she'd kept close for all these years. The cowering girl who'd been rescued by Broderick would have wilted under that direct questioning. That girl had also died on London Bridge as much as if she'd jumped to her watery death that night. "I trust you're here for some other reason than lecturing me?"

An appreciative glint lit the other woman's eyes. "Here," she said, pushing the brown leather folio closer to Reggie's fingertips.

Grateful for the business diversion that was always safer than any talk about Broderick Killoran, Reggie picked up the folder. Loosening the ribbon, she withdrew the stack of documents.

"I found another place," Clara said needlessly. "I have a meeting scheduled for us later this afternoon."

"I see," Reggie murmured, working her gaze over the details inked on the page. "The price is right," she murmured.

"It's far less expensive than any other property we've visited."

"And the funds we save on the purchase price could go toward the repairs," Reggie noted distractedly. She flipped to the next page, searching for the building address, and froze. She was already shaking her head. "No." This wouldn't do. It was one thing, leaving the Devil's Den and establishing a business of her own . . . "We'd be a mere three streets away." A short walking distance between Reggie and Broderick . . . and their halls. It would put them in direct competition with the men who dwelled in or visited these streets.

The other woman pushed the sheet with the address back toward Reggie. "You're not being logical in terms of the business end of this."

She bristled. "I've been nothing but logical about this entire venture since I brought it to you." That effectively silenced Clara. For ultimately it had been Reggie who, months earlier, had raised the possibility of a partnership. One that would make them shared proprietors, no longer reliant upon work at the Devil's Den . . . or on any man. Reggie attempted to reason with her. "I remain as committed as I've always been to our plans. However, I will conduct myself with honor, and this?" She turned the damning page around. "This is not honorable."

"Honor," Clara spat. "Was it honor that made the last man I gave funds to in exchange for property take those monies and run off?"

Reggie's heart twisted. "Oh, Clara. I didn't kn—"

"I don't want your pity," Clara said flatly. "I want you to think logically. Men aren't honorable."

No, most weren't. Life had proven as much to Reggie. But Broderick . . .

"Do you think Broderick Killoran would make the decision to purchase or not to purchase an establishment because of a misplaced sense of righteousness?" Clara demanded, as if she'd followed the unspoken direction of Reggie's thoughts.

No, the man who'd turned a seedy tavern frequented by society's vilest thugs into a gaming empire to rival any in England would never let emotion drive his actions. This, however, was different. He'd saved Reggie, and that was a debt that could not be repaid and at the very least commanded a modicum of loyalty.

She made to return the document to the folder, but Clara put a hand on hers and stopped her. "Keep it."

"I cannot do this. . ." *Nay* . . . "I will not purchase anything just three streets away. Nor is mine strictly a matter of honor. Broderick would crush any place in the Dials that even remotely threatened his bottom line."

With slow, precise movements, Clara stacked the remainder of the papers and reorganized them so they were perfectly ordered. Shutting the folio, she shoved it across the desk toward Reggie. "Is it purely loyalty that drives you?" She held Reggie's stare. "Or is it that you need as much distance as you can place between yourself and . . . him?"

Reggie's gut clenched. If she'd been so transparent that this woman, whom she'd known less than three years, had gathered the depth of her weakness for Broderick, who else knew?

"No one knows," Clara said with a gentleness that she'd only shown to the young women who answered to her at the Devil's Den. She scooted her chair closer until she sat beside Reggie and then covered Reggie's tense hands with her own. "This was not my dream, Reggie,"

Clara continued with that same tenderness. "You presented me with an idea of something that has never been done."

Yes, she had.

"Do you recall that night?"

"I do," she said softly. Unable to sleep, Reggie had gathered her wrapper and slipped out into the gardens Broderick had built for Gertrude. She had come upon a quietly weeping Clara. "You said the idea was rot," she pointed out. "That men wanted only one thing from women and it wasn't their voice. Not unless they could have a woman on her back, too."

A wry grin twisted Clara's lips. "I was wrong." It was a foreign admission men and women she'd lived amongst didn't freely make. She gave Reggie's hands a light squeeze. "Just as you are wrong now in not going forward with this."

"I have not said no," she said, a defensive edge sliding into her reply. "Only to this place."

"And every place before it," Clara interjected. "I'm merely asking you to come with me today. The appointment has been made. There is no harm in simply visiting the place." She let that dangle there, enticing Reggie with a promise of a future.

Reggie dropped her gaze to the folder. Honor, logic, and self-preservation all warred for supremacy. And it surely marked her a faithless snake that she wanted to visit the property anyway. Broderick be damned. She wanted to put herself, her future, Clara's future, and other nameless-for-now women's futures, those women in desperate need of security, first.

And yet mayhap she was proving herself still the naive miss she'd been from the country, new to London, for she could not bring herself to betray the man who'd helped her when she by all rights should have perished in the Dials.

In the end, her allegiance to Broderick won out. "Find additional properties." Reggie shook her head. "But it won't be this one."

"You deserve to be more than the lackey for some man who doesn't need you and who'll eventually cast you out." Quiet even as it was, Clara's voice still rang with the conviction of one who knew.

Reggie jumped to her feet. "He wouldn't do that." He wasn't like Lord Oliver.

She's a lovely fuck . . . worth the price . . .

Her breathing increased, and she dug her fingers into her skirts, her jagged nails penetrating the thin wool fabric. She'd not think of him. Or of that night. Or of every mistake that had brought her to this point . . .

Sadness twisted the other woman's exotic features, wrenching Reggie back from the misery of her past. "Reggie, that is precisely what I said. And look at me now. Dependent upon you partnering with me so I might try my hand at a new beginning. And you? You'll abandon your plans all because Broderick Killoran rushed to your rooms to see why there was blood all over his carpets," she said with so much pity that shame coursed through Reggie.

God, how she hated Clara for being right. But she hated herself for wanting so very badly for her to be wrong. For Broderick had entered other rooms belonging to women who'd been hurt or injured, but Reggie had more often than not been at his side. He'd spoken gently, also wheedling details from them.

Not in a single instance, however, had he personally tended those bruises, scrapes, or cuts.

Fool. She was a fool, just as Clara suggested . . . wanting to see more where there never would be.

Clara touched her arm. "We need to both be thinking of our futures, Reggie. What will happen when Killoran decides he wants to become the next White's or Brooks's and rids himself of the female staff?"

"He hasn't given any indication that those are his intentions."

"Competing with Ryker Black's family?" Clara eyed her like she'd sprung a second head. "You're too clever to be naive."

And the rub of it was, the other woman was correct. Broderick was always wanting more. Taking more: The clubs. Power. Noble connections.

The door flew open.

Reggie and Clara exploded to their feet.

Reggie's heart kicked up a beat. "Stephen," she greeted. Hurriedly gathering her papers and folio, she filed them away in her bottom drawer. *Blast and damn.* One of the stealthiest pickpockets in London, he'd plucked fortunes with the same ease he had secrets used by Diggory and his henchmen. "Is something wrong?" From the corner of her eye, she searched for some hint that he'd caught the talk between herself and Clara.

"I got to talk to ya." Stephen spared Clara a quick, derisive glance and then jerked his head at the door. "Time for ya to go."

"You miserable little bastard. You need someone to teach you manners," Clara said crisply.

Reggie winced. No truer words had ever been spoken, and yet Stephen was still just a boy. A boy who'd endured greater hells than most grown men. He'd forever locked horns with the woman who'd come to them from Black's establishment, with Reggie playing at peacekeeper between them.

"Ain't gonna be ya." He sauntered into the room like a prized peacock. "Ain't gonna be anybody. But certainly not ya." As proud as if he owned the Devil's Den himself, he plopped himself into the seat Clara had vacated and dropped his ankles on the edge of the desk.

That relaxed pose he'd imitated from his eldest sibling, however, merely painted Stephen in a boylike image. He was very much a child playing at adulthood.

"Stephen," Reggie reprimanded in her governess tones. Giving his dirt-stained boots a little shove, she knocked his feet back to the floor. "If you'll excuse me?" Reggie asked as she handed Clara back her folder.

They exchanged a look, Clara silently pleading.

Reggie shook her head once.

As soon as she'd gone, Stephen again dropped his small feet on the corner of her desk. "Wot was that about?"

Meeting that insolent question with a blanket of silence, Reggie leveled the boy with a stern glance.

His button nose scrunched up.

"Now." She folded her arms and reclaimed control of the situation. "I don't believe you're here to speak about Miss Winters." Hers was a statement.

"No." Stephen narrowed his eyes. "Oi ain't."

Although the staff and former gang members left over by Diggory regularly derided her for her lack of ruthlessness, she'd gleaned enough from her time in the streets to know the importance of unsettling one's opponent. "Why were you at that residence?"

Stephen's color went slightly ashen. "Ain't yar business." Except this time he sounded scores less confident. He swallowed loudly. "Did ya tell him?"

That question came out on a whispery croak that tugged at her heart. For all the ways in which Stephen was crass, cold, and oftentimes unkind, he still was just a boy. In these streets that stripped a person of their humanity, it was too easy to forget that.

"I had to tell him something," she quietly said. "He's your brother. He's concerned about you and deserves to know—"

"Did ya tell him where I was?"

In Grosvenor Square. "I didn't." She paused. "Should I have?"

He stared at the tips of his feet and answered with a question of his own. "Ya going to?"

Reggie placed her palms on the back of her chair. "Well . . . it depends."

"You want to know why I was there," he grumbled, slipping into his perfect King's English.

"I want to know."

Stephen scoffed, instantly shattering all pretense of vulnerability. "Do you think *Broderick* wants to know that Clara missed her shift?" He narrowed his eyes. "He of course will want to know why she missed that shift."

Just like that, she had the tables flipped on her by a child.

She carefully picked her way around her mind, searching for her next move. It was one thing to put herself at risk, but Clara, who'd been forced out of her last employment, was only recent to their ranks. Nor would any of Broderick's loyal staff speak to the woman's defense.

Stephen dragged out her bottom desk drawer with the tip of his boot and propped his feet on the edge of that makeshift footstool. Looping his arms behind his head, he smirked.

Despite that bravado, the truth remained she couldn't simply turn a cheek to whatever he'd been on about. Given that he'd burnt down the rival gaming hell, she could not risk that others might be in danger because of him.

"Tell me why you were there and what you intended." As Diggory had always said: a purse was a purse was a purse. One didn't follow a fat one and sacrifice a smaller, safer one.

A dark glimmer lit the boy's eyes. "An' if I do, ya won't go to Broderick?"

She wouldn't lie to him. "I don't know the answer to that." Having herself been the victim of false promises and assurances, she appreciated the value of truth. "It depends on what you have to say."

Tears welled in his eyes, and he dropped his feet back to the floor. He focused on the tips of his boots like they contained the answer to mankind's existence. But it was too late. She'd already detected that glassy sheen. Proud, spitting, and snapping most days, Stephen never showed a hint of weakness. This evidence of his vulnerability caused a physical ache. "Ya got a kerchief? Oi got something in my eye, is all." He glared at her, daring her with his tear-filled eyes to challenge that.

Shoving to her feet, Reggie went and gathered an embroidered handkerchief from her armoire. She appreciated how proud he was. When she returned to his side, Reggie said nothing. She simply held out that scrap.

Stephen yanked it from her fingers and blew noisily into it. When he spoke, his words emerged muffled around the fabric, his tones so threadbare she had to lean down to hear. "Devlin 'ad issues with the gent."

She creased her brow. Devlin, one of the children who'd been hired recently, brought into the club by Ophelia, was of similar age and spirit as Stephen. "Devlin?" she asked, reclaiming her seat.

Stephen offered a jerky nod, confirming she'd heard correctly. A strand tumbled over his small brow, highlighting once more his tender years.

"H-his da owed the nob a hefty sum, an' 'e took his timepiece as payment. Da ended up 'anging, anyway, and Devlin wants the piece back. To remember his da by." He scoffed. "Not sure why anyone would want to remember one's da." Her own father's beloved visage slipped forward, and with it a wave of agony and heartbreak so acute it threatened to drag her down. She clung to Stephen's telling, as it stopped her from wandering down that path of regret and pain. "Devlin was going to do a nick from the gent, and Oi knew Oi could nab it more easily." Stephen kicked her bottom drawer closed and glowered at her. "And Oi would 'ave if ya 'adn't showed up."

Reggie searched his face. He wasn't being truthful. It had been there in the first syllable of his lengthy explanation.

"Ya going to tell 'im?" Stephen asked hesitantly. When he was never hesitant.

"No." He perked up in his seat. "*You* are going to tell him and allow him to get that piece back for Devlin."

His little shoulders slumped. "Foine." Ducking his head, he jumped to his feet. "Oi'll tell him."

She stood. "*When?*"

"Later. 'e's meeting with MacLeod."

"Now," she countered.

He folded his arms across his chest. "Mayhap Oi should mention about Black's girl running around when she's supposed to be working?" He smiled a frosty grin that raised the gooseflesh on her arms.

He'd cut Clara loose. He'd always been suspicious of the woman who'd come from his rival's club. "Fine," she bit out.

KnockKnockKnock.

Broderick possessed a distinct knock.

It wasn't the slightly hesitant ones by the guards and servants who lived in a perpetual state of hero worship for the proprietor.

But rather a firm, steady, confident thump that demanded a person not tarry.

All the color bled from Stephen's cheeks. "Are you going to tell him where you found me?" he whispered, his voice barely audible.

KnockKnockKnock.

"Are you going to tell him yourself?" she countered in hushed tones.

He nodded frantically.

"Just a moment," she called out.

When she opened the door, hazel eyes filled with suspicion sharpened first on Stephen's face and then on hers.

Ducking under her arm and around his brother, the boy bolted, leaving Reggie alone.

"Broderick," she said with a forced smile.

He inched an arrogant brow up.

Reggie clutched at the edge of the door, digging her fingers into the panel. "You wish to come in," she blurted.

"I'd rather not discuss personal matters in the hall," he drawled, his words a melodious flow with a slightly husked timbre that had even the most jaded woman inside the Devil's Den sighing and soft-eyed.

Reggie, however, had learned the perilous path a woman might be led down by those euphonious tones long ago and knew better than to go weak-kneed over a man's voice. Wordlessly, she stepped aside, allowing him entry.

Broderick brushed past, ever formal, ever in command. He laid dominion over every path his boots crossed, including these chambers that she'd called hers for more than ten years.

At first, his presence in the same rooms where she slept had left her mouth dry with fear . . . a dreaded anticipation that he'd at last collect that debt she owed, paid in the form of her flesh.

Until it had become as clear as the freckles on her pale-white face: the last thing he wanted or desired was a romantic entanglement with her.

Regret sat low in her belly.

Not taking her gaze from him, Reggie pushed the door closed.

Broderick worked keen eyes over the rooms. "What was that about?" There was a casualness to his sweep, and yet she knew this man oftentimes better than she knew herself. He touched his razor-sharp gaze on every corner and crevice.

"Nothing." Venturing over to the long-cold hearth, Reggie gathered her wrinkled cloak up from where it lay strewn and carried it to her armoire. "He was asking after me." The lie slipped out with an impressive ease. To stymie any further queries, she nodded to the cheroot in his long, elegant fingers. "You are smoking," she observed, tucking her cloak away. "You only partake in those scraps when you're troubled."

Broderick inhaled of that small scrap and exhaled a perfect circle. "I require help."

Her stomach clenched. It was dire indeed if Broderick, a man who ruled the Dials, asked anyone for assistance. In the more than ten years she'd served in his employ and called him friend, he'd humbled himself but once—to the owners of their rival establishment, no less. But then, in his quest to form connections with the nobles, he'd go to any lengths.

"Gertrude," she predicted. She drew the doors of the armoire closed with a click. With but one remaining hope of a familial connection between the Killorans and the peerage, all chances would rest upon the eldest and most underestimated of the Killoran girls. As one who'd been viewed in a like manner, Reggie felt a kindred connection to the partially blind woman.

"She needs to marry," he confirmed.

It had been obvious. She'd been expecting it. Even so, a different kind of regret turned over in her chest, chasing away a foolish longing for what would never be with this man. "Gertrude doesn't need to marry a nobleman, Broderick." Those girls, even Gertrude, who was near in age to her own eight-and-twenty years, were more like the daughters she'd always dreamed to have. "I'll not help you in this," she said with finality. She'd rail and fight for their happiness as if they were her own. "Gertrude deserves to marry where her heart leads her." Reggie balled her hands. "And she certainly deserves better than a nobleman who'll never appreciate her."

Because in the end, those fancy lords saw those outside their social sphere only as baubles beneath them to be toyed with.

Broderick tightened his jaw. "This isn't a debate or a discussion." It had been a fight that had dragged on with each Killoran girl. "I've already secured Gertrude's agreement."

"What?" she whispered. Sadness assailed her . . . for what that meant for Gertrude.

"She has agreed to a London Season." He took another draw from his cheroot, his lips forming the faintest grimace that she'd come to recognize whenever he smoked. A telling gesture that hinted at one who hated those loathsome scraps as much as she detested their pungent odor. "She knows there is no other choice." He gave a distracted wave, sprinkling several ashes to the floor.

Reggie let fly a sound of impatience. "You managed to ensure Cleo's cooperation and Ophelia's, and now Gertrude's." The man could make a sinner out of a saint. "But it does not mean I'll support you in this." Nor could she make heads or tails of what need he had of her in this latest scheme to tie the Killorans to the *ton*.

Stubbing the cheroot out within the empty Derby chamberstick, Broderick abandoned the scrap. "Stephen was kidnapped."

She shook her head slowly. "I don't understand."

Broderick opened his mouth and then stopped. Glancing to the door, he quit his spot over at her desk, joining her at the hearth. "Nine years ago," he spoke in hushed tones that, even with the mere handsbreadth between them, she struggled to hear.

Confusion clouded her mind, and she struggled to make sense of what he'd revealed. She shook her head. "I don't . . ."

"Diggory gave the orders for another boy to be brought within the fold." The color bled from his cheeks as he spoke. "Two of Diggory's thugs found that child." This new version of the always unflappable Broderick Killoran left her at sea—rattled and fearful in ways she hadn't been since her long-ago flight through London. "Unbeknownst to me, they brought a *marquess's* son."

Her legs wobbled under her, and with a soft shuddery exhalation, she slid into the wooden folds of the woven rushes. "Oh, God." This family had come to mean as much to her as those whose blood she'd shared. And their existence was about to be torn up. "When . . . how . . . ?" Reggie couldn't muster a single coherent thought as the horror of what Broderick revealed weighed heavy around her. She settled for the least weighty of the questions. "When did you find out?"

Searching about, he grabbed the padouk chair from her writing desk and dragged it over so he faced her. The seat creaked under the weight of his powerful frame. "Ophelia's husband's investigation—"

"To find the Marquess of Maddock's son?"

"Yes, the one." He nodded. "Steele's investigation turned up a string of boys through the years who'd been kidnapped from the nobility and forced into Diggory's gang."

Numb, Reggie sank back. Bile stung her throat as the oldest, darkest memories of her mistakes, and of the man who'd sought to sell her in a like manner but for different purposes, came flooding back. Stephen had been . . . kidnapped. Ripped from a life that was safe and familiar—no doubt a beloved child and a coveted heir, who'd instead been thrust into the seven levels of Hell that existed within the Dials.

"Reggie . . . Reggie?"

Blinking slowly, Reggie fought to attend him, this man who knew more—but not all—parts of her dark past. And whose very existence was now in peril. "I'm sorry," she said hoarsely. "You were saying?"

"It was Ophelia who put together the facts. She revealed all when she was . . ." *Imprisoned.* His throat muscles jumped, and that—his inability to speak of his sister's recent imprisonment at Newgate—filled her heart. After being betrayed by the gentleman who'd vowed to love her forever, Reggie knew better than to trust a handsome face or pretty words. But this? A gentleman who cared for his sisters and offered protection for even the lowest class of street folk weakened her sturdiest defenses.

And yet . . . "You've known since before Ophelia went to Newgate," she stated blankly.

"Yes."

Reggie glanced away lest he see the hurt that was surely there in her eyes. "I . . . see." Despite her closeness to the Killorans and her devotion, no one had shared this darkest of secrets that hung ominously over the family. It was a silly detail to fix on, given the Killorans' dire circumstances.

Fighting back her own selfishness, she focused on the true victim in this. "Does Stephen know?"

Grief twisted Broderick's chiseled cheeks. "Yes." Again, the evidence of that love for his sibling of the streets chipped at her heart.

Reggie dragged her chair closer, so close her knees brushed Broderick's. "All hope is not lost. The gentleman will surely realize that Stephen is alive now because of you and your sisters." And then Gertrude needn't sell herself to maintain the Killoran empire.

Broderick held Reggie's gaze. "*I* assigned the man to find an orphan," he whispered, scraping a hand through his hair, tangling that halo of lush golden curls. "I unwittingly commanded the man who coordinated Stephen's kidnapping." His jaw tensed. "I knew Lord Maddock would never simply take my word. I knew I needed to find Walsh and Lucy first and drag them before the marquess." Broderick set his jaw. "Walsh already had the marquess's ear."

His revelation knocked her back in her seat. It wouldn't matter that the Killorans had taken the boy within their fold and loved him as their own. All the boy's father, all the *ton*, and for that matter, all the world, would see was that Stephen had been taken and resided with the Killoran gang. Nay . . . that Broderick had given the orders. Her eyes slid briefly closed.

A heavy hand settled on hers, the warmth of that touch enveloping her and driving back some of the horror of all Broderick had revealed. "We need those connections more than ever."

His "we," however, implied her . . . but that couldn't be. Before it had been strictly greed and a desire to climb ranks. This . . . she shivered . . . he would swing for this.

Reggie stared at his olive-hued fingers covering her own, concealing her cracked and chipped nails, a product of all the work she did within these halls with her own hands.

"What do you require?" she brought herself to ask. For him and his siblings she would do anything.

"As I said, Gertrude agreed to a London Season." His thick golden lashes swept down, obscuring his eyes. "Under certain conditions."

"Good for Gertrude." She managed her first smile that day, one brimming with pride for the woman who'd begun to exert herself within the club. "What were her terms?" If Gertrude had volunteered to sacrifice her happiness to save her brother and her family from the financial fallout that would come with this scandal, then Reggie hoped she'd asked for—

"She wants you to serve as her companion."

Every muscle from Reggie's cheeks to her toes turned to stone. For she'd previously been incorrect with herself. She'd do anything for the Killorans—except that. "What?" she asked, her tongue thick.

"The assignment would last for the duration of her Season." With a calm that belied the tumult in her breast, Broderick looped his ankle across his opposite knee.

A loud buzzing filled her ears. Enter Polite Society?

After a long stretch of silence, he added: "You will of course be well compensated."

She flinched. He'd mention . . . monies? Hurt simmered in her breast. And oddly, this time hurt was safer, for the acuteness of it dulled the memories of her past mistakes. The very ones that saw her dependent upon this man before her.

"I've already secured a townhouse in Mayfair. Before we go, I'll need you to examine our ledgers and assemble a list of names."

He'd already taken it as a foregone conclusion that she'd accompany him. *Because when have you ever said no to him . . . ?* "What *manner* of list?"

"I want a list of those gentleman who are in greatest debt to the Devil's Den. And I want those patrons ranked by title and influence."

Everything was by rank in this club with this man. Broderick's obsession with status and title guided his every decision, and it was just one of the many, many reasons Reggie could never be truly a part of his life. That, and the fact that he had no wish for her to be part of it.

She bit the inside of her cheek.

Broderick rolled his shoulders as though they were stiff, and that slight, deliberate shrug sent his muscles rippling.

That subtle movement released a flood of butterflies in her belly.

Have some pride, you foolish woman . . . He just upended your future and talks of thrusting you back into a world you vowed to never set foot inside again.

At her silence, Broderick drummed his fingertips on the side of his gleaming black boot. "I trust this is daunting . . . the prospect of your moving amongst Polite Society."

A panicky laugh built in her chest, and she forcibly held it in, the effort of that causing a sharp ache. What would he say if he knew the truth? That she'd once dwelled in a duke's household and moved amongst the company of those people he so exalted? Granted, she'd served in that nebulous role of not quite a servant and certainly not a member of the noble family, but she'd acquired a very clear understanding of that world.

Bitterness sat like a stone in her.

No, she could not—nay, would not—reenter that cruel, unfeeling world.

A frown pulled between Broderick's brows. "Reggie?"

She gave her head a slight, clearing shake. "I am honored that you have confidence in my ability to accompany your family to *ton* events." Whether he detected the sarcasm in that reply, he gave no outward indication. "However, you would be best served by finding a proper young lady to steer you." Oftentimes, she wondered if Polite Society would recall the young woman they'd condemned as a whore. Reggie had no intention of truly finding out the answer to that question.

Broderick lifted an eyebrow. "Ah, yes, but Gertrude wants you."

That he himself concurred with Reggie cut deep in a way that she despised. Restless, she shoved to her feet, desperately in need of some distance between them. "You've not thought this through," she clipped out, needing to make him see reason.

"Careful," he warned.

Unsettled by the ice in his eyes, she forced herself on anyway. "Honored though I am that Gertrude would choose me as the one to accompany her about Polite Society, it would be ruinous for her." That statement was not driven by purely selfish reasons to be spared the duties, but rather by a cold, unyielding fact that came from her time amongst the *ton*. "Everyone will know one of your gaming hell employees has been tasked with caring for your sister, Broderick. And what will they say? Hmm?" Even if she hadn't thoroughly blackened her own reputation, her moving freely amongst lords and sailors alike inside the Devil's Den had done so enough where what Gertrude wished, and Broderick requested, was an impossibility. "Do you think *that* is how you're going to secure the *ton*'s approval?" she asked, her voice pitched even to her own ears.

"Let me be abundantly clear," he said, flashing a cold smile. He slowly stood. And blast if he, with his nearly six inches over her, wasn't the only man capable of making her feel small. "I do not seek *anyone's* approval."

"So what is this really about, then, Broderick?"

His eyes hardened as he came slowly to his feet. "Don't presume you're entitled to more than I offer about my decisions."

Reggie swallowed hard, and an unfamiliar disquiet swept through her. For as long as she'd known him, had seen his ruthlessness carried out or displeasure turned on cheats, thugs, and ineffectual workers, it was also the first time she'd been the recipient of it.

Pride, however, brought her shoulders back. "Your single-minded determination to connect the Killorans to the nobility goes back far beyond Stephen. So do not suggest this venture to be vastly different. It's not."

They locked gazes in a tense, silent battle.

And then, as quickly as he'd turned that merciless edge on her, it was gone. "Gertrude wants you there, Reggie. She knows you." He caught her hand, giving it a light squeeze, and heat radiated from the point of his touch. Her heart tripped several beats, and she glanced briefly at their interlocked fingers. "She trusts you," he said in a melodious murmur that could convince a saint to sin. "And you understand her."

Her pulse quickened. That appeal on behalf of his sister, evincing such devotion to his family in a world where that gift was so lacking, reminded her all over again why she'd first lost her heart to him.

Reggie wanted to do this not only for Gertrude . . . but also for Broderick. She owed him her very life. And a lesser man without his honor would have hurled that, and the security and safety he'd provided Reggie, in her face. But God help her . . . she couldn't. "I am so very sorry for Stephen," she said softly, disentangling her hand from his. "For all of you." In the end, every Killoran would be stricken with the loss of their brother. "But I cannot help you in this."

Broderick's mouth fell agape, that shock surely a product of Reggie not having said no to one request or order he'd put to her through the years.

"You cannot?" he finally said. Not even for Gertrude . . .

It hung there, unspoken and unfinished, but as clear as if he'd shouted it.

For Gertrude asked nothing of anyone. Reggie briefly closed her eyes.

How she wished she could be at Gertrude's side, and if Gertrude needed her anywhere else, including hanging by her fingernails at the edge of the world, she'd be there.

She shook her head, once more.

"I . . . see." His tone indicated he saw anything but.

Nor could he. Her secret shame was hers alone. Despite the close bond of their friendship, she'd never shared her greatest mistake. How could she have, to one who'd so masterfully built himself up to be the person he was—one reliant on no one but himself. "I'll remain behind and oversee the club while you join Gertrude," she said in a bid to soften her rejection.

"MacLeod has already been appointed to that role."

His statement should not have surprised her. Though he'd provided his sisters and Reggie a role in the club, at the end of the day, men always chose other men to oversee their most important of business—Broderick included. Reggie arched an eyebrow. "Because you don't trust that I'd be capable?" He might trust Reggie implicitly enough to share the greatest secrets about Stephen and offer her his ledgers and records to freely study. He'd not, however, ever put his establishment in her, or any woman's, hands. "MacLeod, who barely looks at your books, and who's not had a single meeting with a vendor, is more capable than me?"

Women . . . using their own talents and skills and not their bodies to survive. A place where women do not have to rely upon the mercies of any man . . .

Broderick leaned close. The crisp, masculine sandalwood scent of him filled her senses, weakening her defenses. "Because that is not the favor I need of you, Reggie," he murmured, his chocolaty-smooth baritone managing to turn that otherwise hideous moniker into something seductive in its beauty. A dangerous half grin ghosted his smile, revealing even, pearl-white teeth and dimples in his cheeks. "Have I ever given you reason to doubt me?" he pressed softly.

She forced her breathing into an even cadence.

This was Broderick at his most dangerous, one who used his charm and wicked appeal to effortlessly bring others 'round to his wishes.

This was also the first time that he'd turned that charm upon her.

Reggie, however, had made perilous missteps with men equally skilled in tempting a lady out of her own thoughts.

"Don't use that seductive tone on me, Broderick." She pursed her lips. "Save it for the prettiest serving girls you want to work an extra shift to please your ducal patrons."

He reared back. "Egads. I wouldn't *seduce* you, Reggie."

The horror etched in his face and coating his words ripped a hole in a heart that had beaten too long for a man who would never see her. "I know," she said too quickly. "Of course I don't think you would. I . . ." *Stop rambling.* Mortified, she curled her toes tight into her arches until her feet ached, all the while welcoming that discomfort.

"When have you ever known me to say I was without choice?" Broderick asked somberly, directing another, *safer*, question her way.

Never.

"This isn't solely about you wanting to make your damned connection to the nobility," she snapped. "This is about the manner of gentleman you'd contemplate pairing her off with."

He bristled. "I wouldn't marry her to just any damned bounder."

"No," she snapped. "Just the most powerful one with the greatest debt to you." Reggie shook her head, disgusted. "You underestimate your sister if you think the only gentleman who'd marry her is an indebted-to-you nobleman." Anger, hurt, and fury roiled in her chest and drew the words rapidly from her lips. "A wastrel. A whoremonger whose only desire, whose only *wish*," she hissed, "is for more coin to toss down at your tables. Now, if you'll excuse me?"

Broderick reached for the door handle. "I'd ask you to reconsider your decision," he attempted once more.

He, who asked for nothing from anyone. She felt herself weakening and wanted to be there for Gertrude and him. And yet she could not. "There is nothing that would make me change my mind."

Broderick moved a piercing gaze over her face. "I respect you and call you friend."

Friend. Bitterness sat heavy on her heart.

Broderick took a step closer, and then another, until she was forced to tip her head back to meet his gaze.

"It was why I put Gertrude's request to you." He lowered his face close; his breath, tinged with tobacco and brandy, fanned her skin, her heart quickening at the masculine pull of those scents. His next words, spoken on a steely whisper, penetrated the daze he'd cast. "Be not mistaken; regardless of your very clear opinions on my actions and the benefits of a match between Gertrude and a nobleman, I'll have your cooperation . . . whether you freely give it . . . or not."

And with that silken threat, Broderick bowed his head and left.

Fingers shaking, Reggie closed the door. She promptly collapsed against it, taking support from the oak panel.

Leave. Pack your belongings, take Clara with you, and go. They had funds enough to survive until they set up their music hall.

As soon as the thought entered her mind, reality quashed it. Her setting up a business that would draw away patrons would be seen only as a betrayal. And regardless of the time he knew a person, Broderick didn't tolerate those who moved against him. No, her motives wouldn't matter. Her dreams. Only his empire did.

She knocked the back of her head against the panel.

Damn him. Damn him for always having possessed this single-minded fascination with the peerage. That lot of cold, ruthless, soulless bastards who'd steal a young woman's happiness and cast her out without a hint of remorse for all she'd lost. The day he'd implemented changes, bringing those dissolute lords into the club as patrons, she'd been filled with a sickening dread. It had remained, day in and day out, growing, as consuming as the fear that one day *he* would walk through those doors. But this . . . She pressed a shaking fist to her mouth and bit down hard. Broderick would disguise a demand as a request, all the while stripping her of a say.

She could not go back there.

Would not.

Not for Gertrude nor Broderick nor anyone. Yes, he'd saved her, but she'd also given him her loyalty and service, all the while holding futile dreams for more . . . with him.

I was so devoted that I failed to see how precarious it was to trust that he had a like devotion until I had it all yanked out from under me . . .

Before her courage deserted her, Reggie rushed back to her armoire and grabbed her cloak . . . and left.

Chapter 6

Mayhap you are thinking . . . my sister can save me.
Let me disabuse you of such foolish hopes. No one can . . .

She'd said no.

With frustration coursing through him, Broderick returned to his offices to find a small, familiar figure stationed outside the door.

Seated against the panel, his knees drawn up to his chest and his cap pulled low over his eyes, Stephen followed Broderick's approach.

Mistrustful. Wary. Cynical.

They were all ways in which the boy had been twisted by the Dials. *Because of me. It is all because of me.*

His chest tightened.

As soon as he reached him, his brother popped up.

"Stephen," he greeted, forcing a casualness past the wad in his throat. "Would you care to . . . ?" Stephen reached past him and let himself in. "Join me," he finished dryly.

Once they'd entered, his brother kicked the door closed with the heel of his boot. The mud caking those dirty soles fell to the floor in small clumps.

"Your hat," Broderick called over as Stephen plopped himself into his usual seat across from the desk. The threadbare cap that he'd worn since he'd picked his first pocket and set his first fire—it was as much a part of him as his angry soul. That article, however, had also proven a shield that hid his eyes, and Broderick wasn't above removing that protection to aid his ability to read the boy.

With a curse, Stephen swiped the cap from his head. Slouching in his chair, he watched Broderick with suspicion spilling from those dark irises.

Helping himself to a brandy, Broderick joined his brother at the opposite side of his desk. "Why do I take it this isn't to be one of our usual meetings?" His spirited, stubborn brother visited often, and when he did, Stephen spoke openly and with enthusiasm about a day in the future when eventually he'd run this club. Only in the past, where Stephen had peppered Broderick with questions about the gaming hell business, patrons, and dealings of the Devil's Den, now he remained silent.

"What are you going to do?" The boy held up a small, folded note with a familiar seal inked into the crease.

Broderick searched inside his jacket. *Bloody hell.* With a curse, he held his hand out. "How . . . what . . . ?"

"I'm not just a fire setter—"

"An arsonist," he automatically corrected.

"I'm the best pickpocket, too," the boy said with an inordinate amount of pride, puffing out his chest.

"Stop picking mine." Broderick snatched the damning letter from his brother's hands.

All the boy's earlier bravado flagged, and he glanced down at the tips of his boots. "You're going to hang." It wasn't a question.

Yes. That was the likely outcome.

With a calm he didn't feel, he stuffed the note back inside his jacket. "It certainly makes a noble connection between our family and some powerful peer more . . . vital," he said quietly. It had always been the goal he'd carried for the Killorans. That hadn't changed, nor would it ever. That link would provide the last of his sisters with a security not afforded to those outside the illustrious ranks of the peerage. And moving amongst that world, Gertrude would at least be the one Killoran who could manage to watch after Stephen when he was returned to his noble father.

"Only a connection to the king 'isself can save ya."

Nothing could. Broderick had accepted that. Not him anyway. There was, however, hope for his family and those who depended upon the Devil's Den.

"If ya're hoping Gert's gonna make that match, ya're even stupider than her damned cat, Brave."

"She's already agreed to a London Season." It had been a capitulation that had come far easier than from either of their younger sisters. She'd made that sacrifice on behalf of the Killorans. *Nay, on behalf of you.* She believed it was about saving Broderick and the Devil's Den. Just as Stephen did . . .

Guilt and shame made his tongue heavy, making it impossible to smoothly deliver words as he so often did. He coughed into his hand.

Stephen shrugged. "Don't matter wot she's agreed to. No one's going to marry 'er with 'er eye."

Anger coursed through Broderick. Ultimately, though, Stephen was just a boy in desperate need of guidance. A child who would have turned out vastly different from the dangerous, hardhearted person he had if it hadn't been for Broderick. His chest tightened. "Look at me, Stephen," he quietly ordered.

The younger boy hesitated and then brought his head up so he faced Broderick.

Laying his palms on his desk, Broderick leaned forward, shrinking the space between them. "No one speaks ill of a Killoran, and we certainly don't do so to one of our own. Is that clear?"

Stephen ducked his head. "Yeah. It's clear." He kicked the toe of his shoe over the floor. "But I'm not really a Killoran," he whispered, slipping into a flawless King's English better suited to the noble he was. "And I don't want to go back."

"It's not your choice. It's not mine, nor Cleo's nor Ophelia's nor Gert's." A vicious pain, sharper than the last blade plunged into Broderick's person, lanced him. At last, they would speak of it. Stephen's fate and future had only been whispered about amongst Broderick and his sisters and never again mentioned to or with the boy after he'd first received the news of his circumstances.

Quitting his seat, Broderick came around the desk and squatted beside his brother. "You will *always* be a Killoran," he said somberly. He covered Stephen's dirt-smudged fingers with his palm. "We are not family for any blood that is shared but because of a bond that runs far deeper." Even after he eventually left.

"If she marries a more powerful nob than . . ." *His father.* The fires of hatred burnt strong in the child's eyes, chilling Broderick. ". . . *him*, might he arrange it so that I can remain here?"

Broderick scrubbed a hand over his mouth and then let it fall to his side. "I can't make this go away for you, Stephen," he said quietly. For everything else he'd righted for the club and the family, this was something that could never be undone.

His brother's throat worked, that slight bob of his Adam's apple the only hint of the grief tearing at him . . . and a small show of it, at that.

"When . . . *he* . . . your father," he forced himself to say, "comes for you, we'll have to let you go."

"But why hasn't he come for me already if he wanted me?"

There was an odd blend of both resentment and hope to that query that shattered Broderick all over again. "I . . . don't know," he said, settling for the truth. "I cannot presume to know why the marquess is doing or, in this case, not doing what he is." Broderick held his brother's eyes. The only answer was that the man was as mad as the gossip columns professed him to be. *And I'll one day soon have to send Stephen back to the marquess . . .* "Eventually, you'll have to leave. And I trust the marquess won't allow us near you. If Gert weds into the same social circle, she'll always be close."

"So it's to watch after me when I go to Mayfair, then," Stephen said, his voice ringing hollow, his eyes avoiding Broderick's. "Gert marrying." He spoke in the deadened tones of one who'd given up hope. "Not to spare me."

"That is not the only reason," Broderick quietly conceded. "Gertrude will benefit in having a fortune and powerful connections." They would provide his last unwed sister with a future Broderick himself was incapable of. "There are the staff and servants employed here dependent on—"

"Do ya think 'e'll 'ang ya?"

Broderick didn't pretend to misunderstand. Still, with the boy's inclination to protect his family at all costs—be it burning down businesses or threatening lords—he measured his response. "I believe he's within his rights to feel whatever rage he does for me, and for what he lost."

"'e can go to 'ell."

No doubt having lost his son and wife, the man was already there.

Stephen pulled his dagger out of his boot and passed it back and forth between his palms. "Ya were with Spark," he casually remarked. Broderick scrutinized that distracted movement. Since when had his brother begun referring to Reggie by her surname? "Wot ya be needing her for?"

"Generally, everything," he muttered, coming to his feet. He went and grabbed his brandy. And as panic twisted his brother's features, Broderick took a long swallow. "I should ask you the same."

Stephen spat on the floor. "No. Oi didn't do anything. Wot did she say?"

"She told me I should keep a closer eye on you." Which was wise advice.

His brother exploded. "She can go to hell."

"Enough." He'd not tolerate the boy disparaging her. Not Reggie. Broderick sharpened his gaze on his brother's tiny frame. "What's this about?" It was time they stopped dancing around whatever had truly brought Stephen to his offices this time.

"Oi don't trust 'er."

"*Reggie* Spark?" Unfailingly loyal and devoted to him, his siblings, and the Devil's Den, today had been the first time in the whole of their time together she'd ever said no to fulfilling a task or request he'd put to her. "Don't be ridiculous. Because she was concerned about you?"

"It ain't that," Stephen said, slashing a frustrated hand through the air.

Broderick managed his first smile since his world had been flipped over. "You don't believe any woman is to be trusted." How many times had the boy said as much about the serving girls and prostitutes and servants? For that matter . . . "You don't believe any*one* should be trusted."

Stephen gave an emphatic nod. "And it's true. They ain't to be trusted." He paused, wrinkling a dirt-smudged nose. "Except for Cleo, Ophelia, and Gert."

Stephen might be a miserable little fellow, but he was loyal to the family, and he loved deeply. "Reggie is family," Broderick reminded him.

"No, she ain't. She's just some peculiar harpy you rescued from the streets who was following after me."

That disparaging assessment raised a frown, chasing away his patience for Stephen's latest temper. "A harpy is a winged monster."

"Precisely."

Reggie, with her crimson curls and endearingly freckled, heart-shaped face, was more siren than monstrous mythical figure. As soon as the dishonorable thought slid in, he scowled, equally annoyed with Stephen . . . and himself for lusting after her, if even in the privacy of his own musings. "Reggie is more than whatever you're making her out to be."

"Yeah?" Stephen folded his arms. "What is she, then?"

That brought him up short. "Well . . ." He'd never given a specific title to her role within their household and family. Most of the staff referred to her as his assistant. She was, and always had been, just . . . *Reggie.* "She oversees the books and accounting whenever I require it." That task was one he hadn't and never would entrust to a single person outside of him or his immediate family. But it had also been about more than that. Having her—the one person unafraid of him who'd speak candidly and also manage to freely smile—at his side made his life . . . enjoyable.

"So she's a bookkeeper," Stephen stated flatly, thankfully freeing Broderick from his confused ponderings.

"No." His brow pulled. "Well, on occasion, when I require her to fill that role."

Stephen stared at him like he'd sprouted three heads. "You aren't making much sense."

"She's everything I need her to be in a given moment," he settled on. For that was precisely what Reggie had been over the years. Whenever he required assistance with the club or his family, Reggie had unfailingly seen to either . . . and oftentimes both at the same time. He set his glass down. "She's cared after you and your sisters for years now." As such, she was deserving of far more than Stephen's vitriol.

"She's a governess, then." Stephen spat again. "I caught her following me. I don't need no nursemaid looking after me."

"Stop spitting on my floor," Broderick muttered. "Furthermore, she's not a governess. If you stop sneaking off, you'll not give her reason to follow after you." He rubbed at the ache at the center of his forehead. "She'll be Gertrude's companion . . ." Now it was just a matter of bringing Reggie around. Bloody hell, she'd chosen the wrong time to discover she was as stubborn as any damned Killoran. Broderick took another drink.

"She said no."

"So you heard that," Broderick stated.

"No. I guessed and you confirmed."

Bloody hell, the boy was clever. Finishing off his drink, Broderick crossed over to his liquor cabinet. That was what accounted for Stephen's sudden antipathy toward Reggie. Unflinchingly loyal, if one even glanced wrong at the Killorans, the boy would proclaim that unfortunate soul a forever enemy. "She said no," he confirmed. He forced a smile. "But when have I ever accepted those words as any kind of fact?" People, actions, moments, could all be bent and twisted until capitulation was granted, and a *no* transformed into that far preferable, always agreeable, other one-syllable word, *yes*.

His grin went unanswered. "Not as loyal as you took her for, then."

Fetching a bottle and snifter, he carried them over to his seat and took a position at the head of the office. He uncorked the bottle and, tossing down the stoppard, poured himself a drink. "I would remind you," he pointed out, the stream of liquid hitting crystal punctuating his words, "that you have been of a like opinion as Reggie on the topic of the peerage."

Stephen blanched. "Oi ain't nothing like her. An' Oi'll be damned if she comes with us to the fancy end of London."

Abandoning his negligent pose, Broderick sat forward in his chair. "Do you have something to say, Stephen?" He'd schooled each of his siblings. They knew better than to dance about issues with veiled innuendos as his brother now did.

"Ya've been careless with her." With that cryptic pronouncement, he reached inside his jacket and pulled out several folded sheets. He shoved them across Broderick's desk. "It's fortunate for ya that Oi'm here."

Broderick worked his gaze over those pages that contained name after name of members of his staff. He froze.

What in blazes is this? "How . . . what . . . ?" Broderick tried to make both thoughts and words make sense.

"How did I get them? Easy enough taking anything from Spark. I made up some fake, sad story to distract her, and filched those."

God, no. Numb, Broderick shook his head. *Impossible.*

"Oh, and if you need me to tell ya what they are . . ." Broderick didn't. He knew. He bloody well knew. His brother went on with entirely too much glee. "That's wot betrayal looks loike." Stephen spat on the floor, and this time Broderick let that gross offense go.

Jerking his gaze back to the numbers and tabulations on the sheet, he examined them. The computations included details about the purchase price of a building, along with calculations for monthly liquor expenses and tobacco ones. All figures that used Broderick's own vetted vendors and their prices.

Why . . . she intended to establish her own club . . . and just three streets away. The wind knocked out of him, Broderick sank back in his seat. And here he'd found himself waxing on in his mind about her as a woman who'd never leave the people she loved unprotected, while all along she'd intended *this*. Pain slapped at his senses and consumed all logic. He should have learned at his own father's hand the inherent foolishness in trusting that there were selfless people who put the welfare of others first.

She'd not only gone behind his back, gathering up vendors and suppliers based on her time here, but also planned on stealing his staff away and hitting his bottom line.

His jaw tightened. Nor had she intended to take just any of his staff. Rather she'd sought to steal the most productive, reliable women who'd developed a following within the club, who kept most noblemen coming back each night. God, what a fool he'd been. He'd crafted a plan that included her as a key part of it, to protect his family and staff. Was there no one whom he could truly trust?

Snapping open the next page, he went still.

"MacLeod," he gritted out. She'd intended to steal out from under his nose not only the leading women staff members at the Devil's Den but also his head guard. Fighting the red haze of fury threatening to engulf him at this, a betrayal from a woman he'd called friend and confidante over the years, he drew in a deep breath. "When did you get these?"

Stephen shrugged. "Not long ago. She was talking with Winters."

Again, Clara Winters. He seethed. He should have known better than to bring in Ryker Black's former madam. Fixing on his rage with Clara was a good deal safer than making sense out of Reggie's defection.

Why? Why?

"Ya need to get rid of her," his brother counseled. "Nothing else to it."

Yes, he did. To be deceived once and then keep that perpetrator in one's fold marked one not only as weak but also as a fool just moments away from the next betrayal.

But this was Reggie. Surely there was more to understand here? More to explain why, despite the role he'd afforded her in this club and their relationship that went back ten years now, she would carry out that treachery.

I would have helped her . . . I would have given her guidance had she wished it, and . . .

Except would he have? Would he have truly given his blessing for her to create a rival establishment? Certainly never in the same streets. They'd have only ever been in competition, and he might respect Reggie, like her, even, but that relationship would never supersede his business here.

Broderick stared into the amber contents of his drink.

Nay, if he were being honest, he could admit, at least to himself, that he wouldn't have allowed or encouraged the venture. He would have crushed it. Which was likely why she'd gone about it in secret, keeping the truth from him. All the while stealing his suppliers and securing better rates for herself, if the numbers were any indication, and taking his staff and—

Broderick tossed back a long swallow, welcoming the fiery trail it blazed.

"Oh, Christ," he whispered, as a slow dawning horror seeped into his fury-laden mind. A wave of cold swept over him. With fingers that shook, Broderick set his glass down and clasped his fingers before him to hide their tremble from the boy who sat on, silently observing him in his tumult.

He'd revealed . . . all to her.

His stomach pitched.

"What is it?" Stephen urged, and the thread of anxiety woven through those three words marked an unusual display of vulnerability.

Broderick forced a response out past tense lips. "Nothing," he lied. But then, was it really a lie? For in a few short weeks, everything had gone wrong—including Reggie.

Reggie, to whom a short while ago he'd revealed the most dangerous secret that could take down Broderick, his family, and all those dependent upon him.

Twenty minutes ago, he'd not possessed even a remote doubt about trusting Reggie to that damning secret. Now his future hung not only in the balance . . . but also in her hands.

Christ in heaven.

"I require a favor of you," he said, needing his brother gone. Broderick memorized the address marked on the page and then refolded the damning sheets, following the crease line she'd set with her own hands. "I need you to return these to Miss Spark's rooms before she discovers them gone."

Stephen hopped up and smartly saluted. "Ya got it." Taking them with eager fingers, he tucked them back into his jacket.

"Say nothing to anyone," Broderick warned, holding his brother's eyes.

"Ya going to sack her?" Stephen asked, his voice hopeful. "She can't be trusted. Surely ya know that." To a boy whose only remembrances were of the time he'd lived on the streets and whose home these years had been London's most dangerous gaming hell, Stephen had grown into a person who lived by the street code. If one betrayed a man, one was dead . . . that death physical, symbolic, and more often than not, both.

Unlike Stephen, Broderick had spent his earliest years and youth coddled and oblivious to the depravity that existed outside that once safe world. Mayhap that was why he'd never questioned Regina Spark's loyalty to him or to the club. He flexed his jaw.

"I'm not certain what is to be done with Miss Spark." She represented just another damned problem atop an ever-growing host of them. For he could not, as his brother encouraged, simply toss her out. Not anymore. Not with her knowing everything she did.

A protest sputtered incoherently on his brother's lips. "But y-ya can't keep her here. Ya 'ave to know that?" There was a thread of desperation contained within that question.

"Yes," he concurred. "I know as much." Now, however, the question of what to do with her had been complicated by the secrets he'd shared. "You need to go."

Stephen dragged his heels and then, with a sigh, started for the door.

"Stephen?" Broderick called after him, freezing the boy in his tracks.

The boy angled a glance back in Broderick's direction.

"You did well," he said softly.

Crimson splotched his pale cheeks as it so often did at hints of praise and affection.

Still, he lingered.

"'ow long do ya think Oi 'ave?"

Broderick respected the boy too much to feed him a falsehood. "I don't know."

It was the topic they all danced around but no one openly spoke of. Until this morning's meeting had revealed what would invariably have to be discussed: the kidnapping of Stephen long ago that would have a marquess down upon them with charges surely brought, the family absent a member, and a fortune lost in the process.

Stephen grunted. He turned to go. "Mayhap 'e'll let me stay? Wot fancy nob would want a bastard loike me around?"

The one who'd sired him . . .

And me. His gut twisted. *I want you around.*

"Run along," he said quietly, tipping his chin toward the door.

Stephen jammed his cap back on and raced off.

As soon as he'd gone, Broderick downed his drink; the liquid stung a hot trail down the back of his throat. With a grimace, he abandoned his glass.

As they said at the gallows, three times lucky.

And given the Killorans were one vengeance-driven nobleman away from a noose about their necks, never had a saying proven more true.

After the boy had gone, Broderick surged to his feet. A curse exploded from his lungs; full of all the fury and resentment teeming inside, he focused all those energies on the one problem within his control.

Reggie Spark.

She intended to steal his staff, including his best guard, and open up a rival establishment. Despite that treachery, Reggie was the one matter that could be most easily resolved.

Through his earlier anger, hurt, and frustration at her betrayal, a clear head at last won out.

He stopped.

All he needed was to ensure Reggie's silence and gain that which she'd been so reluctant to give—her cooperation.

Ultimately, Broderick always emerged triumphant. An icy grin ghosted his lips. And he had no intention of failing where Regina Spark was concerned.

Chapter 7

Have you found a way out? Have you still convinced yourself that is a possibility?

The next morning Broderick stood upon the dais at the center of his club, surveying the room, taking in everything and missing nothing.

It was an eclectic mix of people who wouldn't look at one another on the streets, but in the Devil's Den, just like in Satan's real inferno, all sinners comingled without regard to rank. Lords shared spirits with sailors, who kept company with merchants.

Prior to Broderick's inheriting the club from Diggory, the hell had operated altogether differently. Back then, only the most lethal, ruthless men in the rookeries sat at the tables and imbibed watered-down spirits.

Broderick had transformed this place, a hell in every sense of the word, into an empire which catered to all. He'd had the broken, scarred tables and chairs burnt as kindling and replaced it all with gleaming mahogany commissioned for the club and suitable for any nobleman's residence.

When his father had proven himself a thief—and a bad one at that—Broderick had survived long after him and made a new life for himself here with Diggory's three daughters and Stephen. They'd become his new family, and he'd been determined to offer them that which his own miserable father hadn't—security.

This club sustained them, and any threat against it through the years had been quashed.

This time would be no exception.

From across the crowded gaming hell floor, his gaze landed on Gertrude. Her modest citrine skirts stood out in stark contrast amongst the scantily clad women and gentlemen surrounding her. Gertrude worked her way over to the dais.

No doubt triumphant in her *victory*. Pleased that she'd *bested* him.

"'ello, Miss Killoran," the guard, Nerrie, at the entrance of the cordoned-off area greeted as she climbed the steps. The burly man with a barrel-like chest attempted to make himself smaller to allow her a wider path.

"Nerrie," she returned, with a smile.

That smile faded as soon as she set her foot on the first step. Her gaze held on Broderick's masklike features, and then she slowly continued the climb.

They remained in silence, shoulder to shoulder, arms folded in a like manner, both examining the crush of guests that filled every last corner of the club.

"It is busy," she stated with her usual somberness. "Not even noon, and there's not a space to be had at the tables."

He grunted. The Devil's Den was *always* busy. Their fortunes were vast. Unlike their rival club that catered only to the peerage, Broderick had enough business sense to realize coin was coin, and he'd built the Killoran fortune off the monies from street thugs and lords alike. And for all the pretend shows amongst Polite Society of shock and disdain for their world, ultimately they all craved a shred of the excitement to be found in the Devil's Den. It was why a nobleman would one day wed Gertrude, and why others had courted his younger, now wedded sisters.

He motioned to the floor. "Soon, this will no longer hold true," he said cryptically, his gaze focused on the noblemen surrounding the roulette table, loudly calling out numbers and plays while the clink and jangle of their coin punctuated their shouted wagers. "Soon the tables will be empty, and lords will look on in disdain at the family who . . ." He scowled and wisely silenced the remainder of that dangerous revelation. Instead, he focused on that which he *could* control. "You knew she would say no."

And he hadn't. He'd trusted Regina Spark implicitly in every way. Had expected her to say yes because he needed her to, and because she'd been like a member of their family. But then, Stephen's revelation had proven that to be a lie several times over.

How wrong he'd been on so very many scores where Reggie was concerned.

A guilty blush pinkened his sister's cheeks. Having been kept largely from acts of treachery and crime as a girl because of her partial blindness, she'd not developed the same ease at subterfuge and dissembling as the rest of their clan. "Broderick . . . ," she began.

"Am I incorrect?" He leveled a probing stare on her.

Her silence marked her answer.

"And all the while *I* was foolish enough to believe her devoted enough to be there for you."

Gertrude winced. "Broderick," she chided. "That's unfair. Reggie's never been anything but loyal to us."

Cheers went up, and Broderick silently cursed the jubilant gents gathering winnings at that table.

After the celebration died down, he spoke casually in hushed tones reserved for Gertrude's ears. "I don't believe you comprehend the gravity of our situation."

"How dare you." His sister pursed her lips. "I understand precisely what is at stake."

"Do you, though?" he asked crisply. "Have you given thought to all the men, women, and children who'll find themselves out on the streets of Seven Dials, living like animals?" The color bled from her cheeks. "Do you realize my very neck"—both literally and figuratively—"is on the damned line?"

Gertrude caught her lower lip between her teeth. "Surely you *know* a Season is a waste of our efforts."

Not for what he sought for her. A sound of impatience escaped him. "Do you believe that because you're a Killoran?" For each of his sisters' strengths, they had never seen their true worth. They hadn't realized that for their lack of noble blood, they may as well have been born queens for the strength in them.

"I never doubted Cleo or Ophelia could or would make a match." Gertrude paused. At her silence, he glanced over. "It is *you* who doubted me." He flinched. "Don't try to deny it," she said before he could speak. "It is because I am blind, Broderick," she said matter-of-factly. "Gentlemen don't want a blind bride. And you—"

He scoffed. "That is rub—"

"Know it, too," she spoke over him. "Or you would have sent me first instead of Cleo or Ophelia. They were the ones who could secure you that connection."

His neck heated. "You don't know what you're talking about," he said tightly, doing a sweep of the floor.

"Don't I?"

Of course she would see every prior decision he'd made in that light. Because Gertrude, just like all his siblings, knew when he set his mind to something, it was not a matter of if it would happen, but when. As such, she would see only the surface of that decision to not send her. She'd taken it as an indictment against her, hadn't seen that his had been a bid to protect. A truth he'd never admit, for it would only hurt her for altogether different reasons. Either way . . . "You'll have what you requested." Or rather . . . who.

Gertrude sharpened her gaze on him. "What?"

He tugged at his lapels. "I'm insulted. That you'd doubt my—"

"What. Did. You. Do?" she bit out.

Over the top of her head, Broderick caught sight of MacLeod at the doorway that connected the gaming hell floor to the corridor leading to the private suites. The burly guard lifted a folded sheet in his hand.

Whipping her head back, she followed Broderick's stare. "Broderick?" she demanded.

"You're determined to have Miss Spark as your companion for the Season, and as such, I intend to see you receive what you require. If you'll excuse me?" He stepped around her.

Sputtering, Gertrude rushed after him. "But . . . but . . . *what* are you doing to secure her assistance?" She knew him. The fear in her eyes spoke of one who knew the ruthless practices he'd employed over the years to secure what he wanted when he wanted.

"Does it matter?" he drawled, not breaking stride, forcing her to match his longer steps. All the while, patrons lifted their hands in greeting and made way for Broderick and Gertrude.

Ever the consummate host, Broderick returned those greetings and waves.

"Yes," Gertrude snapped, slightly out of breath. "It very much does."

They neared the back of the club, and he lifted his finger. "Ah, then you should have indicated there were limits to what you'd do to have Miss Spark."

Gertrude gripped his arm, forcing him to a stop. "Since when has Reggie become *Miss Spark* to you?"

Since she'd offered him lies and then placed her own desires before the good of the Killoran family. Broderick was unendingly loyal . . . so much so that one crack in that devotion revealed itself. At which point, anything went in terms of Broderick's dealings with him . . . or in this case, her. "I'm merely meeting your demands." Glancing dismissively past her, he gestured MacLeod forward.

From where he'd lingered in the wings, allowing Broderick and Gertrude privacy, the guard sprang forward. He handed over a note.

Unfolding it, Broderick worked his eyes swiftly over the page and then tucked it inside his pocket.

"She's leaving now, Mr. Killoran."

"What are you doing, Broderick?" his sister whispered as all the color leached from her cheeks.

"I'm securing Miss Spark's cooperation." And ensuring her silence.

With that, he stalked off.

"If you think I'll simply accept those shadowy statements," she hissed, matching his strides, "then you are out of your bloody mind. I've changed my mind. I'll go have your damned London Season," she spat, her skirts snapping about her with a like anger. "Leave Reggie out of the matter."

"It is too late," he stated, accepting the cloak an efficient servant came rushing forward with. For he'd learned enough—albeit inadvertently—that there was more at play around Reggie's denial, and as such, it moved beyond whether or not she joined Gertrude. He accepted his hat next, affixing it atop his head. "You have already insisted on it—"

"I've changed my mind."

"Let this serve as a lesson . . . be more decisive in the future." He lifted a hand, and the guard, Locke, immediately joined them.

"A lesson?" she squawked, and the guard took a quick step back under the fury that blazed to life in her gaze.

"Are you . . . k-keeping me prisoner here?" she stammered, color firing her cheeks.

Broad across the chest, Locke's enormous frame swallowed the hall. Bald, without a single strand of hair on his head and curiously devoid of eyelashes and eyebrows, the man ducked his head sheepishly. "Apologies, Miss Killoran."

With his sister's furious calls and demands following in his wake, Broderick took his leave. A better man would feel some compunction at ordering his sister to be waylaid by one of the club's guards.

Broderick wasn't a better man. He was one with single-minded purposes and intentions. He tightened his jaw.

As he entered the kitchens, Stephen, who leaned against the wall, a sentry over this space, stuck a finger toward the door.

Nodding, Broderick continued his path. A young servant rushed forward to open the door, and he sailed through just as Reggie's wool cloak disappeared around the edge of the building.

Broderick's determination and mercenary approach to any venture he undertook had only ever been matched by his youngest sibling. Oh, Cleo and Ophelia were stronger and fiercer than most men in the Dials. But at the end of the day, they were not so jaded they'd step over another in order to strengthen the Killoran empire.

Broderick reached the end of the alley and followed the same path those brown skirts had disappeared down.

He instantly found her. Nearly six feet tall, it had always been impossible for Reggie Spark to lose herself in crowds. A task lent an even greater improbability by the flame-red curls that even now, with her bonnet in place, escaped and flew around her shoulders like a crimson calling card.

Never, however, had that calling card proven more valuable than it did in this moment.

Keeping close to the buildings, Broderick set out in pursuit.

Chapter 8

Is today the day your empire falls . . . ?

Dank heat slapped at Reggie's face as she marched purposefully through the Dials.

The offending stench of East London rot and stale air flooded her nostrils, an unnecessary reminder of this place she called home.

Suddenly, her nape prickled.

She slowed her steps.

Shivering, she did a quick search of those she now kept company with: whores calling out wicked promises to potential customers, toothless vendors hawking their wares.

Reggie might not have ever developed the same street skills as the Killorans, but she had sharpened her senses enough to pick up on traces of danger around her.

Or mayhap her guilt accounted for that whisper of dread.

She tightened her grip on the blade that was never far from her person. A gift given to her years earlier by Broderick, that dagger was as much a part of her as the freckles on her face. Of course, he had handed over that *gift* as matter-of-factly as he would a loaf of bread or glass of water and then spent weeks instructing her on how to defend herself.

Now she held it close, taking comfort in the reliable hilt.

Don't be a blasted ninny. You're not one to shirk because of shadows. Not anymore. She hadn't been that girl in a long time.

Forcing herself back into movement, Reggie continued on.

The pace she'd set combined with the early heat to send sweat beading at her nape and trickling down the high collar of her modest cotton gown, winding an infuriatingly itchy path down the middle of her back.

Yet in these streets filled with sinners Satan wouldn't dare cross, Reggie knew better than to dash about alone with even the hint of her arms exposed.

An old beggar woman called over from the opposite side of the cobbled roads. "Ya want yar fortune read, girl?"

Not breaking her stride, and not so much as bothering with a glance in her direction, Reggie pressed on. She didn't slow her steps until she reached the corner of Monmouth Street.

Shoving her bonnet back with her spare hand, Reggie shielded her eyes from the sun and searched.

One.

Two . . .

And finding . . . *three.*

She squinted. Surely not . . . Mayhap she had read the address incorrectly in that folder.

Forcing herself to move, Reggie walked the remaining twenty paces until only the busy street stood between her and the address in question.

Raising her hand to her brow once more, she peered at the brick facade. Bricks that surely once gleamed bright crimson had faded to a lackluster coral hue, wearing cracks and breaks that marked the passage of time.

This was what her friend Clara had called their hope for the future?

Disappointment swept through her.

"Get out a me way, ya ginger wench." That coarse Cockney wrenched a gasp from her, and she jumped back, narrowly missing the speeding hackney.

The pair of horses kicked up the thick puddles as they trotted past, splattering the front of her cloak with grime and unknown waste contained within.

With a curse she shook out her skirts. Bending, she swiped her now muddied bonnet from the edge of the sidewalk.

And then froze.

A lone rook making a morning drink of the puddle paused. He cocked his head, the subtle movement tipping his thin beak sideways. The creature ruffled his raven feathers but remained belligerently standing in the midst of Monmouth Street, staring at Reggie. His unblinking, bluish-black eyes locked with hers.

One's bad, two's luck, three's health, four's wealth . . .

Reggie trembled and did a frantic search for another rook, but that usually social creature sat solitary in his study of her.

It is an omen . . .

How many times had she teased her father for his unfailing belief in those signs around them? Yet just now she proved to be very much his daughter. For standing outside the decrepit building that was meant to represent her future, there could be no doubt that this was not the dream she'd aspired to.

And for a long moment, she contemplated returning to the Devil's Den and accepting a safer but emptier future.

Reggie briefly squeezed her eyes closed.

She opened them . . .

Another rook stood beside the lone one who'd so watched her.

Her heart kicked up a beat. *Two . . .*

Reggie stood and sprinted across the street, skirting several street lads who had the look of thievery in their eyes.

She reached the five limestone steps and paused to admire the striking turquoise double doors. So previously fixated on all that was wrong with the building, she'd failed to note the heart-shaped adornments etched upon both panels; framed by a trim of wood roses, there was a breathtaking beauty to them. A beauty that defied the cracks in the paint and wood along the base of the door.

It is called a turquoise, poppet . . . a stone so powerful it protects against evil and ill health. As long as you wear it, you will be safe . . .

Her throat thickened as she allowed herself to think of him once more—the father who'd loved her.

When her life had crumbled under the treachery of false love, it had been so easy to sell off that gift she'd carried. Until now. For the first time, she yearned for that slight reminder of those she'd left behind.

These double panels . . . were a sign.

Finding the apropos Greenman door knocker, Reggie gripped the handle clenched through his teeth and rapped loudly.

Her back prickled, and tugging the folds of her cloak close, she surveyed her surroundings, doing a search of the bustling streets, grateful when that door at last opened.

A pinch-faced fellow with thick whiskers along his cheeks stared up at Reggie with a tangible disapproval. Nearly five inches or so shorter, the solicitor representing the seller had perfected the art of peering down his bulbous nose at people he'd himself determined were his lessers. "You are late," he clipped out.

"You came," Clara whispered, coming forward.

"My apologies," Reggie demurred.

The solicitor gave her another long look before reluctantly waving her in. *"Hmph."*

It took a moment for Reggie's eyes to adjust. In the spirit of conservation practiced at such meetings, only a handful of sconces had been lit. The candles' glow, however, cast a faint-enough sheen to illuminate the heavy dust hanging in the air. Fishing out a kerchief, she pressed it to her nose.

Staring over the scrap of fabric, she took in the hall. Dilapidated tables and broken chairs littered the space, and the wood floor had long since lost its shine, having been replaced instead with the remnants of spilled drinks and water stains.

Her heart sank.

So it was to be a one-crow day, then.

"Broken furniture can be fixed," Clara pointed out, accurately following Reggie's thoughts.

"Yes," she concurred. "But it isn't just broken furniture." She nudged her chin. "It is an entire *establishment* that is run-down."

"Hmph," Mr. Elliot, the testy man-of-affairs, grunted. "The price is fair."

The other woman gave her a silencing look.

Reggie had amassed substantial funds through the years, serving Broderick Killoran, but she was not like any of the Killorans, rich in money . . . or any other way. "It's broken—everything," she said with a wave of her hand. Her plan with Clara to purchase, restore, and build a music-hall business in the Dials was a venture Broderick wouldn't have lost a nod of sleep over, but for Reggie there wasn't an unlimited supply of wealth. Everything was costly.

Clara grunted. "That's what you've said about any place we've visited." She cast Reggie a glance out the side of her eye. "I didn't believe you'd show up." There was a reluctant admiration in the other woman's voice.

"I hadn't believed I would, either."

"Come, then," Clara urged with the same ease she'd once commanded the former prostitutes inside the hell. Her responsibilities had changed and diminished since Broderick had put an end to that profitable venture.

And in that way, Reggie from the Kent countryside was more like the shadowed madam who didn't speak of her past.

She fell into step beside Clara.

Her friend spoke in perfunctory tones as they walked. "It has potential."

"The potential to what?" A small laugh escaped Reggie. "Fall down about our ears?"

Of a like height, Clara strode with long, sure strides as she pointed out details to Reggie, attempting to sway her on a place that had only those turquoise double doors to recommend it. "The stage requires but minimal refurbishing, and there is already a dais for the orchestra. Wood can be repaired, and walls painted, but an establishment in this area is nigh impossible to come by." Clara stopped and, taking Reggie by the elbow, forced her to halt. "And do you know what else is nearly impossible to find, Reggie?"

Life. Happiness. Love. The answers were really endless.

The other woman held her gaze. "A man who'd be willing to sell a property to two women, one a whore and the other one who's worked inside the most disreputable hell, and whose reputation is equally suspect for it."

Yes, because the truth remained that though Reggie had never been forced to sell her body, society would care only about the surface appearance. The only fact that mattered to the world was that she called a gaming hell home. There was no reputability to be had. And as Clara pointed out . . . few options.

With a sigh, Reggie resumed her inspection.

Clara fell back silent as Reggie walked, this time with slower steps as she took in every detail and considered not only Clara's words but also her own circumstances.

She'd never allowed herself to think of leaving the Killorans. They had represented the only stability and safety she'd known since she'd left her family's cottage. She had been content with the role she'd found herself in as de facto older sibling.

Now she contemplated this next step: building her own empire with Clara, a music hall that would supply work for women such as herself and Clara . . . and girls who, presented with no options, had entered a life of prostitution.

Life was changing . . . as it invariably did. Sometimes when one was fortunate, those shifts came slower, and one was allowed a prolonged sense of comfort to be had in the familiar.

But then sometimes life spiraled like the old wooden merry-go-round in Kent, spinning in dizzying circles until one couldn't make sense of a world that existed only in blurry images and vibrant colors.

Reggie drew to a stop beside the square tabletop piano. She depressed one of those faded-yellow keys, and it whined mournfully of its neglect. This instrument was so very different from the treasured one her father had gifted her and seen carefully maintained.

And yet . . . it had been so long since she'd sat at any pianoforte that she could have been playing half of one and it would have inspired the same euphoric sentiment within her.

The pull of this piano drew her closer. How much she'd missed holding an instrument in her hands. First, she'd done so as a girl, and then as a governess instructing woefully unappreciative-of-song charges. With a sad smile, she ran her fingers over the chipped keyboard, and the medley of her childhood played in her ears, drowning out the discordant whine of the out-of-tune pianoforte.

"'Tis the last rose of summer
Left blooming alone;
All her lovely companions
Are faded and gone;
No flow'r of her kindred,
No rosebud is nigh,
To reflect back her blushes
Or give sigh for sigh."

Reggie stilled her fingers. . . . *you could instruct a choir of angels, poppet!* The memories of her playing to her father's praise and a captive audience of her beloved siblings slowly faded with the last hum of that final chord.

She opened her eyes and confronted reality once more.

Reggie tipped her head back and evaluated the chandelier, stripped of most of its crystal.

Clara joined her. "What are your thoughts?" she asked, her murmurings containing the traces of her nervousness.

For this dream could not come true for Clara without Reggie's additional monies.

She measured her reply. "It is . . . in need of work."

As if in a farcical cue, a three-foot shard of the mirror hanging behind the stage splintered off and shattered upon the dais.

Reggie winced.

And now a broken mirror to boot.

"It doesn't count if you do not break it," Clara muttered at her side.

They shared a smile.

Clara's was the first to fade, giving way to her usual somberness. "Look at it." She took Reggie by the shoulders and directed her so she faced the stage. "Truly look at it without thinking about h—" Clara abruptly cut herself off, and Reggie stiffened. "Truly look at it without thinking about how much wrong you see and think of all that is *right* and what it might be. Not a saloon," she spoke, an impassioned fervor to her tones, "but something that's not been done here in London . . . a hall devoted solely to music."

Leading her by the hand, Clara drew her closer to the stage and farther from the solicitor. "Women of all ages, dependent upon no one, using their own talents and skills and not"—a brief spasm contorted the former madam's face—"their bodies to survive. A place where women do not have to rely upon the mercies of any man." She fixed a piercing, pointed stare on Reggie. "Does all that sound familiar? Hmm? Because it should."

Reggie's cheeks burnt. Yes, those had been the very ideas she herself had put forward when it had been Clara who'd been the skeptic. "It's complicated now," she said, willing the other woman to understand.

"Well, then?" The bewhiskered gentleman called from across the hall in his nasally tones. "What is it to be? I don't have all day to entertain you two." He raised the monocle dangling from a chain to his eye and gave them both the once-over. "There are other potential buyers interested." He paused. *"Male buyers."*

Reggie jutted her chin out. "And do you rush those potential buyers along, too?" she snapped. For all she'd lost the day she'd left first her family and then the safe post of governess to a duke, she had found an ability to speak her mind. It was a gift she'd discovered with the Killorans. "Or is it merely those of the female sort you take umbrage in having any business dealings with?" That challenge echoed from the rafters.

A pair of rooks took noisy flight, flapping their wings and sending errant feathers fluttering to the middle of the room.

Clara groaned.

"The insolence of y-you," he stammered. "You insult the property and then challenge me?"

Reggie opened her mouth to tell him precisely what she thought of him but caught Clara's pleading eyes. Clara, who oversaw all the female staff within the club and begged for nothing, and asked for even less. "We are going to lose it," she whispered.

Curving her full, rouged lips up in a sultry smile, Clara turned her considerable charms on the crotchety solicitor. "Forgive my friend," she purred in a husky contralto.

High color flooded the solicitor's cheeks, and he dropped beady eyes down to Clara's generous bosom.

Reggie watched the interplay unfold, as Clara used her body to silence the pompous bastard before them.

The former madam drifted over. Her generous hips swaying and her satin skirts molding against her voluptuous frame, Clara presented herself as a carnal display before Mr. Elliot.

Reggie hadn't been an innocent miss for some years now. Yet even having lived and worked inside a gaming hell where girls had plied their trade, Reggie felt a blush climbing her neck and cheeks.

"It is a lovely establishment," Clara whispered, dusting a speck—real or imagined—from the solicitor's shoulder. "As for your reservations," she went on. She paused to straighten his lapels the way a devoted wife might a loving husband's. "I assure you, we are both capable." She dropped her voice. "Very capable."

Mr. Elliot finally lifted his gaze, shifting that stare reluctantly over to Reggie. "What is it going to be?"

Chapter 9

I'm going to take away everything that matters to you . . .

The next morning, with a nervous pit in her belly, Reggie sailed through the double turquoise doors of her future establishment.

The miserable solicitor followed her approach with a condescending gaze. "I see you are capable of being on time."

Biting back the caustic response on her lips, Reggie forced them up into a semblance of a smile for the miserable solicitor she had the misfortune of having to deal with—again. "Mr. Elliot, a pleasure to see you," she lied. Reggie loosened the strings of her bonnet and shoved the article back so she had an unobstructed view of this place that would belong to her and Clara.

Where a handful of candles had been lit at her last visit, now the room was pitch-black; the bright morning light at her back served as an ominous juxtaposition to the place she now entered.

Despite the oppressive darkness of it, and for every last reservation that had gripped her, now there was a euphoria. It froze her in her tracks as she stopped abruptly and simply took in her surroundings.

Where yesterday she'd seen all that was wrong, today, in the light of a new day, Reggie looked upon it as something altogether different—hers.

Hers, when nothing, not even the work she'd done at the Devil's Den, had truly been for her.

There was a euphoria that came from that empowerment. In a world ruled by men with women fighting for any shred of control, Reggie had accumulated funds through her hard work and was charting a new course on her own.

With a renewed sense of invigoration, Reggie tugged free her gloves and stuffed them inside her pocket. "I would like to sign the documents as quickly as possible," she clipped out in the precise tonality used by Broderick that had so easily brought about compliance.

Mr. Elliot pursed his mouth. "If you have a problem waiting for my employer, then you are free to leave."

You'd love that, wouldn't you, you nasty bugger . . .

"I will wait," she forced out through a tight smile. Refusing to give him the pleasure of her frustration, Reggie presented the rotter her back and took a slow turn about this place that would soon belong to her.

Regardless of what her future would now be, her time, as long as she was still employed by the Devil's Den, still belonged to Broderick. If he summoned her, he'd find her missing, and then he'd wonder where she'd gone off to—

You'll eventually have to tell him . . .

She thrust back the reminder. For she would. When the papers were signed and it became impossible for him to talk her out of her plans with Clara.

Reggie stopped at the center of the stage. Hitching herself onto the edge, she drew herself up.

Another chandelier stripped of its crystals hung overhead.

She closed her eyes, and this time she saw in her mind everything this place would one day be.

A gleaming stage awash in candlelight while singers danced and sang before a crowd of appreciative patrons. The lively strains of an orchestra's music would fill the auditorium.

Nay, it wouldn't be a saloon, little better than a gaming hell, where men came to drink and smoke. There wouldn't be courtesans on the laps of drunkards, but rather women employing real talents in a venture that was something *new*.

New, like her life was becoming.

Mr. Elliot called out, breaking her reverie. "I've been asked to leave so you might conduct the formal arrangement in private."

Warning bells went off. Reggie spun back to face the squat man now laying out a series of papers upon one of the tables. "Beg pardon?" The nervous timbre of her query bounced off the rafters.

The solicitor didn't bother to glance up from his task. Removing a quill and inkwell from the travel desk, he set them out in a meticulous row. "It is not my place to question," he said with a pointed edge that she'd have to be deaf to miss. At last finished setting up a makeshift desk for the formal meeting, he finally spared her his focus. "If you have reservations about conducting business as any other male client would, then perhaps you'd be wise to consider a different plan, Miss Spark."

Reggie curled her fingers tightly. So that was what this was, then? A bid to send her running in fear? "I'll wait until your esteemed employer arrives," she said coolly. She scraped a frigid stare over the solicitor and, drawing on the memory of a ducal command issued by her previous employer, added, "You are dismissed."

Muttering loudly under his breath, Mr. Elliot gathered up his belongings. On a huff, he took his leave.

The doors landed shut behind him with such force they brought the moth-eaten, faded velvet curtains down in a noisy heap.

Curtains falling is an ominous sign peril is to come to thine . . .

Unease grew in her breast. "Enough," she whispered, that familiar lore filtering through her memory. As a girl she'd listened, enthralled by every folk story and legend and superstition shared by her eccentric father. Now she wished she'd done as her mother had instructed and attended to him a good deal less. Dragging a chair over to the heap of velvet, she hefted it up. Dust specks danced in the air, stinging her nose.

"Achoo."

Grunting at the surprising weight of the dusty fabric, she climbed onto the seat. The wobbly oak chair rocked under her, and she steadied herself before tossing the curtains over the metal rod. "There," she said, pleased with herself.

She'd not let this day be ruined. Not by miserable Mr. Elliot. Not for her irrational fear of shutting doors and falling curtains. And not for any regret at all she was leaving behind.

Reggie crossed to the documents awaiting her signature. The crack in those heavy curtains now let in a stream of sunlight that erased some of the trepidation she'd long carried of dark, empty rooms.

Nor had hers been an irrational trepidation. Rather it had been a fear she'd long carried with her since that dark night when . . .

Reggie gave her head a hard shake, refusing to let thoughts of him in. Refusing to think of every last mistake she'd made that had brought her to this point—a woman alone, on her own.

There had been a time she'd been fresh to London, a girl who'd never left the placidity of Kent. The kaleidoscope of noises, sounds, and people in the Dials had sent terror clamoring in her breast.

That fearful girl of long ago was gone . . .

Ten years ago, nearly to the date, Broderick had saved her.

On this day, Reggie would save herself.

She scanned the official document, the complex legal language that women were so often refused any kind of say in. Reggie flipped to the next page.

She lingered on the page in her hands, staring absently down at her name etched on the legal document. So why did sadness creep back in and dull the joy of this moment?

Because new beginnings marked endings, and from this day on, when she stepped inside this badly neglected establishment, the familiarity she'd known would die.

Liar. It had never been about familiarity.

Reggie slid her eyes closed and allowed the memory in.

You look to be in need of help, love . . .

For just like that, Broderick had arrived at London Bridge, an avenging hero, escorting her off as if she'd been some fancy lady. He'd led her to a life of security and safety, a seeming impossibility with a monster like Mac Diggory ruling the streets of London.

From deep within the hall, a lone floorboard squealed.

"Hello?" she called, fiddling with the clasp at her throat. "Mr. Elliot?" Her question bounced off the plaster walls, her only company.

Shivering, she drew her cloak closer about her person and moved deeper into the establishment. She'd ceased believing in monsters and dragons long ago. Time had proven there was greater peril to be found, not in fictional tales but in the men and women around her. Her foot depressed a loose floorboard, and it creaked and groaned forlornly, increasing the already-frantic beat of her heart.

Reggie stopped beside the pianoforte, resting her fingertips lightly upon the nearest keys.

The off-tune G chord whined, and she swiftly yanked her hand back. Her neck prickled as something that had once been a familiar sentiment, that had been kept safely at bay but would never be truly forgotten, stirred: *fear.*

It was a living, breathing force that never truly left a person; it had lain dormant in Reggie, put to rest by the blanket of security Broderick had provided.

But it was always there.

She wet her lips. “H-hello?” she called out again. *Danger.* It hung in the shadows and blanketed the room. “Is anyone there?” she demanded.

Reggie battled with the logic that had driven her life these past ten years.

“Don’t be silly,” she whispered, in desperate need of any voice, including her own. “No doubt he’s keeping you busy, as you kept him yesterday.” After all, the pompous solicitor had been quite clear in his tangible disdain for Reggie and her *insolence*.

And yet . . .

Reggie had grown up in the English countryside, but she had lived long enough on the streets to sense danger. And it churned within her entire being—an instinct not to be ignored. One that said, *Run.*

Sprinting over to the table, she grabbed her bonnet. Her fingers curled hard around the brim. The brittle straw crunched damningly loud in the otherwise stillness. Heart racing, she bolted for the front of the club.

She’d return. When she and Clara were both able. But this, coming here alone, had been folly.

Suddenly the door opened, and she raised her bonnet reflexively to her eyes as sunlight doused the room, temporarily blinding her.

The stranger drew the door shut with a decisive click.

Reggie stumbled back several steps, and relinquishing her bonnet, she yanked out her knife. “Stop,” she ordered, proud of the steady deliverance of that directive. “I . . . ” Her thoughts and words faltered. A peculiar buzzing filled her ears as the fear that had sent her into flight exploded within her.

“Never tell me you’re leaving already, Miss Spark?” A frosty grin iced the lips of the towering gentleman before her. From the ruthless glint in his hazel eyes to the unyielding harshness of his aquiline features, he stood before her a stranger in all ways that mattered.

Reggie clutched a hand to her throat. “B-Broderick,” she whispered.

He peeled immaculate white gloves off with meticulous precision, finger by finger. Slowly. Deliberately. He drew each fragment of this moment out, a panther toying with his prey. A lethal, unforgiving creature poised to pounce.

This is bad.

Broderick let the silence stretch on. Toying with her.

All the while, rage gripped him.

Reggie was to have been the one he depended on, the one constant for his family, and with one act she'd gone and stripped that all away.

She'd deceived him. And *no one* deceived him.

It was an offense that went unforgiven and forever remembered.

That included the guards and staff within the Devil's Den who'd worked for him, all the while unfaithfully funneling information to the late proprietor's wife.

Those men and women who'd betrayed him, however, had been different.

They'd been ones he'd inherited from Diggory. People whose first loyalty had been to their original liege and his deranged, now dead, wife.

They'd not been people he'd rescued from the streets and stuck his neck out defending when Diggory and all his henchmen had ordered Regina Spark thrown from their midst for her absolute lack of usefulness.

He'd never asked for her loyalty in return. He'd simply . . . expected it.

And now, Reggie's guilt stared back at him, reflected in her eyes.

"Hello, Miss Spark," he finally said, shattering the quiet.

The long column of her throat moved, and she cast a desperate glance beyond her shoulder to the documents neatly laid out upon a table. When she returned her gaze to his, the usual spirited glimmer had chased back all her earlier worry. "What are you doing here?"

Brava. He'd expected her to wilt. To cry, perhaps. He should have known better. And had she done so, had she cowered and shook as she'd done at finding him before her, it would have made it vastly more difficult to go through with his plans for her.

He leaned a shoulder against the doorway. "I trust I should ask the same of you."

She flinched . . . but did not back down. "You followed me." Mayhap a day ago, before he'd read the information brought to him by Stephen, he'd have felt a suitable amount of remorse at having done so.

"And do you intend to stick a blade in my belly because of it?" he drawled, nodding pointedly to the dagger clutched in her white-knuckled grip.

Reggie followed his stare and then swiftly dropped her arm to her side. "I have never given you reason to follow me about," she said tightly, returning her knife—a knife he'd provided her—to the pocket sewn along the front of her cloak.

It was amazing the conviction she put behind her pronouncement.

"Now," he went on, venturing past her and removing his cloak as he went. Broderick stopped beside the makeshift workstation. "Shall we begin?" He tossed his garment in a purposeful display of mastery along the back of her chair.

The faint tread of her boots striking the floorboards indicated she'd moved. "Begin?" she echoed, confusion steeped in her tone. With all the enthusiasm of Eve confronting the serpent in her gardens, Reggie hovered across from him. Yet again, however, she didn't bow to fear.

Then the truth hit him. "You still have not pieced it together?" He made a tsking sound. He saw the question in her eyes as clearly as if it had been spoken. "I'm disappointed. You've always been far cleverer than this, *Miss Spark*."

Her eyes darkened. "Stop playing games with me," she snapped. She might not have gleaned the reason for his being here, but she would be astute enough to fix on the formality he'd erected between them. Her eyes glittered with outrage. "I'm not one of Diggory's former street thugs who you'd intimidate."

No, she was the woman who intended to steal his staff and negotiate for herself better rates and prices on liquor, while keeping it all a secret between them. Betrayal stung his throat.

He tossed his arm wide, drawing her attention to the table. "Why, I'm merely here to conduct our transaction."

All the color leached from her cheeks, and her freckles stood out starkly in her horror.

"That is," he went on, settling into the wobbly wood seat, "if you'd still like to move forward with the purchase of this"—he flicked his gaze about the run-down hall—"fine establishment?"

"*You* own it," she whispered.

"Oh, only just recently."

Reggie's thick, fiery lashes swept down. "*How* recently?"

He smirked. "I found myself the proud owner just last night."

A shuddery gasp exploded from Reggie's lips. Her legs swayed under her, and she sank lifeless into the seat across from him.

Broderick made a show of studying the contracts his solicitor had hastily written up. Ones that would turn this place from his hold over to Reggie's. He drew out the moment, feeling her eyes on him, taking in his every movement. That mastery of any exchange he'd learned not from Diggory, the gang leader who'd taken him under his wing, but from the duke his late father had once served. From that peer, just a step below royalty, Broderick had appreciated the power of silence and had come to use it as a tool to unsettle his opponents. At last, he shifted his attention briefly to the tense spitfire opposite him. "Shall we begin?"

Except . . .

Reggie seethed, the fury emanating from her aquamarine irises threatening to burn him. "Let's," she clipped out.

Knocked briefly off-kilter by that show of resolve, he attended his documents. "Now." Gathering the stack of papers in hand, Broderick flipped through, searching for one item in particular. "I understand you had terms agreed upon with the previous owner? What was the sum of the purchase price?"

Tension crackled in the room.

He glanced up.

And if looks could kill, he'd have been smote before Reggie Spark's feet. "Come, the all-*powerful* Broderick Killoran knows all." She dropped her palms on the table and leaned forward, striking in her fury. "Surely you gathered how much I intend to offer for this place."

Not what she'd negotiated. Not the price settled on between her and the previous owner.

But rather, how much she intended to offer . . . which spoke of a woman who had no intention of moving away from that payment amount. One who intended to go toe to toe with him despite his having secured the upper hand.

And through his outrage an appreciation flared.

"Three thousand pounds," he murmured. "An impressive sum for any woman to amass. For anyone, really," he added. "But especially so for a woman in a society that limits her opportunities and options."

A low, throaty growl worked its way up Reggie's throat. "I earned those monies." She thumped the table with her fist. The folders and papers still littering the surface jumped from the force of that knock. "It was *never* charity." Her cheeks went flush with a palpable anger that highlighted the lines of her high, prominent cheekbones.

Fearless.

She was fearless in every way. None dared go toe to toe with him. And Reggie, who'd been his right arm through the years, he'd expected at the very least remorse from. Never . . . this. This passion. This strength.

And through his earlier appreciation, Broderick felt something more.

Desire stirred . . . for Reggie Spark. Of course, his body had no appreciation for logic or the wrongness of that response to this woman who had served in his employ and who'd even now betrayed him. Rather, his was a primal response to the spirit that emanated from within her.

"How indignant you are," he purred. Her thin eyebrows with their natural arch snapped together. Broderick held her gaze. "But if you believe I couldn't have found someone to do precisely what you've done for significantly less payment, and with a good deal more loyalty than to make off with my best staff, you're as naive as the day I brought you into the Killoran fold."

Her body jerked like he'd run her through.

I will not feel bad . . . I will not feel bad . . . He knew she'd brought them to this moment. Even telling himself that, replaying the mantra and reminder in his mind, guilt sat low in his stomach. For everything that had come to light these past twenty-four hours, he'd shared more with this woman than he had anyone outside of his sisters.

"What do you intend?" she spat. "To stop me from purchasing this place?" He heard the worry there. It lent the faintest quake to the question that another might have missed. But he'd built his empire off gathering any hint of a person's weakness.

Tilting back on the legs of his chair, Broderick rested his hands behind his head. He scoffed. "Of course not. What kind of monster do you take me for?"

Distrust remained sharp in her aquamarine eyes. "One who'd snoop about and buy this place out from under me."

The minx didn't miss a bloody beat.

He latched on to the former part of her charges. "You accuse me of snooping?" He chuckled. "That would imply you had been clandestine in your efforts." He hardened his features, shedding the false veneer of amusement. "I taught you better than to be this careless."

"Yes, you're a master of treachery and deceit. Aren't you?" she asked, her expression deadpan.

A muscle twitched in his jaw. How dare she turn this on him? How dare she play the offended, wronged party here? Broderick planted the legs of his chair back on the floor. "Careful," he warned. "My tolerance for any insults from you was a great deal more considerable before I learned of your duplicity."

"Duplicity?" she hissed. Reggie dropped her spindly elbows on the table, as she effectively framed her fury-reddened face. "You of all people would begrudge me having something of my own?"

"I would begrudge you stealing my staff and better rates for yourself," he coolly returned, effectively quelling whatever words she'd intended to hurl next. "So let's not have you play the offended party here." Giving his lapels a tug, Broderick sat back in his chair. "Now, shall we resume our negotiations?"

"Negotiations?" she spat. "Is that what this is? You forget, I know you." And she knew everything, including the greatest sin he'd shared with her less than a day ago. Under the table, he curled his hands. "This is nothing more than your usual show meant to intimidate me. To remind me of who holds the power."

The problem with having confidantes is they know a person more than could ever be safe. It was why holding the trump card and wielding it with precision determined whether one thrived . . . or died.

And he'd no intention of caving. "Am I to take this to mean you don't wish to continue with the purchase of this establishment?"

All the color faded from her cheeks until her tense ruby-red lips stood out stark amidst her pale face. "Go. On."

"Splendid," he said with false cheer. "Let us proceed." Broderick fished through the legal documents. His skin prickled with the heat of her stare on his every movement. "Let us first begin with the new terms of the arrangement." Finding the page he'd sought, Broderick slid it wordlessly across the table.

Not making any attempt to pick it up, Reggie glanced down at it and then back to him. "What is this?" she asked bluntly.

"It is a number."

She ground her teeth with a ferocity that was sure to give her a headache. "I see that. What is the . . . ?" Reggie gasped, and she caught the end of that sound of shock behind her palm, stifling the remainder. "You intend to charge me double?" she choked out, her gloved hand muffling that query. "And for *this* place."

"Tsk. Tsk. Surely you don't expect me not to make a small profit on my venture." He flashed her a smile. "Nor should you disparage the hall. It would make you a *lovely* establishment."

Overhead, two birds flapped their wings wildly as they darted to another beam. Several black feathers rained down, one landing at the center of Reggie's red curls. "How dare you make light of me . . . and this?" she demanded with a breathtaking display of courage and strength. It lit her eyes and colored her cheeks, transforming her from an ordinary woman into a Spartan warrioress, the manner of mesmerizing beauty whose fire burnt from within and whom red-blooded men would gladly risk being singed by. "I know this is about more than making a profit on this place." She leaned forward, the delicate hint of jasmine that clung to her stirring his senses, at odds with this place and everything the Dials represented. And damned if it wasn't heady for it. "So out with it." He remained riveted on her lips moving as she spoke, her voice dripping with fury, only fueling this inexplicable desire for a woman who'd gone from friend to adversary. "What do you want?" There was a faintly husky quality to her contralto.

"What do I want?" he repeated back her question that, by the sheer nature of the words strung together, enticed. His gaze of its own volition moved from her face to the rapid rise and fall of her chest.

Shock went through him, holding him immobile at the absolute inanity of this unwanted, perilous hungering for Reggie Spark.

Broderick swiftly returned his focus to her flushed face. His was merely a primitive response born of the battle that had sprung between them.

Except—

Reggie nibbled at her lower lip, her slightly crooked front teeth troubling that flesh. And from that distracted movement sprang a sea of wicked visions: her mouth under his, on him, their tongues dueling in a bid for supremacy as fierce as the battle Broderick and Reggie waged in this crumbling hall. "A man such as you knows precisely what he wants of his opponent."

Her absolute calm in the face of his own tumult effectively killed that reckless hungering.

Broderick kicked his legs out under the table until the tips of his boots brushed hers. "Why, I believe I was abundantly clear yesterday, Miss Spark. I want you to serve as a companion for my sister."

And she would. Broderick ultimately got what he wanted from a person. He'd take what he needed from Regina Spark.

Friendship be damned.

Chapter 10

Mayhap you're foolish enough . . . desperate enough to believe if you insert yourself into Polite Society that some powerful peer might save you . . .

What?

Reggie's mind raced.

Surely that was not what this was about.

Surely Broderick couldn't have schemed to purchase her building out from under her and exercised this display of control and power . . . all for the purpose of forcing her hand?

"You cannot be serious." Incredulity crept into her voice. "You've done all *this* to coerce me into joining you in Mayfair?"

He lifted his broad shoulders in a shrug. "Yes."

The world had gone insane. There was nothing else for it.

Yesterday, she'd experienced Broderick's charm turned on her for the first time in all the years she'd been in his employ. And today, he'd turned on her the patent ruthlessness he'd used to destroy his enemies and make the lives of his opponents hell.

"I don't believe you," she finally said. Despite all the ways he'd proven himself to be a stranger to her, she knew him enough to detect there was always more with Broderick Killoran. "That can't be all this is about."

"Clever woman." There was a raw sincerity to that pronouncement, and she hated it. For it didn't match with the ruthless schemer who'd snatched her dream out from under her.

Nor was it just her dream he threatened. Through her blind allegiance to Broderick, she'd also cost Clara the security she craved.

Bitterness tasted like vinegar on her tongue as she witnessed the death of a friendship and had a confirmation of every last warning Clara had attempted to give her. "If I were truly clever, I would have signed the damned paperwork the moment I had the opportunity instead of rushing back to"—*you*—"your club." Clara had proven correct. In making more of her relationship to the Killoran family, she'd made herself weak. It was a mistake she'd not make again—not where this man was concerned.

"Yes." He sat upright. "But you didn't, and so we are here now, renegotiating the terms of this place."

Panic clawed at her chest, but she kept her face in a careful mask, refusing to let him see how greatly he'd shaken her. "You cannot truly want me there, Broderick," she said coolly. He'd never wanted her in the ways she'd yearned for him to. "With your love of the nobility, you know very well that it would be far wiser, far more advantageous, to have a proper lady escorting Gertrude." And not some interloper who'd tossed away her good name and virtue long, long ago. "She will understand that."

He fished a cheroot from inside his jacket, along with a small box. "She would," he acknowledged as he withdrew the double-folded sandpaper and, dragging a match through, sparked a crimson ember. He touched his cheroot to the tip and, tossing the box down on the table, took a long inhale.

So, he was uncomfortable, too.

Good—the evidence of it steadied her. His unease marked him as human. It reminded her they'd been friends far longer than they'd been at odds, and as such, she knew his weaknesses—mayhap more than he'd ever detected hers. That gave her strength.

Broderick studied her from over the perfect ring of smoke he exhaled. "Gertrude also freed you of any obligation."

Reggie forced her next words out in modulated tones. "Did she?" She made a show of studying her fingernails. All the while she felt his penetrating stare taking in her every movement.

He took another draw from that pungent scrap. "She did." Flicking the ashes at the tip of the cheroot, he sprinkled them on the floor. "And I would have accepted her decision to be joined by another companion."

Another more honorable, ladylike one. The unspoken implication there stung. But his veiled words were worse, for they quashed the earlier hope she'd allowed herself. "You *would* have?"

Broderick held his cheroot to his lips, smoking away with an infuriating calm. Just watching her. Baiting her. "You know too much."

Her stomach sank. Of course. "Stephen," she said, her voice hollowed out. *Bloody hell.*

The tobacco scrap dangling in his fingers, Broderick tapped his palm against his opposite hand in a small, mocking clap.

The ramifications of what he implied . . . what he suggested, tore a hole in her heart. "You believe I would betray you?" How little she truly knew this man.

"Yesterday I would have said no." He took another draw from his cheroot and then put it out on the corner of the table. "But that was before I learned of your plans." The mask slipped, and he leaned forward, his features a study of disbelief and confusion. "Sally? Willifred? Mariel? And all my best serving girls?" She held steady under that barrage of accusations. "MacLeod?" he demanded on an angry whisper. "My head guard?" There was hurt there, from this man who revealed not even a hint of emotion to his siblings.

Fearing every last pathetic secret she carried, Reggie dragged her eyes away from his and trained them on the stage. Needing him to understand . . . and yet unable—and unwilling—to share that most humbling of reasons, that she wanted *him*. That she loved him. That she always had and always would. Her heart spasmed. For nothing could come from her telling Broderick anything of that secret she'd kept close.

"Will you not say anything?" he fairly entreated.

In the end, she'd rather have his resentment than his pity. "I had my reasons," she said flatly, offering a vague response that preserved her pride.

"They don't matter," he said in his patent proprietor tones. The ones he'd reserved for those left over by Diggory who'd betrayed him.

Clenching her hands, Reggie buried them in her lap.

"What matters is how much you know about . . . certain matters," he declared with a finality that roused her earlier panic. "As such, my options with you are limited." He ticked up a finger. "I could have you removed. Or"—he waggled that long digit—"well, as I see it, that is really the only option. Wouldn't you say?"

Gooseflesh rose on her arms. There had been countless others before who'd roused terror within her . . . but never Broderick—until now. "Don't say that," she ordered, that command faintly breathless. He'd proven himself single-minded in his intent to build up his gaming hell empire. Ruthless to those opponents who crossed him or stood in his way. He'd never cut a man, woman, or child down like Diggory had done with chilling frequency. "You aren't Diggory."

That reminder was as much for him as it was for her.

He smirked, and her fingers twitched with the need to slap the expression from his face. "I meant remove you from the Devil's Den."

"So this"—Reggie's suddenly heavy tongue made her words come out garbled—"demand that I serve as Gertrude's companion is really just you making me a prisoner?"

"I don't see any other way around it." Broderick may as well have been one who chatted with her about the tobacconist's latest shipment, and not one who sought to strip her of power and control. "As you aptly pointed out, I don't *need* you serving Gertrude. I just need you close."

How odd. Five words she would have once traded years from her life to hear from this man, spoken in a way that left her cold inside.

"You'll serve as companion to her and a governess to Stephen until . . ." Stephen returned to his true family. Broderick's jaw flexed. And through the misery of her own circumstances, sadness for Stephen and all the Killorans swept her.

Reggie stretched a hand toward Broderick's. He flicked a stare over her palm. His eyes were filled with such antipathy her cheeks blazed hot. She yanked her fingers back.

The unfeeling proprietor of the most wicked gaming hell was firmly back in place. "You'll serve until I determine your time is through."

Her throat constricted, hating that they'd come to this. Reggie eyed him a long while, dragging out the silence, maintaining her scrutiny.

With her decision, she'd made them into combatants fighting one another, both refusing to bend. And still, even as she knew she was in the wrong, she despised his inability to see that something other than greed drove her.

Hers was an act of self-preservation. One that she could not reveal without losing the remaining vestiges of her pride.

The slightest frown formed on Broderick's lips.

At that crack in his guard, she spoke. "In the years I've known you, Broderick, you've proven to be stubborn, confident, arrogant." He preened, and she resisted the urge to roll her eyes. Reggie leaned across the table, holding his gaze. "And logical. You always made decisions and carried on discussions with an absolute clearheadedness."

Color marred his chiseled cheekbones. Nay, a man as proud as Broderick wouldn't ever take to having his attributes and character so neatly dissected and laid out. She sought one last time to appeal to that cogency and relied on that which had driven him all these years. "I'm not a lady."

"I know that," he said automatically.

Another wave of bitterness assailed her. What if she'd been born to that class he'd always desired a connection to? Would he have seen her then? Is that what it would have taken?

I never wanted him that way . . . I wanted him to see me as a woman he admired, respected . . . and loved . . .

But then, just as she'd erred before in matters of the heart, she'd committed that same grievous offense here. With a man who now played a game with her future.

"You don't know the world of the *ton*. A young lady is only as respected as the woman she calls companion," she persisted. Reggie might not have been born a lady, but she'd served their ranks and knew their ways enough to know how that world worked. "To Polite Society, the fact that I've lived in a gaming hell with courtesans makes me no different than a whore myself. It would only taint their view of Gertrude." And that did not include all the other ways in which those lords and ladies would be right about Reggie's reputation.

"You're no whore," he said crisply, as though he were offended on her behalf. As though he was so very certain of her virtue. "Their opinion of you is neither here nor there."

Shame filled her. "Your sister's reputation is inextricably linked to her companion, whomever that may be."

"The ones who matter are the gentlemen who will not care about her lineage."

She sneered. "Ones in need of a fortune." He'd sell a sibling for that coveted connection.

"Ones who appreciate her for who she is," he said quietly.

That sent her back in her seat as he knocked her off-balance once more. *Damn him.* Damn him for revealing that devotion he'd long had for his siblings. It was easier to hate him when he proved to be the driven, ruthless bastard who'd not accept no at any turn.

She stared at him a long while. "You are woefully naive if you expect to find such gentlemen in their midst." They were all snakes and vipers. People who didn't give a second thought to ruining a young woman's life.

"Your experience comes in seeing the lords who patronize the clubs," he remarked with a shocking amount of conviction to his erroneous assumption. "There are other manners of gentlemen. Those with honor."

I once thought you were one of them . . . "You believe that?" Who could have thought that Broderick would be naive in this way?

"I *know* that." He laid his palms along those documents that had the power to both free and trap her.

She'd not debate him on the point. It would require her to reveal her every sin and folly. She'd sooner dance a jig through the Dials without a stitch of clothing on than share anything with him now. She searched his face, seeking a hint of humanity . . . a shred of warmth . . . and finding none. "If I say no, what then?" she asked, already knowing the answer.

"Then"—he slashed a hand toward the stage—"this venture you propose will have to continue in some other place."

Grateful for the protective shield the table provided, Reggie clawed at her skirts. It had taken her and Clara months to find this one place. But they could find another . . . nay, they would. Reggie shoved back her chair. "You can go to hell with your attempt at manipulating me. I'll find another place." One farther away from him and these streets . . . as she should have done in the first damned place.

"I didn't take you for a coward," he called after her.

Reggie's steps drew to a slow stop. *He's trying to get a rise out of you . . . he's trying to twist you around his skilled finger . . .* As such, she should continue walking, pack her bags, and put Broderick, his damned club, and all the many mistakes she'd made far behind her. She turned. "And I took you as one clever enough to know not to insult the one whom you need something from but who is also privy to all your secrets." Reggie dipped her voice to a low whisper. "All of them."

He exploded to his feet and was upon her in three long strides.

Gasping, Reggie staggered back. A table blocked her escape, knocking her into a seated position atop the surface. She arched her neck back, meeting his fury-filled gaze.

"Let us be clear," he whispered. "I don't take threats from anyone, Miss Spark. Regardless of how long I've known you." He lowered his head so close their lips nearly met. His chest brushed hers. "If you threaten me and mine, I will destroy you. Make no mistake of it."

Only Broderick Killoran could issue a threat in a silken whisper that painted it as seduction instead of ruin. Her chest rose hard and fast, with each rapid intake bringing her body flush to his.

Nor was it fear or anger, but rather her own pathetic weakness to his nearness. And for a man who would ruin her. She saw it in the ice in his eyes and the hardness of his chiseled features. "What will you do?" she taunted, her breath tangling with his. "Have one of your men off me?"

His eyes drifted to her mouth. Desire flashed in his eyes.

Her breath quickened.

Except Broderick feeling any desire for her was impossible. He had neither wanted her nor noticed her in any of the ways a man who longed for a woman did. But then he cupped her cheek. Caressed it with his palm. And just like that, he cut her indignation out from under her and tossed her ordered thoughts into upheaval. His callused fingers against her cheek were so different from the only other man whose touch she'd allowed. Broderick's were the hands of a man, in every way. One unafraid to work. One who'd killed to protect her years earlier. It was a chip he could call in, and yet . . . he hadn't when any other man would. That noble gesture had just been one of so many reasons she loved him.

When he spoke, his mouth nearly brushed hers, that illusion of a kiss heady for what it promised. "There are far worse fates a man . . . or woman . . . could suffer than a physical death." That steely threat knocked loose the haze he'd cast.

Reggie shoved herself upright, forcing Broderick back. "I'm not afraid of you." Did she give that assurance for him? Or for herself?

He smiled slowly, displaying that wolflike grin he donned before any battle. "Then you are far less clever than I credited. Because you see . . . not only do I own this place, but my solicitor has also made inquiries on every establishment you've visited. Any building for sale in London." With each triumph he hurled, she felt the blood draining from her cheeks. "Why, I even know the ones that are merely rumored to be for sale in the near future."

This was the danger in dueling with one who possessed more money than God himself. With his fortune, Broderick could force anyone's hand. Her and Clara's funds combined would never be a match for the wealth he possessed. And all her earlier confidence sagged.

"Shall we discuss the terms if you accept?"

She wanted to spit in his face. To hurl a "go to hell" at him and march off. But as a woman who'd tossed aside her virtue for a cad and made the life she had in the Dials, there was too much at stake.

Giving a snap of her skirts, Reggie marched past him. As soon as she'd retaken her seat, she lifted her chin in his direction. "Get on with it."

With that damned swagger that came as natural as breathing to him, he rejoined her. "In the event you accompany *my family*"—that pointed emphasis striking like a knife between the shoulder blades; how easily he'd just cut her from the Killoran clan—"I'm prepared to offer you the same agreed-upon terms for ownership of this establishment for this sum." Locking gazes, he reached inside his jacket and held out a folded sheet.

Reggie swiped the page from his hands, and unfolding it, she scanned the single amount written there.

"Four thousand pounds?" she choked out. She tossed the page at him. It bounced off his chest and fell to the table. It was a fortune for any person . . . except him.

"I know. How incredibly fair I am. I'd contemplated five." He flashed that charming, lopsided grin that had always done wicked things to her heart's beat.

Until now. Rage simmered in her chest. "Can you not leave me to my affairs and go on with your life?" How had her world been turned so inside out that she could utter those words to this man who'd snatched her heart long ago?

His smile deepened, never reaching his ice-cold eyes. "I'm afraid that is an impossibility. I have to make *some* profit on it. As it is, I've lost time at my own club, conducting business with you."

Reggie made one last grab for control. "I can find another place." She hurried to clarify. "Outside of London." She winced at the stridency of her tone. "If I go anywhere else, I'll be no competition to you."

He chuckled. "Is that what you think this is about? *Me* fearing competition from *you*?"

His slightly mocking emphasis set her teeth on edge, and she fed her fury, for it kept her from mourning the splintering of her heart.

Placing his palms on his knees, Broderick leaned forward. He let his false grin drop. "Whatever you intend to do, whatever next move you make, I'll be three steps in front of you."

That steely promise raised the gooseflesh on her arms. This was the man who sent terror clamoring in the breasts of all unfortunate enough to call the Dials home. It was Broderick as she'd never before known him. Still, she'd not back down. "What are your terms?"

"You remain in my employ until I give you permission to leave. At no time are you to be alone. Be it a guard, or Stephen, or myself, someone is to shadow your movements."

She choked. She was to be a prisoner, then.

Broderick continued. "The extent of your obligation is to accompany Gertrude to *ton* functions: balls, soirees, dinner parties, the theatre."

Just agree, a voice needled at the back of her mind as he ticked off those requirements. Reggie knew Broderick Killoran enough to know that he'd never concede a point or battle. At most, she'd be required to serve mere months in that hated role of companion.

Her pulse pounded loudly in her ears.

Could she truly do this? Could she risk facing Lord Oliver again and the greatest mistake of her youth? One that had put her in this vulnerable, helpless place she now found herself?

Jumping up, Reggie strode away from Broderick. Needing space between them. Needing to think. She stopped in front of the pianoforte and stared blankly down at the chipped keys.

In her mind she saw another seated at this instrument, fingers flying over the keys, while performers moved about the stage. Other women who'd not find themselves in the vulnerable position she now found herself . . . dependent upon the mercy of a man. Upon the mercy of any man. Even ones they erroneously took for *friends*.

Fool.

Yes, she *could* do this.

She could journey to the posh end of London she'd vowed never to set foot in again. She would risk seeing *him* again, and having the whole world speak about her sins.

But she would be damned if she didn't have a say in the terms of their agreement.

She faced him again. "I'm not staying in Mayfair."

"That is not negotiable. You'll stay where I am."

She shivered. There was an air of a threat underlying that declaration. "Very well." Reggie placed her hands on her hips. "I want this establishment turned over to me now." He was already shaking his head. She didn't allow him a word edgewise. "In the times I'm not serving Gertrude, I want the freedom to visit and conduct work here as I wish." For when he eventually set her free, she wanted to know that this new home would be awaiting her.

"You have to be mad to believe I'd sell this to you now. Tsk. Tsk. Where would be my leverage, Miss Spark?"

So she was "Miss Spark" again.

Very well, that was far easier in the frosty negotiations they now carried out.

"Draft new papers. In the event I fail to carry out my responsibilities, you are free to absolve me of my ownership."

"What of Miss Winters?" He arched a single elegant eyebrow. "Is she comfortable with those negotiations?"

Of course he would have gleaned Clara's role. "What other choice does she have?" she spat. Reggie hugged her arms tight. If the ten years she and Broderick had shared as friends had meant so little, how would he be to one such as Clara, who'd only recently joined the Devil's Den . . . and had come to them from a rival establishment, no less?

"I want your assurance that you'll cede my portion of ownership over to her."

"And what would prevent you from shirking your responsibilities, being sacked, having Winters take on total ownership, and simply hire you?"

Reggie opened and closed her mouth. My God, how had his mind arrived at that devious conclusion? He'd been correct earlier. She'd always been rot at subterfuge. "You may include a clause that bars me from taking employment with Miss Winters." She settled for the easiest resolution.

Broderick caught his chin between his thumb and forefinger, contemplating Reggie.

She simmered, her body poised for a fight on this point.

"Very well," he acquiesced. "But a guard is with you at all times."

Fury lanced through her. "Am I to travel in shackles, too?" Reggie sneered. "That would certainly earn you the respect of the peerage you so desperately crave."

He flushed; splotches of indignant rage suffused his cheeks. "We'll begin with just the guard," he said, refusing to take the bait she'd hurled at him.

"I'm no man's prisoner. I want independence to conduct my affairs without your spies about."

His eyes formed slits. "That is nonnegotiable. Is there anything else?"

She wanted to leave. To end this meeting and find a place to privately rail at her folly in trusting him. "Nothing," she spat. "I want nothing from you."

"Come. You did this to us. *You,* Reggie."

A shuddery smile tugged at the corners of her lips. "There was never an 'us.'" Not truly. Not in any way.

He considered her for a long moment with that piercing, penetrating stare capable of stripping a person of their secrets. And for one horrifying, agonizing moment, fear struck. Fear that he knew the secret she'd kept from him all these years. That he'd at last gathered her reasons for leaving were largely grounded in what she could never have—with him. He spoke. "You act the wounded party, Reggie." That use of her nickname sucked the palpable anger from the room and restored a familiar ease to their discourse. "Do you think I wanted this?" He shoved the legal documents across the table at her. He didn't allow her to speak. Nor did Reggie in this instance have any words for him. "I trusted you more than nearly anyone. I shared things with you about the club that I didn't even reveal to Cleo." Cleopatra, who'd been like a second partner at the clubs before she'd gone and married.

And yet . . . Reggie hadn't wanted that to be all he'd shared with her. She'd wanted him to share himself—the past he kept secret from all, the family he'd had before he found himself in the same hellish existence Reggie had. She looked away.

"And you?" he spat with such vitriol she forced herself to meet his stare.

Betrayal blazed bright within his always guarded eyes. Reggie's throat worked.

His rage had been easier than the sting of his disappointment. "You were intending to not only take my best staff from me, Reggie, but also planning to leave with barely a *goodbye*?"

"I was going to tell you," she said, her reassurance lame even to her own ears.

"And what? Hmm? Knock on my door and give a short notice at the hell as though you were simply any member of the staff and not . . ." He gave his head a shake, leaving that statement unfinished.

Her ears pricked up. "What?" she asked, unable to call the question back. Neither did she want to. For she needed to know just what she had been. She held her breath, weak as she'd always been for this man because of that yearning.

He gave her a sad smile and completed his thought. "My friend." Her heart dipped. "You were my friend."

Were, which implied a friendship that had come and gone.

Sadness flooded her: for the loss of that bond, but also for the loss of something that had never been. "Me leaving," she said tentatively, "does not have to mean we become enemies." That is never what she'd wanted to come out of her departure. "My having an establishment of my own doesn't undo the years of friendship we shared."

The indifferent mask was back in place. "Whatever bond we shared is dead."

His pronouncement carved a place in her already-broken heart.

Broderick proceeded to gather the documents and papers strewn about the table. How many times had he carried out those same mundane movements before her? She stared on, unable to look away; sadness filled her. Every casual exchange they'd shared may as well have existed within another lifetime for all that had come to pass in these last moments. "I'll have new documents drawn up with the terms carefully spelled out."

"Thank you." She pulled a face, detesting that response born of automaticity that had been chiseled into her as a respectable young girl in Kent.

He didn't spare her another glance. "You are dismissed."

Reggie jerked.

Like a servant. Drawing on every last lesson of deportment she'd doled out, she climbed slowly to her feet. Shoulders back, chin up, she gathered her cloak and shrugged into it. Broderick now saw her as nothing more than hired help. In a sense, that was all she'd truly ever been. Oh, he might dress their relationship up as friendship, but he'd paid her well, and she'd dedicated her time and energies to the Devil's Den.

Reggie placed her bonnet on and, hating the quake of her fingertips, tied the strings under her chin. "Mr. Killoran."

With that she swept out and left him there in the club that would one day be hers, feeling very much like she'd struck a deal with the Devil himself.

Chapter 11

Any hope you have is false. Nothing and no one will save you . . .

"Where are they?"

It was the fifth time since Stephen had joined Broderick outside the Devil's Den, beside the loaded carriages, that he'd grumbled that question.

It was the same question Broderick himself had been asking for the better part of thirty minutes.

"They'll be along," he said tightly, staring at the double doors hanging open.

"Ya told them to be here twenty minutes ago."

Broderick frowned. He knew very well the directive he'd sent around that morn to Gertrude and Reggie. The carriages had long been loaded with trunks and valises, and his sister remained inconveniently absent.

Though it isn't your sister whom you're worried about . . .

Reggie Spark, who'd given him countless reasons to be wary of her, was the true source of his unease.

"Maybe she snuck 'round back?" Stephen piped in, hope contained within that supposition.

Broderick caught his speedy brother by the back of his collar. "Reggie doesn't sneak," he said impatiently. She was a spitfire who'd gone toe to toe with him at every turn yesterday in ways that he'd never expected. He'd always gathered there was a strength in her, but never before had she turned that fire upon him.

"She don't sneak. Now we know that ain't true," Stephen pointed out. "She does." He flashed a gap-toothed smile. "Just badly," he added, nudging Broderick in the side. "Freakishly tall to be of any use in the Dials."

Broderick scowled. "Watch your words," he warned, immediately quelling whatever else Stephen had been about to say.

Color splotched Stephen's cheeks. "Ya'd defend her?"

"Men don't talk unkindly about women."

His brother wrinkled his nose. "Yeah they do. All the time. Lord Tamley said Sally's tits were even smaller than her brain." A muscle leapt in Broderick's jaw. His brother referred to the disparaging words hurled by drunken patrons. That was what Broderick had unwittingly exposed a marquess's son to: crude talk about whores and serving girls. Stephen kicked a lone pebble toward the steps of the club. The stone caught a crack in the pavement and bounced to a stop. "And Cowan said it anyway."

"Said what?" he demanded.

"About Reggie being too freakishly tall and that she ain't yar usual preference for a fuck—"

"Enough," he barked, his cheeks going hot with rage at those vile charges against her. He wrestled with his cravat.

"Cowan's words," Stephen said with a shrug.

Broderick gnashed his teeth. "I'll sack the bastard." Another one of Diggory's leftovers. The bloody servant wouldn't work in the Dials again.

"So you haven't kept her around because you're tupping her?" Stephen pressed.

Broderick swept a hand over his eyes, and then he let his arm drop to his side. "I have never been anything but respectful toward Miss Spark. Reggie is"—*was*—"a friend." And regardless of what had come to pass these past two days, he'd never so disrespect her that he'd tolerate Cowan or any other man, woman, or child in his employ disparaging her.

Stephen swiped the back of his hand over his nose. *"Hmph,"* his brother said noncommittally. "Cowan said that was the only reason you trust her."

Not only had he disparaged Reggie but he'd also cast aspersions on the reason for her influence at the club? He'd bloody the man senseless before he sacked him.

"Bloody hell," he gritted.

"You asked," Stephen protested.

"I know. It's . . . let it go. I assure you, Cowan is wrong . . . on *both* scores." Proper as any lady in London, Reggie Spark wasn't the manner of woman who'd take any man as her lover . . . including a blighter like Broderick.

"So why ya keeping her around, then?" his brother persisted.

Had he always been this tenacious?

"I am not . . . *keeping her around*." He was keeping her close, as he would anyone who came upon the information about Stephen's parentage and Broderick's role in the boy's kidnapping. He'd not share Reggie's fate with the Killorans with his brother. His world had been upended enough. "This isn't appropriate discourse." In the Dials there was no limit to the type of talk a person, of any age, could take part in. Not, however, for the world Stephen would soon enter.

And he'd do so with a knowledge of the streets and life that no young child should carry with them. Glancing to the doorway and finding it still empty, Broderick dropped to a knee. "It isn't appropriate to use that language or to speak as you've done about Miss Spark, Stephen." Again, guilt assailed him. For he was the one responsible for stripping this child of his innocence.

Stephen pulled his brows together. "Why?"

"Because you just do not," he awkwardly explained.

"That ain't much of a reason."

Broderick grimaced. "No," he muttered to himself. It wasn't. He'd failed Stephen in so many ways. At the very least he could eventually return him to his father with this most basic form of decency explained. *I should have done so long before . . . I should have worked harder to see that he didn't become this angry, scarred creature.* He tried again, calling forth lessons given him by another man long ago. One who'd been good and decent and like a father. "How you speak, the words you use, matters. To descend into cursing suggests a lack of intelligence and an inability to find the appropriate words to convey how you're feeling." That guidance had come not as a castigation by the duke his father had worked for, but rather as a gentle explanation.

"But I like cursing."

He winked. "It's because you haven't found the other words you need yet." Lord Maddock would find all the appropriate tutors to school the boy . . . and manage what Broderick hadn't. "And you don't speak ill about any woman, do you hear me? *Regardless* of her birthright," he tacked on.

"What about women who betray ya?" Stephen asked dryly. "Can a fella talk about them?"

So his brother had been listening in. Broderick lightly cuffed his brother under the chin. "Not even them." How did a boy of eleven become such a master of turnabout? He shoved to his feet and glanced yet again at the doorway.

Thunder rumbled ominously, and a solitary raindrop landed on his nose.

Bloody rain.

He tugged out the enamel watch fob, his last link to the life he'd left behind, and consulted the time. What was keeping them?

"You sure . . ." That hesitant child's voice pulled his attention down to Stephen. "We gotta live there?"

Broderick sighed. "We do." As Reggie had rightly pointed out, Gertrude would already face society's censure for her past and the place she'd called home. "It would open her to"—even more—"gossip, if she were to return each night to a gaming hell."

"Ain't wise for ya to be away from the club," Stephen persisted.

Nor had he ever been gone from the Killorans in all the time he'd served Diggory and then taken the hell over. "I trust it won't be long before she's wed and—"

Stephen's face crumpled, and with it, Broderick's heart.

With a black curse, he glanced to the nearest servant. "Where in blazes are—?"

Gertrude stepped outside, her hands folded primly before her and the hood of her muslin cloak drawn up. Leveling him with a harsh glare, she swept down the steps.

At last.

Impatient, he looked beyond her toward the still-empty doorway. Searching for the still-missing companion. Gertrude stepped directly into his line of vision. "Where is . . . ?"

"Not. One. Word," she clipped out.

"Reggie . . . ?"

"I said not one," she spoke over him.

Stephen's jaw went slack as he looked between Gertrude and Broderick.

This increasing show of spirit was still unexpected and unfamiliar from the one sibling who'd always been . . . *not* difficult. If he weren't so bloody frustrated, he'd have been proud of that resolve.

"In the carriage, Stephen." Broderick didn't take his gaze from the gaping double doors. From the corner of his eye, he caught his youngest sibling reaching for the handle behind him. "You will ride in the other one with Gertrude," he instructed.

Stephen spoke over Gertrude's shocked gasp. "Why you riding with her?" he bemoaned.

Shifting his gaze over to the obstinate little boy beside him, Broderick gave him a hard look.

"Oh, fine," the boy mumbled, and cursing under his breath, he stalked ahead to the other conveyance.

As soon as Stephen scrambled inside, Gertrude unleashed her temper. "What have you done?" she whispered, fury coloring her tone.

Aware passersby and servants baldly stared on, he spoke from the corner of his mouth. "I've done nothing."

"Reggie is silent and sad. She did not wish to do this. What did you do to gain her capitulation?"

"Miss Spark agreed of her own volition to serve as your companion."

"Oh?" Gertrude demanded snidely. "And just what did you threaten her with to bring about that sudden change of heart?"

And blast if he didn't feel heat mottle his cheeks. "What did she say?" Had she returned yesterday and played the victim, presenting him as the villain?

"Do you know what she said?" He stiffened. "Nothing. She refuses to speak out against you or share any of what happened." Gertrude's throat bobbed. "Except to say that after I was married, she would no longer be employed by the Devil's Den."

A niggling of discomfort needled at his chest. After she'd stormed off yesterday, he'd been so struck by his own outrage that he'd not focused on the fact that when they left, she wouldn't return to the Devil's Den as his right hand. That their relationship as he'd known it was at an end. Even with everything that had come to pass, a sliver of regret slipped in. She'd been as much a part of the family and the clubs as Cleo, Ophelia, Gertrude, or Stephen.

The fight left Gertrude. "What transpired between you two?" she repeated, imploring with her eyes.

Of course, Gertrude had always been incapable of sustained anger and fury. That had set her apart from the rest of the Killorans.

"I don't—" He was saved from replying by Reggie's sudden appearance.

She lingered in the doorway.

Just then, the wind gusted, tugging her stubborn red curls free of her neat coiffure. They whipped about her shoulders as she stood there with the regal bearing of a queen.

"I'll discuss it with you later," he promised.

Gertrude looked as though she'd fight him on that order, but then snapping her skirts, she marched off to the other carriage. And that she believed his lie was just further proof of how different Gertrude was from the rest of them.

Broderick drew the door open and waited. Reggie cast one last look back inside the club before joining him.

"Miss Spark," he greeted with a cool formality, needing to erect barriers between them. The folly of trusting too deeply was one he should have learned firsthand from his own father's treachery against the one who'd been kindest to them.

He held a hand out to assist her up. Reggie brushed by him and, gripping the sides of the doorway, drew herself inside.

Broderick hesitated before following behind. Doffing his hat, he tossed it down on the empty place beside him. He'd had enough of this. He was not in the wrong here, and he'd be damned if she'd make him out to be the villain.

The servant closed the door behind them.

A moment later the carriage sprang into motion, for the first time leading him away from his club to another residence, albeit a temporary one. And yet, as they rolled through the streets of the Dials, a melancholy filled him.

Quashing that pathetic, mewling sentiment, he reached inside his jacket. "Here," he said gruffly, extending a sheet toward her.

Reggie stared at it a moment and then accepted it with stiff fingers.

"I thought I might use this time to review your commitments for the coming weeks," he explained as she unfolded the page and read. "Your services are required for the following events. I've secured invitations"—with Cleo and Ophelia's assistance—"to an array of *ton* functions. Balls, soirees, trips to the theatre, and other affairs. I'll also be hosting a small gathering. In addition, you're to accompany her to the modiste to be fitted for new gowns."

He saw her eyes moving over that page, methodically taking in the schedule.

"Per our agreement, any days where Gertrude does not have an obligation and doesn't require a chaperone, you'll be free to go about your affairs."

Infuriatingly calm, Reggie folded the page and tucked it inside her pocket. "And . . . have you shared with your siblings . . ."

"Your betrayal?" he supplied for her. It was a mark to her strength that she didn't so much as flinch, and it merely increased his damned appreciation for her, and annoyance with himself for admiring her. "They'll all be informed soon enough."

"They won't want me near, Broderick," she said quietly.

"Undoubtedly. But they'll still see we need to keep you close."

Her throat muscles worked. "And there is nothing I can say to make you see reason?"

"Our terms are set, Miss Spark."

With all the aplomb of a queen, Reggie presented her shoulder, dismissing him.

From the corner of his eye, he stole a peek at the woman. Taller than most men, she'd still managed to make herself somehow small, pressed as she was against the far corner. Pointedly ignoring him was what she was doing.

Refusing to let that rankle, Broderick yanked open his window curtain and stared out.

Several raindrops pinged the window.

"Bloody marvelous," he muttered.

Thick grey clouds hung heavy overhead, rolling by at an interminable pace that mocked him for his notice.

It was a silly, nonsensical detail for a man who'd clawed his way from the gutters and claimed the throne of the king of the underworld to notice.

It was unfortunately, however, a telling part of himself he'd been unable to leave behind since he and his father had set out from Cheshire atop a stolen mount in the dead of night.

And it was an ominous sign that in his journey back into that world of respectability, the same thick clouds of gloom should greet him.

"Rain washes away one's sorrows."

Broderick stared at his visage reflected back in the window, for a moment believing he'd imagined that hushed murmur.

He faced Reggie.

Letting the brocade curtain slip from her fingers and flutter into place, she turned reluctantly back. "My father used to tell me that rain washes away the sorrow because it represents life and new beginnings."

It was the first she'd ever mentioned her family. As part of that unspoken code of the streets, he'd never pried, and she'd never shared. Now . . . the questions he'd carried but eventually buried about the woman before him rose once more: Who was Regina Spark? Or rather, who *had* she been before he'd come upon her at London Bridge all those years ago?

The answer of course didn't really matter. Soon she'd be gone, and with her, her secrets and story.

Liar. You'll miss the damned chit.

At his silence, her stare lingered on his face. "You always hated the rain."

His body stiffened.

A wistful smile brought her lips up at the corners. "You curse whenever it starts."

It was just one more glaring way in which he'd let his guard down around her. Unnerved by that truth, he returned his focus to the passing streets, grateful fifteen minutes later when they at last arrived. He grabbed his hat in one hand.

The carriage hadn't even rocked to a full stop when Broderick shoved the door open and jumped out.

Servants immediately came rushing from the brick-finished townhouse.

A flash of lightning streaked across the sky, briefly turning the grey sky bluish-purple. Placing his hat on, he did a sweep of the Mayfair streets and this new place that would serve as a temporary home.

From within the panes of the neighboring windows, lords, ladies, and servants all stood with their noses pressed to the glass panels.

This was to be what followed them wherever they went. He'd accepted the Killorans would be an oddity but had trusted that strangeness would work as an advantage for Gertrude in the attention they'd receive.

Now, as Gertrude and Stephen disembarked and filed in, huddling close, matching steps with one another, he saw before him that which he'd not considered—the unease they would feel in this foreign world.

The intermittent drizzle gave way to a steady, pounding rain.

At long last Reggie ducked her head outside.

She hovered in the carriage door, gripping the edges with a white-knuckled death grip that drew his attention to her callused, ink-stained hands and chipped nails.

They were the hands of a woman unashamed to work, and yet he frowned . . . she'd deserved more than those coarse palms.

As the wind kicked up its fury, it became increasingly clear the woman frozen at the entrance of the carriage had no intention of accepting the hand of the waiting footman.

Quitting his spot, Broderick returned to the carriage. "I understand your affinity for the rain, madam; however, I'd rather we continue on inside."

His presence seemed to jerk her from whatever momentary fog had gripped her. She blinked wildly. "Of course," she blurted, and accepted his hand, allowing him to help her down.

They continued on ahead, the people still pressed against those windows, until Broderick and Reggie disappeared inside.

Chapter 12

Your time is nearly up . . .

She'd been summoned.

Only this summons was nothing like the ones that had come before in Reggie's ten-year tenure with the Killoran family.

It had been issued not in the Devil's Den, where she'd resided for years now, but rather in Reggie's new *home*.

With Reggie in a different role.

Nerrie followed close at her side, a hand on his waist, in the ready position for a fight.

"I assure you, I don't intend to make off with Mr. Killoran's silverware," she said in a bid to break the tension.

He gave her a regretful look. Of course. His employer had spoken, and whatever orders he'd given Nerrie and the other guards had erased any niceties from his staff and left Reggie . . . alone, once more.

She firmed her jaw. Very well. So she'd been cut out of the Killoran clan in every way. She'd been alone before him, and she'd be without him and his people after. Under no circumstances, however, would she make apologies for defending herself or Gertrude.

After an interminable march through this labyrinth of a home, they reached a pretty arched ivory doorway.

Braced for battle and schooled by the man she was now meeting on taking the offensive, Reggie stepped into the room.

And the argument she'd prepared swiftly died.

Of everything she'd contemplated—being turned out, having Broderick renege on the terms of their arrangement—this certainly hadn't been what she'd expected to find waiting for her in the brightly lit, yellow parlor.

Madame Colette, the most sought-after modiste on New Bond Street, conversed at the center of the room with Broderick. That plump woman blushed and preened before Broderick. Broderick, who, when he chose to wield his charm, could have talked Satan out of sinning. Neither of them gave any indication they'd observed Reggie's arrival.

And should that come as any surprise? Broderick never saw you standing there.

Nonetheless, knowing that as she did, a miserable niggling of jealousy rooted around her belly.

She curled her fingers tight, hating herself for the pathetic creature she was.

With the ease with which he'd manipulated her into joining him in London, and with the threat he posed to her future, she shouldn't feel anything for Broderick. Nothing but the sting of resentment and bitterness. Alas, the heart knew . . . *nothing*, it seemed.

The pair looked up.

All warmth immediately faded from the modiste, transforming the plump beauty into a dour-faced harpy. As her gaze locked on Reggie in the entranceway, she pursed her lips. It was not, however, the stranger's antipathy that cut to the quick but rather the icy coldness Broderick reserved for her.

And coward that she was, Reggie was the first to look away. "You summoned," she stated crisply. Of their own volition, her eyes wandered the room, taking in the bolts of fabric and handful of seamstresses at makeshift workstations.

"I did. Madame Colette has been"—he drew the woman's hand to his lips and placed a lingering kiss on the inside of her wrist, earning a breathy giggle—"extraordinarily generous with her time, and she's agreed to perform a fitting here."

Only Broderick could manage to secure an appointment in his household with the most sought-after modiste in London.

The woman preened under his adulation. "You are *too* kind, Mr. Killoran."

Reggie rolled her eyes. "Yes, most kind, is he not?" Neither seemed to hear her droll retort. Or if they did, they paid her no notice. God, she despised how every woman had ever fallen down at his feet, herself included. She hated that she'd allowed herself to be charmed by him years ago. Oh, her reasons had not been born of his subtle flirtations or long, seductive glances, but rather of the care and regard he'd shown his siblings . . . and Reggie. "If you'll excuse me?" She sketched a curtsy. Broderick's eyes narrowed on that deferential dip. "I'll gather Miss Killoran."

She made it two steps.

"Stop, Miss Spark."

Broderick's smooth baritone earned sighs from several of the young seamstresses.

Reggie gritted her teeth. She'd once appreciated that melodic flow of his speech, so controlled and yet with a hint of sin underlying each word. His was the kind of voice that made a lady toss aside logic in order to know what other promises were contained within that slightly husky tone.

Drawing on the years of long-buried-but-never-forgotten time as a governess, she forced herself back with measured movements that didn't set so much as her hem aflutter. "Mr. Killoran?" she murmured, clasping her hands as demurely as an abbess before her. "Is there something else you require?"

Those thick golden lashes she'd spent years envying him for swept down as he leveled a piercing stare upon her. The sharp intensity of that look was softened by a single lock that slipped over his brow.

Reggie's heart did a pathetic jump.

"Madame Colette is not here for Gertrude."

It took a moment for his words to sink through the bothersome haze he'd cast. The modiste wasn't here for Gertrude. Then who in blazes was—

"She is here for you."

"For me," Reggie repeated dumbly.

"You," he said coolly.

And just like that, he'd upended her previous bravado. "Wh-what?" she squeaked.

"Your wardrobe, Miss Spark." Broderick flicked a glance over her person, and she drew back under that cool scrutiny. "You'll require a new wardrobe."

On cue, the modiste clapped her hands together once. "Shall we begin?" Not bothering to wait for an answer, the plump woman swept over to an ivory sofa that had been overtaken by heinously bright fabrics and lifted several bolts to reveal one of gold-and-silver satin.

"No. No, we shall not." Reggie held her palms up, warding off the modiste, preferring the fight she'd been prepared to face to . . . *this*.

Gasps exploded around the room.

Madame Colette's jaw fell agape as she glanced over to Broderick.

Reggie lifted her chin. "I am grateful for your . . . *generosity*." Generosity he'd thrown in her bloody face not even a day ago. She'd take not one more thing from this man.

Ever perceptive, he narrowed his eyes at that slight taunt.

"For my purpose here"—as a dutiful servant and prisoner—"my garments are just fine." The last thing she wished for was to have her drab dresses stripped away and replaced with the finest satins and silks. Not when she'd spent the better part of her adult life using her coarse garments as a protective shield against the leering stares that had once been directed her way.

The young seamstresses looked around at one another.

Broderick's gaze locked with Reggie's, and she shivered at the frost there. He'd no intention of conceding this point. He was one who didn't surrender in any battle. But then, she'd never gone to war with him, either. The clock ticked away, leaving with each passing moment another level of tension upon the room. "Leave us," he said quietly.

So he'd seen that fight, or mayhap he'd simply seen the logic in not wasting a single shilling on a wardrobe for a mere companion. Either way, a thrill of triumph humming in her veins, Reggie dropped another—albeit hasty—curtsy and turned on her heel.

"*Not* you, Miss Spark."

Bloody hell.

Of course it would never be that easy with this man.

The small army of seamstresses filed past her in a neat line like perfect ducklings, with Madame Colette close behind. Each young woman shot Reggie a disapproving glance as she went.

After the door had closed behind them, Broderick stalked toward her with sleek, panther-like strides. He was a predator toying with his prey, and every instinct screamed to flee. "Do not challenge me in front of anyone, Miss Spark. Not my servants. Not my family." That hit with a daggerlike pain and precision in her chest. For the Killorans had been the family she'd lost. "Not my guards. And not those who I employ at any level." Broderick finally stopped, several steps between them. "Am I clear?"

Do not let him intimidate you . . . he's used that lethal whisper in front of you . . .

But never on her.

Refusing to be cowed, Reggie gave a toss of her head. "Come, never tell me you're worried that a gaggle of young girls will not find you suitably impressive." The sting of jealousy pulled that from her before she could call it back.

"Is that what you think this is about?" he murmured, drifting closer.

And despite her resolve, Reggie faltered. Broderick Killoran had torn down the empires of rivals. He'd shredded the reputations of men who'd slighted him. She'd be wise to not toy with him. In a bid to escape so she might regroup before battle, she stepped sideways.

He shot an arm out, laying a palm against the door, blocking that path. "Hmm?" he pressed.

Her pulse jumped. "I don't know what this is about," she brought herself to say. "But I do not need a new wardrobe. And I'll be damned if I accept that extravagant offering from you." Reggie feinted in the opposite direction.

Broderick brought his left hand up, anchoring both palms alongside her head, effectively trapping her in his arms. The fabric of his jacket strained under the rippling muscles of his forearms, muscles she'd seen before without the hindrance of either a jacket or shirt when she'd tended him after a street fight. Her mouth went dry at the mere remembrance of that whipcord strength bared before her eyes.

"You always were too proud for your own good, Regina Spark." The hint of tobacco on his lips, mingled with brandy, whispered across her cheek.

Her heart quickened. It was the first time he'd ever referred to her by the whole of her name. And done so with his breath wafting over her cheeks, fanning a loose curl at her temple, which wrought chaos on her resolve. The masculine scents that clung to him were not unfamiliar in the gaming hell she'd called home, but on this man, they enticed. Tempted.

She breathed in deep.

How many times did I dream of being this close to him?

He lowered his brow, closer, closer still, erasing the space between them, sucking the air from the room so that only the two of them existed.

His gaze dipped to her mouth, lingering there, and the world stopped spinning.

Reggie didn't blink for endless seconds.

He is going to kiss me . . .

A virtuous miss might have mistaken the passion darkening his irises. But Reggie was no innocent and felt the pull of that desire for what it was, and after years of being invisible, she reveled in that hungering.

She, who'd vowed to never again suffer through the unpleasantness of any embrace, wanted to know this man's kiss. Because with an intuition as ancient as Eve born of the first taste of sin, Reggie knew. Knew that being in Broderick's arms, surrendering her mouth to his, and opening herself to him, would be nothing like the sloppy embraces she'd made herself suffer through with Lord Oliver. That it would be . . . magic.

She tipped her head back to receive that kiss.

The powerful muscles of his neck moved hard under the force of his swallow.

"You are a reflection of me and my family, and of our wealth." As he spoke, Broderick's lips nearly brushed hers, and yet that steely pronouncement effectively doused her ardor and snapped her back to the harsh, ugly reality of this exchange. He worked his gaze over her drab day dress, and she went hot with mortification. "Given that you will attend formal gatherings, your garments must reflect your role as Gertrude's companion, *Miss Spark*."

Broderick stepped back.

Reggie. Her chest constricted. She'd spent so many years hating his use of that hideous male moniker, only to now find, as he failed to utter it, how very much she missed it. Nay, she missed the ease that had once existed between them, and she felt a sudden urge to cry at the loss of his friendship.

"No one will say the Killorans are impoverished." He leveled her with a stare. "And no one will speak ill of anyone in my employ." She winced. "When your wardrobe is readied, you'll begin your services." Just any member of his staff was what she was. It was what she'd always been.

But then, her ears pricked up at that latter part.

"When my wardrobe is ready?" she asked cautiously.

He inclined his head. "Until then, Cleo and Ophelia will serve as Gertrude's companions."

Her mind raced.

She'd been granted a stay of execution.

Albeit a slight one.

Drifting past him, she wandered to the fabrics on display throughout the room. She dusted her fingertips over a bolt of sapphire silk. "Very well," she grudgingly conceded. "But I do not wish for anything . . ." He drifted closer. "Anything that will earn me any notice," she said quickly.

"Ah," he said as he captured a lone red curl that had tumbled to her shoulder. He rubbed that strand between his fingertips in a possessive hold. "An impossible feat for a spitfire with hair the shade of sunset."

Her chest quickened. With just the slightest touch and but a handful of words that contained only the faintest hint of seduction, Broderick was able to cause this weakening in her. But then, that was the potency of Broderick Killoran. He possessed an effortless ability to bewitch. Why, even now, he toyed with her. Just as another man had. Lord Oliver, who'd destroyed part of her.

You've been seduced by one man . . . do not allow yourself to be a fool for yet another who only seeks to manipulate you.

Reggie slipped her hair from his grip. "I don't need more than two dresses. I'm a companion, Broderick. Dull colors, drab garments, are suitable attire for a servant." And safest. "Not . . ."—Reggie held aloft lavender satin best reserved for a debutante—"cheerful, extravagant garments."

He clasped his hands behind him and wandered over. "You know so very much about serving as a companion."

Largely a statement, there was still the hint of a question there. Her mouth went dry, and she struggled to throw some flippant reply back . . . that would not come. "I . . ."

For . . . she did know something about it. Too much. And what would this man who'd built an empire from nothing but his hands and hard efforts think of all the failures that marked her soul? So instead, she offered him nothing but a lie. "Don't be s-silly."

Their exchange highlighted the fact that for all they'd shared over the years, most of who they each truly were remained a mystery to the other. They'd taken pains to hide away their pasts and focus on this world they lived within now.

Broderick stopped on the opposite side of the upholstered Chippendale piece.

"No," she finally said, letting the fabric fall back to the scalloped edge of the sofa. "I don't." She'd never been a companion, but rather a governess. The slightest distinction kept that from being a full lie.

He should leave. She'd already capitulated, and they'd struck an agreement that saw him victorious in their debate. Yet, he remained . . .

Broderick examined the display of nauseatingly cheerful scraps of fabric, surveying them with the same intensity he did his ledgers and accounts. "This"—he said, pausing to pick up a chocolate-brown muslin, one that would be perf—"will never do." Tossing aside the modest fabric, he picked up a long bolt of emerald satin. Broderick guided her around so she faced the floor-length, gilded mirror.

"Wh-what are you . . . ?" Her words ended on a breathy cessation as he brought his arms around her in a loose embrace. He snapped the fabric several times until it draped about her in an illusion of a gown. The green satin, finer than anything she'd worn in the whole of her life, fluttered against her skin like a butterfly-soft caress. And yet it was the hard-muscled wall of his chest at her back, their bodies brushing, that brought her eyes briefly shut.

He was so close he must have heard her heart pounding in response to his nearness. The catch of her breath. The whispery sigh that slipped from her lips.

In the smooth, immaculate glass panel, his gaze held hers. "Look at yourself."

"I am," she whispered. Only she didn't see the freckle-faced, gangly woman with hideously red hair and slightly crooked teeth. Rather, she saw the two of them together—her and Broderick.

And in that mirror reflected his gaze, locked on the sight of her. His eyes widened, and then he hooded his lashes once more. He layered the satin against her, her body so attuned to his that she felt everything: the faint tremble to his hands as he wrapped that fabric about her, the quick fall of his chest. "Everyone connected to the Killorans shines, Regina." Her pulse quickened. *He's as aware of me as I am of him.* And there was a heady empowerment in that realization. She reveled in that power. "Everyone," he whispered, his lips nearly brushing the shell of her ear. "Including you."

Including you.

That was, of course, all this was about: how the *ton* viewed the Killorans. That was all it had ever been about with him, as long as she'd known him. That reminder shattered his mesmeric hold and the illusion she'd allowed herself. *Fool.*

She tugged the fabric from her person, freeing it from his hands. "No one with the name 'Reggie' shines," she muttered. Tossing it aside, she retrieved the bolt he'd previously discarded. "And I *like* this."

He snorted.

"What?" she asked, her indignation creeping up. "Because it is not the brightest nor the most extravagant, it does not mean it's not lovely in its own right."

His lips twitched, the corners tilting up in the faintest half grin. "I don't believe I've seen you in any shade other than brown."

She started. He'd noticed the dresses she'd worn.

He caught the slight puff of her brown wool dress. "I notice everything," he murmured, following her thoughts with an unerring accuracy.

Her chest constricted, and for an endless, terrifying instant, she believed he toyed with her. That along the way he'd at some point gathered the truth of her affections. In the mirror, Reggie searched his face for evidence of that knowing. Finding none, relief chased off the horror. "Well, I like it," she repeated. "It's the color of chocolate and . . . and . . ."

He arched an eyebrow.

"Oh, hush." She held the muslin close to her breast. "It's a perfectly fine color."

Broderick touched the tip of her nose. "Precisely." He glanced to the door. "Enter." His voice boomed around the parlor.

Madame Colette pushed the panel open and swept inside.

"You shall find Miss Spark far more agreeable," he promised as the modiste approached. "No browns for her." He continued over Reggie's protestations. "No matter how much the young woman might insist. I want her in rich greens, lavenders, deep shades of blue." Broderick's gaze locked with Reggie's. "I don't want simply 'fine' for my sister's companion. I want a masterpiece."

Reggie slapped a hand over her eyes. "Companions do not *neeeeed* masterpieces." She let her arm fall and tried to reason with him. "We simply need dresses. Proper ones. Modest ones. *Uninteresting* ones."

"All of that means the same thing," he drawled.

She gritted her teeth. "I know. I was attempting to make a point that servants do not wear extravagant gowns. Isn't that right, Madame Colette?" With her palpable loathing for her clients missing those noble connections, Reggie could certainly count on support there.

The modiste angled her body in a way that made it clear there were only two participants in this conversation, and Reggie was certainly not one of them. "I only do masterpieces, Meezter Killoran." Madame Colette patted the back of her turban.

"Of course, madame," he purred. Quitting Reggie's side, he moved to gather the other woman's spare hand. He trailed his lips over her wrist. "She'll need a gown readied in two days' time."

No! Reggie sprang forward on the balls of her feet in protest.

"Two days?" Madame Colette squawked, slipping out of her already-poor French accent. "Why . . . why, that is *impossible*. It takes no fewer than two days for a seamstress to craft a day dress. Let alone a masterpiece. And . . . and . . . that is if the girls are working without a moment's rest."

Relief brought Reggie back on her heels.

Through the modiste's tirade, Broderick had retained hold of her hand. Over those smooth fingertips, he eyed the woman like she was the only one in the room. It was a skill he'd turned against any staff member or servant whose cooperation he required. Reggie, however, had always seen right through it and had refused to fall over herself at that ploy. "Ah, but you've not two . . . but . . . six young women here. Not just any women." The gaggle of seamstresses arched forward on the balls of their feet, hanging on the promise he dangled.

Reggie tapped her boot, that annoyed *thump* muted and dulled by the thick Aubusson carpet.

"But the finest seamstresses at Madame Colette's," he finished, ushering in a collection of sighs.

His gaze crept just beyond the woman's shoulder, over to Reggie.

Had he always been this infuriating? *"Really?"* she mouthed.

He winked.

"Non, non, non. Friday, Meezter Killoran, at the earliest."

Reggie waved her fingertips in the air. "My current wardrobe will do splendidly until you have time to create your latest . . . masterpiece."

Alas, she remained invisible for all the notice paid her.

"Two days. One hundred pounds more."

The modiste's eyes bulged in her face.

At that weakening, Broderick pounced. "A woman of your talents and skills," he murmured, walking a slow circle about the modiste. "You are surely capable of anything."

It was foolish in the extreme to feel anything over his blatant attempt to charm a bloody gown from the sharp-tongued woman. Especially because Reggie knew the exact game he played. And yet another unwanted wave of jealousy stung her.

Madame Colette tittered. "One gown." Reggie's earlier hope proved fleeting. Bloody hell, he'd charmed the miserable harpy into this. "Not one more." She clapped her hands once. "Now, shoo, you scoundrel. You've left me with a"—the modiste finally spared Reggie a glance—"near impossible task."

Broderick flashed that pearl-white smile that dimpled his left cheek. "But not impossible."

"You are shameful," Reggie mouthed as he stalked past. *"Shameful."*

He winked. "And you'll have your gown in two days' time."

Her heart sank. *Blast.* "I already have"—Broderick was already through the door—"a gown," she said under her breath, the audible utterance buried behind the firm click of the door.

The earlier levity instantly faded from the group of seamstresses and the modiste.

"Now, Miss Spark." The slight, sneering emphasis there indicated precisely what the modiste thought about Reggie Spark from the Dials. "It is time to turn you into a silk purse."

Chapter 13

The question you must be asking . . . when am I coming for you . . . ?

The first Killoran meeting inside their new Mayfair residence took place the next morn.

"I found Lucy and Walsh," he said, not mincing words. Removing the stoppard from a decanter, Broderick splashed several fingerfuls of the amber spirits into a glass. He took a long drink and grimaced. "It did not go well."

Cleo sat forward in her seat. "What happened?"

Running through a methodical accounting of everything that had transpired since his meeting with Walsh, Broderick filled his siblings in on the ever-pressing threat posed by Maddock.

Through his telling, Ophelia's frown deepened. "Who located them?"

He looked over to his middle sister. A question darkened her gaze. Broderick shifted in his seat, the leather folds groaning in protest.

With a growl she stomped over and slapped her palms on the side of his desk. "You hired another detective?" Other than her husband, that was.

"I'd been working with him long before you married O'Roarke," he gritted out. "Furthermore, you are missing the damned source of concern in all this."

"No, I'm not," Ophelia spat, as stubborn as she'd always been. Of all his levelheaded, collected sisters, her temper had always burnt as hot as Stephen's. "Had you enlisted my husband's assistance, we wouldn't even now find ourselves in the circumstances we do."

Heat suffused his cheeks.

And damn if Ophelia wasn't right. "I should have used him, but I did not," he gritted out that admission. "As such, I'm electing to focus on what we might still be able to control."

As one, the sisters looked to Gertrude.

"Hence Gertrude's hasty London Season," Cleo surmised. She turned to the eldest of the siblings. "No one has asked you before . . . but is this what you want?"

Shame stung him at this, his absolute failure to care for his sisters. Of course they'd believe his efforts were solely driven by self-preservation. What reason had he given them to think anything else? He'd proven single-minded and determined to wed them off. They couldn't know he was motivated by fear for their future and the need to provide them security in an ever-uncertain world.

"There's no other choice," Gertrude said quietly.

Ophelia moved over in a whirl of skirts. Presenting Broderick with her shoulder, she sank to a knee before Gertrude. "There is *always* a choice." She shot a glower back at Broderick. "Even when *we're* made to feel like there is not."

He winced. *I deserve that.* He'd sought to maneuver each of them into respectable matches to honorable gentlemen. He wouldn't, however, make apologies for attempting to see them secure.

"You do not have to do this," Cleo put forward.

Gertrude shifted her stare past Ophelia, and she held Broderick's gaze. "I do," she said with resolve in her tone. "Even more than either of you had to."

In so many ways, Gertrude had long been the matriarchal figure of this family. How much each of his sisters had come into their own as women. Not for anything he'd done but because of the manner of people they were.

Ophelia exploded to her feet and redirected her impressive fury at Broderick. "This is your fault," she snapped, gripping the corners of his borrowed desk. "All of it."

Unable to meet her anger-filled eyes, he stared down into the amber contents of his glass. He swirled it in a smooth, counterclockwise circle.

"Do you have nothing to say?" Ophelia cried.

He lifted his shoulders in a shrug. "I don't." It was far safer taking the brunt of their fury than acknowledging a fear over his own infallibility. A need for some other gentleman, respectable and powerful in wealth and connections, to provide the security they were deserving of.

"Ophelia," Cleo commanded, still capable of laying command to any tense fight, be it one between families or those on the street. When she focused on Broderick, his youngest sister was very much the woman who'd been more of a trusted partner than anything else. "What do you require?"

Broderick gritted his teeth. "Introductions at the dinner party this evening for Gertrude." The first event hosted by Ophelia's father-in-law, the Earl of Mar, would mark Gertrude's introduction to Polite Society. It would also see Gertrude seated alongside some of the *ton*'s leading peers . . . gentlemen influential in Parliament, others with connections to the king.

Three pairs of Killoran eyes went to Ophelia. "Of course I'll perform the introductions," she said gruffly. "But neither will I support just *any* match. I love you, Broderick, but I'll not see you marry Gertrude off to some nobleman to save your club."

Nay, to save his sister. To see her settled.

Ophelia looked to Gertrude. "I'll not sit idly by while you sell your happiness for noble connections," Ophelia said softly.

"You forced yourself to London for a Season." Gertrude settled her accusing gaze on Cleo. "As did you. Therefore, I ask that you please trust that I'm capable of knowing my own mind and making my own decisions."

Broderick closed his eyes. When had he made such a damned mess of his family? Everything he touched turned to rot. But then, what did he expect? He was, after all, his father's son.

The matter of this evening's dinner party settled, he brought them to the other topic they needed to discuss. "Gertrude's London Season is not the reason I've called you all here." Broderick glanced around the room. "We have a traitor in our midst."

That brought Ophelia's head whipping around. "What?"

Cradling the snifter of brandy between his fingers, he evinced a calm he did not feel.

It was of course Cleopatra who asked the most important question. "Who?" she demanded, all steely ice as she surged forward with an abruptness that dislodged her spectacles, knocking them forward on her face.

Silent until now, Stephen puffed his chest out. "Oi know who it is." From where he stood at the doorway, he slammed his left heel into the panel, commanding the room's attention.

Every set of eyes swiveled in his direction, and he preened under that uncharacteristic level of importance placed on him.

Broderick silenced him with a look.

"Wot? Oi do."

Yes, it was the youngest of the Killorans who'd gathered information they'd been too trusting to ever suspect.

Not even deigning to glance back, Cleo jabbed a finger at the empty spot beside her.

Muttering under his breath, Stephen dragged his heels across the room until he stopped beside his long-favorite sister. She'd always been the one who managed to gain his compliance, an otherwise impossible feat.

Broderick motioned for her to reclaim her chair, and for surely the first time since he'd entered Diggory's gang and begun looking after the girls before him, she complied. He went on to detail the information brought to him by Stephen.

"Not only does Reggie intend to establish a rival club but she also sought to take the most profitable members of our staff and the most reliable guard." With each enumeration, the sense of betrayal grew, and with it, the anger in his chest. "And she intends to do so not even three streets from the Devil's Den."

Ophelia shook her head. "Impossible."

"Oh"—he rolled his shoulders—"I assure you. Quite possible. Stephen raided her rooms and found the documents." He chuckled, the sound stripped of mirth. "Why, she even negotiated better rates from our suppliers at the expense of our own costs remaining elevated."

"I can't . . ." As one who'd let loyalty and honor drive her every word and action, Ophelia's palpable outrage matched Stephen's and Broderick's in fury. His own sense of betrayal was reflected back in Ophelia's blue eyes. "How could she do this?"

He tightened his mouth. Her reasons didn't matter. "We let our guard down with Reggie." That, however, did matter.

"What a lot of rot," Cleo said quietly, those words more powerful than had she shouted them.

Reggie's treachery was indisputable, and as such, he'd not be battling anyone on this, and certainly not Cleo.

"She is the one who wanted to set up her own hell and take my staff. Including MacLeod and all our best serving girls. What do you call that?"

"First, are you certain she's actually creating a rival club?" Cleo protested.

Ophelia scoffed. "You're looking for anything that would excuse her actions."

As Cleo proceeded to defend Reggie, the truth of the youngest Killoran sister's transformation hit him like a slap to the damned solar plexus. "You've gone soft."

Behind her spectacles, Cleo's eyes formed narrow, threatening slits that would have inspired terror in any other man. "Have a care." Slowly removing those wire frames, she dusted the lenses along the front of her skirts. "Now, regardless of Reggie's plans, I am sure, knowing her as I do . . . as we *all* do"—she looked amongst them—"that she has her reasons." With an air of finality, she returned her glasses to her face.

Yes, Reggie had said as much. He'd not reveal that particular detail. He gritted his teeth. This forgiving note, he'd expected from Gertrude. Not, however, from Cleopatra, who'd proven herself as single-mindedly focused on the success of the club as he himself had been.

"Yes, she 'ad her reasons." Stephen stuck up a finger as he ticked off his reasons. "Money, power, and influence."

"Bah, don't be mad," Cleo charged, and an angry flush mottled Stephen's cheeks.

"Don't call me mad," he cried.

"I'm merely pointing out—"

"Enough," Broderick said quietly, silencing the quarreling pair.

Support of Broderick and Stephen came from the likeliest of their sisters. "That is it?" Ophelia shot back. "That is all you'd say. Damn it, Cleo, the evidence is here before our eyes."

"Do not forgive a man who's betrayed you." Broderick tossed that lesson doled out by Diggory long ago at them. It had guided them all. "Not unless you wish to be destroyed."

"If you live the whole of your life by the code of a killer, then you're no different than him," Cleo said quietly.

He flinched. "I'm not debating Miss Spark's duplicity."

"Nor should you have to," Ophelia piped in. Her face crumpled. "Why? Why would she do this?"

Hers was an echo of the very same question that had haunted him since the discovery of Reggie's betrayal. He'd called her a friend, that relationship a rarity in the Dials. Only Reggie had proven it was something more. "As Stephen said . . . greed. Power."

Cleo exploded to her feet. "Bloody rubbish," she shouted, slamming her fist down on his desk.

The crystal inkwells rattled under the force of that strike.

His sisters began speaking over one another, the room filled with angry charges, questions, and insults.

This was what Reggie had wrought, as well. Strife within the Killoran ranks, when their family had already been torn asunder and was about to be shredded even further by Maddock.

Fishing a cheroot and match out of his jacket, he lit the thin scrap and took a much-needed draw.

You only partake in those scraps when you're troubled . . .

His fingers clenched reflexively about the cheroot as Reggie's soft, lyrical voice floated forward in his mind. She'd gathered his weaknesses over the years. She'd revealed as much when he'd confided in her the truth about Stephen. He'd been too bloody blind to realize all the ways in which he'd proven himself . . . human with Reggie Spark. She knew his weaknesses. She knew the darkest secret about his family.

And she could use it all against him. Now. In the future. When he wasn't expecting it. The day he eventually freed her of her obligations, the threat she posed would always be there. Lingering.

Christ.

He inhaled deep of his smoke. "Enough," he said around a perfect circle of smoke. When Cleo and Ophelia continued going toe to toe, he raised his voice. "I said, enough."

That managed to silence them.

"I'm not looking to debate the reasons or possible reasons or invented excuses to justify Reggie Spark's actions. The papers I saw with my own eyes"—he waved his cheroot—"speak for themselves."

Through it all, Gertrude had remained silent. At last, she spoke. "That is why you've forced her into the role of my companion? Because you fear she'll be disloyal to us."

"She's already been disloyal," Ophelia said gently.

Gertrude scowled. "Don't patronize me. Surely we cannot simply overlook a lifetime of friendship because she wants a business of her own?"

"I made the mistake of confiding in her the circumstances surrounding Stephen." Silence met Broderick's damning admission. "Reggie is the only one outside our immediate kin"—he spared a glance for Ophelia—"and O'Roarke to know the truth." Reggie had in her hands information that could bring him, his family, and their empire crumbling down about them.

Ophelia cursed.

"Surely you aren't implying that she would use that information to harm us?" Cleo asked, directing her gaze about the family.

He flicked the ashes of his cheroot into a nearby crystal tray and then took another pull. The smoke filled his lungs, doing little to calm him. "I've shared what I have this morn so you're aware about Reggie's altered role within the family. In the past, we've shared all. Now, I warn you to reveal nothing. She is . . . a prisoner, and nothing more."

"That is a bit harsh, is it not?" Gertrude scolded.

"It's not," he clarified for the most innocent of his siblings. "It's practical." When Gertrude's future was settled, Broderick would free

Reggie. But he would not barter his siblings' security on her loyalty. And particularly not when she'd already given him reason to mistrust her.

Cleo folded her arms before her. "No."

Of all the siblings he'd expected that denial from, the last would have ever been Cleo.

He dusted his spare hand over his eyes. "You'd never let the matter be this simple," he muttered.

"No, I wouldn't. In the event you've forgotten, let me remind you. The fate and future of our staff is decided . . . by all of us. You do not get to make decisions about the Devil's Den. *Not* without a vote. Sack her or keep her on."

"This isn't a damned matter of staffing." Broderick jammed the tip of his cheroot in the crystal tray. "This is not a vote on employment," he barked, tossing aside the scrap. She'd used the existing code they'd employed years earlier when going through Diggory's former staff and determining who remained on in their posts.

Cleo shrugged. "She's employed by the Devil's Den. I vote to send her away."

"You'd sack her so Broderick can't keep her as a prisoner," Ophelia charged.

"That's right. I would never support making Reggie remain on in that way. And if you've a problem with it, then show it in your vote," Cleo said with a calm that silenced her sister. Holding Broderick's gaze, she lifted her palm. "Who votes to send Reggie Spark away?"

Stephen darted his fingers up, waggling them for effect. "I say we're better off with her gone. Don't trust having her around. I caught her snooping after me."

"Because you gave her reason to," Gertrude chided. "You were supposed to be making up your lessons that night"—Stephen shot a foot out, catching his eldest sister in the shins—*"Oomph."*

"Enough," Cleo clipped out. "We are talking about Reggie's future." She looked around at her siblings. "What is it to be, Ophelia?"

Ophelia looked away.

"Ophelia?" Cleo whispered, shock in that query.

"It's not forever," their sister explained, a defensive edge to her tone. "Only until . . . this is settled."

Not allowing Cleo to press her further, Broderick put the question to the room: "Who votes to keep her on as Gertrude's companion?" He lifted a hand.

Ophelia hesitated, then added her vote to his. "I don't disagree with Broderick," she said quietly. "Even if there are reasons behind Reggie's decisions and actions, as Cleo suggests, Reggie has given grounds for us to be cautious. And given our family's circumstances?" She shook her head. "I'd not begrudge him for monitoring her movements."

"Gertrude?" Broderick prodded when she still did not vote. "Well? Out with it."

Gertrude frowned. "I haven't said anything." No, she'd always sat as a silent observer, taking everything in and measuring her words. She had also long been the moderating voice of the Killoran sisters.

"I know. That's why I want to hear from you."

Gertrude's gaze grew contemplative. "Reggie isn't one driven by greed or jealousy."

"Everyone is driven by greed."

"I'm not," Gertrude pointed out.

His mouth turned up in one corner. "No," he said quietly to himself. "You aren't." The most selfless of the Killorans, she'd care for a rat in their alley with the same attention as she would a servant or sister at the Devil's Den. His smile fell. "What is your opinion?"

"I don't know why she's done what she's done. But we all have our secrets." She glanced around, touching her gaze on each sibling. "All of us." Her eyes darkened, and under the desk Broderick tightened his hands into fists. What other demons did she carry? What other ghosts haunted all of his siblings? Once again confronted with his own failings, he felt regret swell in his chest. Gertrude went on. "She's been part of this family even longer than Stephen, and I have to believe there is a reason she did what she did. But I have to agree it is wise to keep her close," she said, her voice falling to a whisper. She slowly crept her fingers up, joining Broderick and Ophelia.

"Gertrude!" Cleo cried.

"It is settled then," Broderick announced over that explosion. "Reggie remains on staff." As a prisoner.

Someone thumped at the doorway.

Bloody hell with this foreign staff who didn't know the rules on interrupting a Killoran meeting.

"Enter," he thundered.

Nerrie ducked his head inside, his cheeks ashen.

"What is it?"

"It's Miss Spark, sir."

"She's been here but a day," he barked. "Are you telling me she's making trouble already?" And should he really expect anything different from the spitfire?

"No, sir. That is . . ." Nerrie gulped. "She's gone."

"Oi knew it," Stephen cried, slamming his fist against his opposite palm.

All of Broderick's muscles jumped. "Gone?" That slipped out on a steely whisper. Reggie, who was rot at subterfuge and taller than most of the males on his staff, had slipped out in the middle of the damned day?

Nerrie gave a jerky nod. "Y-yes, sir."

Bloody hell. "The meeting is concluded for now."

Ophelia was already on her feet. "I'll find Connor."

"You are all being ridiculous," Cleo cried as her siblings rushed off. "Reggie would not betray us."

Broderick stormed around his desk, but Cleo stepped into his path, blocking him from leaving.

"What?" he snapped.

Cleo settled her hands on her hips. "You're punishing her when you know nothing about the reasons for her decision."

"I'm treating her as I would anyone who threatens our club." Nor would he make apologies for it.

Cleo was unrelenting. "Why do you *think* she's done what she has?"

"It doesn't matter."

"Doesn't it?" she countered, giving him pause. "You live a life based on logic and reason. Look and see that which is in front of you."

He frowned. "If you know something, have out with it."

She immediately went tight-lipped. "It's not my place to say. Ask her yourself." Cleo gave her head a shake. "And when you discover her motives, then tell me it doesn't matter. You bastard."

With that cryptic warning, Cleo left.

"Her motives," he muttered under his breath as he strode through the double doors opened by his butler.

A short while later, his sister's warning forgotten, Broderick guided his horse through the fashionable London streets. As he wound past fancy lords and ladies in their elegant attire, fury pumped through him, burning with its ferocity. He'd been clear in his orders, and not even a day in her new assignment, she'd bolted. Of course, she'd shown her true colors these past days. *She isn't the loyal, devoted friend you've taken her for but one as ruthless in her goals as . . . me.* She'd proven not unlike him, in this. Gnashing his teeth, Broderick forced back the unwanted comparison and focused on finding the woman he'd handed his darkest secret over to. He scoured his gaze over the streets.

And yet . . .

She wouldn't be here. Broderick frowned. She'd been clear that she'd no desire to accompany the Killorans to London's high end.

Which of course could only mean . . .

Broderick tugged on the reins of his mount, bringing him to a stop so abruptly that Chance did a quick circle to slow his steps.

She'd be in the Dials.

Alone.

And with that realization, his anger lifted, and a memory trickled in of their first meeting: Regina as she'd been, her eyes wild, her skin pale and faintly bruised as he'd approached. Had she not accompanied him back, she would have perished.

She was not, however, that same scared woman she'd been. She'd become a fearless warrior unafraid to go toe to toe with him.

Nay, Reggie Spark could take care of herself in these streets better than most grown men. He told himself that over and over again.

That didn't stop the grim possibilities from buffeting at his logic: Reggie on her own, fending off assailants. Reggie being dragged down an alley—

Oh, God.

His stomach churned, and clicking his tongue, Broderick wheeled his horse onward to the Dials.

He'd taught her to take care of herself. He'd taught her everything she needed to survive. Telling himself that did nothing to diminish the terror clutching at his insides.

Half-mad with panic, he rode his mount hard.

Where could she be?

Chapter 14

Is today the day that vengeance is mine?

"He's going to murder you," Clara drawled from the opposite end of the single-drawer tea table.

Reggie didn't even pick her head up from the calculations she was currently completing. "He won't even notice I've gone." She directed that at the page. She paused and silently counted the monies saved with the adjustment to the liquor contract. Bloody hell, where in blazes was she going to make up the lost funds?

"His guards will, and then he will, and *then* he'll murder you," Clara amended.

"*Pfft.* Broderick's men were otherwise engaged." Those lax guards had been too busy charming the new parlor maids to notice Reggie making use of the servants' stairway. "He was visiting with his siblings. There was a . . . family meeting." Meetings which she'd always been part of . . . until now. Now she was the source of the discussion. Reggie's fingers tightened, and the pencil snapped in her grip, shattering into two neat pieces. She tossed the remaining scrap in her hand aside. "And then they have their first foray into Polite Society this evening." What Reggie was or was not doing would be the least of Broderick's focus this night. Rubbing shoulders with the nobility was all that would matter . . . any night, really.

"Brava," Clara praised, managing an awkward clap with the floral teacup in her fingers. "Sneaking past his guards while all the Killoran siblings were otherwise occupied. Some would say that is an insurmountable feat."

Reggie bristled, tired of yet another challenge to her integrity. "Part of the arrangement I made with him was that when my services are not engaged, I'm granted time to see to my own business."

With a snort, Clara toasted Reggie with the cup. "Something has me believe that this freedom"—she motioned to Reggie and the work laid out before her—"is not what he intended."

Reggie caught her lower lip. No, her slipping between Mayfair and the Dials in the middle of the day when anyone might see was likely not the agreement he'd had in mind. Not while any missteps she made would have disastrous consequences for Gertrude's reception amongst the *ton*. Guilt needled at her conscience, but she forcibly thrust it back. She'd spent years putting the Killoran family first before everyone, including herself. Now she faced ruin far greater than that of her reputation if she didn't succeed in her plans. "Then he'll need to be more specific in his future transactions."

Clara's shoulders shook with her amusement as she filled the half-empty cup in her hands to the top. From behind the rim of her teacup, Clara blew on the piping brew. Laughing softly, she offered Reggie another small salute.

She was the only person in all of England to take her tea hot and not lukewarm. Reggie dropped her elbows on the French satinwood table. "May I ask you a question?"

Clara gave a slight nudge of her chin.

She pointed to the steaming floral porcelain pot. "Why do you always drink your tea hot?"

The other woman leaned forward. "Truthfully?"

Reggie nodded.

"Because everyone expects I should drink it one way." She shrugged. "To hell with them."

"Hmph," she said with a dawning understanding. "I . . . can appreciate that." Reggie picked up another pencil. For years she'd been Broderick's loyal assistant. The expectation was that she'd place his wants, wishes, and needs above all . . . including her own interests. And for so long . . . she had. She'd done precisely that. Reggie's gaze fell to the last number she'd tabulated. What a pathetic fool she'd been.

She resumed her new calculations based on the additional expenses they'd lost to Broderick's increased price of the building. The loss of one thousand pounds required adjustments to every other detail that had previously been worked out.

While Clara sat quietly sipping her tea, Reggie let her pencil fly over the page. The click-click-click of the tip striking the table was soothing.

For in this, there was something she'd been without, something she so desperately yearned for: control.

"How did he react?"

"You know," she muttered, blowing back a bothersome curl that fell over her brow. "He charged us one thousand pounds more." A factor which Clara had taken far better than she should have. In fact, she'd displayed no outward anger or upset with Reggie . . . which had only magnified Reggie's tremendous guilt. "And severed my employment as his assistant." Which was bloody fine, as she'd rather walk the long trek to London Bridge again without a pence to her name than ever serve on his staff.

A hand covered hers, and she started, glancing from Clara's palm to the other woman's eyes. "That is not what I meant."

"He . . ." Reggie absently picked up the porcelain chamberstick at the middle of the table. The flame danced back and forth, wafting a faint cloud of smoke toward the ceiling. She trailed the tip of her finger between the outstretched hands of the courting couple, the look of longing that passed between them expertly crafted even in cold stone. Feeling the other woman's eyes on her, Reggie set it down. "He was angry. He accused me of betraying him. And . . ." *Hurt.* There had been the flash of that vulnerability in his gaze, too. Reggie chewed at her lower lip. Whatever warmth he'd once felt for her was gone. And it was better this way . . . for now she could hang up the false hope she'd carried in her heart.

"And?" Clara pressed, leaning forward in her seat.

She shook her head, unwilling to share that intimate hint of vulnerability. "And he made it clear that I'd been stripped of my role and previous duties within the family." Her heart twisted. Not wanting to reveal her weakness for a man undeserving of her pain, she returned her attention to the last column.

"Reggie?"

She hesitated, then lifted her head.

"You are better off."

"I know that," she said automatically.

"No, you don't," her friend gently corrected. Again, she stretched a palm out, covering Reggie's. "But someday, after you say it enough and gain your freedom, then you'll finally realize it."

Disquieted at how easily Clara had read the lie within her words, Reggie cleared her throat, steering them to more neutral topics. "I don't know how to make up the one thousand pounds." She'd always been proficient with numbers, but it would take the maneuverings of a damned wizard to snip enough here and there to account for all that Broderick insisted on taking.

Setting down her cup, Clara was immediately all business. "The liquor distribution?"

She shook her head. "At best, I can find us one hundred pounds there." Nor would the amount cover the cost of the account over the course of the year.

"We can water it down?" Clara's suggestion came with the ease of one not unfamiliar with the practice.

A sigh of exasperation escaped her. "I don't want us to be that manner of establishment." One where cheap spirits were to be expected and the patrons catered to were the manner of men too drunk to even notice or care about the watered-down claret.

"We can cut it altogether?"

Reggie tossed her pencil down, and it rolled off those damning records. "We can't. Not truly. Not if we wish to . . ." *Compete.*

She winced. For her and Clara's hall would have always posed as competition, and whether or not he feared that as he'd mocked, the truth was, setting their business not even three streets away had been . . . wrong. Desperate, but wrong.

Reggie stared down at the most troubling sheet. "We'll have to cut staff," she said reluctantly, turning the page over to the other woman.

Wordlessly, Clara traded her teacup for that paper. Reggie watched as her eyes flew over the numbers and names written there. Clara sighed. "It's hardly promising to cut staff before we even have a staff . . . or a business."

"Yes." Every shilling had been carefully accounted for. From servants to performers to the construction of the music hall, Reggie and Clara had divided the monies to fund each expense. They, however, weren't like the Broderick Killorans or Ryker Blacks of the world. Each pence mattered, and the slightest increase in their expenditures was the difference between surviving . . . or floundering.

"Or . . ." Clara left that single word dangling there.

"What?" Reggie pressed when the other woman didn't complete that thought.

Clara spoke in hushed tones. "I know you want to create something that hasn't been done—"

"No," Reggie interrupted before Clara had finished speaking.

"And someday mayhap when we find our feet we can establish your music hall, but we've no choice but to build a saloon . . . or a bordell—"

"I said, no." Reggie spoke sharply, finally silencing the other woman. She searched her mind. How could she make Clara understand? Reggie dragged her chair closer. "This was never about just simply setting up our own club."

Clara stared back, a gaze hardened by life and betrayal. "This is because of Broderick Killoran."

"It is not," she shot back. She gripped her pencil hard. *With your brains and talent, poppet, you can do anything you want in this world . . .* Her father's brogue rolled around her mind. "It is about beginning again, and allowing other women that same gift, but while using their real talents and not their bodies." Sensing Clara was wavering, she reached over and covered her hand. "What did you say when I first spoke to you?"

The former madam stared down at her painted nails. "I once loved music, too," she whispered, almost grudgingly.

Reggie nodded enthusiastically. It had been a connection they'd bonded over in that late-night talk. "We talked about how our happiest moments had been over song."

She released Clara's hand and dropped her forehead into the charcoal-stained palm. And now, Reggie's history threatened the dream they'd shared. "This is my fault."

"Do not say that," Clara said sharply.

"But it is." Reggie swept to her feet and began to pace. "Because of my relationship with Broderick, you've become embroiled in this . . . this . . ."

"Tangle?" the other woman supplied without inflection.

"Precisely," she muttered, increasing her strides. The rapid whoosh of her skirts tossed one of the pages she'd been working on to the floor. "And I cannot fix this. I cannot afford the builder or even the damned pianoforte." A half laugh, half sob climbed up her throat, and she came to an abrupt stop. "A damned music hall . . . without any music." Covering her eyes, she gave her head a frustrated shake.

"Listen to me," Clara demanded in the sharp tones used for breaking up fights between gaming hell patrons who'd taken a fancy to the same girl. "We will make this work. A music hall. *Not* a bordello." Reggie reluctantly let her arms fall to her side. A sharp glint lit the other woman's eyes. "I would not even have dreamed of a way outside the life I was living if it hadn't been for you. So do not take the blame for this. We will find a way because to fail . . ." She shook her head once. "I've failed before, and that is no longer an option for me, for either of us. You'll suffer through your time with the blighter, and then you'll be free of him."

Be free of him.

That dangled promise should entice.

And yet . . .

Her throat worked.

Clara took her hands and gave them a light squeeze. "I know," she said softly. She blushed and swiftly released Reggie's fingers as if she were uncomfortable with that show of warmth. "Now"—she gripped the chair Reggie had vacated and thumped its legs on the floor—"let us look again at those papers you've been working on all day. And then you need to return before he finds you missing."

From outside the window, the echo of shouts went up below, the familiar ones of drunken revelers, and Clara swiftly came out of her chair to investigate the uproar.

"I'm not missing," Reggie muttered as she slid into the chair. "Furthermore, I've nothing to feel guilty over. I've done nothing wrong."

The curtain clasped between her fingers, Clara paused to glance back. "Do you believe that?"

"No," she said, again resuming her work. "I know that."

"Then that is a good thing." Clara let the curtain go. "Because he's here now."

Reggie jerked her head up so quickly pain shot down the muscles of her neck. "That is impossible." Broderick and Gertrude were attending their first formal event amongst the *ton*.

"Oh, it is quite possible. In fact, I had the right of it earlier. He looks as though he intends to murder you."

Reggie groaned.

Bloody hell.

Chapter 15

There is one certainty: you will pay for your crimes, Killoran.

She'd been hiding in plain sight.

He'd searched all day.

Nay, Broderick and his siblings had searched all day. As had the damned guards, the same ones who'd let the blasted chit slip out from under them.

All their searching had turned up empty.

And during his flight through London, something had happened. That fury had turned over and become something different, something sharper, more acute, and more crippling: fear.

It was as though Reggie Spark had simply vanished, leaving not a trace that anyone could or would find, and on the heels of that had come the realization that he'd be empty were she to go. Nay, when she left.

And all along she'd been the last place he'd have considered looking—his damned club.

His cloak whipping about him and Stephen close at his side, Broderick stormed through the front doors of the Devil's Den.

From his spot atop the dais, MacLeod glanced up, a question stamped on his features. Saying something to one of the pit bosses next to him, he trotted over. "Is there a problem?"

Yes, there was a damned problem. A nearly six-foot-tall, willowy one, to be precise. "Where is she?" Broderick demanded, yanking his gloves off as he went.

His head guard drew his brows together. "Who?"

"Who do ya think?" Stephen bellowed.

Broderick growled, and several dandies new to the club bolted in the other direction. "Miss Spark," he clipped out. "The same Miss Spark who lost her role as assistant in this club and who recently had guards placed on her to monitor her movements."

They reached the back of the club and continued past the burly guard stationed there.

"Did the lass do something wrong?" MacLeod asked, their footsteps falling in tandem as they climbed the stairway to the private suites.

Aside from terrifying him out of his bloody everlasting mind? No. Stephen had discovered Reggie's whereabouts from a pair of street urchins who'd been petitioning for work out back by the servants' doors when she'd arrived.

His patience snapped. "Not a single bloody guard"—not MacLeod or anyone—"thought to send word to me?"

MacLeod's already ruddy face flushed with color. "The lass walked right in. She's been with Miss Winters."

"Course she'd be with that one," Stephen spat. "That means we can't trust either one of them."

"Enough," Broderick clipped out. "MacLeod, return to the floor. Stephen, wait for me in your rooms."

Stephen and MacLeod spoke over one another, their words rolling together. "But I don't—"

"I didn't know she wasn't supposed to be here," MacLeod called up after him as Broderick took the final stair to the landing.

Reaching the former madam's doorway, he didn't even bother with a knock. He tossed the door open, and the two women standing shoulder to shoulder at the center of the room gave not even a hint of outward surprise at his entrance.

Even having confirmation from MacLeod that she was in fact here, relief assailed him.

They'd been expecting him. Immediately any advantage was cut out from under him, as he found himself confronting not one displeased pair of eyes, but two.

Broderick's problem, however, wasn't with his damned former madam.

The terror that had dogged his steps eased from him.

Had it been simply terror? He himself had schooled her on self-defense and well knew she could handle a blade better than most street thugs. Or had it been the fear that she'd simply fled? Away from London. Away from his family. *And away from me . . .* Never to be seen again.

Unable to make sense of those riotous thoughts, he fixed on that which was safer: his fury.

He homed his gaze in on the tall, flame-haired warrioress standing with her shoulders back and a dare in her eyes.

"Out," he seethed.

Clara thumped a fist on the nearby desk, rattling the teacup and chamberstick at rest there. "You don't enter my rooms and order my guests about, Killoran."

Broderick briefly shifted his focus to the pursed-mouthed woman. Almost three years ago, he'd extended an offer of employment to Ryker Black's lifelong mistress in what had never been anything more than a ploy to get under the skin of his damned rival, but she had proven the bane of Broderick's club. Oh, she was damned good at her work, but the woman had made a million kinds of headaches for him since. "I can always sack you," he said coolly.

Clara flashed an icy smile. "Do it, then. Regina and I will both be free of this place soon enough and answer to no one." She flicked a mocking stare over him. "And certainly not you."

He sank back on his heels, knocked off-balance, and then quickly righted himself. "By God, I will sack you."

Reggie stepped between them. "Don't be a bloody arse." Of course the first words Reggie hurled at him would be an insult. He was in the wrong, when she'd gone missing, leaving without a damned trace. "You'll do nothing of the sort." She looked to the former madam. "May we have a moment?"

He gnashed his teeth. By God, had she always been this brazen?

Clara stared mutinously back and, with a quiet curse, stalked out of the room.

Broderick drew the panel shut behind him and turned the lock. "I'm not pleased with you." He hurled his leather gloves onto the Serpentine side table. "I've had men out, searching all day for you." *And me . . . and my family.*

"You're displeased with me?" A sharp, cynical laugh he'd believed her incapable of . . . until now burst from her. "My God, the arrogance of you. I told you I'd not be a prisoner, followed about by your minions."

Broderick narrowed his eyes. His minions? She'd paint him as a lowly street thug of Diggory's ilk? "Yes, you did," he purred. He leaned a shoulder against the doorway, still fighting for equilibrium in a world where Reggie went head-to-head with him. "But lest you forget, I never made you a promise either way."

She reeled. Her mouth moved, but no words came out. And then she exploded forward. "How dare you?" Storming over to the cluttered table, she grabbed up the contract signed in his hand and gave it a sharp wave. The abruptness of those movements sent several strands of curls falling over her shoulder, drawing his gaze unwittingly downward to the creamy swells of her small breasts. He gulped. "You play with your words the same way you do a person's life. But I have it here in writing"—she jammed a finger at the page, her chest rising hard and fast, crimson color staining her cheeks, dimming those freckles—"that my time is my time, and my services were not required."

"My God, I thought something happened to you," he cried.

It was harder to say who was more shocked by the shout that echoed around Clara's room still.

Reggie's lush mouth parted in a moue of surprise that matched his own. "You were worried," she said softly as if she'd been handed a piece to a puzzle that didn't fit in the frame she worked with. "About me?"

Of course he'd been. That was the flippant reply. She had been his friend and confidante, and yet . . .

He crossed over in two quick strides and, cupping her by the nape, covered her mouth with his. Heat. Stinging, searing heat exploded throughout him at the contact as he kissed her as he'd longed to since their meeting in that decrepit hall she now owned. He kissed her with that need which had haunted him since.

Reggie went still in his arms, and then with a low moan, she dropped the pages. They fluttered to the floor in a whispery afterthought as she climbed her arms about his neck and returned his kiss.

After days of having noticed the plump roundness of her lips and the luxuriant feel of her crimson curls, he explored them, tasting her, learning the lush contours, molding his mouth with hers in a way that etched an eternal memory of that flesh.

He slanted his lips over hers again and again, and she met every fiery meeting with a boldness that fueled his ardor. "What is it about you, Regina Spark, that tears at my reason?" he rasped against her mouth between kisses.

She met that query with a low moan and drew him down closer, pressing herself against him, a siren pulling him deeper and deeper and deeper into her snare, and he had the answer as to why those mere mortals had been lured. Because a taste was not enough. A taste of her was a mere taunt. Temptation. Sin wrapped in splendor. And he wanted all of her, rules of honor be damned. For he didn't give a jot that this woman was in his employ or about the years of friendship between them. His body knew nothing but the hunger to know her in the most primitive way.

With a groan, he plucked free the pins holding her chignon in place, and those locks cascaded around them like a fiery-red waterfall. He tangled his fingers into those silken strands, angling her head to better avail himself of her mouth.

Reggie parted her lips, and he swept inside, stroking the tip of his tongue against hers. Searing heat blazed through him at the contact.

Their chests rose and fell in a like rhythm, their breath noisy and desperate in the quiet of the room, a wicked symphony of lust and desire.

Broderick filled his hands with the generous swell of her buttocks, and not breaking contact with her mouth, he anchored her legs about his waist and guided her onto the tea table. The porcelain rattled noisily. Broderick moved between her parted thighs, and they fell open in welcome invitation as though he belonged there, as though she, too, had been set afire these past days and welcomed the burn of that conflagration.

Yes, there would come time enough later for proper shame.

But for now, all he saw, tasted, and yearned for was the feel of Regina Spark.

Reggie's first kiss had been quick and sloppy, stolen from her then fifteen-year-old self by the village innkeeper's arrogant son.

The second—and ones to come after—had all been delivered by a cad who'd promised her forever. They had been no less sloppy, only tinged of spirits and syrup from the sweets he'd had a taste for, and she'd despised every minute of it but yearned for the promises he'd made.

She'd waited for the end of each embrace . . . just as she'd waited for the fulfillment of those false promises.

Broderick's hands at her neck both cradled and commanded, angling her to receive him, opening her to a whole new universe of sensation and feeling. Each stroke of his lips over hers, his tongue against hers, set her core to throbbing.

It had never been like this.

It had always been distasteful and dirty and empty . . . until this.

Until Broderick.

And she wanted the moment to go on. She wanted to explore passion as she'd never before tasted it.

Moaning, Reggie searched her hands down the contours of his broad, powerful shoulders, lower, exploring all as she went, as she'd ached to. She gripped his arms, the tense muscles bulging under her touch, and she reveled in his hunger for her.

Broderick broke the kiss, and she cried out at the loss of that heat, but he was already moving his lips to the corner of hers, caressing the curve of her jaw, over to the sensitive place her lobe met her nape.

"So soft," he rasped against her, his breath a sough upon her hot skin that sent her pulse hammering . . . And then he found the spot where it beat with desire for him. Broderick lightly nipped and suckled, trapping a groan somewhere in her throat, and the sound of it emerged as a wanton plea.

He pressed himself against her, and even through the fabric of her brown skirts, the heat and length of him throbbed. "Broderick," she panted, dropping her head back.

His mouth found hers again, and she surrendered to the hungering she'd carried for this man for ten years. She licked the hard seam of his lips, tasting him as he'd done her.

He gasped, and she, gripping his thick, loose golden curls, brought his mouth back to hers.

The wanton she'd been accused of being, and for which she'd been shamed in the past, she now reveled in what it was to feel passion.

Broderick dragged up her skirts, and a cool blast of night air slapped at her, a balm to the fire he'd kindled within her. He caught her leg and dragged it about his waist, deepening the press of him against her core. She moaned, but he swallowed that entreaty, sinking his hands in her hips, his fingers possessive in their hold.

"Reggie," he gasped, laying her down, stretching her open.

Her head collided with the chamberstick, sending the piece tumbling. It broke in an explosion of noise, glass, and hot wax, shattering the moment and splattering her skirts.

Panting like he'd run a great race, Broderick remained frozen over her, his eyes glazed with the evidence of desire. Her chest rose and fell in time to his, and she silently pleaded with him to continue, to teach her everything she'd never known and everything she'd believed her body incapable of experiencing.

Someone pounded at the door. "Did ya foind 'er?" Stephen demanded, his voice muted by the heavy oak panel.

Her stomach pitched as reality came crashing in.

Broderick's face whitened, and for the first time in all the years she'd known him, he remained motionless, incapable of a response. She nudged his shoulder. "Broderick." Her hushed whisper penetrated the fog.

He jumped back, tripping over himself in his haste to be free of her.

Stephen jiggled the door handle. "Everything all right in there?"

Reggie pushed herself up and, with fingers that shook, shoved her skirts back into place.

"Fine. Everything is fine," Broderick called out, his voice somewhat hoarse. He ran horror-filled eyes over her wrinkled dress. He spun Reggie about and proceeded to draw her hair back into place with an efficiency and skill that could come only from one who'd undertaken the task before.

"Ya sure?" Stephen called. "Let me see ya."

Bloody hell.

Broderick quickly assessed his work, and then, stepping over bits and shards of glass, he crossed over and drew the door open.

Suspicion better suited to one twenty years his senior darkened Stephen's features. He took in the mess strewn about, and then Reggie's rumpled appearance. She quickly slid behind the table to hide the sorry state of her skirts. "What happened 'ere? You two fighting?"

Clasping her hands before her, Reggie looked to Broderick.

"We were in the middle of a discussion," he said with his usual calm restored.

Stephen peered at his eldest sibling a long while. "Didn't sound like a discussion. Sounded like a mighty racket."

Reggie's entire body burnt with the force of her blush, and she sent a prayer skyward for the Lord to open the floor up and spare them any more probing from a boy far too astute for his tender years.

"What we were discussing isn't your business," Broderick said with a finality that would have quelled any further questioning in anyone—

Except Stephen.

With the tip of his boot, he kicked the wax candle, and it rolled forward, sliding under the table and landing damningly at Reggie's toes. "Doesn't look like a discussion, either."

And for one horrifying moment that stretched into eternity, she believed he referenced her and Broderick's embrace. Her face flamed several degrees hotter.

"What it was or was not isn't your affair." He gentled that admonishment by ruffling his brother's curls. Stephen ducked away from that touch, but Broderick looped an arm around his shoulders and brought him in to rub his head. It was a sweet hint of fraternal affection that tugged her heart. Recalling a different time. A different boy. Broderick caught her gaze over the top of Stephen's head, and she forced back the melancholy musings. "If you'll excuse me while I speak with Miss Spark?"

Eager to shake off his elder brother's touch, Stephen ducked under him.

"Stephen?" Broderick called after him.

The boy hesitated.

"See that one of the carriages is readied for Reggie's return to Mayfair."

A muscle twitched in the boy's jaw. "Fine," he spat, and rushed off.

As soon as he'd gone, Broderick drew the door quietly closed behind them, turning that lock once more.

To give her shaking fingers something to do, Reggie dropped to a knee and proceeded to gather up the large pieces of glassware scattered about. She deposited them on the corner of the table, one at a time. Meticulous with the piles she assembled. Singularly focused on that task. All the while, her skin prickled with the intensity of Broderick's gaze.

What did one say after . . . after . . . what they'd shared?

Her heart raced. That embrace had been the single headiest, hottest moment of passion she'd ever felt in her eight-and-twenty years. One she'd spent ten years longing to know in this man's arms.

"That should not have happened."

A shard of glass stuck in her finger; that sharp stab stole a gasp from her. Tossing aside the scrap, she jammed the wounded digit into her mouth. Not looking at him. Instead, focusing on the welcoming distraction of that slight gash.

A stark, cruel humiliation chased away all earlier warmth, ushering in something familiar. Something she'd experienced too much to ever be considered proper and virtuous: shame.

"It is fine," she bit out, sending a different prayer overhead. Wanting his silence. Wanting him to add not one more word to his admission of regrets.

He cleared his throat.

Damn him. Damn him for insisting they have this discussion. She paused in her task and forced her chin up at a mutinous angle.

His aquiline features were a study of dismay. "I . . ."

Say something. Say you wanted that moment as much as I have. Say . . .

"I am sorry," he said gruffly. "I . . . my apologies."

She flinched. *Say anything except that.* He'd blame his passion on his fury. "I said, it is fine," she repeated, terse in her rebuttal.

Broderick scraped a hand through his disheveled golden hair, a halo of golden curls the angel Gabriel himself would have envied. "It is not fine. I . . . *kissed* you," he choked out, as if that truth made him ill.

And here Reggie believed there couldn't be anything more cutting than his apology. Unable to meet his eyes lest he see that pathetic weakness she carried for him still, Reggie inspected her finger.

Why should he not be horrified? Broderick Killoran had always been clear that the connections he craved were to fine ladies, and as such she'd never, ever be the manner of woman he bestowed his attentions on. Bitterness threatened to swallow her.

And for the first time since Lord Oliver's betrayal, tears stung behind her eyes. Refusing to let Broderick see a hint of that pathetic weakness for him, she dropped to a knee and began to gather her pins, placing them into a neat little pile.

Finding a calm as she always had in organizing . . . anything. It required focus and served as a distraction and—

The floorboards groaned as he dropped to a knee beside her. "Say something," he demanded.

Please leave . . .

"There is nothing to say."

His long fingers made quick work of collecting the remaining bits of glass, and without a care for the pile she'd already begun on, he dropped them on the table. "I have it," she said quietly, and when he still did not relent, she repeated more sharply. "I said, I have it."

He abruptly stopped.

And she gave thanks.

Now he'd go.

Only that left her desolate in a different way. "As long as you are in my employ, I vow that will not happen again," he said gruffly. "I can only humbly ask for your forgiveness."

Her body went hot and then cold as his pathetic excuses paled next to this . . . his continued apologies. Refusing to let him see how those words were like a lance upon her heart, she forced her words into a semblance of calm. "Broderick, it was just a kiss." *Liar.* It was so much more. It had been music and mysteries at last answered, and with every stammered word and rambling excuse, he made that moment into something vile and ugly. "It was certainly not the first I've had," she forced herself to add and hurriedly picked up the remaining pins. It would be the last, however.

For she wanted no further part in losing her heart to any man. She hated how it left her splayed open and vulnerable in every way.

She registered his silence and forced herself to look up.

There was a peculiar hardness to his always intractable features, a steely cold in his eyes that raised goose bumps on her arms. Jumping up, Reggie began gathering up the paperwork she'd completed that morn when Broderick rested a hand on hers, staying those movements.

For a dizzying span of a heartbeat, she believed he'd take her in his arms once more. His body had spoken of his desire for her. She'd felt it in his hard length pressed against her belly. And the ragged pants of his breath as he'd explored her. "Before we return," he began in coolly calculated tones that doused that foolish hope, "let me be clear. You are not to venture out without someone with you at all times."

"How could I forget my status as prisoner?" she spat. Her outrage safer than the mewling weakness to come before it. "I already told you I'll not be followed about by one of your minions."

"Because I'd not see you come to any harm," he said quietly, stopping her in her tracks.

Broderick cupped her cheek.

He drew his hand back, letting it fall to his side. Did she merely imagine the reluctance to that movement? "You may be an enemy to me and one day a rival, but I would still not see you hurt."

An enemy and a rival . . . that he cared about? "You see the world in absolutes, Broderick. As long as I've known you, that has been your way." Reggie lifted her palms. "You once saw Ryker Black and Adair Thorne as the enemy, but they've been more, too. They've been *allies*." Just as she'd always been and always would be to this family.

And for a sliver of a heartbeat, she thought she spied a flash of something in his eyes. Understanding? Regret? What was it? But then it was gone as quickly as it had come.

"Have I made myself clear here today, Reggie?"

A sad smile hovered on her lips. "Abundantly." From how he'd felt about their kiss to her continued role as his enemy, he'd only ever been completely transparent.

And she'd be wise to remember that. They would never be anything more. An embrace did not a future make.

And as she followed him from the room, Reggie struggled to gather up the battered barriers about her heart and put them back into place.

Chapter 16

What reason should I have to trust your word? To trust anything you have to tell me about my son's kidnapping and my wife's murder?

Broderick had never run from a battle, conflict, or situation.

Until now.

Until last evening, to be specific.

And if one wished to be even more precise, the instant he'd laid Miss Regina Spark down atop a scarred tabletop and kissed her.

And she kissed you back . . .

She'd twined her long, graceful fingers around his neck and urged him on with her hands and breathy moans.

And God help him, had it not been for the crack of porcelain and the shock of Stephen's arrival, Broderick wouldn't have stopped. He'd have shoved her skirts higher, and laid himself between warm, welcoming thighs, and—

He groaned as the same nagging lust that had haunted him since last night reared itself. It was a mocking reminder on this most important of nights of the vileness of his father's blood that ran through his veins.

"Is there a problem, sir?" His valet paused, Broderick's sapphire tailcoat held in the young man's gloved fingers.

"No problem," he muttered, gathering the garment. Broderick shrugged into it, shoving his arms through each sleeve with such force the servant winced. He held a hand out for the satin cravat.

The man hesitated and then turned the article over.

"Have the carriage called for, and find out whether my sister and her companion"—the minx who'd stolen into his thoughts—"are ready."

"As you wish." With a bow, the servant let himself out.

Staring at his reflection in the beveled mirror, Broderick drew the cravat around his neck and, holding the smaller end of the fabric, folded the longer end around three times. As he went through the familiar movements, his mind remained stuck precisely where it had been since last evening.

Which was, of course, madness. His future, his very life, his family—all were one moment away from being torn asunder . . . And yet Reggie retained that maniacal hold upon his thoughts.

He smoothed the satin as he went and then tugged it up through the knot, flattening it out.

Broderick paused.

Nay, it wasn't just Reggie. Rather, it was that he'd secretly been relying upon her to be there for his family when he no longer could or would be. He'd given her his trust and been reminded all over again that people were as selfish as his late father had proven himself to be.

But *bloody hell* . . . He'd expected more from her. He'd wanted her to be that woman, loyal and honorable in every way.

Throughout the years he'd served as Diggory's right hand, and then even after his murder, attention had been paid to Broderick's relationship with Reggie. His Seven Dials mentor had always assumed he'd been bedding Reggie. Because, of course, in the most dangerous streets of East London, how else could Diggory or anyone else have accounted for Broderick's acceptance of her?

She'd been too tall to steal and too genteel to ever truly thrive in a world where thieves, killers, and sinners ruled.

Broderick had been content to allow them their opinions as it kept her safe and secure in her role within the Diggory gang when any other woman would have been tossed out on her buttocks, forced to fend for herself.

All along, Reggie had been like a mother to his siblings. She'd been a confidante. And she'd been a friend. She'd been a friend long before she'd been an enemy, but a friend all the same. And noble *friends* and respectable employers didn't go dragging skirts about the waists of those women and stepping between their legs.

He finished knotting his cravat, absently inspecting his efforts.

And yet, for the shame of what he'd done . . . of the path he'd certainly have continued on had it not been for those timely interruptions, he remained fixed on one single statement that had fallen from Reggie's lips as an assurance:

Broderick, it was just a kiss . . . It was certainly not the first I've had.

There had been another man who'd known that pleasure; it had been there in the assurances she'd given when guilt had raged over the liberties he'd taken, and also in the unbridled passion of her embrace.

Some man had made kisses casual to her.

And for reasons he didn't care to think overly long on, that realization sent a primal bloodlust pumping through his veins. A need to find the one who'd claimed that gift and made an enthralling Reggie Spark unconcernedly state that *it was just a kiss*. And with that same insouciance, bury his fist into that bounder's face over and over.

And some other man will be there when Maddock ends this game and you are gone. An unexpected jealousy slithered around his insides, along with something else: regret. For his own mortality and the realization that life . . . would continue on without him.

The door opened, and his valet entered, interrupting his maudlin thoughts.

"The carriage is readied, and I've been informed that Miss Killoran and her companion will be downstairs shortly."

"That will be all," he said distractedly. "Please inform my sister I'll be along shortly." With a nod, the servant rushed off.

Broderick waited, and then he withdrew from his jacket the note that portended his inevitable doom: Maddock's pledge to take Broderick apart.

He stared at the inked words, long memorized.

What the marquess, his siblings, Reggie . . . no one knew was that Broderick had accepted his fate—for himself. He'd built an empire from next to nothing, but he was not one to delude himself into thinking he could escape anything.

Cleo and Ophelia were settled. It was the rest who needed to be put to rights: Gertrude, Stephen, his staff at the Devil's Den.

And this evening represented the great hope for all of them.

Broderick tightened his fingers; the page crumpled in his grip. He forced himself to relax his hands and then returned the note to his jacket.

This is where his energies should be solely focused. Not on Regina Spark and his dangerous awareness of her as a woman . . . but rather on the one who sought to destroy not only Broderick . . . but through him also his family, his club, and all those dependent upon him.

Fueled with that purpose, a short while later, Broderick joined his sister . . . his sister with a cat in her arms, and absent one companion. He did a quick sweep, and a rush of disappointment filled him at finding her gone. *And why do I want to see her?* On the heels of that was the still-fresh reminder of her recent jaunt through the streets of London. "Where in blazes is she?" he demanded as he strode down the stairs.

"Oh, hush, you've only just arrived," Gertrude said impatiently.

His sister would safely assume that query came from a place of suspicion. Avoiding her gaze, he looked to Nerrie, who served as a sentry at the doorway. "We're certain she's accounted for?"

"She is," he assured. "I've men outside the servants' stairways." This time. That hint of his failure hung on the other man's pronouncement. Mentored and trained under MacLeod's tutelage, the young, wiry guard had shown all the makings of the most skilled guards on his staff, and as such, after Reggie's flight yesterday, Broderick had set him up as head of security in his new household. The younger man glanced up the winding staircase. "I've guards outside her window, and another outside her door. The seamstresses are here, still."

"Thank you, Nerrie," he said. Yanking out his watch fob, he consulted the timepiece.

His sister stroked the top of her cat's head. "You never did say what happened with Reggie yesterday," Gertrude quietly pointed out.

No, he hadn't. And largely because speaking of Reggie in any way, after an embrace that had seared itself on his memory, had seemed a faulty venture. Broderick stuffed the gold chain back inside his jacket. "She returned to the Devil's Den to work on preparations for her club, and I took the time to explain my expectations for her as long as she serves on our staff."

He felt Gertrude's far-too-clever gaze on him. Pressing him. Did she sense there was more to his exchange yesterday? Broderick retrained his attentions on searching for the stubborn minx. "Bloody hell." He again whipped his timepiece out. "What is taking. . . ?"

Delicate footfalls sounded overhead, faint but distinguishable and long Reggie Spark's mark upon a sea of people who'd perfected the art of stealth. "At last—" He glanced up, and the words withered, died, and disappeared, fleeing from his mind and memory. And with it, they took the rest of the world, except for the fiery Spartan princess at the top of the staircase.

Reggie stood there, and yet . . . at the same time, the siren before him bore no resemblance to the friend who'd kept his books and looked after his siblings.

Candlelight played off the metallic shimmer of her satin gown, the emerald-green fabric clinging to a nipped waist, narrow hips, and a décolletage that placed generous, creamy swells of flesh on proud display. The crystals adorning the bodice, glimmering in the candles' glow, drew his gaze. Tempting.

The gold chain of his timepiece slipped through his fingers. That fob twisted in a dizzying circle, one that matched his disordered thoughts.

Reggie's gaze locked with his, a daring challenge there.

Then she moved, and with it that satin clung to her endlessly long legs, molding the fabric to her thighs as she went, leaving little to the imagination except wicked thoughts involving those legs wrapped about him. Seductive thoughts that would tempt a saint and make a sinner smile. And Broderick, with enough dark marks upon his black soul, added one more as she approached, staring on with an unapologetic boldness.

Reggie reached the bottom step.

And they stood there, their gazes locked, the world forgotten but for the two of them.

Had the hues of her hair always contained the hints of sunrise and sunset, all together?

Say something. Was that silent urging for her? Or for him?

All he knew was in this suspended moment in time, he wanted to hear once more her lilting laughter, or a challenge on her lips, or the teasing camaraderie that had been such a part of their repartee through the years.

Then a little frown pulled her crimson lips down. Reggie smoothed her palms along the front of those skirts and moved her stare away from Broderick's, and he mourned the loss of the brief connection. Nay, he grieved for something far deeper—the bond he'd once had with her.

"Broderick? Broderick?" Gertrude repeated with greater insistence, and the world resumed spinning as all the blood and sound came rushing back through his ears.

"What?" he asked, his voice hoarse.

"I said it is time to go." Gertrude peered at him. "Are you all right?" Yanking off a glove, she pressed the back of her hand to his brow.

He drew back. Insane. That was what he was. Caddish and wicked for lusting after Reggie Spark as he'd been. And pathetic for his maudlin sentiments. He settled for a lie. "Fine. I am absolutely fine."

A liveried servant immediately rushed forward with a muslin, hooded cloak made that morn by one of Madame Colette's girls.

He helped Reggie into the garment, settling it over her shoulders, and Broderick stared on until the fabric fluttered into place, concealing her lithe frame.

Disgust filled him, and he gave his head a firm shake. Lusting after Reggie Spark . . . a woman he'd called friend, and worse . . . one who was in his employ, descended to a level of caddishness of which he'd never been accused.

"Shall we?" Not awaiting an answer, Gertrude, with her cat cradled close, walked side by side with Reggie through the double doors that were thrown open in wait.

Broderick lingered there, staring after the retreating pair. Nay . . . not the pair.

Unbidden, his gaze went to the lush swell of Reggie's buttocks, the slight back and forth sway of her gently curved hips.

He gulped. It was the damned gown. That was the only reason he'd noted the flare of her hips or the creamy-white hue of her skin. Or the way the candles' glow toyed with a hundred shades of red that made up her loose crimson curls.

Nerrie cleared his throat.

Broderick tore his gaze away from Reggie, and his neck heating, he looked at the young guard.

"Would you care for me to accompany you, Mr. Killoran, and keep watch on her? I can gain entrance to the residence and monitor her movements."

"I assure you, I'm quite capable of watching after Miss Spark," he muttered. He hurried after the pair, already settled within the black lacquer carriage, and then pulled himself inside.

The young women sat side by side, forcing him onto the other bench . . . with Gertrude's cat. Even with the largeness of the conveyance, their three tall frames shrank much of the space, leaving Broderick with his knees pressed to Reggie's.

She stiffened.

Did she even now recall the feel of his hand sliding up her firm calves, collecting that very knee, and guiding her legs up around him . . . ?

Reggie jerked herself out of his reach.

And there could be no doubting by the disdain dripping from her eyes that any of the same seductive musings that had both tempted and taunted him since last evening were entirely one-sided. That realization had both a steadying and sobering effect. Broderick fished out two small notes. He turned one over to Gertrude and held the other out for Reggie.

She grabbed for the page, and their fingers brushed. An electric charge passed between them, searing him from the heat of it.

Reggie's lips parted.

"Broderick?" Gertrude prodded. She stared peculiarly at him.

He and Reggie immediately drew their hands back as if burnt. And mayhap he had been for the warmth of her touch.

Broderick curved his lips into a knowing, triumphant grin. So she wasn't immune to him, after all.

"What is this?" Gertrude asked as the carriage sprang into motion.

From the corner of his eye, he caught Reggie already making quick work of the contents there, her long fingers still faintly trembling. She lifted her head and hid those digits in the folds of her skirts. "Your list," she supplied for him. Who knew a sneer could be a sound? And yet Reggie Spark managed it. She layered it so skillfully, in a way that had him flattening his lips.

"His list?" Gertrude alternated her confused stare between Reggie and Broderick.

He directed his response to his sister. "Given the limited nature of time we are facing, I thought it beneficial—"

"To select prospective grooms for your sister?" Reggie scoffed. "Your sister is quite capable of making her own match."

Crumpling the page in a tiny ball, she flicked it at him. That ivory projectile bounced off his chest and landed mockingly on his lap.

Gertrude went slack-jawed.

As long as he'd been a member of the Diggory gang, not a single person amongst them had dared treat him with anything less than respect. Until now. "Do you have a problem, Miss Spark?" he asked, lacing that query with steel as a warning. One that urged her to silence and demanded she see to the task he required of her.

"Do I?" Reggie plucked the sheet from Gertrude's fingers. Had she always been this spirited? Somewhere along the way he'd underestimated her, mistaking her loyalty for meekness. "I have"—she proceeded to jab her fingers at the page—"one, two, three, four, five problems with them." With every battle, she wrested the upper hand and knocked him off-balance. "Lord Landon is a rake who courted not one of your sisters but two of them in the hopes of securing a fortune. Now he'd shift his attention to a third? Lord Mitchell is a consummate gambler in fifty thousand deep. To just you. Lord Harrington revoked his membership because you ended prostitution within the clubs. Lord—"

"That is quite enough," he gritted. An annoying muscle ticked at the corner of his eye.

Gertrude suppressed a smile behind her gloved palm.

Reggie feigned a wide-eyed innocent look. "Are you certain? You don't wish for me to continue? Because I might also mention that Lord Harrington is not only allergic to cats but was also quite cross when Gus mistakenly found his way to his rooms."

Gus picked his striped feline head up.

"Oh, yes. He will certainly never do," Gertrude murmured, patting that damned cat reassuringly.

Broderick dug his fingertips against his temples and rubbed. He'd erroneously believed he'd secured her assent and that would be enough. Yet, again he'd proven himself two steps behind the minx. "You've quite made your point."

With an arrogant toss of her head, she returned the note to Gertrude . . . who promptly crumpled it.

She tossed it on the floor of the carriage just as it rocked to a slow halt outside a white stucco townhouse awash in candlelight.

A servant drew the door open and helped hand Gertrude down. Reggie made to follow, but Broderick called out, staying her.

"Miss Spark?"

She stared back.

"I see I've not been clear where your duties are concerned. Before we go, I think it important to go over some essential details about your altered role within my family." If that intended jab hurt, the spitfire across from him gave not so much as a hint of it. She held his gaze, her own unreadable and stony in ways it had never been. Disconcerted, he hurried to right his thoughts. "I'll not have you insert your opinions on matters as they pertain to my brother and sisters. And certainly not when you undermine their safety and security." Passion blazed to life in her gaze. "Nor will I be challenged at every turn by you." Dropping his hands on his knees, he leaned across the carriage. "Have I made myself clear?"

"Abundantly so," she said, enunciating each of those five syllables. "Now let *me* be clear." He stiffened. "You may have forced me into this task I did not want. You may have cut me from the fabric of your family as though I've been nothing but a servant."

God, she was breathtaking in her fury. With the bright splashes of color that suffused her creamy-white cheeks and the depth of fire in her eyes, he was torn between going to battle with her and taking her in his arms.

Bloody hell. I'm a damned cad, lusting after a woman I forced into the role of companion for my sister. And yet, through that guilt, a powerful hungering for Reggie held him ensnared.

"I'll not be made to feel guilty for reassigning your role within my staff and household, Reggie," he purred. Her betrayal had given him every reason to doubt her and strip her of her role of once valued confidante.

Reggie leaned close, closer still, until he could make out every last, endearing freckle on her flushed face. "Do not think I'm here to serve as a silent companion. I'll protect her from the bounders you'd name as potential husbands for her, and I'll protect her from you."

Any other moment that biting insult would have commanded all his focus. Not this time. Not with this *woman*. His gaze dipped lower. Reggie's shoulders rose and fell rapidly with the force of the breaths she drew. His eyes went lower, and lower still, to the creamy swells of her breasts. When he again met her stare, there was a guardedness to her features.

He caressed a finger warningly down the curve of her cheek. Her breath caught, and he reveled in the evidence of her shared awareness. "Do not ever question my ability to care for my siblings." He wrapped that warning in a husky murmur.

Reggie caught his wrist and drew his hand back, and yet she still made no move to release him. "I'll strike a deal with you. I'll stop questioning your capabilities as a loyal brother when you give me reason to."

And with that cheeky vow, Reggie yanked her hands back, grabbed the edges of the carriage, and leapt down without assistance.

From where he sat, he stared after her quickly retreating figure. She walked with long, unapologetic strides, and yet there was a grace to those steps that carried her quickly across the pavement.

With a growl, Broderick adjusted his cravat.

His sister's cat stretched out on the now abandoned bench, settling himself into the red velvet squabs.

"Oh, hush. You don't know anything about it," he muttered.

The creature stared back with a taunting expression.

Now I've been reduced to conversing with a damned cat.

Giving his head a hard shake, Broderick jumped down and prepared for the Killorans' formal entry into Polite Society.

Chapter 17

You have many enemies. I'm not the only one. I am, however, the only one who will see you destroyed . . .

Reggie had suffered through all number of hells.

There had been the day she'd been caught in a compromising position in the Duke and Duchess of Glastonbury's country estate with the noble couple's son, Lord Oliver. And then on the immediate heels of that, her and Oliver's hasty flight to London, where they'd *intended* to begin again as husband and wife.

Then there had been the night she'd discovered the depth of his depravity and callousness.

The loss of her invisibility, however, proved the greatest lesson in torture.

The Duke and Duchess of Somerset's distinguished guests openly gawked at Reggie. She could feel their eyes on her from her seat on the sidelines of the ballroom. Yes, this was its own special kind of hell.

Seated alongside a handful of other companions, Reggie stared out, deliberately ignoring Lord Cavendish, who'd taken up a seat beside her.

All in the guise of joining his sister and her companion.

And if Reggie hadn't had her innocence quashed by another rake years earlier, she might have believed there were some devoted brothers amongst the ranks of nobility.

Alas, working as she did inside a gaming hell, Reggie had observed a different side of that very earl. He was frequently drunk, and he preferred to avail himself of the charms of whores—often several of them at the same time. And then he tried to seduce those same women when Broderick ended prostitution inside the clubs. No, she was wise enough to never be fooled by a cad's seeming brotherly devotion.

Just then, that devoted brother pressed his thigh hard against hers.

She gritted her teeth and drew away from that bold touch.

The lords of London had been content not questioning her honor within the Devil's Den, but the rules of respect all changed when she stepped outside that world. Every last patron knew she was neither lady nor proclaimed sister to Broderick. As such, the protections she'd enjoyed in the club ceased.

Of its own volition, her gaze wandered the room, searching, searching . . . and through the dancers performing the intricate steps of a country reel, she found him.

The one good man amongst them. Not a gentleman by rank but honorable in all the ways that most mattered.

Broderick spoke with Gertrude, Ophelia, and Connor, and together they presented a loyal family front, as at ease and in command here as they were at the Devil's Den. With a glass of champagne dangling between his elegant fingers, by all intents and purposes Broderick very much belonged to this glittering world. She smiled wistfully. That was Broderick, though. Where mere mortals such as Reggie knew their place in the order of society, Broderick inserted himself where he would and took that place as his right.

He didn't flinch under the focus paid him but rather took it as his due.

But then, why should he not? Every last lady present devoured him with her eyes. From fresh-faced debutantes in blinding-white skirts to the protective mamas at their sides, each woman clamored for a hint of his attention. She wrinkled her nose. Why, even London's leading lords—some members of the club, most not—courted his favor.

As if he sensed her gaze, Broderick found her over the heads of the other guests.

A charged energy passed between them with the same intensity that had sprung to life while they'd fought one another for control inside her music hall. Her heart hammered. There was a heat in his eyes that seared her, that challenged her even as the room around them continued on in a dizzying whir of sounds.

For a slip of a moment in time, even with the length of the room and dancers twirling between them, passion glinted in his eyes. His stare hot, like a lover's caress. And then a dark frown pulled at his lips.

Ophelia said something, calling Broderick's attention away, and the moment was lost.

"You look as happy to be here as I do."

Reggie gasped. "Cleo," she squeaked.

The young woman who'd been like another sister to her grinned wryly. "Not quite the greeting I'd expected."

Reggie jumped up. "Forgive me. I was . . ." *Woolgathering. Making eyes at your brother.*

Cleo winged an eyebrow up.

"Attending Gertrude," Reggie finished, praying Cleo would not challenge her on that statement. Hoping that she'd not pry here . . . or anywhere.

Lord Cavendish stretched his legs out and, looping them at the ankle, stared with bald interest at Reggie. "Put yar eyes back in yar head." Cleo leveled him with a sharp glare that immediately sent his attention swiveling in the opposite direction. "Join me."

Looping her arm through Reggie's, Cleo led her along the perimeter of the ballroom, steering her inside an alcove. "Bloody bastard." The moment the curtain fluttered, allowing them privacy in the darkened space, Cleo spoke. "He must have threatened you."

"Lord Cavendish? Hardly. He's made a nuisance of himself, but he's not—"

"My brother," Cleo cut in dryly. "I meant my brother." Reggie stiffened. "Did he promise to interfere in your purchase?"

Reggie sighed. For her and Broderick's shift from friendship to enemies, she'd not sow the seeds of discontent within his family. She loved all the Killorans too much to be the source of tension amongst them. "I think it best if we not speak about what transpired between your *brother and me*."

"Come," Broderick's youngest sister scoffed. She gave Reggie a slight shove, pushing her down onto the bench. She claimed a seat on the one across from her. "This is me. You've been like another sister. I know you and your . . ."

Secret. Reggie's breath lodged in her throat. Cleo knew her secret. The one Clara had gathered but otherwise remained unknown to all.

Cleo lowered her thin eyebrows until they disappeared under the wire rims of her spectacles. "He purchased it, didn't he?"

Reggie sighed. "Your brother has a right to his fury."

"But only because he doesn't know the details surrounding your decision," the other woman said earnestly.

Far cleverer than any person ought to be, Cleo had gleaned early on the feelings Reggie carried for Broderick Killoran. It had been a revelation they'd not spoken of since the night she'd tended the younger woman's wounds after Stephen had set that fateful fire.

Reggie smiled wistfully. How much Cleo had changed. Once, she'd have never forgiven a person for even contemplating going against the Killorans, let alone one who'd set a plan into motion as Reggie had.

"You're leaving because it's too hard being with him."

And yet she was as astute as she'd ever been. Reggie's stomach muscles clenched.

"I'm leaving because it's better for me if I do," she supplanted. It was a slight distinction, but one that mattered. It shifted the focus to where she'd not allowed it to be . . . ever. *Herself.* "This decision isn't about your brother. This is about me."

"I don't begrudge you your decision," Cleo said quietly, her hushed words nearly lost to the thunderous applause of the guests outside the alcove as they concluded the latest set. "I once believed there couldn't be another gaming hell than the Devil's Den and all competition needed to be quashed. Adair"—the young woman touched a hand to her heart—"Adair showed me the world is wide and there's a place for many in it."

It was an endearingly generous thought . . . that her brother would never be of a like opinion on.

"My husband will be looking for me, but I wanted to give you this." Reaching inside the pocket of her sapphire satin gown, Cleo fished out a small scrap of paper. "You've never put yourself first." She pressed the paper into Reggie's gloved hands. "It is long overdue."

Furrowing her brow, Reggie opened it.

Her confusion deepened.

Martin Phippen.

That single name, wholly unfamiliar, written in Cleo's hand.

"Mr. Phippen is both an architect and builder," Cleo explained. "He oversaw the repairs of the Hell and Sin Club after . . ." After Stephen had burnt the gaming hell to the ground. The young woman coughed into her hand, her ravaged features still reflecting the undeserved guilt for that night. "After the fire," she went on. "And he's responsible for the design and construction of the Paradise Hotel, Ryker Black's latest venture."

Reggie attended that name. "Why are you giving me this?" she asked cautiously. These past years had taught her to be properly suspicious of everyone's motives and actions. No truer lesson had been handed down, solidifying that reminder, than Broderick's recent theft of her dream.

Cleo kicked her in the shin.

Reggie grunted and leaned down to rub the offended limb.

"Woipe that look off your face," Cleo snapped, her language dissolving into Cockney tones that had long marked her upset. "You think I'd deceive you?" she demanded, master of her speech yet again. "I'm trying to help you, because that is what family does."

Family.

Her throat tightened. That is what the Killorans had always been to Reggie. Since Broderick had shared her betrayal with his siblings, she'd become invisible to Stephen, Ophelia, and even Gertrude. "They'll come around," Cleo said gruffly, correctly following the path her thoughts had traversed.

"Perhaps," Reggie softly returned. But no doubt she'd be gone long before that ever happened. "Your family, they carry powerful grudges."

Cleo chewed at her lower lip. "You can always . . . tell him."

Reggie's mind was slow to process that suggestion, and when it sank in, she recoiled. Share the pathetic depths of her feelings with Broderick? "You mustn't say anything," she urged on a frantic whisper. She'd cast aside her pride and shamed herself too many times in the course of the past ten years. She couldn't do it again. Not for Broderick. Not in front of him or anyone. Not in any way. Taking Cleo by the arm, she lightly squeezed. "Promise me you shall not tell him. I—"

"I won't. Your secret is yours." Cleo touched a fingertip to the corner of her eye. "But I will insist that you think about yourself."

And like the phantom figure who'd robbed nobs all over the Dials, Cleo slipped from the alcove with such stealth the curtains barely fluttered.

Alone, Reggie sat back on her bench and stared at the paper in her hand. It was just a single name, but it heightened the reality of her new beginning . . . and a future carved out with her own hands, by work she herself had done over the years. It represented freedom.

The curtains parted and then fell back into place. "Miss Spark, how very unexpected it is, seeing you again."

Reggie froze. Her fingers curled reflexively around the note given to her by Cleo, and she clung to the name scrawled there to keep from lifting her head.

For the moment she did, it became real. He became real.

"But then," the owner of that voice taunted, "this would not be the first alcove we've stolen within, would it?"

Oh, God. She wanted to clamp her hands over her ears and blot out that hated voice.

Reggie bolted forward, but his bulky frame blocked the only path to freedom.

The blackhearted devil shot a hand out, catching her upper arm in an unrelenting grip.

She bit the inside of her cheek to keep from crying out at the pain of that hold.

No. No. No.

"Oh, forgive me." That purred apology was anything but, husked in lurid tones that had once seduced a younger, more naive, stupider version of herself. Now she sensed the evil contained within. "It's not Miss Spark, though. Am I correct . . . Miss Marlow?"

Her stomach pitched. *I'm going to be ill . . .*

Say something. Order him gone. Order him to the Devil.

Her mouth went dry as terror clawed at her mind, robbing her of rational thought.

And by the feral grin on Lord Oliver's slightly fleshier face, he well knew it and reveled in the upper hand he'd wrested from her.

He raised a hand, and she recoiled, hunching her body protectively.

You little whore . . . you will do whatever I tell you to do . . . and with whomever . . .

With a smirk, the duke brushed a ginger curl back from his brow in an affected gesture.

He was toying with her, as he'd always done.

"Get away from me," she whispered, and she hated her own inherent weakness for the threadbare quality to that pitiable command.

A flute of champagne dangling between his white-gloved fingers, he swirled the contents in the slightest circle. "Tsk, tsk. And here I'd thought there would be great joy at being reunited with your former love." He sipped at his drink.

And through the terror and misery of having him step back into her life, a seething and potent fury swept her. A welcome, deserved hatred that shook loose the shock and brought her back up. "What do you want?" she demanded.

He paused; it was an infinitesimal slip of time but one she saw and took strength in.

Reggie wasn't the young, weak girl she'd once been. Broderick had helped her to see her own strength and worth. She'd not let a cad like Lord Oliver bully her about. Not any longer.

"That's hardly the greeting for the man you were to marry."

She seethed. "The man who made me a whore."

Lord Oliver touched his spare hand to a chest. "You wound me, love." He lifted his glass and toasted her. "I never made you anything." He lowered his voice to a husky whisper. "You saw to that all by yourself." As casual as if he were raising a lady's finger for a requisite kiss, he grabbed her right breast, squeezing hard.

Her skin crawled, and for a horrifying moment she was transported back to another time. And she was that small, pathetic creature too afraid to say no to even his filthy touch. Fearing the inevitable backhand. The unexpected fist.

Break and belittle. It had been a tactic he'd wielded with militaristic precision.

It chased off her fear, leaving in its place fury. Color burnt her cheeks. Not this time.

Snarling, Reggie swatted Lord Oliver's hand, knocking his hold loose. With her opposite palm, she unsheathed her dagger and touched the tip of her blade to his throat.

He blanched, going absolutely still.

And mayhap she'd been shaped in Mac Diggory's image, for she reveled in the stark terror spilling from his slightly soft frame. "I'll ask you one more time, what do you want with me?"

Lord Oliver swallowed and forced a chuckle that sent his throat muscles bobbing.

Under that slightest of movements, the lethally sharp tip of her dagger pierced his skin. A single crimson bead wound a trail down his creamy-white flesh, staining his cravat with a minute drop.

"Come now, Regina," he cajoled, those same tones he'd used when coaxing her out of her virginity. "Surely you don't intend to slice a duke's throat in the alcove of another powerful peer."

"You're a duke now," she said dumbly.

"Indeed," he purred, his relish clear in even that two-syllable reply.

She faltered but made no move to lower her knife. Of course his ascension to a dukedom had been inevitable, but still, this understanding elevated him to all-powerful in ways he hadn't been before. "I'd rather swing than allow you to hurt me." Again.

Never again.

"Ah, but what about the family which has taken you in?" Her heart wound a path from her chest, dipping to her stomach, and then crashing to her toes, along with reality. "I, along with all Polite Society, understand Mr. Killoran seeks a proper match for his sister. A scandal in a ballroom between us?" He flashed a wide grin; the cloying hint of garlic and sweetness on his breath set her gut to churning. "Why, I trust that would ruin all hopes. Don't you?"

Reggie stood immobile, breathing hard and fast. Wanting to tell him to go to the Devil and provide a path for him to get there.

And yet he didn't threaten her . . . he threatened Broderick and his family.

Silently cursing, she let her arm drop. "What do you want?" she asked succinctly.

Lord Oliver set his glass down on the ledge behind him and then yanked out a kerchief to dab at that slight wound she'd made on his throat. "With *you*?" he scoffed. "What would I want with you, the whore who robbed me?"

"You bastard," she spat. "I didn't rob you."

He chuckled. "It doesn't escape my notice that you do not dispute being a whore."

Shame came, hot, swift, and with a stingingly familiar force. For there could be no disputing what she'd done in the past . . . what she'd given to this man. What she'd been. Before Broderick had taken her in and let her carve a new beginning.

For all the anger she'd carried these past days, love swelled within her breast for every gift he'd given, and more for the strength he'd helped her find within herself. And for those gifts, she could not see him harmed. Not even to spare herself. "You have one minute," she warned, "and then I'm leaving."

He frowned.

Yes, of course, dukes didn't partake in discourse. They spoke, and the world listened and didn't volunteer a word edgewise. Reggie, however, didn't belong to this world. She never would. Nor did she wish to. Not even when she'd believed herself in love with him.

"Mr. Killoran wants a title for his sister."

She stiffened. Of all the things she'd expected from his treachery . . . that had been the last she'd anticipated. And yet why should it be? Why should his motives in seeking out Reggie, Gertrude's companion, knock her aback? "No," she said curtly before he could put another word forward.

The duke flicked an imagined scrap of lint from his midnight-black sleeve. "I didn't put my request to you."

"You request nothing," she snapped. "You take what you want and give nothing in return."

"Yes," he acknowledged unapologetically. "Generally, that has been my way. That is a luxury afforded dukes. This time, however, is different."

A warning knocked around the back of her head. *No!*

He spoke, confirming her dark suspicion. "I've lost my fortune."

"To whores, wagers, and drink," she spat.

He smiled. "Indeed. However, I now find myself in need . . . of funds."

Reggie's mouth moved with no words coming out. She was already shaking her head. "No."

"I'm not asking you." He stroked a finger down her right cheek, flesh that had suffered so many blows from the very hand he worked over her face now. "I'm telling you."

She stumbled away from him, knocking against the back wall and toppling onto the bench.

"I'm going to court her and make her my duchess."

Her stomach heaved, vomit climbing her throat.

"Over my dead body."

He laughed softly and leaned down, erasing the distance between them, making the already-small space of the alcove narrower and darker.

She flinched, but he merely flicked her nose. "I can arrange that. A whore who robbed me years ago and lived the years in between as a gaming hell owner's mistress? Killoran wouldn't survive the scandal, and you?" He scraped a derisive glance up and down her frame. "You simply wouldn't survive."

Her tongue felt heavy in her mouth. "What do you want from me?"

"Your silence. And I'm so generous, Regina, that I'm willing to not only spare you but also pay you."

"Pay me?" she echoed.

"Word is that Killoran would pay anywhere up to seventy-five thousand pounds for the man who takes the blind one off his hands."

Fury blazed through her, and she proved herself more ruthless than she'd ever dared believe. For she wanted to stick a knife through his vile heart and spare any woman his evil.

Encouraged by her silence, he continued. "All I want is a promise of your silence, and some . . . backing on your part. It is my understanding you are close with Miss Killoran."

Her teeth chattered. He'd have her betray Gertrude. Nay, he'd have her betray all the Killorans.

"I can't do it," she whispered. Gertrude would be crushed and destroyed as Reggie herself had been at the hands of this monster. And then when she was, Broderick would gladly kill him in return and find himself on a hangman's noose either way. Because he'd never, ever let his sister be bullied about by any person—man, woman, or the king himself.

He touched a finger to her lips, and she flinched away from that hated touch. "Take a week to think on it," he went on as if she hadn't spoken.

A week? "There's nothing to think—"

"I understand you are in the process of establishing a business?"

No.

Reggie's hands went to her throat.

"How very . . . quaint." His lip peeled in a mocking sneer. As quick as that harsh smile had come, it faded. "Come, Regina," he soothed in those same calming, tender tones he'd used after she'd been beaten and bloodied on the floor at his feet. "It will be good for everyone," he vowed. "Killoran will have a duchess as a sister."

Reggie lifted her chin, daring him with her eyes and next words. "And if I say no?"

He laughed softly, and Reggie darted her gaze about. Her heart pounded with the fear of discovery. "My goodness. You've grown bold over the years. What if you say no?" he repeated, his tone dripping with mockery. "There's nothing for you to say yes or no to. What you'll do is remain silent about our having known one another."

And through her terror came the realization. "You need me to be silent," she murmured.

It was empowering, having something this man sought . . . and needed. It gave her strength and made her more than the downtrodden, spiritless girl she'd once been. He caught her by the throat, crushing her scream into silence. With a bored air, he backed her against the wall.

Reggie clawed at his hands as he clenched and unclenched his fist, that merciless game where he teased her with her own air.

"Every fist you ever took was because you were deserving of it."

Look what you made me do . . . This is all your fault . . .

Struggling to drag a breath of air into her lungs, she searched for her knife, but he slammed his body into hers, quelling her efforts.

"Let me be clear, Regina," he whispered against her ear. "I intend to marry Killoran's sister." He gave her throat another squeeze, emphasizing that point and promise. "And if you say so much as a word, then I'll see your employer, Mr. Killoran, knows precisely the manner of woman he's entrusted his sister's care to." He released her, and she collapsed against the wall, dragging air into her lungs. "Tell me, do you think he'll prove so magnanimous toward a whore who's threatened his sister's reputation and stood between that sister and the title of duchess?"

With that last taunt, he left.

Chapter 18

Ticktock. Ticktock. The end is coming. Make no mistake of it.

It had taken mere moments after their arrival for one fact to become indefatigably clear to Broderick—Reggie's gown had been a mistake.

It hadn't been an error because she was in any way undeserving of the fine French satin . . . but because it had done precisely as she'd predicted: it had earned her the attention of every rake, rogue, scoundrel, and cad present.

Including me.

By God, I am my father in every way. A bastard whose treachery against Lord Andover and his household had revealed not only a thief but also a man who'd taken his pleasures amongst the earl's staff while holding the threat of a sacking over them if they didn't fulfill his wishes.

Loathing for the depraved bastard who'd sired him rooted around his insides, as sharp now as it had been years earlier when he'd learned the extent of his father's failings . . . and evil.

Standing on the fringes of the ballroom, a glass of champagne held forgotten between his fingers, he looked around.

Where in blazes had she gone?

Across the dance floor, he did a purposeful sweep for her.

Nor did his worry stem from the fact that Reggie Spark had become an opponent to be carefully watched and her actions monitored—at all times.

Rather, Broderick's irrational response was born from a primal jealousy at the way those bloody nobs had leered at her all evening.

Because of me. I'm the damned one who insisted on—

"Searching for someone?"

He cursed, spilling the contents of his glass, and faced an amused Cleo.

"Bloody hell," he muttered.

A servant rushed over, relieved him of the empty flute, and darted off. Waving off the next footman who came bearing a silver tray of champagne, Broderick tugged out his kerchief and dusted off his fingers.

His sister arched an eyebrow.

"Where's Regina?" he demanded.

"What . . . ?"

"Don't play games with me." He'd seen her not even twenty minutes ago taking a turn about the damned floor with Reggie. He, however, had mistakenly relaxed his guard, trusting Cleo would cut any gent who came near. She'd gone soft. "You were far better at subterfuge before you married," he muttered.

"Lost 'er, did ya, guvnor," she taunted, and heat crept up his ears.

Actually, he had. Somewhere between her stroll with Cleo and his exchange with the Dowager Duchess of Argyll, who'd sprung Ophelia from Newgate.

Suspicion darkened Cleo's eyes. "Why does it matter where she's gone off to? Reggie ain't one who'd run around the host's home filching finery."

He bristled. "Of course she's not." No, Reggie had always possessed a gentility that made her better matched to a ballroom than a gaming hell. Who had she been before they'd met? He'd always simply accepted that her secrets were her own, but now . . . he wanted to know. Broderick raised a hand, briefly concealing his mouth. "Have you not noticed how they're eyeing her?"

Cleo blinked slowly. "Who?"

Bloody hell. She required new spectacles. "The damned gents present. They're *ogling* her." He gnashed his teeth. Or they had been before she'd gone and sneaked off.

His sister whistled. "Ya're mad. There weren't nobody 'ere eyeing Reggie."

Broderick had noted the bounders the minute she'd descended the damned staircase and the candles' glow had toyed with the lustrous strands of her crimson curls. "Oh, trust me," he gritted out. "They were."

His sister emitted a snorting sound.

His frown deepened. "Do you find something amusing? I know what I saw." Broderick jerked his chin in the direction of one of their best patrons, a consummate rogue and dedicated gambler. "Lord Cavendish played the devoted brother and joined his sister and the young lady's companion."

Another inelegant snort escaped Cleo. "You're taking umbrage with a gent watching after his sister?"

"Yes." He puzzled his brow. "No." *Bloody hell.* "Yes. In this instance I am. He merely sought a place alongside Reggie."

"And you gathered all that from?" Shaking her head, she stared expectantly back.

In the way Cavendish had, with his eyes, stripped that emerald creation off Reggie's willowy frame. *"Pfft."* He adjusted his immaculately knotted gold satin cravat. "I know men." His father had been a scoundrel, and Broderick had made his fortunes catering to other men's vices.

Cleo studied a finger and picked at a jagged nail. "Seems a lot of information to note about some nobs and Reggie. The same nobs," she pointed out, "who have spoken with her as they did any other worker at the Devil's Den."

"Yes, but this is different." And that had also been before.

"Oh?" That syllable hinted at one who saw absolutely nothing.

"Now she looks like *this*," he hissed.

Cleo tossed her hands up in exasperation. "Like what?"

As if she were one of those mermaids who'd traded her fins for long, graceful limbs and moved amongst mere mortals like the siren she was. "You know what I'm talking about," he clipped out, doing another search for the taller-than-most-guests lady with flame-red curls.

"No, Broderick," Cleo confirmed. "I really have no bloody idea what you're saying."

"Her gown," he said distractedly. Where in blazes had she gone?

"Her gown?" Cleo repeated. "I have it on account from Gertrude that you were the one who insisted Reggie trade her brown dresses for her current wardrobe."

He curled his hands into fists. And what a blasted mistake that had been.

"And furthermore . . . what do you think? She was lured off by one of those rogues to some clandestine meeting?"

Broderick opened his mouth and closed it. He tried again.

Except Cleo's droll query roused unwelcome images. Unwanted ones. A rake luring Reggie off. Tempting her. Running his hands over those exposed, creamy-white shoulders.

Tendrils of something potent, something that felt very much like jealousy, slithered around his chest, making words impossible.

His entire body turned to stone.

By God. Surely, he was not jealous over—

Cleo jabbed him hard in the side with her elbow. "I was jesting." She narrowed her eyes on him. "And furthermore, why are you, of a sudden, so concerned with where Reggie is or isn't?"

His mind stalled.

Of course he was not jealous. It was nonsensical and irrational.

Mindful of the attention even now being paid as he and Cleo, two of the most lethal members of the former Diggory gang, stood there, Broderick spoke in hushed tones reserved for his sister's ears. "She's here to serve as Gertrude's companion."

"Gertrude, who is even now speaking with Ophelia and Connor," Cleo pointed out.

He continued over her. "Any scandalous actions on Reggie's part will be a reflection on Gertrude."

Cleo eyed him like he'd sprung a second head. "And all of a sudden you're so very concerned with what people might say about us?" She moved closer. More than a foot shorter than his own height, only Cleo was capable of looking down the length of her nose at a taller man. "You never cared about how our past or reputations might impact our future amongst the nobs. I suspect, deep down, you know why you're really searching for Regina."

He pleated his brow. What was she suggesting?

"Now," Cleo said, taking a step back. "If you'll excuse me? I've dragged Adair here far longer than either of us wish to be."

That was it?

She turned to go. "Oh, and Broderick?" she tossed over her shoulder. "If you are looking for Reggie, she's in the alcove at the corner of the ballroom."

His gaze automatically shot to the curtained alcove in question. When he glanced back, Cleo had gone, disappearing into the crowd with the same fleet-of-foot skill she'd had as a girl picking pockets. All the while his sister had known precisely where Reggie had been, and yet she'd allowed him to panic about . . .

What? As she'd taunted, what reasons had he had to be agitated? She'd spotted the lie through his expectations for Reggie's conduct.

Shifting his attentions back to the very person he'd spent the better part of thirty minutes now searching for, Broderick started through the ballroom, passing men just a smidgeon below royalty and weaving around the leading lords and ladies of London's ballrooms. It was the realization of a long-held goal, and yet all his focus remained on a pair of thick brocade curtains.

Broderick reached the corner of the hall, and with his back kept deliberately to that hiding place Reggie had made for herself, he stepped back and entered.

As soon as the curtains fell back into place, the hiss of a blade sliced through the darkened space. And its tip pricked his throat.

He'd gone lax. There was no other way of accounting for his being caught off guard. He made himself go absolutely motionless. "Is this to be my repayment for forcing you into the role of companion?" he drolly asked.

"Broderick?" Reggie demanded on a furious whisper. She drew the knife away from his throat. "What in blazes? I could have killed you."

"Yes." Adjusting his rumpled cravat, he faced her. "You would have found yourself—"

Reggie lifted her foot and strapped her dagger just above the inside of her ankle, killing the rest of that flippant reply. "Where is your sister?" She paused midmovement, her skirts rucked about her leg, and whipped her head up. "You should be with her. I should be with her," she swiftly amended.

She'd asked a question. What was it? All logical thought had fled. *My sister. Gertrude.* "She is currently dancing with Lord Landon."

Some of the tension left Reggie, and she retrained her efforts on her dagger.

His throat moved rhythmically as a wave of lust bolted through him, and he proved himself as caddish as Lord Cavendish himself, for he could not look away.

While she bent her head over her task, Broderick used the opportunity to study that generous expanse of flesh exposed, a firm, muscular calf belonging to a woman unafraid to work. Of their own volition, his eyes drifted higher, following that swath of skin, and those shameful, wicked questions that had recently stirred at last had an answer—she was freckled everywhere.

An enthralling pattern of those dark flecks kissed long, graceful limbs.

Reggie lowered her dress back into place, and his sanity was restored. He tore his gaze away. "Where have you . . . ?" The question trailed off as he took in those details he'd been previously too preoccupied to note: Reggie's perpetually red cheeks stood out stark white; her eyes, rounded with fear, had the look of the hunted so familiar to one in the Dials.

She'd pulled a knife on him, in the middle of a crowded ballroom, no less. Reggie wasn't one to act impulsively or draw a weapon without provocation. He did a quick search of her, lingering on the handful of loose curls that had escaped her intricate chignon.

He narrowed his eyes. "Has someone offended you?" Fury shot through him, a seething, simmering rage that briefly darkened his vision.

"What?" She blinked slowly. "No," she squeaked. "Why would you . . . ? Who would . . . ?" Her ramblings came to an abrupt cessation. "What are you doing here?" she asked this time with a greater calm. "You should be mingling with the duke's guests."

He frowned. Is that what accounted for her peculiar reaction around him? "Are you trying to be rid of me, Reggie?" The idea that she wished him gone . . . rankled.

"Yes," she said with a blunt honesty that earned one of his first real smiles of the night.

He claimed a spot on the narrow bench built into the wall.

Reggie stamped her foot. "This is not a game, Broderick. We cannot be discovered together."

He spread his arms behind him. "*Pfft.* I'll speak with whomever I wish and wherever I wish." Nor would he treat her as a servant, lesser than the other people present.

"The rules of your world don't apply here. You're in their world now."

Broderick searched her face.

He'd convinced himself that her feelings on entering Polite Society hadn't mattered. Nor had her long-held derision for the *ton*. And for the first time, he felt a modicum of shame at his selfishness.

"What?" Reggie watched him with suspicion in her expressive eyes.

"You think this is all about my appreciation for the nobility."

She didn't pretend to misunderstand. "I know it is." He'd have to be deaf to fail to hear the thinly disguised chastisement buried in her tone.

Gertrude's face flashed to his mind, and a familiar panic knocked around his chest. The omnipresent threat hanging, posed by the marquess.

Ticktock. Ticktock—

"I have no choice."

"We always have a choice."

It took a moment to register that quiet murmur uttered by the woman seated across from him.

And suddenly his patience with her thinly disguised disapproval snapped. "Tell me, were you born to a noble family, Reggie?"

"Me?" She snorted. "Hardly." And yet she conducted herself with the regality of a queen.

Questions swirled anew about the enigmatic woman before him.

"It's why you found yourself at London Bridge."

She jerked as if he'd put a bullet in her belly, and for an instant he wished he could call back the words that had ushered in a haunted glitter in her eyes. And yet, at the same time, he wanted them spoken.

Reggie rushed to her feet. He caught her loosely about the waist, keeping her from fleeing. Keeping her at his side. Her chest rose hard and fast, and she yanked free of his hold. "You know nothing about why I was at London Bridge that night," she whispered.

Before she left and he hanged, he wanted those secrets she kept. He wanted the memory of her—even the darkest ones—to be whole in every way.

It was the first they'd ever spoken of it. "You offered yourself to me," he reminded softly.

"Why are you doing this?" She stared at him with stricken eyes. "Do you hate me this much?"

Stung by that question, he frowned. "Do you think I would deliberately shame you?"

"I don't know what you would do anymore."

He flinched. It was warranted, and she was right to have that suspicion, and yet . . . he'd never deliberately hurt her in that way.

But you'd hurt her in others . . .

Cleo's recent admonishment whispered forward.

And when you discover her motives, then tell me it doesn't matter . . .

Just as he didn't know what had brought the then eight-and-ten-year-old girl to offer her virtue for a sovereign. That had been the value she'd placed on herself. That realization all these years later struck in ways his younger self had been too jaded to see. "I'd spare her that fate you knew."

"And do you believe your siblings would ever allow that to befall Gertrude?" she demanded. "You'd rather place that trust in a *nobleman*?"

That took him aback.

Reggie took a step closer, and in the narrow quarters, her movements had the tips of their toes touching. "Do you know what I believe?"

She didn't allow him a place to so much as breathe. "This is about *you*." He stiffened. No one, not even his siblings had questioned his motives, and yet this spitfire would call him out. "This is about your love of the peerage." She peered at him, working her gaze over him. A woman searching for secrets and answers. "And do you know . . ." The fight seemed to go out of her as she fell back on her heels. Reggie hugged her arms around her middle. "I cannot in this instance say whether you'd turn away the most powerful peer if he provided you what you so desire." With a disgusted shake of her head, Reggie turned to go, but then she paused, facing him once more. "You remain so convinced that a nobleman might save Gertrude and the Devil's Den." She plucked at her skirts, those distracted movements wrinkling the shimmery fabric and leaving creases within the fine garment. "But Broderick, oftentimes what appears to be at the heart of our salvation is just a different form of strife."

And with that ominous warning, she slipped out.

Chapter 19

Be warned, nothing can save you. I am coming for you. Just as you and yours came for mine, I am lurking. Waiting.

Lying at the center of the stage with Clara at her side, Reggie stared overhead at the still-glorious mural vibrantly captured above. The wide-smiling cherubs dancing in their pastel skies and clouds served as a mocking juxtaposition to the doom hanging over her.

And now because of their connections to her . . . over Clara, Gertrude, Broderick.

And all the Devil's Den.

She squeezed her eyes shut.

A week. Or was it now six days? A panicky laugh built in her chest.

Her partner in business turned her head. "That bad?"

"Worse," Reggie squeezed out.

"Killoran?"

And oddly, this time, the one who'd upended both her heart and her existence was not to blame. Reggie was the one responsible for all her own problems. She always had been. Lord Oliver's face flickered forward, and she slapped her palms over her eyes in a bid to blot out the thought and memory of him. And yet the threat hovered. Lingered.

"What is it?" Clara urged.

Emotion clogging her throat, Reggie shook her head. "I can't." Not yet. Even though Clara, whose fate and future were inextricably linked to Reggie's, was deserving of every last detail. "I found a builder."

The other woman abruptly sat up. "What?"

Remaining in her supine position, Reggie fished into her pocket and pulled out the scrap given to her by Cleo. She handed it over.

The other woman yanked it from her fingers.

"It's all there," Reggie said, not even looking at the note she'd received the previous evening from Broderick's sister. "According to Cleopatra, the builder would offer us an extremely fair and generous rate and also a promise to begin and end construction in no more than a month's time. Perhaps sooner, depending on how he finds the conditions."

"Yes," the other woman blurted. "Of course he can come in. I'll arrange a meeting with him and discuss the contract." She alternated her stare between that page and Reggie. "It must be dire."

Reggie glanced over, a question in her eyes.

"We've been searching months for an architect who'll one, deal with women, and two, work with a whore, and three . . . who we can afford." She waved the page. "And yet you've found all three and appear as though you've just attended your own funeral."

Reggie sank her teeth into her lower lip. "It's bad," she whispered. . . . *Look what you made me do . . . This is all your fault . . .* Lord Oliver's charges rolled through her head, and she clenched her teeth to keep them from chattering. "I'm poison." Tears flooded her eyes. She blinked them back, willing them away. "You never, ever should have agreed to any venture with me."

"Stop that," the other woman demanded, slapping the page down.

"It's true." Drawing in a shuddery breath, she sat up. Before her courage deserted her, Reggie recounted her meeting with Lord Oliver, taking care to leave out the most shameful ends of her relationship with the gentleman. When she'd finished with a pared-down version of the history between her and Oliver, silence met her telling.

"Oh, bloody hell," Clara said quietly, wiping a hand over her eyes.

"Precisely." In the past ten years she'd crossed not only one of the most powerful peers in the kingdom but also the most ruthless kingpin in the Dials. Drawing in a breath, Reggie shoved herself upright and, drawing her knees close, looped her arms around them. "You should do it alone." She'd not begrudge Clara a new beginning because of her own mistakes.

"Stop it," the other woman clipped out with far more loyalty than Reggie deserved. "Do you remember what I first said to you when I moved here?"

"Go to hell?" Reggie reminded her dryly.

The other woman laughed. "Yes, well, that was when I thought you were as cold as everyone else on Killoran's staff. You told me—"

"That in these streets, we're taught to mistrust everyone and their motives," Reggie said softly.

"But that you were once like me, an outsider to this place, and you knew what that felt like." Clara's voice cracked in an uncharacteristic display of emotion. "And that whenever I wished it, I'd have a friend in you." She hardened her jaw, killing all previous hint of that vulnerability. "As such, I'll not abandon you."

"You wouldn't be abandoning me," Reggie insisted, undeserving of that loyalty.

Clara arched an eyebrow. "Where would you even go?"

For a moment, another place far away from these diabolical streets floated around her memory, the endlessly rolling green hills of the Kent countryside. The family she'd left behind. But in her mind, they existed as she'd left them, a father and two brothers frozen in time, an unaging trio. Tears stuck in her throat. There was no going home. There was no going back from what she'd done. And if she did quit this life and return, Lord Oliver, now that he'd found her, would likely—and gleefully—come for her. And worse . . . her family.

And that's assuming her once proud papa could forgive the daughter who'd whored herself to a nobleman and then dwelled in a gaming hell—

"Reggie?"

"I don't know," she brought herself to say. There was no place for her. She'd deluded herself into believing the Devil's Den was a home. And for a short while it had been. She held the other woman's gaze. "I will not begrudge you if you wish to cut me from this." Reggie spoke over her protestations. "I'm the reason we lost one thousand pounds more to Broderick. All of this is my fault."

"I've already said I will not abandon you, and I won't. That bastard," Clara muttered. "Him," she hurried to clarify. "Not you." She grabbed one of Reggie's hands and squeezed hard. "I would never abandon you, but neither can I do this alone without your funds or assistance." She motioned to the sheet music Reggie had been writing. "If I'd had the idea to start out on my own, I would have established another hell. Another bordello. It's all I've known. You reminded me that I wasn't always a whore. That I was once a singer." It had been a piece of Clara's past that she'd reluctantly shared; her forgotten-but-not-lost love of music, however, had only strengthened their bond.

They fell into silence that Clara was the first to break. "And we're certain," she began hesitantly, "the match might not be a welcome one for Gertrude or Killoran?"

It took a moment for the implications of that question to settle around her slow-to-process mind. "What?" Surely she wasn't suggesting Reggie turn a blind eye while Gertrude married that monster? But then, she'd not shared the ugliest, most humiliating aspects of her time with that devil. How he'd beaten her. Choked her. Mocked her.

"Killoran is determined to have a title at all costs," the other woman pointed out.

"Not like this," Reggie said vehemently. *Not with this man.*

"Are you so certain?"

"Yes." In this, she was.

"Then why didn't you tell him last evening?"

Because the moment Lord Oliver became real between Reggie and Broderick, her past would no longer be her own, and her sins and her greatest shame would belong to a man who'd held her heart for the past ten years. "I wasn't ready," she quietly confessed. She'd never be ready. How did one ever truly, freely share all the sins Reggie carried? Ones that had left her as tattered as any Covent Garden doxy. "I've made many mistakes." Too many to count. "But I know Gertrude deserves more than a husband like him," she spoke with a finality meant to signal the end to Clara's plans to turn Gertrude over to the recently minted duke. Reggie had sold her virtue, her pride, her body, and now the other woman would add her soul to the mix. For the disappointment of that, there was also an ache that settled around her chest. What had driven the other woman to such desperation that she'd sacrifice another in the name of survival?

"Reggie . . ." Clara scooted over and, matching Reggie's positioning, faced her. "You think me ruthless. Whether she's a duchess or a whore at the Devil's Den, or a lover of some undeserving lord, can one ever truly escape that fate? That is a woman's lot."

"No." Reggie was already shaking her head. Yes, that had been her fate, and Clara's, and too many other women's. For that Reggie knew better than to give of herself in any way to a man. "I can't believe that is every woman's lot." Mayhap it was naivete or innocence or hopefulness on her part. "Broderick never laid his hand upon a woman." And he never would.

Clara scoffed. "Because Broderick Killoran once showed you a kindness? His actions since should have opened your eyes to the truth of who he is . . . because it's who they all are," she said, drawing out the last five syllables for emphasis. "Men aren't good and kind." Hardness iced her eyes. "The one man I thought was proved how very easy it was to turn me out."

"But this is not about Broderick or Ryker Black or the Duke of Glastonbury."

Reggie winced as that carefully omitted admission slipped out.

The other woman went motionless. "He's a *duke*. Oh, Reggie." There was such disappointment there that Reggie flinched.

"He wasn't a duke at the time," she said lamely.

Clara groaned. "Reggie, as a duke's son, he was always a duke. You don't cross a duke. You don't anger them. You steer clear of them—"

"I know that now," she said impatiently. He represented the single greatest folly of her eight-and-twenty years. In giving her heart and virtue to Oliver, she'd lost every part of herself in the process: her family, her innocence, her hopes, and now, if she didn't do as he wished, her future.

Clara dropped her chin atop her knees. "All right. There is a way out of this . . ."

They stared in silence at one another.

"There isn't." Reggie was the one to finally say it. "Not unless I'm willing to trade my future for Gertrude's." *And Clara's.*

It hung unspoken between them, clear, with Clara not needing to even toss that accusation at Reggie.

With a resigned sigh, Reggie stacked books. "I have to return."

Stephen's daily lessons would conclude soon and thrust Reggie back into the role of companion. To a woman who, since Reggie's betrayal, had said fewer than a hundred words altogether to her.

"Your loyalty will be your downfall, Regina Spark," Clara said, joining her on her feet.

Reggie collected her cloak. "Some might say the same of you," she pointed out, shrugging into the wool garment.

"It is different," the other woman muttered.

"Is it?" she countered, latching the grommets at her throat.

"Those Killoran girls always had one another. They've had Killoran and even that miserable cur of a younger brother." Since Clara had come to the Killorans from the Hell and Sin Club, the boy had never been able to see past his hatred and mistrust for her association with their rivals. "We have lived with only ourselves to rely on. That is the difference. And that is why you should not sacrifice your own existence for a family who won't even remember you when you're gone." The matter-of-fact pragmatism to her delivery hurt more than had Clara hurled the words as a mocking barb.

Wordlessly, Reggie picked up the small stack of books. As they started for the door, she tried to speak. "I . . ." Apologies were useless. Promises to make it right, impossible.

Clara waved that off. "I'll pay a visit this afternoon to Phippen's offices."

"And you have the calculations we've gone through on . . . ?"

"The building redesign? Yes."

On a venture that Lord Oliver could see dismantled with nothing more than a few ill-placed words about the proprietress. The walls closing in on Reggie's existence narrowed all the more.

As Clara reached for the handle, letting Reggie out, the former madam made one last appeal. "Reggie?" Reggie paused. "How forgiving will Broderick be if he finds out you've brought the wrath of a duke down on his family?"

Either way, she was doomed.

For there was either her soul on the line or her future.

Her stomach sick, Reggie closed the door behind her.

Nerrie, standing alongside a lamppost, immediately sprang to attention, the presence of that guard dogging her steps a reminder of her role in the household. She was no friend or family to the Killorans. She had been a member of their staff who'd served their purpose, and now she brought nothing to the proverbial table.

Not giving him so much as a backward glance, she stomped off, her gaze fixated on the carriage.

Nerrie quickened his stride and fell into step beside her.

"It ain't because he doesn't trust you, ma'am." Nerrie, who'd always been the most loyal of the guards to her. Where she'd caught the mocking whispers and aspersions cast about her role in the Devil's Den, Nerrie had proven different.

He'd also proven how easy it was for a person to cut Reggie from the fold.

"Hmph."

The guard tugged his hat free. "It's true. Oh, he's angry with ya about . . ." Nerrie gestured back behind him to the club. "But he doesn't want ya running around these streets without protection."

Reggie hardened her jaw. If the guard believed that, he was as much a fool as Reggie had proven to be in trusting Broderick. "I don't need anyone looking after me. I'll see to my own safety."

Shifting her small burden over to her opposite arm, with her spare hand Reggie pulled the door open and climbed inside without assistance.

With a downcast set to his features, Nerrie climbed atop the driver's box.

Once alone in the carriage, rumbling through the streets of the Seven Dials, Reggie considered Clara's words and warnings. How easily the other woman had spoken of putting Reggie's well-being before that of Gertrude.

The conveyance took a slow turn onto another street, and Reggie's gaze collided with a waif-thin girl leaning against the wall. Her hair hung in a tangle of limp blonde strands about a soot-stained face. The street-side doxy lifted her skirts for a passing gentleman. And he stopped, drawn closer to the gift the girl sold of desperation. Even with the space between them, the deadness to the girl's eyes reached through the leaded-glass windowpane, an echo of that seen in the gaze of any woman who'd ever been forced on her own in these streets.

Reggie stared at the young woman, unable . . . unwilling to look away from the tangible suffering until the carriage carried her away.

That had been her.

And that will be me again. There could be no doubt that if she were to stand in the way of Lord Oliver, he would exact retribution. The threat he'd made last evening hadn't been an empty one.

Reggie warred with herself. He'd promised her money so she could finally be free. So that she'd never have to look over her shoulder in fear that he'd be there.

And yet, having him step back into her life, she confronted the truth: he would always be there—from the haunted memories she'd always carry to the absence of the family she'd once loved and then lost because of her sins.

He would always have a hold over her . . . but she would have her hold over herself be stronger.

Even as it meant he would destroy her. It was an inevitability. A certainty. The Duke of Glastonbury would never calmly accept being thwarted by a village girl whose virtue he'd taken.

And then Broderick would know.

Nausea roiled in her belly.

Her past would no longer be a shameful secret that belonged solely to her and the duke who'd ruined her. She squeezed her eyes shut. He'd destroyed her life. She'd not allow him to do the same to Gertrude.

The carriage drew to a stop a short while later. Collecting her books, Reggie took assistance this time when Nerrie held a hand up.

With a murmured word of thanks, Reggie accepted her things and hurried along the pavement.

She was greeted in the foyer by a smirking Stephen. "Spark."

Reggie stopped abruptly. Why wasn't he in his lesson? That incongruity, a warning, tripped along her spine. There was no place for incongruities in life. They only ever spoke calamity. It was an age-old lesson of the Dials.

Looping his thumbs inside the waistband of his trousers, Stephen sauntered over with a cocksure arrogance surely inherent in any noble child's blood.

That dread strengthened, sending warning bells clamoring at the back of her mind. "What is it?" she asked without preamble. Ignoring the servant who came forward to gather her cloak, she took a step closer to the miserable cur.

"Gertrude found herself a suitor," he announced with a smirk.

She rocked back on her heels. Her heart picked up its beat. "She did?"

Stephen narrowed his eyes. "Did you think she wouldn't?"

"No," she exclaimed. "Of course I did." Just not one worthy of her, and there never would be. Relief coursed through her, and along with it . . . something else—hope. The duke had given Reggie a week to come 'round to encouraging his suit, and she'd been so consumed by the initial terror that she'd not considered there was another way out—for Gertrude and herself. She shrugged quickly out of her cloak. "Who is he?"

"A duke."

Chills scraped her spine. "A . . ."

"Duke." Stephen preened. "Glaston-something—"

"Glastonbury," she whispered. A dull buzzing filled her ears, drowning out Stephen's voice.

"Spark? You listening to me?" Stephen asked, a faint and unexpected worry there.

She snapped to. She didn't have time to stand here and debate the belligerent child. "Where are they?"

"He's in Broderick's office. Gert ain't back yet."

Oh, God. Panic threatened to choke her. "If she returns, be sure that she goes to her rooms and stays there." Reggie started forward.

"Spark?"

Reggie paused, glancing back.

Stephen flashed a lopsided grin. "Broderick isn't going to be happy that you've been running about seeing to your own business." He hung a fake noose about his neck and rolled his eyes sideways.

Muttering under her breath, Reggie resumed a path down the hall—albeit a quicker one for Broderick's office.

A suitor.

Lord Landon. He was tenacious in his determination to link himself to the Killoran family. First he'd courted Cleo and then Ophelia, and now Gertrude. How odd that he should now be the safer, best option for the young lady.

She staggered into Broderick's office and stopped.

By all intents and purposes, with the hothouse flowers in his hand, the gentleman seated in the winged leather chair before Broderick's desk may as well have been any proper lord courting a proper miss. But he was not just any gentleman. He was not any man. He was a devil with a soul blacker than Satan's, and Reggie well knew the evil that coursed through his veins.

"Hello, Miss Spark," he greeted with a cold smile. "What a pleasure it is to meet again."

Chapter 20

Retribution will belong to me, and no marriage your sister might make will save your worthless soul.

As Broderick entered through the front doors, Stephen sprinted over with such force he knocked into Broderick.

He caught the boy by his shoulders.

"I think there's trouble," Stephen panted.

Shrugging out of his cloak, Broderick tossed the garment over to a servant. Just once, he wanted to know a damned sliver of peace where doom wasn't around the corner waiting to upend his existence. He ordered the servants gone and turned to his brother. "What is it?"

Stephen tugged at his sleeve. He spoke, his breathless words hushed, rolling together. "She's causing trouble. Told ya, ya can't trust her. Gert's got herself a suitor, and she's interfering. Doesn't want us to—"

Broderick held up a staying hand. "Enough."

"Survive. It's her revenge. I know it."

"I said, enough," he said more firmly, cutting into Stephen's ramblings. "Who is causing trouble?"

Stephen slammed his fist against his open palm. "Damn it. Didn't ya listen to a bloody word Oi said? Spark."

Spark, whose name had become synonymous with "trouble." Broderick scrubbed a hand over his eyes. And then one of the things his brother had uttered registered. He dropped his hand to his side. "Gertrude has a—"

"Damn it, Killoran. Keep up," the boy cried. "Oi said she has a suitor. Not just any suitor." He paused. "A real live duke. Fancy looking. Wants to speak to you. Reggie just went in to see him."

A duke? "Who?"

"Duke of Glaston-Something-Or-Another. Dukes are more powerful than marquesses, ain't they?" Stephen whispered. "One of the whores said they're more powerful than anyone except a prince or a king." He slammed his fist down again. "And Spark is trying to stop it."

Bloody hell on Sunday. Why in blazes would she do that? He was already striding for his office.

Stephen hurried to keep pace. "Why do you think she'd do it?" Stephen whispered. "She's trying to destroy us. She knows we need that match. Only thing that makes sense."

No. That wasn't Reggie.

But then, neither did you believe she'd plot to steal your best staff and guard out from under you, either.

His brow dipped. "Is the gentleman a patron?" Reggie had been clear she'd never support a match between Gertrude and any lord in debt to Broderick.

"No." Stephen gave his head a shake. "Never seen 'im in the Devil's Den even once. Didn't recognize his name. Glastonbury," he blurted. "His name was Glastonbury."

His frown deepened. Then why should she interfere in the gentleman's courtship?

"She told me to not allow Gert near the gent. Told me to keep her in her chambers."

He continued past his brother, heading for his office. A pair of parlor maids stepped aside, allowing him to pass. With every step came more and more questions. Why would Reggie turn away a suitor? What motives could she possibly have? Or was it as Stephen said and her actions were driven by malice?

Impossible.

Broderick reached his office, and his gaze quickly took in everything.

The first thing he noted was the gentleman's nearness to Reggie. His bulky frame, angled toward hers, hinted at a familiarity between them.

Broderick hated him on sight.

The pair at the center of the room spun to face him.

Relief swept over Reggie's expressive features.

"Your Grace, how may I be of assistance?" Broderick asked, coming forward, deliberately omitting a bow for the pompous peer.

"I thought I might speak with you about a matter of personal importance pertaining to your sister." The duke glanced pointedly from Reggie to the doorway.

At that slight but telltale directive, Broderick narrowed his eyes on the visitor who'd order anyone in his household about. Those orders came naturally to one of his rank and bespoke . . . a ducal arrogance. That arrogance of Polite Society was the pomposity Reggie had spoken of and hated so much.

Reggie, however, remained fixed to the center of the room. Her lips moved, but no words came out. And then: "No."

The duke swiveled his stare in her direction.

Reggie drew in a slow breath and then brought her shoulders back. "His Grace would not make Gertrude a suitable match."

A ruddy flush marred the duke's slightly fleshy features. "Have a care, Miss Marlow," he warned.

"Get out," she ordered, leveling that order on the duke.

"Miss Spark?" Broderick gave her a warning look.

"Miss Spark?" the duke jeered. "You've not even given him your real name."

The color leached from Reggie's cheeks.

Broderick straightened. They knew one another.

The duke faced him. "I've come with honorable intentions to court your sister. And this one?" he said in nauseatingly affected tones. "She seeks revenge against me for crimes she is guilty of."

Reggie flinched but stood, her carriage as proudly erect as any military commander. "I'm guilty of nothing."

The duke turned his back dismissively. "Miss Marlow, otherwise, known as your"—he slashed a gloved hand in her direction—"Miss Spark." Numb, Broderick looked to Reggie. A stranger to him, with this man privy to her past. "She was my sister's governess," the duke said.

Broderick flexed his jaw. "Is this true? Did you serve in the duke's employ?" It was widely accepted and understood that every person in the Dials possessed secrets. But that this man should have them and Broderick find himself sitting an outsider, learning those secrets not from her but another, brought his hands curling into tight fists.

She wet her lips. "No. Yes." She tried again. "I was employed by his father."

Broderick stared on, the exchange like a volley match with his head swinging back and forth between the participants.

The duke pressed a hand to his chest and stared back at Broderick with stricken eyes. "I pledged my heart to her, my troth, and in the end, she sold herself to my closest friend for a bag of coins and a fancy pendant. And now"—he spun, lashing out at Reggie—"you would put yourself between a possible arrangement between . . ."

"Liar," she cried.

A thick tension fell over the room. The duke seethed. "You would question my honor?"

"I would and I am."

"Do you deny that you were my lover?" the duke demanded.

Reggie recoiled as silence met that charge.

Jealousy—violent, blinding jealousy—stabbed at Broderick. Making a mockery of the illusion of friendship he'd upheld with this woman who'd been a friend and confidante . . .

She peeked over at him, like a naughty child seeking absolution. Some of the fight went out of her. It was a confirmation. And it gutted Broderick.

His Grace adjusted the diamond stickpin in his cravat. "And what of my purse, Miss Marlow?"

Reggie shook her head. "Those monies were mine," she whispered. "I earned them."

"You are a thief."

An unfamiliar sentiment held Broderick in its grip—fear. "Enough," he said quietly, that order coming in part from a need to silence any other admission from this man's lips. "Miss Spark," Broderick said evenly. "If you'll excuse us?"

Reggie's stricken eyes met his. "I . . . of course." She released the death grip she had on her skirts and spoke calmly. "I would have you know he is a liar." Breathtaking in her boldness, she withered the duke with a hard stare. "And you can be assured if you allowed him to marry Gertrude, he would make her life misery." With that, head held high, she marched around the duke and quietly took her leave.

As soon as the door had closed, Broderick made for the sideboard. "My apologies," he said evenly, fetching two glasses and a bottle of brandy. Carrying them back to his desk, he poured two snifters full and held one over to the duke. Broderick made no move to sit but rather settled his hip on the edge of the desk. "Miss Spark is . . . spirited."

The duke accepted the proffered drink. "No apologies necessary," he assured, waving his other hand dismissively. "The young woman was always more spirited than is prudent for a lady to be. Particularly a young governess."

Broderick sipped at his brandy. "So you were quite familiar with my sister's companion?"

His Grace leaned forward, the leather folds of his chair groaning under that slight shift in his weight. "As a rule, I do not speak about my relationships with lovers."

All the muscles in Broderick's face went to stone. "Indulge me."

"Our affair took place ten years ago," the duke was swift to reassure. This was Reggie's past. This was the story of ten years ago. And he despised that the telling now came from this man. "I was young." The duke paused. "And I was in love with the idea of being in love with someone wholly unsuitable."

Wholly unsuitable.

Broderick offered the other man a steely half grin. "I trust no less suitable than a bastard raised on the streets who's lived more years than not in a gaming hell."

The other man must have heard something layered there in Broderick's speech. He blinked slowly and then sat upright. "You misunderstand."

Broderick arched an eyebrow. "Do I?"

"It was not the young woman's station that made her unsuitable but rather her actions. I was in love with her, and she was in love with the baubles and gifts to be had."

He stared over the top of the other man's head.

I don't need more than two dresses. I'm a companion, Broderick. Dull colors, drab garments, are suitable attire for a servant . . . Not cheerful, extravagant garments . . .

"Never tell me. She seduced you?"

"Indeed. Against all better judgment and my family's warnings." The duke spread a hand wide. "I was young. Just out of university. I believed myself in love with her."

Broderick's palm tensed around the snifter in his hand, his fingers straining the crystal stem. He forced himself to lighten his grip and then swirled the contents of his glass. "And you made the woman hired as your family's governess your lover."

The duke's ears turned red. "Yes . . . but"—he dropped his voice to a hushed whisper—"I did so fully intending to marry her. My family would never have approved, and as such, we eloped." That admission speared Broderick for the unexpectedness of it . . . and more.

She'd given herself to this man. Had, by this lord's accounts, very nearly married him. Broderick raised his glass to his mouth. "And yet you did *not* wed the lady." He paused. "Or I trust you do not intend to court my sister while being wedded to her companion?" He flashed another grin, taking the steely edge off that question. All the while, a slow-building hatred swirled in his gut, poisoning him against a duke who sought permission to court his sister.

A chuckle rumbled from the other man's chest, shaking his frame. "No." His laughter instantly died. "I was spared that fate by a friend." Glancing beyond his shoulder, he dropped his voice to a whisper. "Suspecting her of duplicity, he offered Miss Marlow a small fortune in return for her . . . favors." Broderick's body turned to stone. "The young woman *accepted*, and because of my friend's intervention, I was"—he glanced down briefly at his drink, a spasm contorting his features—"spared."

Broderick gave his glass another counterclockwise swirl. "Loyal friendship is a gift, indeed," he said neutrally. He briefly shifted his gaze over the top of his snifter, spearing the man with a look. "What was the gentleman's name?"

"Lord Adinbrooke."

Not a patron.

Broderick set his drink down. "I must confess to some . . . difficulty in reconciling the woman you are speaking of with the woman I know."

Not once in the years he'd known her had she asked for anything. She'd accepted his offerings with words of thanks, but when he was insisting his sisters don satin, Reggie had quite happily donned her coarse wool skirts.

"I trust this *would* be very difficult."

Broderick thinned his eyes into slits. "It is made more difficult as I knew the young woman ten years ago."

There was a slight stiffening in the duke's frame.

"She had neither baubles nor coins nor fripperies to her name." In threadbare garments, her hands cracked and bleeding, she would have never been mistaken for a privileged nobleman's mistress.

His Grace quickly regained his composure. "I don't know how to account for that," he said with a shrug.

No, neither did Broderick. Again, they were secrets belonging to Reggie, involving this very gentleman before him. He unfurled from his relaxed pose. "Do you know what I believe, Your Grace?"

The duke watched him cautiously. "What is that?"

"I believe Miss Spark is in fact correct." Broderick flicked a hardened stare up and down the man's frame. "You are a liar."

Sputtering, the other man came to his feet. "I beg your pardon. I am a duke."

Your single-minded determination to connect the Killorans to the nobility goes back far beyond Stephen. So do not suggest this venture to be vastly different . . .

The accusation Reggie had tossed at him days ago stung all the sharper now when confronted with the reasons for her resentment. "And I'm a man who can identify liars of any rank. If you believe I would accept any suit from a man who dallied with a young woman in his employ and then left her unmarried, you are a bloody lackwit."

The duke's eyes bulged in his face. "Well, I've never . . ." Giving a snap of his coattails, His Grace stomped over to the door.

No, it was likely he'd never been called out for his crimes.

"Glastonbury?" The duke stopped. "It is my hope that my sister will make a match with a nobleman . . ." He held the nobleman's gaze.

"But I'd have her find a man who is truly noble and honorable, and not a cur like yourself."

"How dare you? You'd question my honor." Red in the face, His Grace marched back to Broderick's desk. "Do you want the truth? You guttersnipes don't know a thing about Polite Society." He curled his lip in a derisive sneer. "You'd defend Miss Marlow as though she were some fine lady." Broderick stiffened. "But she is not. Nor has she ever been." Spittle formed at the corners of the duke's mouth. "She is, and was always, a whore. *My* whore."

Rage flooded him. Pure. Vitriolic. And lifelike in its intensity.

Broderick jerked his left elbow out, catching the other man in the cheek.

The duke cried out and cradled the wounded flesh. "My God."

Shooting out one hand, Broderick gripped the other man by his jacket and dragged him close. One inch taller than Broderick, the man was at least three stone heavier. Size, however, meant nothing in the Dials. "You may be a duke, but as you pointed out, I'm a guttersnipe from the Dials. Have a care with Miss Spark's name."

"You are mad," the man whispered, stumbling away. He smoothed the lapels of his rumpled jacket. "She has you under her spell." Understanding lit the duke's eyes. "The whisperings have been correct. She is your mistress now."

Now.

It was a throwaway utterance from an all-powerful duke. One solitary syllable. And yet a single word that marked the passage of ownership.

Only, Glastonbury didn't speak of a notorious mistress who'd shifted affections or clients or any property. But rather, he spoke of Regina.

A triumphant smile turned the duke's lips. "Why, it *bothers* you," he observed as if he were one remarking upon a newly discovered wonder of the world. "You plebeians with your pathetic emotions. You are jealous that I tupped Miss Spark." Ice glinted in his eyes. "And I'll have you know, I did so quite often—"

Broderick was on the man in two long strides. He buried his fist in Glastonbury's nose, welcoming the warm spray of blood from the bulbous appendage.

The duke cried out, crumpling to his knees.

Broderick bent down and stuck his face in the other man's. "You mistake me as one who cares about your rank," he whispered. Breathing hard, he caught Glastonbury by the front of his jacket and dragged him up onto unsteady feet. And with bloodlust pumping through his veins, he propelled him against the wall.

Chapter 21

You've made this entirely too easy . . .

With her belongings organized in neat piles according to color, Reggie gave a snap of her white cotton petticoat. The errant wrinkles shook loose, and she gave it another snap for good measure.

Focusing on that minute task kept her clinging on the brink of sanity.

This was what she'd wanted.

Reggie folded the petticoat in half.

Her freedom from the Killoran family.

She laid the neatly folded article atop the other crisp, white undergarments and reached for another.

Freedom, however, had come in the unlikeliest way and for the most unwanted reason.

Gus leapt up onto the bed and stalked across the coverlet, his claws sinking into the delicate satin as he went, making a mess of her piles, and then he stopped beside her. He nudged his small, soft head against her arm.

With a sigh, Reggie tossed a chemise aside, forgotten, and scooped up the grey-striped tabby.

Holding him close, she buried her head against his neck. He purred, the slight rumble bringing her a measure of calm.

The life draining out of her limbs, Reggie sank onto the edge of her mattress and simply clung to the cat.

The duke had destroyed her once before, and nearly ten years to the date, he'd done it all over again. This, however, was so very different from the shame of her past. Now her sins had touched the Killorans. And Broderick knew all. Or at least the perverted half truths fed to him by the Duke of Glastonbury. She tried to draw breath through her painfully tight lungs.

Gus squirmed and, tiring of her embrace, scrambled out of her arms and darted across the room.

Reggie resumed packing. Gathering the coarse wool day dress, she folded it.

And the worst of it was, after she'd said her piece and warned him about Lord Glastonbury's evil, she'd not been able to glean even a hint of what Broderick had been thinking. Or feeling. He'd been an empty palette, emotionless.

A sob squeezed from her throat and tumbled from her lips. What should he feel? He'd come to Mayfair craving respectability and a link to the peerage, and instead Reggie had visited scandal upon his household.

A knock came. The expected one.

Even as she'd anticipated it, however, her heart turned over.

When she drew that panel open, he'd no longer be the friend unaware of her past but a man in possession of her secrets and shame. Reggie came to her feet. On wooden legs, she crossed over and gripped the door handle.

And for one cowardly instant, she shifted her fingers to that lock. Thought of turning it. Thought of maintaining the illusion of the uncomplicated relationship they'd once shared and simply leaving without having to discuss . . . this.

Broderick knocked again. "Regina?"

Regina.

Not "Miss Spark," because he now knew it for the lie it was. And not "Reggie," because that had been the casual moniker of a friend.

Biting her lip, she drew the door open.

Broderick ran his gaze over her. "May I come in?"

He'd asked when he had every right to force his way inside and shred her for the threat she'd visited upon them.

And she would have preferred him loud in his anger to this . . . stoicism.

Wordlessly, she stepped aside. He strode forward, in masterful command of his steps, and then stopped, glancing around. Uncertain. At sea. Shattering the myth of infallibility. His gaze went to the pile of belongings still to be tucked into the valise and the sealed trunk at the foot of her bed.

And still he said nothing.

Reggie shut the door quietly behind them and leaned against the panel. She braced for his barrage of questioning and curses. Yet he offered her silence.

Where the duke who'd broken her before had laid command to when she'd speak and how she'd modulate her tones, this man allowed her that small-but-vital piece of control. She loved him all the more for that gift.

"I was ten and seven when we met," she began softly. A woman by the Dials' standards but naive in her understanding of good and evil.

Broderick clasped his hands behind him. "He is the reason you didn't wish to serve as Gertrude's companion," he finally said, breaking his silence.

"Yes." Her voice emerged threadbare, and she swallowed back that weakness.

"He indicated you . . . eloped." His gaze did another sweep of her belongings.

Look at me. Look at me, she silently screamed. Imploring him. Because this, his inability to so much as meet her eyes, spoke to her dirtiness in his. She caught her lower lip between her teeth. What else had he said? "I was young," she said lamely, hugging her arms around her middle. Age offered no pardon from one's sins or crimes. "I trust he shared all the details," she said, unable to keep the bitterness from seeping in. Every last sordid, shameful secret of her past.

He finally faced her. "I want to hear it all from you."

Why did it matter? He already knew. She saw the truth in the guarded way in which he now studied her, and she knew by his presence here. "My father inherited a baronetcy."

"Your father was a baronet." Surprise lit Broderick's usually guarded expression.

Oliver had not shared that detail, then. But then, the only hereditary honor outside the peerage would have never made her worthy of Oliver . . . or with his aspirations, Broderick. "By a matter of chance. He was just a commoner." A musician by trade who'd earned just enough in coin from his compositions to maintain a modest cottage for his three children.

She didn't want to wander this path. She didn't want to think about the father and brothers she'd left behind. And how she'd traded a loving family for a heartless cad.

A delicate brush of knuckles along her jaw brought her chin up, a fleeting caress that brought her eyes briefly closed and gave her the strength to continue. "How did a baronet's daughter come to be the governess in a duke's employ?"

A panicky half laugh, half sob built in her chest. *Bad luck. Desperation.* "An old, distant cousin died, and the baronetcy passed to my father." She stared at her belongings laid out; more items sat there than what she'd had in the whole of her life then. "Our journey to Kent was to be a grand adventure. I'd not even traveled outside of Manchester before that. We found ourselves in a new home, in a new place, and with a new distinction for my father. But nothing changed." Her throat worked. Not truly. Not for her family anyway. But for Reggie? From that moment on, nothing had ever been the same. "As far as our fortunes were concerned, there were no more funds than there had ever been. Papa inherited a small farm that hadn't yielded a proper harvest in the ten years before he arrived. We needed money." *My girl, my girl . . . you wished to see London and palaces . . . and now you shall . . .* "And then I was presented with an"—her upper lip curled—*"opportunity."* In the immediacy of Lord Oliver's treachery, it had been so very easy to resent her father for having sent her on to the Duke of Glastonbury's estates. As a woman grown, she acknowledged the truth. "My father knew I wished to see the world outside our little corner of England. He knew I craved . . . excitement." She gave her head a sad little shake.

A primal growl rumbled from where Broderick stood. "And so he sent you away as the hired staff for a duke." Such vitriol dripped from that statement, Reggie glanced briefly back at him.

A vein bulged at the corner of his eye. The evidence of his fury sent warmth coursing through her. She'd not, however, allow Broderick to lay her sins at the feet of her father. "What could be more exciting for a girl who'd only ever known a three-room cottage with one all-purpose servant than to find herself governess for a duke's children?" From that, she'd learned danger, evil, and darkness, in spades. Unable to meet his piercing eyes, she wandered away, stopping at the windowsill.

Reggie pulled back the gilded silk curtains and dropped her forehead against the lead panes. The sun's warmth left upon the glass acted as a balm, the illusion of a human touch. She stretched her fingers to the panels, trailing them along her own visage; the same freckles of her youth remained, but the faint lines at the corners of her eyes and the harshness of her mouth marked the passage of innocence. "I never thought to wonder at the sea of governesses who'd come and gone in the post." Her mouth twisted in a wry grin. "Oh, the villagers talked. Naughty charges. That's always the claim, isn't it? Blame the children, while the sins of the gentlemen"—in this case, the brother—"are forever pardoned."

What she wouldn't give to go back and trade it all. To have remained behind, longing for a glimpse of the outside world, while remaining unknowingly insulated from the reality that was life. "I learned soon enough. It hadn't been troublesome children to worry after," she whispered, speaking the words aloud not for the man immobile in the spot she'd last left him, but rather, for the first time—for herself. "Or the stern duke and duchess." There was something healing in breathing her sins in all their shame into existence. "Rather, it was the rakish heir I should have feared." A lesson learned too late.

She briefly closed her eyes. What a fool she'd been.

And yet to undo any of it would mean she would have never known Broderick . . . or his siblings. And for all that had come to pass, including these past days of resentment between them and the broken heart she'd take with her when she left, she'd not go back, even if there were some magic that might change back the hands of time. She'd not trade the moments they'd shared as a family, or all the lessons she'd learned about strength, courage, and loyalty.

But, oh, how she'd miss him.

Broderick didn't want to hear any more. He wanted to know even less. Reggie's tale was a familiar one that ended with a lady ruined and a rake going unpunished for the crimes he'd committed.

And coward that he was, having had the blackhearted cad who'd stolen her innocence in his very home, stating intentions to court his sister, made the agony of her past all the more acute. More real.

It was the rakish heir I should have feared.

He fisted his hands and, in a bid for pretended calm, leaned against the wall. "He seduced you." The words burnt his tongue.

"I fell in love with him," she corrected.

That quiet utterance stuck in his chest, the unexpected sting as sharp as the dagger that had sliced through Broderick's side fourteen years earlier. This was a feverish jealousy that moved through him in a primitive response that defied mere friendship and threw into tumult every understanding he'd previously carried of his relationship with Reggie.

She'd loved Glastonbury.

Suddenly, Broderick wished he hadn't tossed the bastard out on his arse. He wished he had him here still so he might bury his fist in his face all over again, shattering that damned noble nose.

Reggie's gaze caught his, and she must have seen something in his eyes. Some hint of the volatile sea of emotions roiling inside him. She shifted those wide aquamarine pools to the floor. "I *thought* I loved him. I realized I was so very much in love with the idea of being in love, and he was exciting and scandalous, and I'd never before met any man such as him and—" She abruptly cut off.

Did she take his silence as an indictment against her? Did she believe he somehow found her less worthy?

She turned back toward the window, and he ached to call out to her, urging her to face him.

"We were discovered in a"—her grimace was reflected in the windowpanes—"compromising position, and I was dismissed from my post. He insisted he could not live without me. Insisted that he would not, and we . . . planned to elope." A slow, agonized exhalation spilled past her lips, and he straightened, abandoning his relaxed pose.

"What did he do?" he asked on a steely whisper.

Reggie held on to the opposite ends of the window frame; her fingers curled into those sides, leaving her long, willowy frame in a tragic profile of supplication. "He didn't marry me," she said on a broken laugh that chilled him from within. "At first, he said he could not secure a special license, and then there was a need for funds, and . . . there was a host of reasons but never a marriage." As she spoke, there was a faraway quality to her voice. "If I'd been cleverer, I would have seen that he didn't take me to Gretna Green but to the slums of London." Reggie released her death grip upon the window, and the curtains fluttered back into place behind her. "That he intended to bed me but never wed me."

Broderick pressed his eyes briefly shut, and bile climbed up his throat. "You couldn't have known that." At their first meeting, even with the ill quality of her garments and the dirt smudging her face, he'd known Reggie Spark hadn't been one born to those streets. That she'd been like him in that way. She'd been too trusting. Too innocent.

"Not at first. But don't pardon my mistakes because of that ignorance."

"You were innocent," he said softly, taking a step toward her.

Reggie backed away. "I was stupid," she said with such bluntness he frowned. "I did not know who he was at first. All I saw was the dashing rogue who could charm a chambermaid with the same ease he could a countess." Bitterness dripped from those words. "He was a nobleman who actually spoke to me and didn't treat me like a fragile flower." Her words rolled over the next as she quickly spoke. "He spoke of a world that we'd create together . . . once we had the funds. And he used that glib tongue, and even when I should have so clearly seen that which was before me . . . I could not." Her gaze grew distant. "Or mayhap it was because I didn't *want* to see." Reggie's throat moved quickly. "I learned soon enough."

A chill scraped his spine.

With that ominous statement, Reggie returned to her bed. She began rearranging the existing piles already coordinated by color into neat, symmetrical piles of evenly stacked garments.

Broderick joined her, standing shoulder to shoulder. She remained fixated on her task, not offering him so much as a glance.

"What did he do?" he asked gravely, needing to know the demons that held her in their snare still. Needing to know the full extent of Glastonbury's crimes, so he could hunt him and destroy him with a ruthlessness befitting retribution found only in the streets.

Reggie gave her head a tight shake.

Broderick took her lightly by the forearm, forcing her to finally stop. "He *is* the reason you didn't want to serve as Gertrude's companion." *And not caring about why she didn't wish to come to Mayfair, I forced her to face that monster once more.*

"I couldn't see him again," she whispered, her voice so faint and so broken it barely reached his ears.

And yet that was precisely the hell Broderick had unwittingly visited upon her. With a groan, he yanked his fingers through his hair. *I forced her into the role.* She'd been a friend, a woman he'd been closer with than any other, his own sisters included, and in coercing her into the position and stealing away her choice, he'd proven himself no different than Glastonbury. He slammed his eyes shut. "Why didn't you tell me?" he groaned.

"Tell you what? That I was some nobleman's whore?"

"Do not say that," he commanded.

"What would you have me say?" she cried, spinning out of his reach. "Should I have told you how even though I despised his touch, I allowed him to use my body anyway?" He stiffened. *Oh, God.* He could not take this. "Do you want me to tell you how he beat me, and I let him do it, again and again?" A tortured groan spilled from his lips, and he reached for her. In her haste to escape his touch, Reggie tripped over herself. Her eyes were the ravaged ones of a woman whose soul had been shattered. "I stayed anyway," she rasped, her slender frame trembling. And then she sobbed. Collapsing to her knees, she hugged her arms tightly around her middle. "I s-stayed," she wept.

With a groan he fell to his knees beside her and dragged her into his arms. Reggie resisted, digging her fingers into his chest, and then she collapsed into him. She wept as if she might break, her tears soaking through the front of his jacket.

He didn't offer her false words or assurances. Or toss forth all the words of rage and threats he had for the bastard who'd dared touch her. For none of it would take away her suffering.

And so he simply held her.

These had been the secrets she'd carried alone and for so long.

Broderick buried his cheek against the silken crown of her curls, stroking his palms in soothing circles over her back. This had been what had driven her to the darkest streets of the Dials. What if he hadn't been there? His gut clenched, and he thrust aside the worry.

For he had been there, and their lives had merged in that moment, entangling forever.

Long after she'd ceased crying, they remained on the floor, wrapped in one another's embrace, and he continued to stroke her back gently. "It's not your fault," he said softly.

Her body tensed in his arms.

She released a shuddery sigh.

Broderick tipped her face up to his, needing for her to see his eyes and the truth there. "It is not your fault," he repeated. The guilt she'd taken on belonged to the bastard who'd hurt her . . . a man who'd violated her trust and her virtue . . . and something more: her soul. "None of it," Broderick said urgently. "It never was."

Reggie slid her gaze away. "It was," she said, sagging slightly against him. "I let him—"

Broderick placed a fingertip to her lips, stifling that self-guilt. "He was a monster. He wronged you. He hurt you." He'd harmed her heart, soul, and spirit. "And despite all the suffering he wrought, you emerged triumphant. You pulled yourself from his clutches—"

"You did that," she said tiredly, and then she drew back. He mourned the loss of her in his arms.

Reggie laid her back against the mahogany bed frame, and drawing her knees close to her chest, she tilted her head up at the plaster ceiling.

Broderick scooted over, joining her. They sat so close their thighs brushed.

"You approached me at London Bridge," he murmured.

Her body tensed beside him. "To sell myself," she whispered, and then glanced quickly about, as if fearing someone lurked nearby who could gather the secret they'd both tightly held on to.

And at last he asked the question he'd yearned to have an answer to for the past ten years: "Why?"

At her silence, he glanced over.

She dropped her cheek atop her knees. "For two sovereigns, he offered to let his friend bed me."

The loyal gentleman who'd saved Glastonbury.

Rage momentarily blinded him to everything so all that he saw, heard, and tasted was hatred.

"I gathered the purse that had been handed over, jumped out the window . . . and ran." Reggie lifted her head, and steel infused her spine as she sat upright, breathtaking in her fury. "Because to hell with him."

And with those five words, he fell. He fell so hopelessly and helplessly in love with this woman that everything that came before this moment ceased to matter.

"If I was going to have to sell myself, I'd choose who it was."

And she'd chosen him.

How easily it could have been someone else. Any other ruthless blighter in the Dials or caddish lord who'd have taken the gift she offered and left her nothing but a handful of coins in return.

And in the end, he'd failed her.

His chest ached. Drawing breath from his lungs was a chore. Needing to move, needing to run, he shoved to his feet.

The sight of her belongings brought him up short.

The floorboards groaned faintly as she stood.

He surveyed those piles she'd made. That had always been patent Reggie. From his family to his finances, she'd been one to organize—everything. He'd taken for granted that she'd be there, and in that, he'd taken *her* for granted. She was leaving.

"I know I cannot stay here," she murmured, her thoughts as always in synchronic harmony with his own. "He'll ruin you for protecting me."

"You believe I'd cast you out to save myself?" Broderick demanded sharply. Never mind that he had already roused the fury of that powerful foe himself. "Your opinion of me is that low?" But then had he given her any reason to trust him of late?

"Broderick, think," she said with a calm at odds with the tumult inside him. "He will be sure that everyone knows."

"I don't care." Society could go hang.

He started as the truth slammed into him—he meant it.

His life, his club, and the lives of so many hung on the balance of his being connected to Polite Society. But he could not . . . would not ever sacrifice this woman to achieve those ends.

A panicky laugh gurgled past her lips. "*You* don't care what a duke thinks? Come, Broderick—think. You, your family, the Devil's Den. I can leave now, and you can explain to the duke that you didn't know."

"I care about you."

Her lips parted.

Broderick cupped her cheek. "I'll not sacrifice you for a bastard like Glastonbury . . . or anyone." And with that vow, he left her there, silently staring after him.

Chapter 22

Yes, you've made this entirely too easy . . .

The Killorans were ruined the following morning.

Or rather, their ruin was printed in every last gossip column in London.

Nor was it a mad marquess who'd brought them low, but rather a duke bent on revenge.

Seated behind his desk, Broderick tossed down the scandal sheet in his hands. Three sets of eyes bored into him.

Faintly accusing.

Largely questioning.

He sighed, suddenly wishing he'd never allowed the fierce lot of them free say to question any and every decision or action that involved him or their club. Because the last matter he cared to discuss with any of them was the reason he'd thrashed the Duke of Glastonbury within an inch of his life. Jealousy, hatred, and resentment all wrapped together inside for the bastard.

Wordlessly, Gertrude turned the newspaper she'd just finished reading over to Cleo.

He clenched his teeth. "Do you really need to read every damned paper?"

"Oh, yes. We really do," Cleo said happily. She skimmed through the *Times* and then snorted. "This one claims you broke his nose."

"I didn't break it," he mumbled. Though he would have relished the pleasure of shattering that damned noble organ.

"You're certain?" Gertrude ventured. "Because by this account"—she briefly held up the page—"of slamming the duke's face into the floor? You very possibly could have."

"It wasn't the floor." It had been the wall. "And I didn't break it," he clipped out. There'd been blood, but he'd broken the noses of enough men to know when the bone cracked.

"Even so, if you did, there are actually procedures he might have done to—"

"I don't give a damn about the bastard's nose," he snapped.

Gertrude went owl-eyed and immediately stopped speaking.

Cleo snorted. "I haven't lived amongst the fancy sort long, but I know enough that this"—she tossed the paper over to land with a slap in the middle of his desk—"is not the way you're going to find yourself respectability."

He winced. No. "He was deserving of it." The papers had dragged Reggie's name through the pages as the former lover of a duke turned gaming hell owner's mistress. He curled his hand. Aye, he should have broken the damned nose.

"Either way, it's rubbish," Ophelia said, impatiently skimming those pages. "*Reggie* as your *mistress.*" She scoffed. "*Of course* the *ton* would come to that foolish idea," she muttered, collecting another newspaper and skimming the front page. "They don't understand loyalty and family quite the same. Otherwise they'd know she's like another sister to you."

There'd been nothing the least bit fraternal about the feel of her in his arms, the breathy moans spilling from her lips, swallowed by his mouth. Cleo fixed a probing stare on him. Broderick's neck went hot, and he fought the urge to adjust his suddenly too-tight cravat.

Ophelia cleared her throat. "The state of the duke's nose aside, I have a solution to the problem," she said quietly.

"Which one? We've a number of them," Cleo muttered from her spot at the window. Periodically, she scanned the streets below.

All his muscles knotted as he was besieged by the weight of his failings. By his inability to right the wrongs of his past. At not having answers as to how to fix this.

Ophelia smiled, looking entirely pleased with herself. "Yes, well, there are any *number* of problems I've solved. As you know," she went on, "there's the obvious threat of Lord Maddock. There's . . ."—she briefly faltered, sadness crossing her features—"the matter of properly restoring Stephen to his rightful position."

"Family," Broderick somberly intoned. "Restored to his rightful family."

"To a nobleman who, if he had any real honor, would have claimed his son the moment he learned the truth," Ophelia rasped.

Yes, his sister was correct on that score. The marquess had chosen to use Stephen as a pawn on a chessboard, treating him like an object to be used to torture Broderick. It only spoke to the man's madness. And yet . . . "He is the one who has a rightful claim to Stephen," he reminded his sister in somber tones.

Ophelia's features twisted in a mask of grief. "Yes, well, if I may continue?" she demanded hoarsely. "There is also Gertrude we have to consider . . ."

The eldest of his sisters bristled, sitting upright in her chair. "I beg your pardon?" Fire flashed in her gaze.

Ophelia waved a hand. "I meant no insult."

As his sisters quarreled on, he stared over the tops of their heads.

For the first time, he was unable to erase the threat hanging over him, his club, and his family. And yet Reggie had been correct. For all the frustration over his fallibility, there was a pride a father surely felt at the women his sisters had become. He would hang. Maddock's note all but promised it, each line of that letter dripping with the retribution he'd exact.

When he was gone, his sisters would remain—proud, strong, and courageous women who'd bow to no man. They'd stand tall when he eventually faltered. For they had one another.

And what of Reggie? What would become of her? A woman, making her own way in the world without family. And for the strength to be found in his sisters, Reggie had done something not even Cleo, Gertrude, or Ophelia had been forced to do: she'd forged a path in the Dials—alone.

And she'd do it again. After her time here was done.

Even as admiration swept through him for who she was, for the first time since he'd discovered her plans to leave, he felt something new settle low in his belly—guilt.

Out of his own hurt at her ability to simply leave, he'd set out to crush her as he had countless others before. *I saw Reggie as the enemy. I saw her venture as competition.* Broderick slid his eyes closed. He'd been so accustomed to destroying all in order to be—and remain—the best that he'd let that ruthless drive come before their friendship and her future.

Now he confronted the truth . . .

I don't want her to struggle.

There was room enough for both Reggie and him. Nor did he wish to wrest control from her. He wanted to see the world she ultimately created and support her, and it shouldn't have taken an understanding of her past to have accepted the rightness of that. A lightness filled his chest.

"Are you attending us?" Ophelia snapped.

Feeling three sets of eyes on him, Broderick flushed. *No.* "I am," he lied.

"We were in the middle of discussing the sacrifice you've required of us over the years," Ophelia went on. What a bastard he'd been. Ophelia briefly looked to Gertrude. "The same sacrifice you've recently asked that Gertrude make: marrying a nobleman." His sister smoothed her palms over her lap. "Now, Cleo and I came to Mayfair to marry a nob. We did it for the good of the club and for the connections you so desperately craved."

How empty that wish had been. When he walked the steps of the gallows, it wouldn't matter the connections he had with those respectable peers. His family—Reggie—they were all that had ever mattered. He'd been so consumed by his own thirst for wealth and power that he'd failed to properly appreciate the gifts that he did have.

He struggled to swallow around the emotion clogging his throat.

It had always been about them. Only now did he see how greatly he'd wronged his siblings—and Reggie. He'd wronged her, too. He'd manipulated them, using their love for one another. When it had never been anything more than a ploy to see them secure and safe.

So many mistakes.

But he could put them to rights now. This could be the last good he did before his time was up.

Gertrude finally spoke. "What exactly are you saying, Ophelia?"

"That there are other paths to respectability that do not require your sacrifice."

At that, Gertrude's mouth tightened. "Because I'm a wallflower. You don't think I can make a match."

"It is because of the scandal created by Broderick—"

Broderick spoke over Ophelia. "No," he announced. "It is because you deserve to find love as Cleo and Ophelia did."

Stunned silence met that pronouncement.

"What?" Ophelia blurted.

All along he'd believed Gertrude's security was dependent upon how powerful, how connected her husband was. Only to discover that having the love of a good, honorable man was what mattered. Cleo and Ophelia were testaments to that. Each of his sisters had married men who'd lay down their lives with no questions asked to protect them. "It doesn't have to be a nobleman," he said quietly to himself.

His sisters exchanged a look.

"Broderick?" Cleo asked hesitantly.

Ignoring his youngest sister's prodding, he kept his focus on Gertrude. "I want you to find love with a man deserving of you. I don't care what station he is born to." His throat bobbed. Reggie had opened his eyes to that. "As long as you're happy." Before he was gone, he'd have her know that. "I want you to find joy in someone who brings you a like happiness. Someone who is your partner. Who builds you up but who is also unafraid to challenge you to be a better person. Someone . . ." Like Reggie.

She had given him that gift. She'd shown him that a person's worth wasn't linked to their rank but rather to the strength and beauty of their spirit.

Shocked silence rang around his office.

"But at what cost, Broderick?" Gertrude quietly intoned, her meaning clear.

She'd sacrifice herself for me. All the while failing to realize he'd intended the opposite: her salvation when he fell.

In desperate need of a drink, Broderick stood and stalked over to the mahogany sideboard. "Out with it, Ophelia," he said, grabbing the nearest bottle and glass. Splashing several fingerfuls of whiskey into a tumbler, he took a long drink and grimaced.

"It is far easier to hang a gaming hell proprietor from the Dials than a nob from Mayfair," Ophelia pointed out.

Broderick dropped a hip against the sideboard. "It depends on which fellow you're asking," he drawled, lifting his glass in mock salute.

Gertrude scowled. "Your death isn't a matter to jest about."

Smoothing his features, he inclined his head. "My apologies. Ophelia? If you would continue."

Ophelia patted the back of her pixie tresses, those previously long, lustrous, near-white strands chopped off when she'd been in Newgate. Another failing. Another sister he'd failed to protect.

He grabbed the bottle and poured another drink. Eyed the contents of his glass and then topped it off.

"As I was saying, it's easier for Maddock to lead the charge for your execution when you're . . . you're . . ." She motioned to him as he made to set the bottle down. "You. It would be vastly different if he sought to execute a proper English lady's husband."

He paused, hovering the bottle just above the smooth surface of the liquor cabinet. "Why would they execute a proper English lady's husband?" he asked, puzzled, glancing around the room.

Cleo released the curtain, and her spine snapped erect.

"They wouldn't," Ophelia said, tossing her hands up in exasperation. She stared expectantly back.

He shook his head.

Ophelia nodded.

"She means you," Gertrude said with a quiet, dawning understanding.

Broderick froze. "Me, what?" he blurted.

Ophelia rolled her eyes. "*You* will marry a proper young lady with noble connections."

He . . . ?

His pleased-with-herself sister gave another nod. *"Youuu,"* she repeated, drawing out the syllable. "You've only ever wanted noble connections." She gave a pleased little toss of her head. "Well, now you can have them."

All he'd ever wanted . . . had been precisely that—a connection to the peerage.

She spoke of his marriage to a nobleman's daughter. It was logical. It was clever. And it did fit with every last wish he'd ever carried for respectability. A link, cemented not through his clubs but through marriage, had represented the culmination of what he'd aspired to. What he'd always wished to *be*.

Marriage to one of those ladies would give him entry to a world he'd longed to return to ever since Lord Andover had cast him out.

So why did the idea of it—marriage to a proper lady—leave him . . . empty? Cold inside.

For the first time since he'd put his request to Gertrude, he reconciled himself to the truth of how narrow minded and foolish he'd been. He'd asked her to bind herself to someone as a matter of business while denying her the right to be loved and love in return.

Reggie, however, had seen and known, and had fought him and his intentions for Gertrude at every turn. *And she opened your eyes to this, as well.* It was an awakening. A dawning understanding that had at last taken root and grown.

He'd been so fixed on building an empire, he'd not given thought to marriage. To any woman, *regardless of station*. His love, life, and mistress had always been the Devil's Den. Given that he'd treated his sisters' then-potential matches as more business transactions than anything, the least he should seek for himself was a like match.

It was therefore the height of hypocrisy and selfishness that he found himself wanting . . . more. A tall Spartan beauty with a tangle of crimson curls flashed to his mind. Wanting Reggie. He wanted Regina Spark. A woman who'd go toe to toe with him. A woman who'd be part of his life and business, whom he could share both with.

He froze. *My God. I want to marr* . . . The air hissed through his teeth.

"Broderick?" Ophelia prodded.

He set his glass down hard, splashing liquor over the rim, staining his fingers, marring the table. "I . . ." His voice croaked. Tugging at his cravat, he tried again. "My existence isn't one that allows for a wife."

It could, if it were the right woman . . . one who understands you. Who challenges you and demands you be better in every way . . .

Cleo scoffed. "You aren't the only Killoran who runs a business." Ophelia lifted her fingers in a proud, affirmative signal. "We are capable of love, marriage, and business all at the same time. It just takes work. And no Killoran has ever been afraid of work."

Nay. But neither were his sisters destined for the gallows. For Broderick, soon there wouldn't even be an existence when Maddock finally came calling.

Ophelia clapped her hands. "Given that Broderick *isn't* in love, debating love and marriage is rather a moot point. What we can and should focus on is his survival." Her lower lip trembled in the faintest hint of misery before she stilled it. "Marrying a lady and hoping the marquess is too polite to come for one who moves in his ranks—"

"He's a recluse," Gertrude pointed out. "He doesn't move in any ranks."

"—is really the only hope that I can see," Ophelia went on as though her elder sister hadn't spoken.

And just like that, a different noose was tossed around his neck, tightening, squeezing. He dragged a hand through his hair. "Our rivals were nearly destroyed when they married ladies." It was a pathetic grasp on his part at avoiding a fate that, as Ophelia pointed out, could spare his life.

Ophelia waved a hand. "You aren't like them." She shook her head. "You aren't like us." She spoke over his protest. "You joined our family when you were already a young man. You were well read and spoke the King's English. No one believes you are somehow the same. Not even us." She lifted a finger. "A nobleman would be glad to have your fortune, as would one of their daughters." Broderick finished off another drink, downing it in a long, slow swallow, welcoming the trail it blazed down his throat. He quickly refilled it. "You will have your links to the nobility." She dangled that promise that would have once been everything.

"No!"

It took a moment to register that explosive denial didn't belong to Broderick but another.

Splotches of crimson filled Cleo's cheeks. She adjusted her slightly smudged spectacles. "No," she repeated with a decisiveness that erased Ophelia's pleased smile.

"No?" Ophelia echoed.

Cleo nodded. "He can't marry"—she glanced over at him, and there was a frantic desperation there in her eyes—"someone he doesn't love."

"Do you think I don't want him to marry for love?" Ophelia cried, exploding to her feet. She stormed over to Cleo and jammed a fingertip toward the floor. "I do. I want him to know everything, every happiness that you and I know in our marriages." She dropped her voice, and when she again spoke, emotion husked her words. "But do you know what I want more? I want him alive." She looked back at Broderick, and a sheen of tears glazed her eyes. "I want you alive," she whispered.

"Did ya feel the same way when Connor was going to marry another in order to save ya?" Cleo snapped.

"It's not the same thing," Ophelia cried, lunging forward on the balls of her feet. "There is no woman he loves. If there were . . ."

If there were . . .

Reggie's freckled face flashed behind his mind's eye.

His heart knocked an odd, panicked rhythm against his rib cage. His palms moistened.

"Wot?" Cleo spat. "Then you wouldn't ask 'im to sell himself to some desperate nob and 'is daughter?"

"Broderick?" This time, Gertrude yanked him back from a muddled mess of thoughts that didn't make sense. "What do you want?"

Filled with a restiveness, he strode to the window. Locking his fingers behind him, he stared out those crystal panes to the streets below.

What did he want? After his own father had ripped up the Killoran name and left Broderick with nothing more than shredded honor, an empty currency in the Dials, his aspirations had always been clear. *These* were the streets he'd aspired to. He'd craved respectability. Honor. He'd equated all with a link to the *ton*.

And approval. He'd clawed his way from the bottom, reaching for the top, in the hope that he'd one day atone for his father's sins.

What his sister put forward, however, moved far beyond mere connections. Just like he had sought safety and security for them, she desired the same for him.

Nor was the irony lost on Broderick; she'd essentially turned his own plan on him.

His gaze caught on a passing couple, a young lady with crimson curls and a cane in one hand, on the arm of a gentleman. He leaned down and whispered something into the lady's ear, earning a laugh and a blush. She gave her partner's arm a playful swat. The ease of that exchange stirred a melancholy.

Broderick followed that pair, so comfortable with one another, watching the way they leaned into each other, the tall gentleman's gait deliberately matched to the crippled wife at his side. There was no frosty indifference there, but a couple who moved . . . as friends. What did he want? Broderick stared on as they continued past his townhouse before disappearing within a pink stucco residence.

That. I want that closeness. But not with any woman. He wanted it with Regina Spark.

He gave that truth light in his mind.

A realization that came too late.

A coldness washed over him.

For what he wanted didn't truly matter. It never had. His life had always been about something more: his family . . . and all those at the Devil's Den dependent upon him. He provided a home, food, and safety to people who appreciated the rarity of each gift.

And soon Reggie would be gone. She'd begin a new life on her own in her own establishment. There was no future there. Not with her. And then what became of all those reliant upon him?

An odd ache settled in his chest, and he discreetly rubbed at it. His efforts proved futile in even that.

He'd thieved, killed, and deceived countless souls. And now, if he went forward with this, he'd add selling himself to the list of sins that blackened his soul.

Ophelia glanced around. "It is settled, then?"

The noose gripped him by the neck and squeezed all the tighter.

There was, however, one last attempt at salvation he might seek, one that didn't include a bride.

One that was long overdue.

Chapter 23

No doubt you have convinced yourself there is still a way out . . .

With the Killorans assembled for another family meeting, Reggie found herself with the unenviable task of watching after Stephen.

Oh, bloody hell.

"Yeah, well, Oi don't want to be with you, either."

Splendid.

"I didn't say anything," she gritted, walking at a brisk clip through an empty Hyde Park.

Stephen quickened his strides, keeping up. "Yes, you did. With your eyes."

How did a boy see so blasted much? "Then mayhap you should try being a little friendlier."

"To you?" He snorted.

Reggie stopped abruptly and dropped the basket in her fingers onto the dew-soaked grounds. "You've been horrid to me since the night I found you outside that nobleman's residence," she snapped.

The color leached from his cheeks, and he rushed over. *"Shh,"* he ordered, slapping a finger to his lips.

She dropped her hands to her hips. "No. No, I won't be quiet. I was looking after *you* that night. I saved your blasted cap because I know it's your favorite." She flicked a hand at the very article. "And I said *nothing* to your brother about where you'd been." When she should have. After the fires Stephen had set and the unpredictability of his volatile temper, she'd owed it to Broderick to report all the details of that night. She took a quick step toward him. "And yet you've treated me as though I'm an enemy."

He flinched. There were few insults greater to one who lived in Seven Dials than that one. "I didn't want Broderick to trust you." He paused. "I thought you'd tell Broderick where you found me."

So that was what this had been about? She sharpened her stare on his face. "Well, then congratulations are in order. I gave you my word, and you succeeded in driving a deeper wedge between your brother and me on nothing more than a fear I'd turn your secret over to him." Though that wasn't altogether true. She was the one most responsible for the lack of trust that had developed between them. Stomping over to the basket, Reggie jerked open the lid and pulled out the gingham blanket inside. She gave it several hard snaps, and then not sparing another glance at her sullen charge, she sat.

Stephen hovered, shifting back and forth on his feet. There was not a prouder, angrier boy in all the Dials than the one beyond her shoulder. And yet . . . he wanted to join her. The moment she invited him over, however, he'd bolt like one of Gertrude's skittish cats. Reggie fished her notepad and pencil from the basket. With the tip of his scuffed boot, Stephen kicked a rock at her feet. The pebble grazed the hem of her skirts. She opened her book and flipped through the pages.

"Generally, if you wish for a person's attention, you say their name." Not even glancing up, Reggie held one of the stones aloft. "You do not kick things at them."

"Got it," he mumbled. He kicked another pebble; this time the well-aimed tip of his shoe sent the projectile flying in the opposite direction. "It's all your fault." His lower lip trembled.

"What?"

"Gert could've married herself a duke, and you came along and ruined it."

Her stomach sank. He knew. "Your sister would have never been happy . . . or safe with him."

"But he's more powerful than any lord in London, and you angered him and now Broderick."

She went absolutely motionless. "What?"

"'e beat him up. Real good, too. Might've broken 'is nose."

Reggie's mouth moved but the words ceased coming. What? Her thoughts ran together. He'd . . . beaten Oliver? "Why, why did you do that?" she whispered, dropping her face into her hands. It was an act that would never go unpunished, and Broderick, who craved respectability above all else, had raised the ire of a duke . . . for her.

Stephen sat next to her. "You all right?" he asked hesitantly.

No. "Yes."

"Did he . . ." His words trailed off, and she glanced over. "Did he hurt you?"

Reggie stared ahead. A breeze dusted the Serpentine, sending a small ripple across that otherwise placid surface. "He did."

Stephen said nothing for a long while and then cleared his throat. "I don't really hate you, you know."

It was a significant admission from a boy who hated everyone.

"And I don't think you're a miserable little bugger." She paused. "All the time." She softened that by ruffling the top of his head.

Stephen ducked away from that show of affection and adjusted his cap.

Her heart pulled. How different he would have been—how less fearful, more nurtured—had he found himself the cherished boy of a marquess. While his gaze was directed out at the swans, she studied him. How very different he'd been from her own brothers. Who had Cameron and Quint become in the years since she'd last seen them? Her throat worked. They'd be grown men now.

Stephen nudged her with his elbow. "What?"

She drew a breath. "Nothing." Reggie retrained her energies on the music notes she'd already put to page.

"They were going to have a meeting."

She furrowed her brow.

"Ophelia called it. They were coming over and didn't want me around."

The little boy stole a glance around and then spoke in a hushed whisper that she strained to detect. "Do ya think it's about 'im? My . . . my . . ." He shook his head, unable to force the remainder of that sentence out.

His father.

The man who sought to destroy Broderick and everything he'd built . . .

The man who was the reason Broderick prepared for his eventual hanging.

A lone warbler gave a mournful cry. "I don't know what it's about," she confessed. "I'm not afforded the same privileges I once enjoyed."

Stephen dropped his chin atop his knees and rubbed back and forth.

They settled into an easy silence, with Reggie resuming her work on the first musical arrangement for her eventual hall.

Stephen nudged her foot with the tip of his boot.

She stared over questioningly.

"Do ya want ta play with the racket and balls?"

For this boy, who cursed like a sailor and still thieved for his own amusement, there were so few glimpses of that innocence. Not allowing him an opportunity to change his mind, she fetched the set from her basket. "Here," she said, thrusting over one of the rackets.

"Ya ever play this before?" he called over as they got themselves into position.

She gestured for him to move back. "Oh, quite often." *I won again, Regina . . . Can we play another . . . ?* A wistful smile hovered on her lips.

He volleyed the first shot. "With who?"

The ball sailed past her racket and hit her in the knees.

"What?" she blurted.

Stephen rolled his eyes. "Who did you play with?"

"I . . ."

The approaching echo of a horse's hooves saved her from answering. Together they stared off into the distance, squinting as the rider drew closer. There was something familiar about that powerful mount. Shielding his eyes with his racket, Stephen moved his other hand to the dagger at his waist in a gesture of self-defense ingrained into all who lived in the Dials. Atop a monstrous black mount, a gentleman raced at a reckless pace, tearing up the grass as he went.

"Bloody nobs," Stephen spat, releasing the hold he had on his weapon. "They think"—he faltered, his voice fading to a whisper—"the world is their due."

"Come," she said gently, urging his focus away from the gentleman too arrogant to make use of the riding paths.

Stephen remained immobile.

She whipped her head between him and then the rider. What . . . ?

The boy dropped to the ground and crawled on hands and knees behind the boulder at the edge of the Serpentine. "Reggie?" he implored.

Letting go of her racket, she crawled over, joining him. She ducked down and made herself as small as possible against the smooth surface of the rock.

"You're hiding," she whispered.

"Shh." Pleading with his eyes, Stephen touched a fingertip to his lips and peeked around the edge of the boulder.

The rider, just beyond the clearing now, slowed his mount to a trot.

With his reins in one hand, the gentleman lifted the other to dust off his brow. All the while, he did a sweep of Hyde Park; there was a frosty deadness to those near-obsidian eyes that chased away the warmth of the morning sun. The stranger wheeled his mount but then stopped. He leveled a stare back over his shoulder, focusing on the abandoned blanket littered with items.

Stephen's cheeks lost all their usual youthful color.

After a moment that stretched out into eternity, the nobleman urged the stallion off in the opposite direction.

Her small charge's body sagged against their makeshift shelter, and he made no move to abandon their hiding place. They remained there in a safe silence until only the chitter of insects filled the morning sky.

"Can we leave?" Stephen whispered.

Reggie nodded. She hastily gathered up the items scattered about and, falling into step beside Stephen, moved quickly through the empty Hyde Park.

Stephen was the first to break the quiet. "Ya going to ask who that was?" he demanded, anger mixed with resentment. He was spoiling for a fight. She'd not, however, give it to him. That anger would only further destroy him.

"No," she said gently, not demanding answers or expecting them. From the boy's volatile response alone, she already knew who the dark-haired rider had been. "One doesn't pry into another's past," she reminded, dragging forth another unwritten rule of Seven Dials.

"One does if one's past catches up with 'em."

Another rule and a fair point.

Reggie stopped, and Stephen dragged his heels to a reluctant halt beside her. As she clenched the basket in one hand, she adjusted his crooked cap with the other, straightening the beloved article. "I don't care about the rules of the Dials. I have no right to demand answers about your past."

His throat moved. "He's my da." His da. Her heart ached for the loss known by both father and son. So many lives torn asunder by one unwitting act on Broderick's part. The Killorans' lives had been fuller for Stephen's presence, but another family had been shattered and a boy forever changed.

"And he's going to kill Broderick." Stephen unsheathed his dagger; the whine of his blade sliced through her thoughts. "Oi can always off him."

"Put your knife away," she said gently. "Violence is never the answer."

He hesitated and then tucked the knife back in his boot. "Sometimes it is," he mumbled.

Yes.

If ever there had been a man deserving of a beating, the Duke of Glastonbury was amongst them. Stephen's father, however, was different. "Your father was wronged," she said softly. "And he's hurting."

"Ya'd defend him?" he demanded.

"I'd imagine how he must feel." A heavy ache that would forever be present settled around her breast. "To lose his family. His wife. His beloved son. All the resentment you carry over the fact that he"—*will*—"might take you from your family . . . is how he has felt for more than eight years."

His lower lip trembled, and her heart cracked at that evidence of his vulnerability. A reminder that for all his bluster, he really was just a child. "Come," she said gently, taking his hand in hers. He made to tug it back but then gave a slight squeeze.

They resumed their quick walk to the carriage. Not another word was spoken until they'd completed the short ride to Mayfair.

As soon as the driver yanked the door open, Stephen jumped out. And then, reaching back, he held up a small hand.

Balancing her papers in one hand, Reggie accepted that offering. How she was going to miss him. And yet, if he remained in the Dials, he would always be the angry, volatile, knife-wielding boy. He deserved a new beginning. "Reggie?" he said as they entered through the foyer. She stared quizzically back. "Thank you."

He touched the brim of his cap and then darted off.

Tugging off her gloves, Reggie passed them off to a servant along with her cloak and then made her way through the halls to the music room.

She had not been there long before the faintest rapping sounded at the music room door.

Her papers sprawled over the top of the pianoforte, Reggie glanced over to the front of the room.

"Reggie." Gertrude lingered in the doorway, making no attempt to enter.

"Gertrude," she greeted, pulling the door wide. "Is everything all right?"

The younger woman cleared her throat. "No. No. Everything is fine." She glanced briefly down at the floor. "I am fine, that is." The other woman toyed with her skirts. "I wanted to thank you for your recent defense in the carriage and for saving me from the Duke of Glastonbury's attentions."

"I didn't do either for your thanks," she said gently. She'd done it because Gertrude deserved more. She deserved to find the same happiness her sisters had.

"No," Gertrude remarked. "But you spoke in support of me when I've been nothing but distant. I wanted to say, I don't know what your reasons were for"—her face pulled, but then she settled for—"doing what you've done. But I trust you'd never betray us. And I would rather your plans for the future did not interfere with our friendship." Gertrude held out her palm.

Reggie accepted that peace offering, and the other woman held her fingers a moment. "I am going to miss you so very much when you leave."

Emotion stuck in her throat. "I'm going to miss you, too." All of them. Even Stephen, who'd spent the past years making her life a misery when he could.

"And you . . . have to leave?"

She did.

Her decision was one of self-preservation. And given the scandal she'd brought down on the entire Killoran family, it was best for them as well. Loyal to a fault, they wouldn't cast her out . . . even as they should.

"I need to start over." Away from the Devil's Den.

Away from Broderick.

Her heart spasmed.

"You love him," the other woman blurted.

Reggie opened and closed her mouth, no words escaping; her thoughts twisted. "What?"

"Broderick," Gertrude whispered, that name the faintest breath of sound.

Brows shooting to her hairline, Reggie gripped her by the arm and yanked her into the room. She shoved the door closed behind them. "What are you . . . ? Why . . . ? I don't . . ."

"Of course—I don't know how I didn't see it," Gertrude muttered, pacing back and forth, her hem kicking up about her ankles as she went.

Deny it. Deny. Deny . . .

Nothing came out. Protestations would be futile. Gertrude could piece together any puzzle, and when she did, there was no shaking her free from those facts.

Gertrude stopped abruptly beside the edge of the gold harp and clasped the high curve of that instrument. "It's why you wanted to leave." She spoke with a hushed understanding, and horror filled her features. "And instead, I trapped you here. I threatened your future and"—her throat muscles moved—"forced you to be with Broderick when you sought to esc—"

"Enough." Reggie glanced back at the door. *Oh, God.* If anyone overheard and brought this discussion back to Broderick . . . Panic built in her breast.

"Broderick is not here," the other woman soothed.

But if Stephen discovered she had feelings for Broderick . . . Newfound loyalty won or not, he'd undoubtedly share that secret with his brother.

Reggie shuddered. "How did you . . . ?"

"Cleo said nothing," Gertrude was quick to reassure. "But when we met earlier . . . I just"—she locked her fingers and then stared at those intertwined digits—"finally saw the truth: you care about him."

Nay. She loved him. She always had. Reggie's stomach sank. Cleo. Clara. Gertrude. And more . . . who else . . . ? A secret did not stay a secret forever. Its future was cut all the shorter the more people who knew. Eventually Broderick would discover it, and she'd be an object of pity—and she could not be around when that happened. It would change the bond they'd shared in ways that even her betrayal hadn't managed to. For even with his anger these past weeks, he'd still always been . . . her friend.

A gentle touch on her shoulder jerked her back. "I wanted you to know: this morning, Broderick released me from the expectation to marry a nobleman."

Reggie gasped. "What?"

Gertrude nodded. "Cleo, Ophelia, Stephen . . . myself. We've all fought Broderick for years on this." Yes, they'd been clear in their outrage. "We tried to reason with him and convince him that our having noble spouses didn't matter." She plucked a chord of the harp. "And today, he went against all that." Reggie's heart lifted, joy spreading through each corner of her person. The young woman peered at her. "Why, after years of our debating him on that point, would he do that?"

Reggie hesitated, but Broderick's sister answered her own question. "Do you know what I believe? I believe it is because of you. You've been the only person to have any real sway over him. I believe you spoke to him, and because of that, he saw the wrongness in what he'd aspired to."

"You make far more of my influence with your brother," she said softly. Broderick was a man who knew his own mind.

Gertrude gave her a shaky smile. "And you make far less of it." Her expression of amusement was fleeting, and with the restoration of the young woman's usual somberness, a pit formed in Reggie's belly.

It was a whisper of dread that dusted a person with fear, an innate, heightened sense that came only from having survived the Dials. "What is it?" she asked, curling her hands.

"It was Ophelia's idea," Gertrude whispered, straightening. "I would have you know that."

"What was?" she asked hoarsely.

The young woman hung her head. "Broderick agreed to make an advantageous match."

"What kind of match?"

Gertrude gave her a long, pitying look.

"Oh." It was a whisper-soft exhalation that slipped out. A peculiar humming echoed in Reggie's ears. Numb, she walked over to the pianoforte. She leaned against the heavy instrument, and those chords pinged a haunting timbre.

"He did it to spare me," Gertrude said on a rush. "I believe that. He agreed to do this not because of who he was in the past," she finished lamely.

Reggie's heart splintered and then cracked in half. Who he'd been in the past? It was who he'd always been. Reggie stared beyond Gertrude's shoulder to the flames dancing in the hearth. His marrying another woman had been inevitable. Reggie, however, had believed she'd be gone long before he found the one who'd be his partner in every way—as Reggie herself had longed to be.

Emotion stuck in her throat, a miserable wad of despair that she struggled to swallow back.

For in all the most agonizing imaginings of who that fortunate miss was, Reggie had imagined he'd marry . . . for love. But through that eventual and agonizing match, she was never to have been around to bear witness.

How odd that this should also cleave her heart in two, him marrying his fine, fancy lady for no other reason than—

"Ophelia put forward the idea in the hopes it might save him from the gallows," Gertrude entreated.

Reggie bit down hard on the inside of her cheek.

He'd marry to save his life, and as one who put the fate of his staff at the Devil's Den before all, he'd also make that *sacrifice* for so many others.

She felt Gertrude's gaze searching her face. "Will you not say something?"

Reggie stalked over to the walnut sheet music cabinet. She absently sifted through the disorganized pages, tidying them into proper piles. "There's nothing to say," she said quietly. "This is best for you both. You never wanted to belong to the *ton*, and . . ." He always wanted into that world. He wanted peers for brothers-in-law and a lady for a wife. And ultimately, he got what he desired.

"If he knew how you felt—"

"It wouldn't matter." Knowing what was in her heart had no bearing on his own.

It was better that he'd never seen her standing there. She never would have been enough for him . . .

Gertrude wrung her hands. "He doesn't really want this. Not really."

Reggie smiled wistfully. "Your brother could take two pieces of coal and turn them into a fortune if he so wished." She looked squarely at the sister who'd so staunchly defend him. "Whatever he wanted, whatever dream he carried, he made it into a reality." And when so many faltered, Broderick had stood resolute in these streets, rising up and creating something that had saved so many, Reggie included. "He wanted this," she said softly. "Perhaps it is as you said, and his motives are different . . . but he always craved *more*." And in his eyes she'd always been, and would always be, *less* for her birthright. Or rather the lack thereof.

"You're wrong, Reggie."

Ah, Gertrude. So certain and so optimistic. It was a remarkable gift that invariably died in the Dials. Except with Gertrude. She'd long proven the exception.

"Why are you telling me this?" All of it. Any of it. Reggie's moments with the Killorans were limited, and she was no longer entitled to those intimate arguments that existed between the siblings. Arguments that she'd served as mediator for countless times.

"My Season is officially . . . ended."

The implications of that statement slammed into Reggie.

With Gertrude no longer intent on securing a match, she'd not be expected to attend *ton* functions, and Reggie's role as companion was—

Gertrude nodded. "You are free."

Free.

For all intents and purposes, she'd fulfilled the terms of her agreement with Broderick. She could be . . . nay, would be allowed to leave and start again with Clara. Their hopes for their own futures and the futures of so many other women who'd been so similarly shattered by life could at last be a dream achieved.

It also marked . . . goodbye.

She was required to say something. Express a proper gratitude. Except . . . "I will miss you," she whispered. All of them.

Tears glossed Gertrude's eyes, and where Reggie had fought them through the years, the other woman let them freely fall, proudly owning those emotions. "I will miss you, too." Her voice broke. She started over to the door. Gus darted out from under the pianoforte and rushed after his rightful mistress. Gertrude stopped, glancing back. "You deserve more, and I'll be damned if I let you remain and watch . . ." Broderick marry his flawless-in-every-way miss.

Her heart buckled. The woman he eventually married would be virginal and delicate and would serve in the role of hostess. She'd be everything that Reggie had never been. Nor could ever be.

Oh, God. Reggie hugged her arms tight around her middle. "Thank you."

"Stop that." The other woman offered a watery smile. "You are another sister to me."

With that, she left.

Reggie stared at the doorway. Time was marked by the noxious ticking of the clock, that errant beat that signaled the shrinking moments she'd spend within this household.

Broderick would marry another, and she would be far from this place when that happened.

Reggie slid her eyes closed.

Chapter 24

Your soul is so empty, not even Satan has a use for you . . .

Broderick had stolen, lied, and cheated in order to survive.

He'd never, however, whored himself.

Now he found his survival reliant upon one of those barters of his blackened soul.

The young butler studied the card, his expression impressively blank. "If you'll follow me?" he murmured and, without awaiting to see if Broderick complied, marched off.

Broderick started.

He hadn't been tossed out on his arse. It was what he'd expected. Swiftly concealing his surprise, he hurried after the younger man.

Two inches taller than Broderick's own height and at least ten years his junior, the servant had a fresh-faced innocence that belied the ominous note sent out by the ruthless lord who dwelled here.

But then, perhaps that was what madness did to a person. It drove out the soul and left a twisted version of one's former self who delighted in another man's misery.

You are deserving of that hatred . . . and the noose he wants to hang 'round your neck . . .

The soft tread of their footfalls waged war on the thick silence of the household.

As he walked to the meeting that would ultimately decide his fate and his future, Broderick took in his surroundings.

Portrait after portrait was draped in heavy black satin—with the exception of one. The blue enamel and jewel-encrusted frame hung proudly, surrounded on every side of the hall by a sea of black and mourning.

Riveted, Broderick stared at the trio memorialized upon that oil canvas: a plump babe with big cheeks and a wide, dimpled smile. *Stephen.* He staggered to a halt beside that portrait of his brother as he'd been all those years ago. *Nay.* His eyes weighted closed. Not his brother. Rather, the marquess's son, along with the mother and father who'd given him life. The trinity of proud parents and a beloved son had been masterfully captured by the artist. Joy stood still. Frozen. That family insulated from the hell that awaited them. The hell Broderick had wrought.

I have no right to be here . . . I have no right to ask for anything . . .

Broderick glanced back at the path he'd just traveled. And for a flash in time, he contemplated abandoning this meeting. Accepting his fate for what it was.

And yet to do so meant certain ruin for all the men, women, and children dependent upon the Devil's Den. Cleo and Ophelia now had lives outside of that club which had once been their universe. Gertrude had spent more years caring for the stray animals she'd taken in from the alley than learning the inner workings of the business. Those who'd suffered on the streets would likely fall right back to that empty existence.

"Mr. Killoran?" the butler called out impatiently from the end of the hall.

Broderick forced his feet forward.

At last the butler stopped. Reaching past Broderick, he pressed the handle. "Mr. Killoran," the young man announced.

Where the marble halls and satin-gilded frames had gleamed from the care shown them, the Marquess of Maddock's office provided a contrasting disrepair. Stacks of books and ledgers lay sprawled on every surface, from side table to leather sofa.

"Leave us, Quint," Maddock commanded, his gravelly voice revealing a lack of use.

"As you wish, my lord," the young man murmured and backed out of the room. He closed the door behind Broderick and his adversary.

Seated upon a King Lion throne chair, the burly gentleman was very much the king of this empire. He made no attempt to rise. Hands steepled at his chin, he studied Broderick from over those ink-stained digits.

Assessing. Watching. Evaluating. Soulless, deadened brown eyes that better belonged in the Dials and not these hallowed Mayfair halls.

Through that scrutiny, Broderick made himself absolutely motionless.

"Broderick Killoran," the marquess finally murmured, turning his name into a jeer. "Tsk, tsk. I must confess, I'd greater expectations for the most *powerful* man in the Dials."

That insult rolled off Broderick. He'd earned enough black eyes and bloodied noses as a hotheaded Irish-born lad new to East London, fighting anyone who'd even dared look at him the incorrect way.

Withdrawing from his jacket the letter that had haunted him since its arrival, he laid it atop a mound of ledgers. "What do you want?"

Lord Maddock dropped his hands, laying them upon the arms of his chair. His obsidian gaze remained locked on Broderick. "What do I want?" A harsh, rasping chuckle shook the other man's broad frame. "If you've not already ascertained just what I want from you, then you're even stupider than I credited." His laughter cut off.

This meeting was futile. Everything in Broderick said to leave, but everything he had, and everyone important to him, required he stay. As such, he'd play the mouse to this man's cat and hope there was a crack from which to slip loose.

"Though it makes sense why you'd come to grovel now," he taunted, gesturing to the papers laid out at the center of his desk. "The last of your hopes, ruined by a woman you were bedding and a sister who couldn't make a match."

Rage snapped through him. He planted his palms on those mounds of ledgers and leaned in. "You may toy with me," he warned, layering his words in steel. "You may threaten me and eventually see me hang, but leave their names off your lips."

Lord Maddock again laughed; that taunting, rusty rumble of empty mirth sent heat up Broderick's neck. "So you care about the lady. It's all very splendid. You ruined your last hopes for a powerful connection." He inclined his head, those golden strands an image of Stephen's. "Take heart—nothing and no one could have saved you."

Of course this man would believe that was the reason for Broderick's actions—the desire for noble connections. He'd not see that it was always about putting his family's future to rights. "I did not give the order for your home to be burnt," he said quietly.

"My family," Maddock rasped, surging forward in his chair, the first crack in the man's otherwise steely facade. "My *family* was burnt. My wife. My unborn babe." Little flecks of madness glimmered in the tortured marquess's eyes. And Broderick's insides twisted. The man he'd given his allegiance to was to blame, but Broderick had supported him. "My son was taken from me," the marquess said flatly.

"I had no knowledge of your son's kidnapping." But he'd given the orders all the same. His ownership of that vile deed came from that command.

Maddock went on as though Broderick hadn't spoken. "And then you'd attempt to foist one of Diggory's bastards off on me." He slammed his fist onto his desk. Several piles of ledgers tumbled over the edge and landed with a noisy *thwack*. Flecks of dust danced around the air. The marquess peeled his lips in a sneer that heightened the harshness of his features. And then he settled back in his throne chair, shifting back and forth on that seat, bent on reining in that show of emotion. "This past week, while you raced about London trying to find your sister a husband and yourself a way out of your eventual fate, I've sat here." He spread his arms wide. "Waiting. Reveling in the moment. Because checkmate was declared long ago. But you?" He quirked one eyebrow, continually taunting. Baiting. "You still believed there was a way out. You thought you might find a lord in London who'd intervene on your behalf when I eventually came to collect."

It was an unfamiliar place to be for Broderick. On the opposite end. With someone else pulling the strings of one's life. There was a hopelessness here. A bleak desolation that came in discovering how powerless one truly was.

And this was how so many other men had felt . . . with Broderick at the other end of power. He should leave. There was nothing to say. No begging, pleading, or reasoning that would halt what this man, mad for the losses he'd suffered, intended. And yet he forced himself to stand there because he'd tired of running from him. "I thought perhaps peace might be possible."

"Pfft." The marquess scoffed. "Arrogant and hopeful until the end. But that is what you people do. You survive. You scurry about like cockroaches, escaping gaol, a hangman's noose, a constable's capture. But not this time." His eyes bore the glimmer of a man possessed. "This time, I'm going to end you. I'm going to take down your empire and leave those street rats you call siblings mourning for their guttersnipe brother."

"Stephen is your son," he said quietly.

"Get out," the marquess thundered, exploding to his feet with such force the chair toppled behind him. A crack in his kingdom. His chest heaved, and his face flushed. Maddock closed his eyes briefly. When he opened them, those dark irises had been transformed to their deadened state. "You asked what I want? Your ruin. And I'll have it. You'll not know when it's coming. You'll mayhap think yourself able to escape your fate. Now, get out," he spat.

Broderick quit the marquess's office. Where revenge was exacted swift and precise in the Dials, the marquess was so mad he either didn't know or care about all that might go wrong in one's waiting. And that was the only fledgling of hope to take from this.

The butler, hovering in the hall, jerked to attention. "This way," he said tightly, motioning for Broderick to proceed. When they reached the hall, a servant stood in wait with his cloak. The butler took the garment from the footman and tossed it hard at Broderick.

He caught it against his chest.

"You are deserving of it, you know. Any revenge he exacts." He jerked the door open. "Get the hell out."

Even with that ire directed his way, there was a loyalty to the lanky young man Broderick appreciated. "I know," he said quietly, shrugging into his cloak.

Gathering the reins of his mount from the street urchin he'd handed him off to earlier, Broderick tossed over another purse.

"Ya're Killoran, ain't ya?" the boy whispered, a reverent awe there.

He stiffened.

"They say ya're hiring children. Lots of them."

He had been. Not because of any honorable idea on his part, but because of his sister. It was a hard day when one looked at oneself and found how little good there was in him. "I am." He tugged out a card and handed it over. "Ask for the guard MacLeod. Inform him that I sent you and urge him to find you work."

The painfully thin lad's eyes formed round circles. "Ya 'aving a laugh?"

He started. The high-pitched timbre revealed not a small boy but rather a girl. Similar in age and size to Cleo when Broderick had first entered the Killoran gang. "I'm not. MacLeod will help you." But then, who would help her thereafter? Broderick's stomach twisted.

Climbing astride his mount, Broderick guided the horse on. He rode through Mayfair and Grosvenor Square, those exalted streets home to London's luckiest, and then continued on until the streets grew narrower and the cobblestones grimier but the crush of bodies thicker, even as the night sky rolled in, ushering a cover of darkness that opened up the Devil's playground. Whores crept from the alleys and found their places alongside crumbling walls. Children wove through throngs of passersby, their desperate gazes trained on the next purse.

This was the hell he'd come to call home, and it had been for the family he'd found in his sisters and Stephen . . . and Reggie.

He closed his eyes. Reggie, whose loyalty and friendship he'd repaid with resentment. And sitting there, he confronted the truth . . . he didn't much like himself. He'd been so bent on survival . . . nay, not survival, but rather on being the best, that he'd not given a thought to whom he'd wronged on his way to the top of his empire.

The marquess.

Stephen.

His sisters.

And now, Reggie.

They had all paid the price in some way.

Some sins had been unwitting on his part, but they were marks against his soul still.

And Reggie had known it. She'd called him out on his ruthless determination, seeing what he'd been unable to, the soulless world of the peerage. He smiled wistfully. But then, that had always been Reggie.

More clever than most, she'd forever been unafraid to challenge him when he was wrong.

Loud shouts broke out in the distance, and his mount danced nervously under him.

Giving his head a shake, Broderick wheeled the horse around and then guided him across London toward home. Dismounting outside the townhouse, he handed the reins over to a servant and climbed the steps.

"My lord," the butler murmured, taking his cloak.

Broderick had one foot on the bottom of the stairs when Stephen came sprinting down the narrow hall. He skidded over the slick marble and slid into Broderick.

"Whoa," he said, steadying the boy by his shoulders. A wave of emotion threatened to overtake him.

"Did ya meet him?" he whispered after the servants had slipped off.

Just this morn, there would have been a panic at the risk of so much as breathing aloud the hint of the "him" in question. After his meeting, Broderick was overcome with a calm acceptance.

He sank onto the bottom step and motioned to Stephen. "I did," he said after his brother sat beside him.

"And?" Hope glimmered in Stephen's eyes. Lord Maddock's eyes.

Broderick shook his head slowly.

All light went out of Stephen's gaze. "No."

"Yes," Broderick countered.

And then a shuddery hiss seeped past Stephen's gaping front teeth. "You've given up."

Broderick dropped his elbows onto the step behind them. "I've accepted the reality of my situation," he countered. For there was a difference, and before he swung, he'd leave the boy with that final lesson. "When one lives a life of crime . . . even if it is about surviving, eventually one must face a reckoning for those sins." When one lived a life of evil, eventually it caught up with a man.

"You're a coward," Stephen cried, scrambling to his feet. "I don't care what you say. You've given up. And I was wrong to believe you were strong and powerful. Because you aren't." Each word struck like a blade through the flesh. "You're weak. And a coward, and I wish you'd never taken me in." And with that damning shout soaring around the foyer, Stephen scrambled around him and then darted up the stairs.

Broderick scrubbed a hand over his face.

Damn this day.

A soft tone pierced through the nighttime still.

He slowly lowered his hands and strained for another faint hint of that sound.

Silence again descended on the household.

Then it came, again. The faintest echo from deep within the house, once familiar but long forgotten—until now. Pulled toward that sound, he followed it. He continued walking, drawing forward, deeper into the foreign home. With every step the sounds grew crisper, clearer, and then they stopped, bringing him to an abrupt halt.

He remained motionless, yearning for that melodic pull, and then it came again. Only clipped in a staccato beat. Intermittent. Deliberate. Those strident sounds compelling in their own right for their dissonance, there was a pattern that, as he thought he'd worked it through, shifted and twisted into another arrangement.

Broderick increased his stride until he reached the end of the hall. The door sat slightly ajar, the faintest glow cast by one of the sconces spilling through the entryway. He angled his head back and forth in a bid to make out the figure seated behind that pianoforte.

Her head bent, wholly engrossed, Reggie paused to scribble something on a sheet laid out before her.

Her eyebrows came together into a line.

In the end he was given away not by a careless floorboard or by a misstep on his part.

Hissss . . .

But rather by his sister's damned cat.

Reggie's fingers slid off the keys, and she jumped to her feet.

He winced, grateful for the cover of darkness that hid the guilty color splotching his cheeks at having been caught sneaking. Nay, not sneaking. Watching her. "Miss Spark," he drawled. They were the first words they'd spoken since she'd opened herself up before him. And it was also the first time he'd ever been without them around this woman.

"Broderick." She didn't return that stiff formality but rather nudged her chin up and laid bold command to his name as though she had a right to it. And she had. For so long. How much more he'd preferred those syllables rolling off her lips as an entreaty for his touch.

A proper gent would have offered a polite bow and left her to her privacy.

Broderick had abandoned proper long ago. Restless and haunted by demons, he didn't want to be alone with them. Nay, he wanted to be with her. Reggie, who'd always been there, a confidante and friend. And given the bastard he'd been, he wasn't deserving of her company. He took it anyway. Pushing the door wider, he stepped inside.

Of its own will, his gaze worked a path over her. She'd abandoned her muslin skirts for a modest ivory nightshift and wrapper. At some point the ties she'd belted at her waist had loosened. The cotton article gaped ever so slightly, revealing a tantalizing hint of skin, more enticing than the green silk creation that had expertly draped her frame.

He swallowed hard. *I am a bastard in every way.*

Removing the box of matches and cheroot from within his jacket, he lit the scrap. "I heard you . . . playing," he said, shaking his hand once and putting the flame out.

There were dark circles under her eyes. She was a woman haunted. And that truth ripped at him. "I was unable to sleep and thought I might . . . work."

As Reggie tidied her space, her wrapper fell slightly open, revealing another flash of creamy-white skin and a hint of freckles that teased.

Drawing his mind with questions of how far those alluring little specks traveled and the pattern they made upon her skin.

Reggie piled all the pages together and drew them protectively close, shielding the words written there.

Ah, innocent Reggie. She believed the source of his focus had been the ideas penned upon those pages and not the flash of creamy-white skin now hidden from sight. Glastonbury may have stolen her virtue, but she remained an innocent in every way that mattered. Broderick picked up a lone page and held it before her face, waving it lightly back and forth. "You forgot one, love."

She made a grab for it, and the awkward pile shifted; the pages slid from her hold and rained down, fluttering between their feet.

An impressive sailor's curse exploded from Reggie's lips. Very naughty. Very dark. And not at all Regina Spark.

Finding himself smiling, the first real expression of amusement since his world had been ripped apart this latest time, Broderick fell to a knee.

"I don't require help," she said, her fingers moving frantically to gather up the papers strewn about. Reggie tugged the pages from his hands, adding them to her stack. Aye, she had a right to her suspicion. He wasn't a man to be trusted, and certainly not one to turn over the secrets of one's business ventures to. Only . . . this curiosity wasn't born out of competition but out of a genuine desire to know . . . about her. "You needn't . . ."

Broderick opened his mouth to offer a flippant reply and stopped. His gaze snagged on the neat marks upon the page in Reggie's hand.

He puzzled his brow. Picking up the nearest sheet, he studied it for a long while. Reggie sank back on her haunches. Silent. Unmoving.

Broderick grabbed another page, and this time she was unresisting as he examined her work.

Why . . . why . . .

"The Last Rose of Summer?" At her answering silence, Broderick lifted his head. "It's music."

Surprise lit her pretty eyes. "You can read it."

"And you can write it." He stared wistfully at the instrument. How many years had he spent playing? After he and his father fled the earl's properties, he'd not allowed himself to think back to all those pursuits he'd once enjoyed. They'd been frivolous and offered a man nothing in terms of survival. Broderick smiled sadly. "Most fathers would have been horrified that their son would rather be playing a pianoforte and composing original songs than riding or partaking in other boyish pursuits." A memory flashed behind his mind's eye. His father tapping his foot livelily while he skillfully struck the chords of his fiddle. All the while Broderick had danced a quick Irish step to those songs. *And I'd forgotten all of that about him . . . until this moment.* "My father was a master with the fiddle." That reminder slipped out, for himself as much as the woman beside him. "He made his own."

"I insisted mine play the Sligo style with his fiddle."

"Your father had one as well?" he asked.

"Had one?" She snorted. "He made his own and every night would play." All these years, that had been an unknown bond they'd shared. Before he could formulate a response through his shock, Reggie tipped her head back and forth and hummed a quickened tune. "I favored the o—"

"Ornamentation," he supplied, sitting forward, craning closer to her.

Her eyes sparkled. "Precisely."

They shared a smile.

He sank back. How much he'd forgotten . . . all of this. Any of it. What had become of that beloved instrument? In their hasty flight, the article had been left behind, and Broderick hadn't thought of it since.

Mayhap because you haven't wanted to think of it . . .

Reggie had made him think about . . . so much. Not just life inside his clubs and his quest for power and stability but the joys he'd once known and then let himself forget. And his father. He'd spent all these years hating him so that he'd forgotten the happiness they had shared as father and son.

Unnerved by her scrutiny, Broderick gathered up the remaining pages and set them down on the pianoforte. He stood and then held his spare hand out, helping her to her feet. His palm tingled from the heat of her touch.

He took a draw of his cheroot and blew out a small plume of smoke.

Once she'd finished organizing the stacks upon stacks of papers on the surface of the pianoforte, she picked them up and turned to leave.

"Stay?" he asked quietly. "Please."

Reggie hesitated, and for a moment he believed she'd send him to the Devil as he deserved.

She set down the burden in her arms.

"I am going to hang." Broderick took another pull from his smoke, needing her to understand when no one else did. Not even his siblings because he'd kept them deliberately out.

Reggie's entire body jerked like he'd run her through. "What?"

"I am going to hang," he repeated. He stamped out the remainder of his cheroot and tossed the scrap onto a nearby porcelain tray. At last, he'd uttered the truth aloud. Five words that, before this, he'd prefaced with "probably" and "likely" . . . when all the while he'd known.

The long column of her throat worked. "You don't know that."

"Oh, I do. I know precisely what my fate is." It had been ordained long ago. "Nor did I hope to marry Gertrude off to save my neck." He wasn't so naive as to believe that his sister's making a connection would see him pardoned from the crime of kidnapping a nobleman's firstborn son and heir. "Just as I didn't seek noble connections for Cleo and Ophelia for my own gains. Everything we've built"—because she as much as his siblings and the staff who'd called the Devil's Den home had made it what it was—"it will eventually all be lost. Empires rise and they fall. My club is no different. And neither am I." There; he'd at last forced the words into existence. He braced for the tightening about his throat at the mere mention of his fate. That did not come. There was something freeing in taking ownership of his eventual future. He'd been rushing frantically all over London intending to put his life in order. Only to find himself . . . free. Broderick filled his lungs with a deep, cleansing breath.

Reggie's face crumpled.

He chuckled. "Come, you're going to have me believe you'll miss me when I'm gone."

"Don't say that," she whispered.

Broderick lifted one shoulder in a slight shrug. "It's true." He held her stare. "I'll fall, but when I do, I'll know that all my sisters' fates are secure. They won't find themselves one day at London Bridge offering themselves to some undeserving bounder such as myself."

Chapter 25

You are a blight upon this earth. Your life means nothing to anyone. And the world will rejoice when you're erased from existence.

She didn't want to know his motives.

She didn't want to understand the reasons behind his sick obsession with the peerage or why he'd marry his flawless lady.

It had been easier to resent him when he was the ruthlessly driven proprietor who put his gaming hell empire and his fascination with the *ton* above all.

She'd never questioned the reasons he so admired the nobility, but now she knew.

He was a man putting his business to rights before he hanged. He'd been preparing for this moment long before Lord Maddock had threatened him.

A pressure weighed on her chest. He'd escaped certain doom countless times. She'd patched up wounds that would have killed weaker men.

But this . . . this was different. Reggie's own past had taught her that one didn't cross a nobleman. Not without eventually being brought down. She'd escaped it, as had Broderick. Eventually, they'd all fall to that power.

Reggie trailed her gaze over his face. "You've always sought to create an order to people's lives." He tensed. She took a step closer, willing him to see. "People aren't a puzzle. You can't put the pieces of their existence into a neat frame and make their problems go away."

His jaw clenched.

"There's no shame in being human. You need to let go and allow your siblings"—*and me*—"the freedom of choice." She gave him a small smile. "Even if the decisions they make aren't ones to erase problems or build empires."

"I want her to be safe," he said almost pleadingly.

And then the truth slammed into her.

He was trying to explain his motives—to her. He wanted her to understand why he'd sought a link to those peers she so despised.

"Will she find safety if she marries a powerful peer? What if she weds one such as Glastonbury?" His cheeks went ashen. "It's time you ask your sister what *she* wants. What life she prefers."

"And what of you, Regina?" His eyes scoured her face. "What do you want?"

"Me? I prefer the raw honesty in the ruthlessness of the Dials." Far more than she did the world he was so very determined to join.

A frosty glint lit his eyes. "I'd sooner cut a blighter from the Dials than see either you or Gert married to one."

"At least in dealing with a thief and sinner, one knows precisely what drives them." One didn't risk making a misstep that would see one destroyed, as she'd been so taken down by Lord Oliver. Rather, one knew how to proceed, and invariably it was always with an eye out.

"Answer me this, Regina." *Regina.* How she loved his full command of her name. It bespoke an intimacy that even though false conjured the myth of more. He drifted closer. "Had you been a nobleman's daughter, would you have found yourself on London Bridge with a bounder such as me?" he asked without recrimination.

She stared at the chiseled planes of his cheek, the faintest half-moon scar at the corner of his left eye that she herself had cared for. "I wouldn't," she said softly. Rather, she'd found herself there because of one of those nobs whose worth he elevated. And yet she'd been safer with him than any nobleman. Never once had he expected repayment in the form of her body. He'd required nothing. He'd entrusted her and his sisters with responsibilities no man of any station bequeathed to a woman. And in that goodness, he'd snagged each corner of her heart.

He lifted a finger and wagged it. "That is precisely my point."

Reggie set her papers back down on the pianoforte. "Marrying a nobleman does not mean a young woman will be cared for." Lord Oliver's hated visage flashed behind her mind's eye. "It will see her rank elevated, but you know, Broderick, you have seen the gentlemen who come to your tables. They lose fortunes. They beat women." *Please. Please, don't . . . I'm so sorry. Do not . . .* Her cheek throbbed in remembrance of a fist that had rained down with a staggering frequency. She cleared her throat. "They"—she forced the words out past the thick shame clogging her throat—"bed women outside the bonds of matrimony. You know that. You've *seen* that." And she'd lived it.

He said nothing for a long while. And then: "Not all gentlemen are like . . . him."

Reggie tipped her chin up. "Have you seen honorable ones amongst their ranks?" she countered. The ones who visited the Devil's Den were the basest lords who cared for nothing outside their own pleasures.

"I have." At that somber admission, she drew back. "My . . . godfather was."

"Your . . . ?"

"Godfather," he supplied. "Yes, I had connections to the nobility." He followed that with a wink. "Not by blood, however," he clarified. And then he said nothing more.

"But . . . but . . ." Her questions ran together, jumbled in her mind.

"How did I come to be here?" He plucked free one of the queries there. "A thief's blood runs in my veins." As he spoke his gaze grew distant, and she knew the precise moment he'd forgotten her presence. "My da attended Trinity College with an English earl. They were the best of friends, and when Lord Andover was summoned home upon the death of his father, he took my father with him. Named him his man-of-affairs and set him up on his estates. I never knew my mother. She died birthing me. Instead, I grew up on those properties with my father and an earl who never managed to have children of his own. I wanted for nothing." He absently picked up the music she'd been composing before he'd arrived. Broderick turned it over in his hands, lingering on the notes.

A short while ago she would have wrenched it from his fingers and demanded possession of those pages and her secrets. Now she wanted ownership of his. He set them down. "I had the finest tutors. The best garments and horseflesh. There was nothing I wished for. I was treated as well as any nobleman's son, except for one slight distinction . . ."

"You didn't have noble blood."

He credited that with the reason he'd found himself alone on the streets of the Seven Dials.

"Aye. I merely had a godfather who entrusted my da with . . . everything. His records. The hiring and firing of the household staff." The long, muscled column of his throat moved. "All his finances."

A thief's blood . . . "He stole from him."

Her statement snapped his attention back. His lips curled in the corners in an empty half grin. "Aye," he said with a flawless Irish brogue.

And yet . . . Reggie chewed at her lower lip. "What happened to him?"

"He offed himself." He spoke with a casualness that was belied by the tortured glint in his blue eyes. There it was. The darkest of sins that was taboo to even whisper.

Oh, God. Her gut clenched. At her darkest time, when she'd contemplated a jump into the Thames, there had only been a shamed father and siblings left behind. There had been no child. Whereas Broderick had gone from a privileged life to one . . . alone. Resentment chased away the grief for the young boy he'd been. "No," she corrected. "Your godfather. What happened to him?"

Broderick reached inside his jacket and withdrew that box of matches and cheroot.

Reggie plucked them from his fingers and set them down atop her belongings. "You don't even like them," she gently chided.

He frowned, briefly eyeing those scraps. And then . . . "He tossed us out."

She sank back on her heels. "He tossed you out?" Broderick's traitorous father, she could understand. But . . . "You *and* your father? Even after your father took the coward's way out and your godfather knew you were alone?"

He shrugged. "I don't know that he ever discovered that."

"Well, then he should have." Her voice climbed. "*He should have.* That is what you do when you love someone. You find them. You help them. You support them. You don't let them suffer through life on their own." Hatred sang through her veins on behalf of the boy who'd been failed by so many. A sound of disgust escaped her. "You make him out to be far more than he is. An *honorable* gentleman doesn't punish a child for the sins of his father." Whereas Reggie . . . her dark deeds were her own. There was no one else with whom blame could be placed. She owned her decisions. Every bad last one of them. "Oh, Broderick. What you could never see was that you didn't need a link to the nobility. You have always been noble"—she touched her fingertips to his chest—"for who you are in here."

A faint grin ghosted his lips. "In the end, none of it mattered."

None of it mattered.

Her heart buckled and threatened to take her down from the pain of his resignation.

Those latter four words contained the finality of death he spoke of. Covering her face with her palms, Reggie concentrated on breathing. He, the all-powerful proprietor of the Devil's Den, had faced—and defeated—the most ruthless souls in the Dials. He'd plucked the hopeless like Reggie from the streets and helped restore her spirit. From his strength she'd found her own. And now . . . he'd simply given up?

No.

He'd accepted the outcome with the marquess as the end.

On the heels of the misery threatening to pull her under, there was something more. Something safer.

Fury churned low in her belly and spread through her veins. Reggie took a step away from him. "How dare you?"

"I don't . . ." He stared quizzically at her. "What . . . ?"

"You." She slashed a hand in his direction. "You've inspired men, women, and children who had *nothing,* not even hope, to survive." Herself included. "To live at all costs. And then you'll simply *give up.*" Her voice pitched to the ceiling.

A muscle jumped in his jaw. "I've not given up."

Another person who'd known him less, who hadn't seen the tenderness he was capable of, would have balked at the frosty warning that went unspoken in his words.

"Bah. That is precisely what you've done, Broderick. Precisely," she hissed.

"You don't know a thing about it." He took a step past her.

He was *leaving*? By God, he'd not walk away from this. Reggie rushed over, planting herself in front of him and ending that unlikeliest of retreats. "I know *everything* about it, Broderick. My struggles are not yours." She implored him with her eyes and words to understand. "But I know what it is to feel there is no way out—"

Broderick took her suddenly by the shoulders, wringing a gasp from her. "Because there is not," he cried. He squeezed her lightly. "What I face isn't a threat that can be conquered. It is a father wronged who'd see me hanged, and rightfully so."

Jerking his hands back, he flexed his fingers as if burnt by that touch. That crack in his composure chased away her anger.

And at last, she saw. "You blame yourself."

"It is my fault."

"It was a mistake," she said, not missing a beat.

The muscles of his throat jumped. "Stephen lost the life he was entitled to and was forced into a life of crime because of me."

"No." Reggie shook her head, needing him to see. "What you sought from Walsh was an orphan. A child in need. On his own. That is what you requested, Broderick." She stepped even closer until she was eye to eye with him. "Because for this ruthless image you've built for yourself, there has always been a goodness in you." Reggie pressed her palms to the place where his heart beat, steady and fast. A man very much alive. "Your father gave up," she said softly, and under her palms, the corded muscles of his chest moved. "That is not you, Broderick. You are not one to accept any kind of defeat." She held his gaze with her own. "Not even this."

He dusted his knuckles along her cheek. "I coerced you into accompanying Gertrude. I bought your club out from under you. I'm not deserving of your loyalty."

Poor Broderick. Still believing in absolutes. "It wasn't . . . isn't a club," she said with a forced lightness she didn't feel. Reggie let her smile fade. "We were friends longer than we were enemies."

Broderick lowered his brow to hers. The sough of his breath fanned her lips, the hint of tobacco that still clung to him tickling her senses. "Is that what we are? Enemies?"

If she angled her mouth ever so slightly, it would meet his, and she wanted to again know his kiss. "I don't know what we are anymore, Broderick," she said softly, reality intruding with her words. He was the one who'd set the new terms of their relationship. Why should he care if they were in fact enemies? "Does it matter either way?" *To you?* To her it did. She yearned for his friendship. Pathetic fool that she was, she'd take whatever scraps he'd give her.

"It does." He continued to brush his knuckles along her jaw in a too-fleeting caress. "I don't want my siblings living in the Dials." He paused. "And I don't want you living there, either."

He was done, then, talking about his future. The decisive end to that discourse was there in his eyes and his tone and his abrupt shift in topic.

Unbidden, her gaze fell to the stacks of sheet music, and she stared at the notes inked from memory. Incomplete but whole inside her mind. "There's no other place for me." She'd left home and the family who had loved her, visiting upon them nothing but shame and scandal. There was no returning after that.

She bit the inside of her cheek. Damning him for forcing those long-buried memories upon her. Memories better off buried.

He tipped up her chin, guiding her gaze back to his. "I would have taken care of you."

A vise squeezed about her heart. How was it possible for a vow to both warm one and rip them apart inside, all at once? "I know that." But she'd never wanted him in that way. She'd never wished to be the assistant, always there, ensured by his protection while silently suffering on when he eventually found a woman who won his love.

"It's not too late. If you've changed your mind . . ." He left that there. An offer of forgiveness. And the part of her that would always love this man ached to take that measly piece of him. The woman who'd been stripped of her pride long ago could not make that sacrifice. Not even for Broderick.

She shook her head.

He glanced over at her paperwork. "You're determined to leave."

She'd not see him stay and marry another. Even if that match would save him, it would destroy her. "I am." And she would miss him until the day she drew her last breath.

"Very well." He cracked his knuckles and took ownership of the piano bench. "What manner of work is it?" he asked even as he was opening her folders.

She jumped, her fingers reflexively reaching for that work she'd kept hidden from him.

He cast a glance over his shoulder.

Reggie spoke through gritted teeth. "I'd have to be a fool to tell you anything about my intentions. There's nothing proprietary in an idea."

He grinned. "I've trained you well. You're worried I'd nick it, then," he drawled. She warred with herself before slowly turning those pages over. Mayhap she'd be proven a fool for trusting him and this exchange would have been nothing more than a ruse meant to weaken her, but she believed him. She believed him because of the man he'd proven himself to be over the years.

"Cleo insists you never intended to establish a gaming hell." Her tongue felt heavy in her mouth. What else had Cleo shared with her brother? At her silence, he shot her a quizzical look. "It's a saloon?"

"It's not a saloon."

"A tavern, then?"

Reggie shook her head.

"Then what is it?" He raised his brows. "Surely you know, Regina, that I'll gather precisely what you intend, whether you tell me or not . . ."

She swatted at his shoulder. "God, there is no one more arrogant in the whole of England than you." And with reason to be. Time had proven that whatever he desired, whether it was information, power, or wealth, he ultimately wrested it for himself.

He bowed his head.

She snorted. "You're incorrigible." Reggie smoothed her palms down the front of her night rail. "It is a music hall."

"A . . . ?"

"Music hall," she supplied. She braced for his condemnation and criticism. Encouraged by his silence, she gathered her notebook. "There will be folk music and operas and ballet performances." She rested a knee upon the bench and set the book out before him. "Patrons will not be required to seek out stalls in separate barrooms"—as all theatres did—"but rather will be allowed to consume spirits in the middle of the theatre." When she'd finished, he availed himself of her work folder and said nothing.

"Ah, a music hall."

She wrinkled her nose, trying to make sense of those four words.

"And what manner of music will you play?" He drifted reverent fingers over the oxwood keys and ebony sharps, plucking the strains of "Death and the Lady." "Somber music for your patrons?"

Butterflies danced in her breast. Of course he'd be skilled in even this. When Oliver always mocked music as a lady's pursuit, Broderick had owned those keys. Before she could answer, he began plucking a more upbeat tempo; his fingers flew over the keys, and he sang in an endearing, slightly off-key baritone.

> "There lived a Man in Baleno, crazy
> Who wanted a Wife to make him uneasy."

Reggie giggled. "*And* you sing."

He paused midlyric. "Poorly." He resumed playing. Tipping his head back and forth, he winked at her, and her heart tripped a funny beat.

> "Long had he sigh'd for dear Ally Croaker,
> And thus the gentle Youth bespoke her:
> 'Will you marry me, dear Ally Croaker,
> Will you marry me, dear Ally, Ally Croaker?'"

When he finished, he quirked a brow. "Or romantic shows?"

> "Of all the girls that are so smart
> There's none like pretty Sally;
> She is the darling of my heart,
> And she lives in our alley.
> There is no lady in the land
> Is half so sweet as Sally;
> She is the darling of my heart,
> And she lives in our alley."

As he sang, she studied his bent head, losing every last scrap of her heart that hadn't already belonged to him.

When he glanced up, she fought for a semblance of control.

How casual he was in every regard, while inside she remained a riot of emotions and would always be where he was concerned.

He leaned back on the bench. Removing his fingers from the keys, he held a hand out.

"Well?" she asked grudgingly. It didn't escape her notice that he'd not revealed his opinion about her plans.

"I didn't say anything."

"You didn't need to."

He flipped through those pages, working his stare over the details written in her meticulous hand.

"Hmm."

She tapped her bare foot in an agitated staccato. "What?"

Broderick briefly lifted his gaze. "It's a theatre," he said with an air of finality.

"It is more than that," she said indignantly. She slipped out a rough rendering she'd sketched in her amateur hand and held it up.

His eyes made quick work of the drawing. "The first rule of business is a clear head. It's dangerous to take suggestions personally." And mayhap she was not as good a friend as he took her for, because with this talk of her dream and the business she'd soon have with Clara, she clung to this brief interlude. Where there was no mad marquess nor threat of the gallows hanging over Broderick nor resentment between Reggie and Broderick for all that had come to pass between them.

Reggie squeezed onto the bench beside him. "Very well. I'm listening."

He stared over the top of that page. "Nothing will set you apart." With that flat pronouncement, he snapped the folder closed and set it down. "You'll compete with the established theatres in Covent Garden and set yourself for failure. You won't even survive two months of doors opening." At that dire pronouncement so emotionlessly delivered, unease sank into her stomach.

And if she failed, she'd be responsible for the eventual men, women, and children who relied upon her and Clara for employment.

"The next rule of business," he said, nudging her knee with his. "Never contemplate failure. Rather, focus on how you'll succeed. What will make your venue different, Reggie?"

Picking up her pencil, Reggie tapped it from tip to bottom, back and forth, contemplating her notes. What would set her apart? It was a failing that she'd not considered that before now. Rather, she'd relied upon the talent she and Clara would assemble. But why would patrons visit? "I don't know."

He touched the tip of her pert, freckled nose. "Find what makes you different," he echoed. "Pantomime. Tightrope dancing. A mix of performers *outside* of musicians."

She ceased the distracted tapping of her pencil. "You'd have us become a circus."

"I'd see you thrive," he amended, handing over her pages.

Reggie accepted the notes. "Either way, we don't have the luxury of diversifying our cast of performers or stage setting." With the payments he'd expected, Broderick had eaten into the funds that were to have gone to hiring performers.

"But then who—"

"I'll perform."

That effectively silenced him.

Reggie faced him on the bench. "I'll perform along with several young women Clara knows from Covent Garden. And when I have the funds, I'll find others. Even those women in your employ." He stiffened. "Because the truth is, Broderick . . ." She leaned closer, holding his gaze with her own. "If they are willing, I'll take them. They deserve control of their future, and I'd allow them that, even if you see it as a betrayal."

Broderick stared at her for a long while.

"You're right."

That knocked her aback. "What?" she blurted, her notes slipping from her fingers.

"You are correct." Rescuing those forgotten pages, he set them down on the pianoforte.

Surely he was ill? She touched the back of her hand to his head. Or he'd gone mad? "You don't capitulate that easily."

"So mistrustful." He laughed, catching her fingers, and then butterflies fluttered in her chest as he drew that palm to his mouth. He brushed a lingering kiss upon it. "It was wrong to resent you for starting again. I want my staff to go with you."

She made a sound of protest and tried to stand, but he caught her hand, keeping her next to him.

"I was too selfish. Too bent on control. I wanted to order my life and business, but there was you, all along, Reggie. The salvation that I could not be."

"Stop," she entreated.

"I won't. You are more capable than any member of my staff. You'll care for them. See them—"

"You're doing it again," she whispered. "Putting your life in order."

"Not this time. This isn't about Maddock . . . or me." He sat back on the bench. "This is about you. This is about me acknowledging that you can and will create something wonderful. It will thrive and flourish, and it will be because of who you are. I should have supported you from the moment I learned of what you intended."

Tears blurred her vision, and then a single drop spiraled down her cheek.

"None of that," he murmured, brushing it away.

Why must he do this? Why must he be this tender, supportive man beside her? Those unsteady walls she'd thrown up around her heart these past days faltered, tumbling down.

He handed over her sheet music. "Sing for me."

"You want me to perform?" she rasped, pressing the heels of her palms against her eyes. "Now you're teasing me." Again, Reggie made to slide off the bench, but he caught her.

"How will you play before an entire hall of strangers if you cannot perform for me, alone?"

"Because it's not a performance," she said, her cheeks flushing. "It's"—she slashed a hand in his direction—"you."

"I sang for you."

At that child's argument, she smiled. "That is different."

"And why?" He bristled. "I was quite serious in my efforts."

She laughed. And how very wonderful it felt to laugh—with him. One could almost believe the world wasn't on fire. "Very well." Reggie snapped the sheet music from his hand and adjusted it. She nudged him with her hip, and he scooted to the end of the bench, allowing her room at the center of the keyboard.

Fingers poised over the keys, she drew in a deep breath.

"It's just me."

He was never "just him." He was the one who held her heart and who'd soon marry a proper miss. She shoved the thought from her head.

Hating that unknown stranger for intruding. Hating Broderick for going forward with this. And hating that she couldn't be enough for him.

Regina stroked the keys, bringing the song to life, forgetting Broderick at her side and losing herself in the verses.

"'Tis the last rose of summer,
Left blooming alone;
All her lovely companions
Are faded and gone;
No flower of her kindred,
No rosebud is nigh,
To reflect back her blushes,
Or give sigh for sigh."

She felt Broderick go still beside her on the bench.

"Since the lovely are sleeping,
Go, sleep thou with them.
Thus kindly I scatter,
Thy leaves o'er the bed,
Where thy mates of the garden
Lie scentless and dead.

So soon may I follow,
When friendships decay,
And from Love's shining circle
The gems drop away.
When true hearts lie withered,
And fond ones are flown,
Oh! who would inhabit
This bleak world alone?"

Reggie stopped. The echo of the keys vibrated in the nighttime quiet, even after she'd depressed the last note.

It had been so very long since she'd played or sung, and avoiding his gaze, she came to her feet. To leave . . .

"I was wrong," he whispered, bringing Reggie slowly back to face him.

Passion blazed from within his eyes, burning her with the heat of it, stealing her breath. "W-wrong . . . ?"

He stood, erasing the small space she'd previously put between them.

Reggie's lashes fluttered. "About?"

He swallowed hard. "Your voice alone will do."

Her body swayed toward his. Their lips met in an explosion of heat and hunger.

She parted her lips to allow him entry, and as he swept inside, Reggie met every stroke of his tongue. Their kiss was a duel and a dance. Thrusting. Parrying. Meeting one another in an age-old dance of passion.

Reggie tipped her head sideways, and he caressed his mouth down her nape, lingering his lips on the place where her pulse beat wildly. He sucked at the flesh. Teased. Nipped.

She sank her teeth into her lower lip. She wanted to know him in every way. Before he found his bride and she left this place, she wanted to steal whatever pleasure was to be had in his arms. Reggie gave herself over to his embrace. Turning, she twined her hands about his neck, angling her head to better receive his kiss.

He groaned. Not breaking contact with her mouth, Broderick worked his hands between them, and loosening the ties of her wrapper, he shoved the whisper-soft article down her shoulders. The cool night air was like a sough upon her heated skin.

"So beautiful," he whispered against her lips. He trailed a path of kisses down her jaw, worshipping the column of her neck. A keening moan spilled from her as he filled his hands with her breasts, molding the thin fabric to her skin.

Her nipples peaked, aching for his attention. Through the thin cotton he tweaked those buds, teasing. *Tormenting.* Flicking them back and forth. "Please," she begged, yearning to feel his hands upon her naked skin.

Broderick slid the straps down, releasing the small mounds from their constraints. "Tell me what you want, Regina," he murmured, circling the pink areolae with the pads of his thumbs, that delicate, whisper-soft touch sending a shudder of longing through her.

He was allowing her control. He wanted her to have a voice in her pleasure. And her heart swelled anew with love for him. Reggie slid to the edge of the piano bench and then took his hands in her own. She drew Broderick's large, callused palms to her breasts. Her chest rose and fell fast, and she forced her heavy lashes open, meeting his gaze. "I want you to touch me," she whispered. "I want to feel your touch everywhere."

Swallowing loudly, Broderick fixed his eyes on those twin mounds. With a groan, he dropped a knee onto the piano bench and, lowering his mouth, closed his lips around one of those engorged tips.

Reggie's legs weakened under her, and her buttocks found purchase on the instrument behind her. The keys clanged a dissonant medley, their reverberations echoing around the room and inside her head as he continued his blissful torment.

Then he suckled. Drawing that bud deep, laving the tip. Swirling his tongue around that sensitized flesh. Reggie slid her eyes closed, and threading her fingers through his tousled golden curls, she anchored him close. Each pull and each suck sent a throbbing ache to her center. She felt herself, for the first time, hot and wet, and reveled in that pleasure.

Gave herself over to it. And there was no shame. There was only a violent hungering, and with an incoherent plea, she parted her legs and thrust against him.

The keys chimed and sang to every frantic arch of her hips. A discordant symphony that matched the fire that raged within her.

Broderick drew back, and she cried out, clenching her fingers in the fabric of his jacket to hold him close, but he was merely shifting his attentions to the neglected peak of her other breast.

"Broderick," she moaned, her head falling back. Her plait whipped the sheet music from the stand, scattering those pages about them, forgotten.

He suckled and teased, worshipping that tip until Reggie's speech dissolved into an incoherent half plea, punctuated by the strident discord of the pianoforte.

He sat, and she cried out at the loss of him. His passion-glazed eyes never breaking contact with hers, he slowly drew her night rail up higher. "Since the moment in your hall when you called me out for the bastard I am, I have dreamed of this." He edged her nightshift past her calves, and then higher, exposing her thighs, and ever higher. She lifted reflexively, allowing him to guide the garment up to her hips, so that she lay bare before him.

Broderick reached down and caressed her right calf. "Freckles," he whispered with such reverence it pulled a breathy laugh from her.

"They're hideous." She'd long despised those flecks that marked her skin.

Lowering his head and drawing her leg up, closer, Broderick traced the path of those flecks with his lips. "Beautiful," he said between kisses.

And for the first time in the whole of her eight-and-twenty years, she believed it. Felt it.

He stroked his hands up along the expanse of her leg. "They go on forever." His breath came fast, like one who'd run a great race. That evidence of his desire for her sent a thrill of feminine satisfaction coursing through her, and of their own volition, her legs fell open and her hips arched up.

Broderick groaned, and then dropping to his knees, he buried his head between her thighs, jarring the keys.

Reggie's entire body tensed, and a hiss exploded between her teeth as she caught the edge of the instrument.

"Let yourself feel," he urged, stroking her wet channel with his tongue, suckling her folds.

Reggie closed her eyes and then let her body sag, turning herself over to simply feeling.

Her hips rose and fell in time to the rhythmic stroke of his tongue, their every movement jarring the keys. And they played in her head, a song beautifully perfect in its dissonance as she ceased to exist outside the ache burning at her center.

"That's it," he praised, his breath hot against the inside of her thigh.

Reggie bit her lower lip hard. Needing more. Wanting more. "I've never felt this way," she rasped. *"Neverrrr."* That last word came out as an endless moan as he slipped a finger inside her wet channel.

"Come for me," he urged between each stroke of his tongue.

Reggie gripped Broderick's head, threading her fingers through the light, luxuriant strands. Panting, she pumped her hips, frantic.

Then he sucked her.

Reggie's body stiffened.

She came on a piercing scream. Wave after wave of pleasure crashed through her, swallowing her with its intensity, muting all sound but for the clashing harmony made by those ivory keys.

And she didn't care if anyone heard it, didn't care if they were discovered. She wanted nothing more than for this moment to go on forever.

Panting, Reggie went limp. She caught her elbows on the scalloped wood, the engravings biting into her skin. Tears pricked behind her lashes. "I didn't know I could feel . . . I thought . . ." How many times after rutting painfully between her legs had Oliver called her a cold fish? He'd been wrong. So very wrong, and about so much. A single tear slid down her cheek as she reveled in this newfound power. "He said I wasn't capable of—"

Broderick stood and cupped her gently by the nape. "Don't let him in here. He was never worthy of you."

Reggie pressed her cheek to his chest and breathed deep the sandalwood scent that clung to him; the steady throb of his heartbeat thumped reassuringly against her ear. She stroked her palm over the place where it beat, and his muscles jumped under that light touch.

Because of me . . . his body is responding to my touch . . .

Emboldened and empowered, she caressed her fingers over the corded muscles of his chest, lower to his taut belly.

Broderick caught her hand. "Reggie." Agony wreathed his voice. "Don't . . ."

She faltered, her confidence flagging. "I see," she said dumbly, drawing away from him. Mortified heat burning her cheeks, Reggie presented her back to him and hurriedly dragged her bodice into place. A puffed cotton sleeve twisted, and she struggled to thrust her arm through the tangle.

Broderick stalked over, placing himself before her. "What do you think you see?" he murmured, staying her frenetic movements.

She fixed her gaze at the golden whorl of curls exposed at the top of his shirt. It was a state of dishabille she'd seen him in countless times, and yet there had never been this level of intimacy between them. Her mouth went dry. *I'm a pathetic harlot. Lusting after a man who doesn't want to lie with me . . .*

"Reggie?" he repeated, his melodic baritone breaking across her shameful musings.

She spun away from him. "You don't want to make love to me."

"Is that what you think?"

"That is what I know." She refocused on that damned lacy sleeve, fighting the fabric.

"You're wrong."

She stopped abruptly.

Broderick caressed his hands over her shoulders, and that butterfly-soft caress brought her lashes fluttering shut. His lips caressed her temple, and she leaned into that barely there kiss. "I want to make love to you." Her heart stopped. "I want to lay you down, spread your legs, and join my body with yours." His voice hoarsened. "I've wanted that for longer than I can admit to you." A lightness flooded her; it filled her lungs and heart and being. "Longer than I've admitted to myself." The internal battle that raged within him also ravaged his features. "You are in my employ. And you are deserving of—"

Turning in his arms, she cupped his face, the day's growth upon his cheeks tickling her palms. "Let me decide what I want and what I deserve." She brought her mouth close to his ear. "I want you." His body went taut. "Make love to me," she whispered.

"I am lost."

And yet she'd been found.

He devoured her. All warmth and tenderness stripped away, leaving in its place a carnal hunger as he stroked past her lips and tasted every corner of her mouth.

She moaned, clinging to his shirt, and met every lash of his tongue.

"Tell me to stop," he urged between kisses.

"If you stop I will die," she rasped, and he swallowed those words.

Broderick filled his hands with her buttocks, and sinking his fingertips into that flesh, he drew her between his legs. His length throbbed against her belly, pulsing with his need, and the evidence of his desire for her fueled another wave of heat at her center.

Catching her about the knees, Broderick carried her through the music room and, as if she were a gift to be treasured, laid her gently down upon the sofa.

Her lids heavy, Reggie forced herself up onto her elbows. She stared on hungrily as Broderick pulled his shirt over his head and tossed the garment aside. Every movement sent a ripple through the defined muscles of his chest, his taut abdomen. All corded strength, he evinced a power those Greek sculptors had captured in stone.

Broderick discarded his boots and then paused with his hands on the waist of his trousers.

That slight hesitation clear.

"I want you."

Passion glazed his eyes, and then hurriedly removing that last scrap of clothing, he stood before her in all his naked glory.

Her breath caught. His shaft jutted out high and proud amidst a thatch of golden curls. That enormous length jumped under her scrutiny. "You are perfection," she whispered and stretched out her fingertips, grazing that silken length of him.

Broderick groaned and covered her with his body.

His mouth was everywhere. Worshipping every swath of skin he contacted. He kissed first one breast, then the other, suckling the tip. Flicking it with his tongue.

A long, throaty moan spilled from her throat, and Reggie spread her legs wide, arching her hips. Silently pleading.

Broderick slid a finger inside her, and she cried out, clenching around his hand and then relaxing her thighs. He added another finger, filling her. And then he was thrusting those long digits inside her. Stroking her.

"Broderick," she panted, brushing back the locks that had fallen over his damp brow. "Please," she begged.

He shifted, his shaft nudging the damp thatch of curls at her center.

Reggie reflexively lifted.

"Regina," he whispered, and with a groan he pushed inside her.

He moved over her. Filling her. Stroking her slick channel over and over. Thrusting. Retreating. Thrusting. Retreating.

Reggie met every lunge, her hips arching hopelessly.

"You feel so wonderful," he rasped against her breast. "I've never felt this. Not like this."

Reggie bit his shoulder, her fingers clawing at his back in a bid to get closer. The fire he'd stoked ravaging her, burning every corner.

Their bodies moved frantically, moving together in time. "Reggie," he gasped. Over and over. A mantra. A prayer. Her name. Falling from his lips as he drew her higher and higher, pulling her toward that precipice she'd crashed over before.

Only now with him buried deep within her. Their bodies joined as one. Joined as she'd always yearned for them to be.

Reggie stiffened, and then white light burst behind her eyes. She screamed, a throaty explosion of blissful surrender that shook the rafters.

Her muscles tightened and squeezed, and he thrust deep, touching her to the quick.

"Reggie," he rasped once more. He squeezed his eyes shut and shouted his release, filling her.

Gasping, he collapsed.

In one fluid motion, he rolled them so she lay draped over his chest, and smiled.

Chapter 26

How I relish in the fact that everything you built was for naught.

Everything had changed, and yet all at the same time, nothing had.

Broderick's world had been toppled. The future of his club remained in doubt.

And yet since Reggie had slid her naked frame off his and shrugged into her nightshift, he'd thought of only her.

Whistling a more cheerful rendering of "The Last Rose of Summer," Broderick strolled through the halls for the music room.

The door hung open as it had since the last time he'd gone in search of her. He entered again, doing a quick sweep and confirming that she was still not there. Disappointment swept through him, and along with it, the realization that his days with her were numbered. That soon she'd leave and have her music hall . . . and others would know the gift of her voice and her clever wit and resilience . . .

A pang struck his chest.

Drawn to the pianoforte, with one finger he plucked the notes of that song she'd so hauntingly played. And another image floated forward. Reggie stretched out upon the instrument, a fertility goddess, reveling in sexual splendor.

A smile ghosted his lips.

"Pretty silly grin for a man to be wearin' when 'e's facing down a hangman's noose."

Broderick's finger slid, accidentally strumming a G sharp; that discordant clang brought reality rushing in.

His arms folded across his spindly chest, Stephen glowered back.

"Stephen." Heat splotched his cheeks as he made a show of straightening his cravat. "Shouldn't you be in your lessons?"

Blushing. The minx had set him to blushing.

Stephen pulled the door shut hard behind him and stomped over. "Oi finished them two hours ago. Ya're smiling like the cat who got the cream, and this arrived."

The same pit of dread settled around his stomach as he accepted the note from Stephen. He turned it over in his hands. Only this time, it was not fear for his empire and the inevitable loss of power and wealth and control.

It was a loss of something that had almost been. A dream that he'd not even known he'd carried until now. Nay, until her. He'd let the Devil's Den consume him. It was all he'd been and done. He'd dedicated his energy, his blood, and his very life to seeing it thrive. So much so that the world had continued on around him, without Broderick playing a part in any way that truly mattered. He'd not thought of the dream of a family . . . a wife . . . children . . .

An image flashed to mind. A little girl with riotous red curls and a freckled face.

He crushed the note in his hands.

"Ya ain't even going to read it?" Stephen snapped.

"I trust you'll tell me what it says." Nor did it matter. Not truly. The outcome would, as the marquess had reminded him, remain the same.

"He said it will be this week, Broderick. There's no reason to wonder anymore."

Your time is up . . .

How much of it he'd wasted before. Bent on his rise to power and prestige. And all along? What had it been for? How much did one truly need?

Oh, Broderick. What you could never see was that you didn't need a link to the nobility. You have always been noble . . . for who you are in here . . .

Since his father's treachery against the earl, he'd spent his life trying to prove himself different. He'd thought the way to do so was to amass wealth and power, failing to see what truly defined a man.

"Did you hear what I said?" Stephen shouted in his clipped King's English. "You're woolgathering when you should be plotting. Is this because of her?"

The jaded soul of this child was just one of the dark legacies he'd leave behind. *I allowed him to become this . . .*

"There's no plotting," he said quietly, tucking away the note. "There's no more scheming. It's done." And then something tickled the back of his mind. He frowned. "What do you mean, 'because of her'?"

"Spark," Stephen snapped. "Because she's gone."

"Gone where?" he blurted.

Stephen narrowed his eyes. "You don't know."

Warning bells blared. "What?"

"She left," his brother said with a little shrug.

She left. Just that: two words, and Broderick couldn't move. Couldn't breathe. Surely, he'd misheard—

He stormed off.

"Broderick?" Stephen cried after him.

Abandoning any usual show of calm, he sprinted through the halls, startling squeals from a pair of maids. He stumbled and took off running around them. All the while blood rushed to his ears. Stephen was wrong. He'd misunderstood. Broderick reached her rooms and shoved the door open.

A chambermaid squeaked, dropping the white linen sheet she'd been laying upon the bed. "Mr. . . . ?"

He stalked into the room. "Get out."

The girl bolted past him.

Broderick tossed open the armoire.

He shoved aside satin gown after satin gown, hanging neatly in place.

Brown. Brown. Where are the brown dresses?

Dropping to his knees, he dug around, searching the shoes arranged in a crisp line. He flung each delicate article over his shoulder. Looking for—

"Oomph."

He wheeled around.

The grey tabby in Gertrude's arms hissed at Broderick and leapt to the floor. He raced behind her, darting out into the hall. She rubbed at the spot where a slipper had struck her. "Stephen sent me to you."

"Where is she?" he demanded.

Gertrude cocked her head.

"Reggie," he clipped out.

His sister blinked slowly and then chuckled. "Well, I assure you, you'll not find her in the armoire."

He surged to his feet. This wasn't a damned game. "Gertrude!"

She sighed. "I sent her away."

The earth stopped moving, and he tried to make sense out of those four words. "What?"

"I sent her away," she repeated. Gertrude lifted a finger. "Though in fairness, I describe it more as giving Reggie 'her freedom.'" She smiled.

Smiled. She flashed a damn smile, now? "Freedom, which she took. Which she was deserving of."

His hand went slack, and he released the slipper he hadn't even realized he'd been holding. That emerald shoe landed on the tip of his boot and then with a thump hit the floor. Air hissed through his teeth. "You did what?"

"Do pay attention, Broderick. I explained to her that as my Season was officially concluded, I no longer required her to serve as my companion, and—Broderick!" she shouted as he tore past her, thundering for his horse.

She'd simply left. She'd lain in his arms, given herself to him, and all along, it had been nothing more than a damned goodbye.

Anger pumped through him. Fueling his strides. By God, she didn't get to simply make love and leave without talking about . . .

What had happened.

And what became of *them* from here.

He bounded down the stairs. A servant stood in wait with the door held open. Ignoring the cloak he held out, Broderick snatched his top hat and jammed it on his head. Gathering the reins of his mount, he climbed astride.

Nudging Chance on, he set off through crowded streets at a breakneck speed that earned shouts and cries of fury from the respectable gents who claimed Mayfair as their own.

They could all go hang. Regina had opened his eyes to the truth: a person's worth wasn't decided by blood or wealth or connections.

But then, Regina Spark had always possessed a remarkable sway over his thoughts and the decisions he made in the name of the club and oftentimes fairness.

She eventually had helped him to see the narrow view he'd had of the world, and his place in it. She'd opened his eyes to the truth that rank and title and wealth mattered next to nothing when compared with how a man lived his life and treated others.

And she'd simply left.

Without even a damned goodbye.

He fixed on that. His fury. That turbulent swirl of emotion that roiled under the surface. It kept him from focusing on this latest betrayal, how easy it had been for her to simply leave him.

That bloody establishment he'd stolen out from under her came into focus. Where in the past, this end of the street and that building had been quiet, now activity vibrated, with men carrying boards atop their shoulders through the double turquoise doors that hung open.

Broderick was jumping off Chance before the mount had even come to a full stop.

"You, there," he barked. A tiny lad came loping over. "There'll be more when I return," he promised, handing over the reins and purse to the wide-eyed lad.

Doffing his hat, Broderick skirted the crowd of workers milling about the pavement and climbed the handful of steps.

He stopped at the entranceway.

Since the last time he and Reggie had met in this hall, the broken furniture had been carted off. A loud banging now filled the room as workers ripped up rotted floorboards; the din muted his footsteps as his arrival went unnoted.

And then he found her.

Seated at the sole table to have been left, head bent over a stack of sheets, she pored over the documents laid out.

Broderick narrowed his gaze on the brawny figure who sat at her shoulder. Head close to Reggie's, his jacket off, the man's physique marked him as one accustomed to hard work.

Periodically, Reggie would nod. She chewed at the end of her pencil in an endearing hint of her focus. She paused and gestured to the page.

Whatever her reply, she earned a booming laugh from the stranger, whose frame shook with the force of his amusement.

And then Reggie joined in. Giving that nameless bastard her laugh. Unrestrained, clear, and bell-like, as she'd once laughed with him. A blinding red fury fell over his vision, sharp enough to taste and volatile enough to tense all the muscles in his body.

The tawny-headed stranger glanced up, and his gaze landed on Broderick. The bounder leaned back in his chair and said something to Reggie.

She picked her head up.

And there was no joy there. No pleasure at seeing him, but rather confusion that stretched across the room.

The smile that had previously dimpled Reggie's cheek immediately withered, replaced with a question.

And he found himself hating with a vicious intensity the figure at her side even more for the fact that he'd become a recipient of that warmth.

His skin pricked with the attention paid them by the small army of workers. All activity immediately ceased as they glanced over at Broderick . . . and then back to the bounder who couldn't even be bothered with a proper jacket.

"What is the meaning of this?" he boomed.

A frown puckered between her crimson eyebrows. "I am working."

That is what she'd say. *I am working.*

As though his mouth hadn't been on hers. All over her. As though the scent and taste of her weren't seared in his mind and wouldn't haunt him happily as he took his last steps to the gallows and swung with the memory of that one night in the music room they'd shared.

His neck heated as she turned all her energies back to the tawny-haired stranger and the builders resumed their previously abandoned tasks.

And Broderick, who'd forever been in control of any and every situation, found himself . . . an interloper in Reggie's world and the world she now sat there building with another man. How easily he'd been displaced. *Nay, how easily you've allowed yourself to be displaced.* He'd spent the past week resenting her for her plans instead of supporting her as she'd deserved.

"May I have a word with you, Miss Spark?" he asked quietly when her attention remained wholly focused on the brutishly large figure.

She wrinkled her nose, and for a moment he thought she'd tell him to go to hell and cut his legs out from under him with that show of power. At last, she said something to the young man, who nodded in return. Gathering up a leather notepad, he stood, unfurling to his full height, nearly three inches taller than Broderick and three stones broader in strength. Broderick hated him on sight.

"Martin, if you'll excuse us?"

Martin bowed his head. "Regina."

Who in holy hell was *Martin*? Broderick gnashed his teeth. And more . . . who in blazes had given the bounder the right to her damned Christian name? Nor did *Martin* use the masculine moniker she'd entered the Diggory gang with, but rather he laid possession to those flowing, three syllables—Regina.

All hint of that warmth from Mr. Martin faded when he faced Broderick. With a dismissive glance, he clapped his hands once. The builders immediately abandoned their tasks and filed from the room.

As soon as they'd gone and those turquoise doors had closed behind them, Reggie—*Regina*—proceeded to gather up her papers. And of all the questions he'd put to her, the most illogical of them came spilling forward. "Who in blazes is that?" She opened her mouth. "And since when have you gone by 'Regina'?"

Reggie opted to answer the latter question. "Since I was born," she said dryly, her focus trained on those blasted papers. "You were the one who shortened it." She paused, finally sparing him a glance. "Don't you remember?"

Actually . . . he didn't. Why had he gone about butchering a regal name befitting the Spartan beauty? *Because you didn't see her in that light . . . You saw her as a snarling, wary woman with fear in her eyes that she'd not allowed herself to give in to . . .*

He dragged a hand through his hair.

Only recently, since they'd gone to battle, everything had changed, and he fought to get his placement back.

Reggie smirked, and there was so much knowing contained within that twist of her lips. One that indicated she'd gathered the truth of his remembrance . . . or in this case, his misremembrance, and it allowed her an upper hand where his memory of the past was murky. And she knew more. It was a dangerous end to find oneself on in any exchange.

At last, she stood.

Broderick choked. "What in blazes are you wearing?"

"Oh, come," she chided, striding over to a worktable. In breeches. She was wearing . . . breeches. "You've never been squeamish about what a woman wears."

No, he hadn't. Not with the serving girls and then prostitutes in his clubs. They'd donned scanty garments that put their bodies on full display. But this was not any of the other women in his damned club. This was Reggie—Regina—who'd been alone with a jacketless stranger.

Yanking off his gloves, Broderick stalked down the stairs. "Who was that?" he demanded, slapping the leather articles together.

"Martin Phippen?" She looked up. *At last.* "He is my builder." A builder. Nay, "her builder" . . . a vital distinction of possessiveness for that brawny, burly man whom she'd shared her ideas with and . . . her laughter. She'd shared that, too. "He's responsible for the design and creation of Black's new establishment," she was saying.

Rage pumped through his veins. Only one person could be responsible for a connection between Regina and the builder of their rival establishment.

Cleo.

Broderick swept his gaze over the building plans: Reggie's more rudimentary artwork that she'd shared with him only last evening lay alongside a more meticulous rendering in an artist's hands that included details: her stage, an acrobat ring above the stage. Thoughts of last evening only drew forward other images. Reggie arching back as he buried himself deep within her. Clawing at his back and screaming his name.

And then leaving. She'd done that, too.

Broderick flared his nostrils.

"Is there something else you require?" she asked, already striding over to the doorway.

She thought to toss him on his arse, did she? Over his bloody dead body on Sunday.

He swiftly inserted himself before her.

"You simply left."

That silenced her.

Reggie quickly righted herself. "I was assured by Gertrude that her Season was concluded." She made to step around him.

He blocked her path once more. "We made love."

Her cheeks pinkened, a delicate shade of red that didn't hide those endearing freckles as her full crimson blushes did. "Yes. We did." She wheeled around, starting back toward the table she'd previously sat at with Martin Phippen.

That was it? *What do you expect she should say?* "Why did you leave?" he called out.

She stopped midstride and then belatedly completed that step. "What bearing does that have on anything?" she asked, tiredly.

It had every . . . *bearing* on it. "Don't do that," he said sharply, stalking over. "Don't make what we did—"

"Broderick," she whipped back. "Gertrude's Season was marred with scandal because of me." She touched a hand to her chest. "No good can come from me being there. There's no purpose to my being there."

There was a finality there in her tone that marked the end of their time together.

She started back over to her table and began stacking her pages.

Panic flared in his chest. "We made love," he repeated on an angry whisper.

And this time, he seemed to penetrate whatever wall she'd erected about herself.

Reggie stared at him with wide, stricken eyes, and then all emotion was so quickly masked he might have merely imagined that response. "It was sex, Broderick," she said flatly in this grand reversal of roles.

He sank back on his heels.

With any other woman, any other lover before this, such a statement would have held true. Not with her. It hadn't been just sex, and he'd not allow her to make it out to be as though it were not . . . more. "Don't do that. You know that's not true."

The color bled from her cheeks. "Why are you doing this?"

"Because you don't just get to leave. Not without telling me why."

"Why?" she echoed.

"Everything. All of it," he said, slashing a palm through the air. "You are determined to leave: first to establish your own business." Pain knifed at him. "And now today." After they'd made love, and he'd lost every corner of his soul to her. "I deserve an explanation as to why it's so damned easy for you to walk away."

A frantic giggle bubbled in her throat, but never made it past her lips. "Is that what you think? That any of this has been 'easy' for me?" Her narrow shoulders went back, and her spine straightened. Reggie turned back, and she held his gaze. "Just go," she said simply. "Live your life and let me live mine." Gathering a hammer from a nearby worktable, she fell to a knee and set to work tugging a board free.

That was it—*just go*.

He stalked over, closing the distance between them in three long strides. "No," he said softly. Broderick put to her the question he'd asked her in this very place when he'd first learned of her plans. "This is about me deserving to know why a woman who I made a member of my family sought to steal my staff and my servants and used my club business dealings to her advantage." That managed to pierce the icy veneer she'd erected. "And you insisted there were reasons." He held her gaze. "But you never said what those reasons were for your leaving."

She jumped up. "You are unrelenting," she gritted. "What do you want me to say?" She took a step forward, putting him on the retreat. Her frantic movements knocked loose several curls, and they tumbled over her shoulder, falling to her waist, a crimson waterfall that danced back and forth with her every step. "Are you determined to shred my pride?"

He scoffed. "Of course not." How little she thought of him.

Reggie kept coming, until his legs knocked into a worktable. "Do you want me to tell you that I love you?" she rasped. "That I've loved you for ten years, and that all of this"—she swept her arms around the hall—"was to protect myself?"

He collapsed into that table, rattling the tools scattered there. "What?" he whispered.

Reflected back in her eyes was his own shock. All the color left her cheeks. A quavering hand went to her mouth. "No . . . ," she said quickly. She shook her head as if he were the Devil come to collect her soul.

"You love me?"

Reggie looked away.

Nothing made sense. And yet everything now did. *You see the world in absolutes, Broderick. As long as I've known you, that has been your way . . . You once saw Ryker Black and Adair Thorne as the enemy, but they've been more, too.* Her words whispered forward, haunting him with the truth of his own obstinacy. His mind raced, rapidly putting together pieces of a puzzle that suddenly made sense. This was why she'd sought to leave. "Why didn't you tell me?" Emotion hoarsened his voice.

"What would you have had me say?" A strained laugh filtered from her lips. "That it was too much being around you? That I loved you?"

Her laughter faded, replaced with a stoic strength he'd long admired in her. "I lost my heart to you; I'd not lose my pride, too."

What a bloody fool he'd been. He swiped a hand over his face. Reggie had always been more stubborn and prouder than anyone. She'd never have humbled herself by confessing feelings to him, a man who'd been so blinded by his need to join himself to the *ton*.

And yet . . . how had he not seen it before this angry utterance spilling from her lips?

The same reason you didn't see that which was in your own damned heart. Because you were blind, and she was Reggie, a woman in your employ and off-limits for it.

The silence stretched on, taut and awkward and unending.

Reggie was the first to look away. She pressed her fingertips into her temples. "Now you know, and there is nothing for you to do with it," she said, her voice catching, and then she dropped her arms, fire flaring in her eyes once more. "But I'll be damned if you have me come back and watch you court some other woman and—"

He was across the room in three long strides. Broderick kissed her, stealing away the remainder of those words.

Reggie stiffened in his arms and then melted against him.

"I want you," he rasped between each slant of his mouth over hers. "I love you."

Reggie drew back in his arms; her cheeks flushed. "What?" Her wide eyes roved over his face.

He'd resisted seeing that which he wanted, her standing there . . . So much damned time lost. "I don't have much time left."

Her face crumpled. "Don't say that."

"I don't," he said matter-of-factly. It was why offering her love now was selfish. He would not be the man one day beside her. And that cleaved him in two. "One day there will be someone." And from the corner of hell he found himself spending eternity in, he'd hate that nameless bastard. "A man who woos you and wins you—"

"Stop it." She glared at him. "Don't talk like that."

"A man who is deserving of your love." One who appreciated her in ways that Broderick hadn't until it was too late.

"Stop," she begged.

"Shh," he urged, gathering the lone tear that tumbled down her cheek. That wasn't why he'd told her this. How much time he'd lost . . . they'd lost together. "I want you to have your music hall and my staff as your own, if that is what you desire. But what time I have, I want it to be with you."

He wanted to be with her.

Broderick, whom she'd spent years only dreaming of a future with, would abandon every hope for marriage to a proper lady for her.

Broderick palmed her cheek. "Will you not say something?" he asked, a hesitancy there that had never marked words from this man.

Surely he knew he was all she'd ever wanted. And yet . . . selfishly, this wasn't enough. She didn't want their time to be fleeting and ended by a crime committed by another, doled out by a man bent on revenge.

Her lips trembled. "I want that. I want you. I love you."

He framed her face between his hands, and with an agonized laugh, Broderick dropped his brow to hers. "I love you," he repeated. It had taken the threat of losing her to realize that she completed him in ways that he'd been empty before her. "Marry me?"

A sob burst from her throat, and she threw herself into his arms. He staggered under her embrace and then crashed down, landing hard. "Yes."

A knock sounded at the front door, and Reggie glanced over. "Miss Spark?"

"Your architect." He kissed her neck.

She giggled. "Stop. My builders are here."

God, she was magnificent. How had it taken him so long to see it? Nay, to fully appreciate the true depth of her spirit and strength.

"May I stay?"

She drew back. "Stay?"

He wouldn't impose himself on her plans. He'd take only what she was willing to share. "I don't want to be underfoot—"

Reggie twined her arms about his neck. "You silly man. I want you with me. Always."

He nipped at her earlobe, and she dissolved into a breathy fit of laughter. "Do you know you're the first person to ever call me 'silly'?"

"Surely not?"

He tickled her sides, until great snorting laughs spilled from her. "Minx."

They remained there, the hours passing, reviewing designs and discussing the layout of her hall. Her enthusiasm was tangible, a lifelike joy that came from the dream she had for this place. It wasn't borne of competition or a thirst to crush all who had a similar hope or vision. Rather, she was one who saw the world was wide enough.

Later that afternoon, after they took their leave and made the journey back to Mayfair, she glanced over, a question in her eyes. "What is it?"

"You are remarkable," he said softly. Whatever time they had wasn't enough.

She smiled and slid her long fingers into his. Broderick clung to her palm; callused and coarse, hers belonged to a woman unafraid to work. Just as she'd always been.

They arrived a short while later.

"Ophelia is here," she noted as he caught her by the waist and helped her down. He lingered his hands there.

"Shall we go tell her?" he whispered against her ear.

"Hush." She ducked out of his arms and rushed along the pavement. "People will talk."

Broderick followed quickly on her heels. "Let them." He laughed as the double doors were thrown open.

His and Reggie's laughter immediately died.

A wide-eyed Ophelia stood in the middle of the foyer in her cloak, alongside a stunning, equally wide-eyed woman. She glanced up and down Reggie's trouser-clad frame, and her eyes nearly swallowed her face.

"There you are," Ophelia exclaimed, the first to break the awkward impasse. "I'm so glad you've returned! We were just leaving."

Reggie dropped a curtsy and then started to go. Broderick followed her with his gaze, and she paused, lingering, their eyes locked.

"Broderick?" Ophelia pressed.

"Hmm?" he murmured. "Forgive me."

Ophelia beamed. "Allow me to again present the Dowager Duchess of Argyll. She has been gracious enough as to invite us to her box at the theatre this evening."

"How do you do?" the young duchess murmured, and as he bowed over her hand for the requisite kiss, Ophelia winked.

Broderick narrowed his eyes.

"I've found your bride," Ophelia whispered.

Chapter 27

You took my wife . . .

In the Dials, one honed one's senses, or one perished. It had been a skill that had saved Reggie countless times, and she'd been grateful for it—until now.

I've found your bride . . .

A fingernail moon hung crooked in the sky, casting the faintest glow onto the quiet London streets.

Standing at the edge of the floor-length window, Reggie stared out at the elegant black-lacquer carriage that sat in wait.

That was why Ophelia had, of course, come to visit with the stunning widow. Those barely audible words detected on Reggie's way out, spoken between a brother and sister . . . they changed everything.

She let the silk fabric slip from her fingers and flutter into place.

It was her misfortune to love where nothing could ever truly grow.

"Meowwww." Gus butted his head against her lower leg.

Reggie scooped up the silky grey cat and cradled his body close. "Are you calling me a liar again?" she scolded.

He kneaded the front of her brown day dress.

"That is a yes, then." She buried her face in the downy patch between his ears.

A knock came.

His knock. The sturdy, confident, determined one. And also, the expected one.

Her hands tightened around Gus, and he struggled against her hold. She released him, and he landed nimbly on all fours, scurrying off under her bed.

"Enter," she called into the quiet, and coward that she was, Reggie turned her focus to the floral pattern etched within the gold silk curtains.

The faint groan of the floorboard and click of the door indicated that he'd entered. There were no illusions of propriety where she and Broderick were concerned. There never had been. She'd adored that closeness in the past. Now she hated it for the reminder it served—that to him, she'd never been a lady.

"Hullo," he said somberly.

Drawing in a silent breath through her teeth, she forced herself to face him.

Reggie's breath caught. Damn him for his beauty: Tall. All glorious, golden masculine perfection. No man had a right to his beauty. Attired in a midnight-black jacket, matching brocaded waistcoat, and trousers, and with his tousled golden curls, he was a study of Lucifer upon his immediate fall from grace.

And tonight, another woman would be the recipient of his attentions.

A duchess, no less.

And a widow at that.

The woman he'd marry.

Oh, God.

That truth ripped a jagged hole inside her heart.

Broderick came forward. "Regina," he murmured in greeting.

Jealousy threatened to choke her. Reggie forced her attention back to the window. *I don't even have a bloody reply.* Not one possible response came to mind, nothing that she could put forward that wouldn't reveal the venomous envy snaking through her. For she knew the purpose of the meeting Ophelia had arranged between Broderick and the breathtaking widow. His sister had hand-selected him a bride, and—her lips twisted in a painful smile—a perfect one at that. To give her fingers something to do, Reggie again pulled back the curtain.

It was a mistake.

Broderick stood just beyond her shoulder, reflected back in the crystal panes.

"Look at me," he said quietly.

She shook her head.

"Please."

Reggie closed her eyes. Damn him. Damn him for uttering that plea which never crossed his lips. She forced herself around.

"This changes nothing." And with the low insistence to his husky timbre, she could almost believe it.

Yet it changed everything.

They both knew it.

"You're a liar."

A muscle pulsed in his jaw. "I'm not." He gripped her lightly by the shoulders. "I love you. I want to be with you."

He'd never put himself first. "And I want you alive." Even as she'd lose him, after only just having him. "She saved your sister, and she can do the same for you." A former maid to the late queen consort, the duchess had managed the seemingly impossible: earning a like admiration from the king *and* his outcast wife. As such, with her influence, the duchess could see Broderick spared.

"Do you think I would want a life like that? That I would choose my own life over one together with you?"

She hugged her arms around her middle. "Think, Broderick. There is your club. There are all the staff dependent upon you."

He searched her face, his eyes flashing with such anger and hurt. "What are you saying?" he hissed.

Tears clouded her vision, and she fought them back. "I'm saying I want you to marry her." It was a threadbare whisper, both a lie and a truth rolled together into a contradiction that didn't make sense and yet, at the same time, did in every way.

He released her like one burnt. "I don't *want* to marry her."

"No." Reggie cradled his cheek in her coarsened palm. A hand that would never belong to a lady such as the woman he went off to now meet. "You need to marry her."

Broderick caught her wrist in an unyielding grip somehow both hard and tender. He raised her hand to his mouth and kissed the sensitive place where her pulse beat. "I need you."

"And I need you alive, more than I need you to belong to just me."

A light scratching on the panel interrupted whatever he'd intended to say.

"Mrs. O'Roarke is asking after you, Mr. Killoran," the servant called through the panel.

He cursed. "I'll be a moment."

"Go," she urged.

He caught her around the waist and dragged her close. "This is not done," he breathed against her mouth and then claimed it. He traced the seam of her lips with the tip of his tongue, branding those rounded contours, and then stepped out of her arms.

She silently cried out at the loss, going cold again.

"I love you," he repeated.

And then he was gone.

Reggie hovered at the edge of the window and, through the crack in the curtains, stared down, fixed on the grounds below.

Ophelia and her husband stepped out with Broderick following close behind, a reluctance in his step. He suddenly stopped and looked up toward her window.

Reggie jumped back.

"You fool," she whispered, hating herself for having dared to believe that he would be hers. It was fate mocking her for having carried that dream of love in her heart still, all these years later. Only losing him to another would have been easier had she not had a taste of what had almost been.

She forced herself away from that window and back to the work sprawled out upon her bed. This other dream would have to be enough.

To keep from dissolving into a pathetic, blubbering mess, Reggie turned her attentions to her design plans.

Her door burst open, and she glanced up.

Stephen lingered there.

"You can come in," she encouraged, and he pushed the door closed with the heel of his boot.

He dragged himself up onto the bed. "Do you think he's going to marry her?" he asked without preamble.

The universe was determined to torture her. Or mayhap it was just this eleven-year-old boy who wavered between loyal young brother and surly nemesis. Except . . . she searched for a hint of malice and found none.

"I . . . hope he does," she brought herself to say.

"You do?" He wrinkled his little brow. "I thought you loved him."

Everyone knew.

She sighed, and setting down the page in her hand, she attended him. "I do," she said simply.

"And yet you want him to marry someone else?" She may as well have just sprung a second head for the look he gave her.

"I want him to be happy, and . . . not hang." Her voice cracked, and she coughed into her hand. "I don't want him to hang, and so when you love somebody, you put their happiness before even your own," she explained, willing him to see.

"My damn *father*," he gritted. Stephen's gaze fell to the papers around them, and curiosity lit his eyes. "Is that for your new club?" he asked, scooting over until his shoulder brushed her arm.

"It is for my music hall," she said, welcoming that diversion. Fetching the plans she'd worked on with Broderick's suggestions in mind, she offered them up to the boy.

He hesitated and then accepted the book. Silently, he flipped through the pages. "This ain't a gaming hell."

He'd the outraged tones of one who'd been duped. Her lips twitched, and she quickly hid that smile. "No." It never had been.

"Wot's a tightrope dancer?" he asked, curiosity in his voice.

"Here." Reggie abandoned her sheet music and collected another folio. "Let me show you." Fanning the pages, she found the dog-eared one a quarter of the way through the leather volume. She turned it out.

He stared at the rendering and then lifted quizzical eyes to hers. "They dance in the air."

She nodded. "On a rope," she clarified.

"Hmph." Stephen glanced down at the page once more. "I'd like to see that."

Reggie smiled. "That is certainly the hope." *Find what makes you different . . . Pantomime. Tightrope dancing. A mix of performers outside of musicians . . .* It was an idea Broderick had given her, when he could have so easily allowed her to continue on the path she'd planned, saying nothing. Letting her fail. But he hadn't. She stretched her legs out and hooked them at the ankle. That was the man Broderick had always been to her. Until the assignment he'd recently forced her into, he'd freely supported her.

They fell into an easy silence, Reggie working and Stephen sifting through her papers.

He coughed.

Reggie marked a note for Martin Phippen.

"I said, ahem."

She glanced up.

"Broderick thinks it doesn't matter what he does. Who he marries or what the marquess knows or doesn't know. He says he's going to die. Do you believe that?"

Reggie set aside her pencil and then stared down at her charcoal-stained palms. "I don't know," she confessed.

He pulled a crumpled piece of paper out of his jacket and handed it over.

Reggie clasped the aged scrap. "What is this?" She skimmed the contents and then looked up, in shock.

"They're the ones who took me," he said quietly as he swung his legs back and forth.

I found ya a nob's son like ya wanted . . . Ya said one hundred pounds. We wants two . . . It read in a sloppy scrawl better suited to a child just learning his numbers and outlined the sins of all those years ago.

Walsh and Lucy Stokes.

This was who'd taken him. Two of Diggory's most loyal henchmen. Her heart throbbed with remembered hatred. Walsh, who'd attempted to yank away the protective cover Broderick had offered her within the gang and thrust her into the role of Diggory's whore.

Heart pounding, Reggie gathered Stephen by the arm. "Where did you find this?"

"Found it in Diggory's old things."

"He has to see this," she breathed.

Stephen lifted one shoulder in a dejected little shrug. "He did. Broderick brought it to him, but the marquess wouldn't even listen. Turned him out."

And that fledgling hope came crashing down. Broderick was a man who could talk the Almighty into sinning if he wished.

"Twisted he i-is," Stephen whispered, and through her own grief, she heard fear, so abhorrent to all this boy was, shaking that last syllable.

Reggie carefully smoothed out the aged yellow note, the fading inked words creased and cracked by an angry fist: Broderick's? Or Stephen's? Since she'd discovered the truth of Stephen's birthright and kidnapping, she and all the Killorans had been so fixed on Broderick's survival. How much had they, outside their own sadness and fears, truly considered Stephen's departure? These past days, while Broderick had fought for his own survival, Stephen had been left to contemplate a life with a marquess, called mad, who was a stranger to him.

"I don't want to go," Stephen whispered, leaning his slight weight against her.

She folded her arm around him. "I know. I don't want you to leave, either." Just as Reggie wanted to remain a part of this family.

"He doesn't want me." That admission emerged haltingly from Stephen.

"I don't believe that," Reggie said softly.

He hunched his shoulders. "No?" He didn't allow her a beat with which to respond. "Then why didn't he come when he learned I was his son?"

Why, indeed? Reggie sighed and offered him the only thing she had—the truth. "I don't know why, Stephen," she confessed. "Mayhap he's allowing you time to make your goodbyes to the world you've been living in." Unlikely. "Or mayhap he's afraid, too, of beginning again with the boy he'd loved." A child who was now a stranger. "But you will both find your way together . . . eventually."

Stephen's Adam's apple bobbed. "I don't want to begin again."

No one ever did. Not truly. "Someday," she said softly, stroking the top of his head, "I believe you're going to find happiness with your father. And one day you will have a hard time imagining a life without him in it."

He sniffled. "You really think that?"

She'd have to be deaf to fail to hear the hope threading that question. "I do," Reggie assured him. And she prayed for that gift for the boy's sake.

They shared a small smile.

The door burst open, and they both jumped up, unsheathing their daggers.

Gertrude stumbled inside. "Trouble," Gertrude rasped, her cheeks flushed from her exertions. Bent over, she borrowed support from her knees and held out an official-looking page. "One of Connor's men received w-word," she managed between her great, gasping breaths for air. "Maddock is g-going to act."

Stephen's face went ashen. "Tonight?"

A pit formed in Reggie's belly. "What?" She came forward, retrieving the note from Stephen's shaking fingers, and scanned the contents.

Gertrude's face contorted into a paroxysm of grief. "Connor has had the marquess's townhouse watched." Her voice caught. "T-two constables were summoned to Maddock's."

Oh, God.

For the man bent on destroying Broderick Killoran, he'd found the ultimate revenge. Sending the constables to a theatre filled with members of Polite Society and collecting him before a woman who might have become his bride.

She glanced up quickly. "Stephen, have two carriages ready. Immediately," she shouted when he remained rooted to the floor. That sprang him from his motionless state. He tore past Gertrude, the pitter-patter of his footsteps swiftly fading.

Gertrude dashed over to her bed and retrieved that crumpled page. "Reggie? What are you doing?"

"You need to go to Broderick," she ordered, rushing from the room. Gertrude matched her steps. "Get him out of that theatre. Let him know there is a trap." Shooting out those commands gave her purpose. It kept her from surrendering to the panic clamoring in her breast.

"And where are you going?" she asked as they reached the top of the stairway.

Reggie clenched and unclenched her jaw. "To speak to the marquess."

She had every intention of doing what Broderick had been unable to do—reasoning with a madman.

Chapter 28

You took my son. And now time for you is up.

—The Marquess of Maddock

Broderick sat in the crowded Drury Lane Theatre box, surrounded by members of Polite Society.

Crystal chandeliers hung throughout the auditorium, with the candles' glow flickering off the silk and satin gowns of the ladies assembled. The din of inattentive patrons in full discourse warred with the orchestra set at the center of the stage.

It marked the culmination of the great hope he'd carried. It was all he'd ever wanted: to be part of this world, fully included, as one who *belonged*.

And now he sat here in that very place, seated alongside a duchess, and it was the last place in the world he wished to be.

Broderick's chest tightened.

Nay, he was wrong. This was a place he wished to be . . . but with *another* woman.

He stared out at the tenor performing to a room full of people more fixed on gossip than on the song that soared throughout the room.

> "There dwelt a miller, hale and bold, beside the
> river Dee;
> He danced and sang from morn till night, no lark
> so blithe as he;
> And this the burden of his song forever used to be."

Reggie should be here. She belonged with him. *And I want to share this with her.* Every trill and note sung would have held her enthralled.

Broderick shifted his focus over to the young widow Ophelia sought to partner him with. The delicate planes of her face a study of ennui, she passed a bored gaze around the hall, surveying the lords and ladies present and merely skimming past the performers on the stage below.

Feeling his gaze, the dark-haired beauty glanced over. She snapped her fan open and waved it lightly before her mouth, her encouraging little smile flickering forward and then disappearing behind that satin scrap.

Restrained. Practiced.

There was nothing real or sincere about the tilt of her lips.

Another woman flashed to mind, one who laughed with abandon and whose cheeks blushed bright with her mirth. One who'd never attend a theatre all for the purpose of engaging in gossip.

Ophelia jammed her elbow into his side. "You can at least smile," she whispered from the side of her mouth.

He forced his lips up.

"That's a damned grimace," Ophelia muttered. "Bloody hell. What is the matter with you?" His sister dragged her red velvet chair closer. "She is the answer." As if there were another "she" in question, Ophelia glanced pointedly over at the dark beauty still surveying the crowd. "She represents your salvation."

His salvation.

Yes, because once survival and the future of his club had mattered above anything and everything. How narrow his world had been. He'd placed profit and power above all else.

The tenor, a portly gentleman with a crooked wig, pranced to the middle of the stage.

"I envy nobody, no, not I, and nobody envies me."

Only now acknowledging the truth—there had been safety in that. For it had been something he'd controlled. The Devil's Den couldn't hurt or disappoint. And even as he'd been saved through his ownership of that gaming empire, it had also left his life—empty.

"It is a perfect match. You both enter into it as any other arrangement. You'll have your duchess, and your neck, of course. Bethany's late husband left her in dire straits, so your fortune will—"

"I can't," he whispered.

Ophelia cocked her head. "What?" she blurted. Her husband and the dowager duchess glanced over. She offered a sheepish smile. "Apologies." As soon as everyone's attention was trained forward, her smile faded. "What?" she repeated. "But the marquess . . ."

"I can't marry her."

His sister sat back in her seat. "But you don't even know her. She might make you a perfect bride and—"

"And I don't love her."

That silenced the remainder of her words.

"But you don't love anyone," she noted, a befuddled wrinkle between her brows.

That was to be the legacy he left upon his hanging. Siblings who didn't know how much they'd meant to him. He'd swing, and they'd never know that when he'd joined their family, they'd saved him in ways his own father hadn't. They'd given him a sense of purpose and renewed meaning in a world where those he'd relied on before had so easily cut him out.

"I've been a rotted brother," he said quietly.

Ophelia gasped. "No. Don't say—"

"It's true," he cut off that undeserved defense. In a nearby box, Lord Landon was stroking his fingers across the expanse of his companion's plunging décolletage. Broderick stared at that gentleman, who'd courted two of his sisters, a man whose suit Broderick had encouraged and whose offer he would have allowed. "I thought noble connections were best for you," he said hoarsely, clenching his hands into fists. "I was wrong." *About so much.* "I am so very sorry."

It had been Reggie, however, who'd shown him what was in his heart. Who'd opened his eyes to what mattered.

Ophelia worked her eyes over his face. "You have nothing to be sorry for. You did the best you could. You were a brother to us." Her hand covered his, and she gave a light squeeze. "You saved us," she said simply.

> "I live by my mill, God bless her! she's kindred,
> child, and wife;
> I would not change my station for any other in life."

And after years of searching and fighting to be somehow more, a weight lifted, leaving in its place a peace: in who he was and what he wanted and who he wanted to be, for as long as he had left. "I have to go," he said, climbing to his feet. Eyes throughout the auditorium swung to him. "Forgive me," he said gruffly, taking a step back.

Ophelia stood. "Broderick? What is . . . ?"

The velvet curtains were whipped open, and Gertrude stumbled in.

Their sister blinked, and squinting, she searched the darkened box. "Gertrude?" Ophelia asked, but the elder sister's stare went past her, landing square on Broderick.

"There is trouble," the eldest of his sisters whispered. "We have to leave."

This was the townhouse Stephen had visited.

At last, Stephen's late-night visit here made sense.

His being here had not had anything to do with setting fires or filching the goods of a nobleman.

Standing on the stone steps, she stared at the gold lion knocker, its mouth parted in a silent roar, warning away any who braved this door.

At one time, she had doubted her strength, been unable to see past the mistakes she'd made, and allowed them to define her. She'd seen herself as weak. Broderick had helped her see her strength. She had faced down enough devils and had come out on the other side of survival.

She grabbed the ring dangling from one gold tooth and slammed it hard.

That rhythmic knock rolled around the eerily still Mayfair streets. She shivered and huddled deeper into her cloak.

Her fingers reflexively curled around the two notes in her front pocket.

The echo left by that door knocker faded, ushering in silence once more.

What if he was not here? What if he'd gone himself to witness the fall of Broderick Killoran? Reggie bit her lip. He had to be here.

Ignoring the gold ring, this time she pounded a fist on the black oak panel. *KnockKnockKnockKnock.*

Reggie continued a solid beat until suddenly, abruptly, the door was drawn open.

"May I help you?" That greeting was wrapped in a thinly veiled annoyance.

She brought her shoulders back and faced off with the lanky butler. "Yes. I . . ." All words fled. And along with them, her reasons for being here and the argument she'd composed for Lord Maddock. A low hum filled her ears. Reggie shook her head to clear it.

Reflected back in mirror eyes was her own shock.

The servant clutched at the door. "Regina?" he whispered.

She was afraid to move. Afraid to blink. Afraid that if she did so, his visage would disappear and in its place would remain some stranger. Though one foot taller and several stone heavier, there was no mistaking the heavily freckled face. The crimson curls.

Tears flooded her eyes, blurring his visage. "Quint."

He choked. "I looked for years. It was as though you'd vanished." His Adam's apple jumped. "I thought you were dead."

"You searched for me," she whispered, and tears rolled unchecked down her cheeks. All these years she'd believed that she was dead to her father and brothers for the shame she'd visited upon them. And all the while only a handful of London streets had separated them; and yet Mayfair and the Dials had been worlds apart, where they would have remained perpetually divided, moving about two entirely different spheres.

"Did I search for you?" Hurt rounded his eyes. "*Of course* I did. Father became a broken man after you'd gone. Cameron cares for him now." Father. Cameron. Hearing their names spoken from the lips of her youngest brother made them real in ways she'd not allowed them to be.

She clutched at her throat. "I believed it was better if I stayed gone." How hollow that sounded to her own ears. She'd spent years running, hiding. Finding out ten years too late that it had been herself she'd been running from.

"Never. It was never better with you gone." Quint stepped aside, urging her in. "How did you find me?" he asked, shutting the door behind them.

"How did I . . . ?" And then the shock of their reunion faded. "What are you doing here?" she countered with a question of her own. She took in the palatial foyer of Italian marble so crisp in its shine it nearly hurt the eyes.

"I'm employed by the marquess."

"Your employer is the *Marquess of Maddock*?"

All fraternal warmth vanished. He narrowed his eyes. "How do you know Lord Maddock?"

There was a protectiveness to his question that spoke of loyalty familiar to Reggie. And on the heel of it, a sickening realization. She slid her eyes shut. *Oh, God.* They'd been employed by enemies. When she opened them, he studied her carefully. "My . . ." How could she refer to Broderick as her "employer"? He'd been so much. He'd saved her. And he would forever hold her heart. Reggie straightened her shoulders. "I'm here to speak with him about his son," she said, neatly sidestepping mention of Broderick.

All the color washed from Quint's cheeks. "Follow me," he rasped. He rushed off, taking large, lurching steps so very similar to the ones he'd taken around the Kent countryside.

"Do you know him well?" Reggie asked into the quiet, her gaze taking in the satin-draped portraits lining the halls.

Quint cast her a sideways look. "Yes."

Reggie waited for some elaboration on that score.

Their footfalls, muffled on the carpeted floors, served as the only echo of an answer.

She frowned. It was wrong to expect he should prove forthcoming with information simply because she was his sister. It had been ten, almost eleven, years since they'd last seen one another. Their lives were steeped in secrets and mysteries. It also highlighted that Quint, too, had learned the essentiality of keeping everyone—including those who shared one's blood—close.

They reached an arched doorway, and he knocked once.

"They've arrived?" a gravelly voice called from within.

Three inches taller than her almost six feet, Quint glanced down at her. "No, my lord. Not yet."

Reggie trained her ears. Who did "they" refer to? The constables who'd received the orders to cart Broderick from Drury Lane to Newgate? Or someone else?

Feeling Quint's probing stare on her, she schooled her features. After all, she, too, had learned the art of dissembling and the need for it.

He opened the door and motioned for her to precede him into the dimly lit rooms.

Reggie blinked, adjusting her eyes to the shroud of darkness that hung over the place. Bearing the stale scent of aged books and leather, it fairly ached for a window to be thrown open and a wash of fresh air.

"Who the hell is this?"

Reggie sought the owner of that brutish snarl. Seated behind a cluttered desk, the gentleman with his crooked nose, square jaw, and unkempt hair bore the look more of a street tough than a noble lord.

Her brother cleared his throat. "My sister."

She shivered. It was the eyes that were a window to a person's soul, Broderick had once told her. In them, one might determine anything and everything about anyone. Were they kind? Were they cruel?

"Your *sister*?" And in this brooding figure who scraped a dismissive gaze over her, he was the monster Stephen had made him out to be. Emotionally deadened.

But by that returned query, he was one in possession of her past and his butler's secrets. Surely such a man hadn't been so completely destroyed by his own suffering?

Regina dropped a curtsy. "My lord," she greeted, bowing her head.

"What does she want?"

She frowned. He'd dismissed her outright. She'd not allow him, or anyone, including her brother, to speak about her as though she weren't there. As though she were undeserving of a word with a marquess. Reggie jutted up her chin. "I came to speak with you about your son."

The marquess blanched. His entire body went ramrod straight, making a lie of his earlier indifference. "What?"

Reaching inside her cloak, Reggie fished out the latest note to arrive and waved it. "And also to speak about your intentions for Broderick Killoran."

Quint gasped.

His employer swung a furious gaze from Reggie to his butler.

Her brother shot his hands up, frantically shaking his head. "I didn't . . . she didn't . . ." He glowered at Reggie. "What is the meaning of this?" he demanded.

Ignoring him, she came forward with the latest note to have arrived. The final one that would mark the death knell for Broderick. "You are in the wrong."

Lord Maddock slammed his fist. "Get out."

"I won't." She looked to her brother.

Quint sprang forward on the balls of his feet and then fell back. His options were to throw her out on her buttocks or . . . nothing.

"Get her out," the marquess bellowed.

Match fury with calm. Meet yelling with quiet. They were the rules any skilled governess was wise enough to carry, and lessons aptly used on all—including men rumored to be mad.

"I know this man," she said softly. "He is not the one wholly deserving of your rage."

"Regina."

"He saved me," she went on over Quint's entreaty.

That brought her brother to silence, and the marquess's brows dipped.

Encouraged by quiet on both their parts, she continued forward until she stood before the marquess's desk.

"Get out."

She stood firm. "I won't. I won't leave until you hear me out."

A golden eyelid twitched. "I could throw you out on your arse." He'd do it. Whatever loyalty existed between her brother and him be damned. She saw it in the hardness of his eyes.

Reggie held his stare. "And lose a window into your son's life?" She shook her head. "You won't do that." Uninvited she slid onto the nearest seat, and the reed chair creaked under her weight. Only, seated before this stranger, with her brother looking on, she wavered.

It's not your fault . . . None of it. It never was . . .

For so long she'd felt dirty and ashamed, less for those sins that had seen her ruined.

Despite all the suffering he wrought, you emerged triumphant. You pulled yourself from his clutches—

The echo of Broderick's assurances gave her the strength to share the history behind her meeting with the marquess's enemy. When she'd finished her telling, Quint stood, faintly trembling, his cheeks whitewashed. "He could have made me his whore," she said matter-of-factly. "But that's not who he was. He wasn't and isn't a man who preyed on those weaker. He protected them. He gave them homes and security." She paused. "And he did the same for Stephen." Withdrawing that crumpled scrap, she pushed it across the desk.

He made no move to touch the note, and then with stiff, reluctant movements, he reached for it.

The marquess skimmed the brief contents and then tossed it aside. "You expect I'd believe—"

"You can't see past your own hatred that which is directly before you."

"Regina," her brother warned.

She gripped the edge of the marquess's desk. "Walsh tried to sell me to Diggory." Her skin crawled. "Diggory loved the nobility, and Walsh convinced him that because of both my speech and decorum that I was in fact a lady born. Broderick saved me." Her heart swelled with her love for him. "He insisted I was his and put himself between me and that monster." Reggie turned her palms up, willing him to see. "That is what he does. He saves people. The children he still hires for his clubs, the whores with not even pride left to their names, soldiers without eyes—they are all given a new start."

Reggie searched the stoic stranger across from her. Striving to discover a hint of any of what he was feeling. Despair twisted a person in so many ways that oftentimes they couldn't find their way out. She'd witnessed it in the Dials. At London Bridge, she'd very nearly been that person herself.

"Get out."

Her heart sank. There was no reasoning with him. Broderick, Stephen, they'd both been correct. Gripping the arms of her chair, she pushed herself up.

"Quint," the marquess clipped out.

Her brother hesitated and then made a hasty exit.

"Sit," Lord Maddock ordered. Finally rising, he moved out from behind his chair.

She swallowed. He was enormous. Nearly five inches taller than her own height and broadly muscled, he was more mountain than man. That physique carried no trace of the waiflike boy who'd been like a brother to her.

Pausing at the sideboard, the marquess leveled her with a piercing stare.

Mistrustful. Fearless. Gold flecks danced in those deep brown depths.

They were Stephen's eyes.

Reggie was the first to look away.

Reaching for the nearest bottle, Lord Maddock proceeded to fill his glass. "You are his whore," he noted conversationally.

She stiffened.

"Oh, come." He paused midpour, glancing over. "What other reason would you have for rushing here in a futile bid to save his life?"

A futile bid . . .

Except he'd not thrown her out as he'd first threatened, and she took heart in that.

"I'm not his whore," she said quietly. "I'm no man's whore."

He snorted. "By your own admission, you sought to sell yourself to him."

"Because of his honor, he wouldn't allow it," she shot back, not missing a beat.

That gave him pause. And then . . . "Why pay you when he could tup you without recompense?"

He sought a rise out of her. He was a man so twisted by his own hatred that he'd lost all decency, but her brother gave him his loyalty, and there was surely a reason for it.

"Are you afraid?"

The marquess froze, his glass touching his lips, and over that crystal rim, his eyes bored into her.

"Do you know"—she slowly put forward—"I think you are. You've been searching for your son"—a detail shared by Broderick—"and now you've learned of his existence. You make no attempt to meet him. To see for yourself." Reggie stood and squared off with this man who'd terrorized Broderick with his threatening missives. "Because you are no longer the father you were when he was taken from you."

"Enough," he whispered.

"And you worry you won't know how to be with this child you so loved."

"I said, enough," he thundered, hurling his snifter.

Reggie curled into herself as it slammed into the wall over his desk in an explosion of crystal and liquid. Errant shards hit her shoulder and stuck to the fabric of her wool cloak.

Heart racing, she fought for calm, not allowing him to see he'd rattled her. She dusted those flecks of glass from her person. "You know I'm right."

They locked in a silent, never-ending battle, both refusing to yield the moment.

In the end, the echo of footsteps in the corridor and the return of her brother broke the impasse.

Quint opened the door, his gaze quickly taking in the mess littering his employer's office. He swiftly righted himself. "He's arrived." That cryptic announcement revealed nothing.

A tall man ambled into the room.

Hatred singed through her veins.

Walsh.

"Oi've come to colle—" That cocky pronouncement faded as his gaze landed on Reggie. "Wot's she doin' 'ere?"

Reggie curled her lips up in a slow, icy smile learned from the Killorans, one she'd been wholly unable to master until this hated figure stepped before her. "Walsh," she said as if greeting an old friend. "I see you've found friendship with His Lordship."

"Wot's she doing here?" Walsh repeated, lurching forward. That uneven sway to his gait and slurred speech a mark of his usual drunken state.

"What do you think I'm doing?" she taunted, answering for the marquess. Walsh's eyes flashed with fear, and she preyed upon that. Reggie waved that aged scrap. "Tsk, tsk. Lesson one, never put one's sins down in writing."

Walsh paled. "Oi didn't write that."

Reggie smirked. "You don't even know what 'that' is." She took a step forward. "Or mayhap you do? Mayhap you remember precisely what you put down here." Reggie stopped several paces from him; the stench of cheap spirits and unwashed bodies poured off his body, stinging her nostrils.

And this is the man the marquess would hang his trust in.

"She's a liar," Walsh cried, his voice quavering. "Never wrote any note. Can't write."

"No, of course not, you illiterate fool," Reggie taunted. "But then, Lucy always could." If possible, the drunkard's skin went all the more white. "Lucy, who with her fine speech served as a nursemaid."

The marquess's eyes formed pinprick slits on the haggard drunk.

"Lies," Walsh hissed, lunging for her.

Reggie easily stepped out of his reach, and he collided with a rose-inlaid table, upending the mahogany piece. Energy pumping through her, she put more distance between herself and the monster with murder in his eyes. "This is the man who wronged you"—she directed that warning to Lord Maddock, her gaze never wavering from Walsh—"and with whom you'd tie yourself in a partnership, condemning another to his death, while the one who murdered your wife and stole your son lives high on the coin you feed him."

"You lying bitch," Walsh cried out, reaching into the waistband of his tattered trousers.

Reggie froze, and time stood still as the fire's glow glinted off the head of his pistol.

The door burst open to her brother's shouts of fury.

Stephen!

Their simultaneous cries rolled as one.

"No!"

"No!" He hurtled himself at Reggie, just as the sharp report of that gun thundered around the room.

Gasping, she collapsed, flying back. Reggie landed hard, all the air bursting from her lungs with Stephen's small body draped over hers.

Her chest moved rapidly, and she closed her eyes. Blood seeped through her gown, a sticky warmth that knocked her from her shock.

The room dissolved into chaos.

Quint and the marquess wrestled Walsh to the floor, even as a constable came rushing in. Reggie's arms folded around the slight boy in her hold. Panic pounded at her chest, making breath impossible. "Stephen," she moaned.

He flashed a crooked smile. A weak one. "I saved you," he whispered.

She cried out. Gently rolling him to the floor, she came up over him. *No. No. No. No.* It was a litany that played out in her head. "Why did you do that?" she sobbed, tears dampening her cheeks, and she blinked back the useless drops that blurred his little frame. With fingers that shook, Reggie ripped open his shirt. "A doctor," she screamed.

Abandoning Walsh to the constable's care, Quint raced from the room, tripping over himself.

Blood seeped from the wound at Stephen's side. Another agonized moan belonging to a tortured animal spilled from her. There was so much blood. So much of it.

"Stephen." That hoarse cry brought her head snapping over. Of course—he should be here.

Jerking off his cloak as he went, Broderick stormed into the room. *He is here.*

"He's h-hurt," Reggie said in between wrenching sobs.

Doing a quick sweep of Stephen's wound, Broderick pressed the garment to staunch the flow of blood.

Stephen winced, and over his prone form, Reggie's and Broderick's eyes met. Her own terror was reflected in his gaze.

"Reggie," the little boy whispered, his voice threadbare, snapping all her focus immediately back.

"Yes, love," she soothed through her own tears, stroking his cheek. "What is it?"

He flashed a weak smile, cocksure even through his pain. "Told you I didn't hate you . . ." His eyes rolled back.

Reggie's keening cry pealed around the room.

"No," Broderick chanted. "No. No. No." He collapsed over Stephen's tiny frame and poured his tears into the boy's blood-soaked shirt. Broderick's words were an incoherent jumble of pleading and prayers of forgiveness.

A faint groan split through that heartbreak.

Yanking his head up, his eyes wild, Broderick searched his brother for a sign of a pulse. A strangled cry tore from his throat. "He is alive."

Reggie dimly registered the floorboards shifting under her as someone fell to a knee alongside her and Broderick. Reggie glanced blankly at the marquess.

His jaw slacked. He closed his mouth, but it fell agape. He shoved past Broderick, ripping that makeshift bandage from his fingers. With his other, trembling palm, he traced the birthmark at the corner of Stephen's navel. "I didn't believe . . . I didn't trust . . ." The marquess's eyes weighted closed. "August," he whispered his son's name, and then crumpled over the child's supine body.

Chapter 29

For nearly three days straight, it rained.

Until later that third day, the sun broke through the thick grey clouds, bathing London in a calming light.

"I'm fine, you know," Stephen muttered for a fourth time as Reggie checked his bandages.

He'd been patient with her attentiveness these past days. "I do," she murmured. "There's no one more resilient or stronger than you." Hers weren't words to stroke a boy's ego. He'd endured graver injustices and miseries than most old men took on their way to meet their maker.

Stephen would survive.

"I like havin' you care for me more than my sisters," he said matter-of-factly. "Because you don't treat me different." Treat him different since he'd been claimed by the marquess. "Perhaps he'll let me stay," he ventured tentatively, and Reggie's fingers stilled.

The man who just four days ago had sobbed over this very child and had accepted the truth he'd denied himself over a fortnight wasn't one who'd relinquish his hold forever. "No, Stephen," she said quietly, refusing to lie to him. "He won't." She glanced up at the somber little figure lying on his back, staring mutinously overhead. "But do you know, Stephen?"

He refused to look at her for a long while and then grudgingly moved his attention over.

"A man who searched all those years to find you and who wants you back in his life so desperately, and *still* allowed you time to make your goodbyes, is not a bad man."

Stephen turned his face toward the window.

A knock sounded at the door, and she glanced up, hope filling her breast.

The Killoran sisters filed in.

Reggie fought disappointment. It had been two days since she'd seen Broderick. He'd been called away on business after Stephen had been brought to convalesce with the Killoran family.

And he'd just . . . cut her out.

Before he'd gone, there'd been no talk of his duchess or his promise for the future.

"Your sisters are here," she murmured. Lowering his shirt back into place, Reggie rose to greet the trio as they came forward.

"How . . . ?"

"I'm fine," Stephen mumbled, interrupting Cleo's question. "It was just a flesh wound."

"He's fine," Reggie mouthed.

Gertrude offered the small bouquet over to Stephen. "I've brought you these," she said gently, pushing them into his hand.

"What am I going to do with *these*?" He wrinkled his nose. "Boys don't like flowers."

Reggie's lips twitched, and she accepted the flowers from Gertrude. "Will you put them in the music room?" Gertrude asked.

Stephen shoved himself into an upright position. "I'm fine," he exclaimed when all three Killoran sisters rushed forward.

"He is going to be fine," Reggie repeated once more. The bullet had sliced into his side and exited clean through, leaving more of a vicious gash.

"See?" Stephen shot back for the other women present.

Reggie made to leave and allow the family one of the few remaining moments they had left together. Ophelia stepped into her path.

She bit at her lower lip. "I didn't know," she said on a rush, "about you and Broderick and how you felt about him, or how he felt about you. I simply thought you were like a sister to him," she rambled.

"It's all right," she promised.

"It's not," Ophelia whispered, her voice catching in a crack in her usually unflappable composure. "I introduced him to another woman."

Nay, not just any woman. A striking widow who also happened to be a duchess. Reggie gripped the flowers in her hands. "You didn't know."

"Ophelia?" Stephen snapped, and his sister glanced over.

"Go," Reggie urged them. And as the gathered family continued on, she let herself out. Flowers in hand, she found her way to the room that had proven a sanctuary of sorts. When thoughts of Broderick had kept her awake the past nights and questions swirled about their future, she'd come and played.

And where music had represented a balm and hope for the future, she'd confronted the truth she'd desperately fought: It would not be enough. For she wanted him to share in those joys and endeavors. She wanted him to be her partner through life.

Emotion wadded in her throat.

Reggie entered through the doorway and stopped.

With the tails of his jacket hanging over the back of the bench, Broderick sat before the pianoforte. "You returned," she breathed, motionless. "Where have you been?" She hated the desperation to that query but had no pride where this man was concerned. She never had.

Broderick bowed his head, and his hands flew over those keys, strumming a cheerful tune. Her heart caught.

"Just give me your hand,
Tabhair dom do lámh.
Just give me your hand
And I'll walk with you,
Through the streets of our land,
Through the mountains so grand.
If you give me your hand.
Just give me your hand,
And come along with me."

The flowers slipped from her fingers as she rushed forward, stopping beside him. Each note wrapped in his slightly off-key song, a perfect partner to her melody.

"Will you give me your hand,
And the world it can see,
That we can be free,
In peace and harmony?
From the north to the south.
From the east to the west.
Every mountain, every valley,
Every bush and bird's nest!"

As he finished, she shook her head. "I don't . . ."

Broderick rose from that bench, unfurling to his full, towering height, and then fell to a knee. "Regina Marlow, I love you with all I am and all I want to be. Will you marry me?"

A faint click snapped her attention away from him, and the earth swayed.

Broderick caught her about the waist, steadying her.

The trio in that doorway—three men, different with time but familiar in every way—smiled back.

"Papa," she whispered, pressing a fist to her mouth. Each of them, Cameron and Quint, older but still smiling and dear. So very dear.

"My girl," he whispered.

With a sob, Reggie sprinted across the room.

Her father caught her against him, folding her close. She clung to him, sobbing against his jacket front. The lemon-drop scent of him the same. "*Shh*, my Regina," he said into the top of her head.

"I . . . how . . . ?" She glanced over at Broderick.

"This gentleman came all the way to find me," her father explained. "He said he couldn't marry you unless he had my permission and my presence."

Another broken sob escaped Reggie.

All he'd ever longed for was a link to the peerage, and yet he'd chosen her.

"I love you," Broderick said hoarsely. "I want to spend my life with you. Your music hall and anything else you desire to do or be, I'll support." Her heart melted. "As long as you do those things as my wife and share your life with me."

She struggled to see him through the sheen of tears glossing her eyes, and she dashed a frantic hand over her eyes.

"Well, poppet?" her father demanded, a twinkle in his now rheumy eyes. "Answer the lad?"

"Yes," she exclaimed, on a half laugh, half sob. She raced over to Broderick, and he caught her in his arms, swinging her in a wide arc. Reggie captured his face between her hands. "Yes, I'll marry you."

Broderick claimed her mouth, and she returned that kiss, pouring all the love she'd carried for this man into that embrace.

She looked at her loves: her brothers, her father, then at Broderick. Tears pricked her lashes. Because of her and Broderick's love, they both had an entire world of people they loved and could depend upon. *Neither* of them ever need face the world alone again.

Reggie smiled.

About the Author

Photo © 2016 Kimberly Rocha

USA Today bestselling, RITA-nominated author Christi Caldwell blames authors Julie Garwood and Judith McNaught for luring her into the world of historical romance. When Christi was at the University of Connecticut, she began writing her own tales of love. She believes that the most perfect heroes and heroines have imperfections, and she rather enjoys torturing her couples before crafting them a well-deserved happily ever after.

The author of the Wicked Wallflowers series, which includes *The Hellion* and *The Vixen*, Christi lives in southern Connecticut, where she spends her time writing and caring for her three amazing children. Fans who want to keep up with the latest news and information can sign up for Christi's newsletter at www.ChristiCaldwell.com or follow her on Facebook (AuthorChristiCaldwell) or Twitter (@ChristiCaldwell).